Keep Me Alive

Also by Natasha Cooper

Creeping Ivy
Fault Lines
Prey to All
Out of the Dark
A Place of Safety

KEEP ME ALIVE

Natasha Cooper

SIMON &
SCHUSTER

LONDON • SYDNEY • NEW YORK • TORONTO

First published in Great Britain by Simon & Schuster UK Ltd, 2004
A Viacom Company

1 3 5 7 9 10 8 6 4 2

Simon & Schuster UK Ltd
Africa House
64–78 Kingsway
London WC2B 6AH

www.simonsays.co.uk

Simon & Schuster Australia
Sydney

A CIP catalogue record for this book is available from the British Library

ISBN 0 7432 3106 6

Typeset by SX Composing DTP, Rayleigh, Essex
Printed and bound in Great Britain by
Mackays of Chatham Plc, Chatham, Kent

Acknowledgements

A great many friends provided information and support while I was writing this novel including Robert Avery, Suzanne Baboneau, Presiley Baxendale, Di Bingham, Hilary Bonner, Mary Carter, Broo Doherty, Jane Gregory, Isabelle Grey, Jessica Gulliver, Peter Krijgsman, Ayo Onatade, Manda Scott, Sheila Turner and Melissa Weatherill. Staff at the Civil Aviation Authority press office were immensely helpful, as was Richard Billinge of the Meat Hygiene Service. I am grateful to them all. Of course there were times when I had to adapt the information they gave me to serve the needs of fiction.

Natasha Cooper

For Jane Gregory

It's good food and not fine words that keeps me alive.
(*Je vis de bonne soupe et non de beau langage.*)
Molière, *Les Femmes savantes*

Chapter 1

May, Romney Marsh, Kent

It was like a scene in a war film: three men running through the night towards a small plane, sagging under the loads they carried on their right shoulders. Moonlight glistened on their eyes and on the shiny black plastic that made the packages so hard to hold. Each time one of them stumbled over a tussock, his load slid forwards and he had to haul it back, straining his arm and neck muscles to screaming point.

A tiny slit opened in the plastic. Tim gagged and turned his face away. There was no way he was going to breathe in this stuff.

They had to go back to the van four more times. None of them spoke because speech carried further on these quiet nights than any animal-like sound of grunting or panting. The engines of the van and plane were a worry, but there was no way of muffling them. And there were probably enough roads even on these desolate fringes of Romney Marsh for most listeners to assume it was ordinary traffic they heard, or maybe even a legitimate flight into Lydd Airport.

All three men were breathless by the time the whole lot was loaded. Tim fired up the engines while the other two tied down the packages to stop them sliding around after takeoff.

'Great. Hit the lights,' Tim urged in a whisper that could barely be heard above the engine noise.

Bob tied the last knot and slipped out of the plane, beckoning his brother to follow, and locking the door after him. They ran in parallel down the field, bending every ten feet to set fire to the wicks that floated in big glass jars of oil. The plane began to taxi before they'd reached the end of the landing strip. Bob lit the three flares at the end and stood back as the wheels cleared his head by only a few feet. He could feel his hair lifting in the turbulence under the wings.

'Arsehole,' he muttered, killing the first light.

They had the rest out two minutes later. No one came. No one shouted. It would have been bad luck if anyone had seen them. The flares hadn't been burning for more than five minutes, and no regular flight paths crossed these particular fields.

Bob had made sure of that right at the beginning, when he was checking out the air traffic controllers. He'd learned that the civil ones weren't going to bother a private plane so long as it kept low, and most of the military controllers stopped work at five o'clock anyway. Tim would be right off their radar, so there shouldn't be anyone watching him.

Unless there was a satellite going over, Bob thought, still trying to work out what was wrong tonight. It was as if he had a nail working its way through his shoe, right up into the flesh of his foot. Why?

Even he, with ears like a bat's, couldn't hear the beat of the plane's engine now. They'd always got away with this before. There was no reason why this flight should be any different. But he was jumpy as hell.

'Where did you put the food?' Ron hissed in his ear, making his fists bunch before he recognized the voice or heard the words. His heart thudded in his chest and he could feel his eyes bulging. He rubbed them as he got his mind back into shape.

'Don't creep up on me like that,' he said. 'Can't you think of anything except your next meal?'

'What's the matter with you?'

'There's something wrong. We need to check.'

'Bollocks,' said Ron. 'It was a great takeoff. Let's go and eat.'

'You always were a lazy bastard. Get in the van and shut up. You wouldn't notice anything anyway, even if it hit you in the face.'

Bob prowled around the field, sniffing and peering as he went. Through the oil and the petrol he could smell grass and cow dung and dry earth. There were horses nearby, too, and the warm wind was bringing something flowery from one of the gardens over to the west. That was all OK. Just like it should be. He couldn't see anything wrong either, and there was nothing to hear except the sheep out on the marsh, the wind in the leaves, Tim's hens roosting and a few wild birds scuffling in their nests.

He took one more look around, then swung himself up into the van. The greedy bastard had found the Thermos and the food and was already tucking in. Bob grabbed a steak sandwich before they'd all gone. As he bit into it, the meat juices ran down his chin.

'You can bring something to eat next time,' he said as he chewed and wiped the palm of his free hand across his face. He licked it clean, feeling the ridge of an old scar with his tongue. 'You should be able to lift anything you want from the pub.'

'The boss has eyes in the back of his head,' Ron said, putting his feet up on the dashboard. 'It's easier for you.' He took another bite.

'If you don't get your arse in gear soon and do a bit more of the work, I'll dock your share of the profits.'

It was a long-standing threat, but it didn't bother Ron. He finished his sandwich, rubbing his hands on his jeans. 'If it wasn't for me there'd hardly be any profits. You'd have had the plane coming back empty.'

Bob grunted. 'Better that than what we're doing. I don't like it. I'd rather make less than bring them in. We don't know where they come from, or who's waiting for them, or what they're going to do with them. It's dangerous.'

'So?' Ron laughed. 'We get paid. That's all that matters.'

'Until the day your bloke grasses you up and gets us all arrested. Why won't you tell me who he is?' Bob said, his voice jagged with frustration.

'Because I'm not stupid.'

The man who had been filming them from the trees at the far end of the landing strip waited until he was sure they were settled in the van. He knew they wouldn't move now until the plane came back, so he had at least an hour. He still hadn't figured out where it went, but given the time the flights took and the direction the plane flew off in, it had to be France or Belgium. It definitely couldn't be any further away.

As quietly as possible, he shut up his digital infrared camcorder and stowed it in the pocket of his parka, before sliding his body backwards until he was well shadowed in the trees. There he stood up, grimacing as the blood returned to his cramped muscles. He breathed more freely, too.

It was only half a mile to the place where he'd left his car. He jogged there, moving fluidly once he'd hit his familiar rhythm, glad to be able to stretch properly. The camcorder banged against his chest as he ran. There'd be a bruise later, but it would be worth it. The footage he'd already shot tonight would probably be enough on its own to convince the doubters, but he'd go back to film the arrival of the return cargo once he'd downloaded this lot.

Watery light gleamed ahead of him. There was no real water round here, so it had to be the moon's reflection on the roof of his car. He slowed down and circled the place to make certain no one was waiting for him. He was under no illusion about the lengths to which these men would go if they thought anyone was on to them.

Tonight he was all right. There were no signs of human interference anywhere near the car, and the only sounds were the rustlings of small animals in the grass. A fox had been here, leaving rank and gamy crap somewhere close by. But he wasn't fretting about foxes now.

He eased himself into the car and turned on the laptop he'd left under the passenger seat. It took a while to download tonight's footage and email it via his mobile phone to his secret address. He was about to delete the copy on the hard disk for security when he had a sudden doubt. All servers had problems from time to time; what if his ate the email he'd just sent himself? It would be mad to risk it and have to put himself in this much danger again. He sent another copy of the film to the one person he believed he could still trust.

Waiting for the second email to go through, he thought about the mockery he'd had to take from everyone else in the last few years. It soothed his anger and his bruises to imagine the faces of his tormentors when he slapped the evidence down in front of them and forced them to watch it. No sources to protect this time; no stolen documents to give the lawyers heart attacks; no depending on anyone else for anything: just proof, absolutely incontrovertible proof.

When the coloured bar on the screen cleared to show that the email and its attachment had gone through, he deleted the copies from the computer. An expert would probably be able to disinter them from the cyber garbage on his hard disk, but he wasn't afraid of experts; only the kind of thugs he'd been filming tonight.

With the laptop clean enough to fool any of them, he bent down to put it back under the passenger seat, locked up and jogged slowly back to his observation point in the oak trees at the edge of the cherry orchard.

His eyes had readjusted to darkness by the time he got there, and he could see the old van still sitting at the side of the make-shift airstrip like a ramshackle caravan. The whole expedition had taken well over forty minutes, so there shouldn't be too long to wait now. He extracted the camcorder from his parka and lay down again, blessing the weekends he'd once spent with the Territorial Army. If nothing else, they'd taught him how to wait out the night in the open air and how to conceal himself, making up his face with green and brown gunk and keeping his eyes well shadowed from the treacherous moon-light.

It was weird to be able to think about the future with excite-ment again. Weird but good. He'd get his career back now. Better still, they'd all be all over him. He wouldn't have to take crap from anyone ever again.

The money spent on the camcorder would have been an investment, not a stupid waste. Even the rapacious interest he was being charged on his credit card would be worth paying. He felt a mad kind of affection for the three thugs who were bringing him closer and closer to everything he'd wanted for so long.

It was Ron who heard it first. He prodded his brother in the ribs and jerked his head in the direction of the coast. Bob wound down his window, listened for a moment, recognized the throb of Tim's engine, then nodded. The two of them clicked open their well-oiled doors and slid down on to the dry grass. They had to judge the lighting of the flares carefully. Too soon and they risked someone noticing the outline of the airstrip; too late, and Tim would have to circle round and make his approach again.

That would up the risk. Worse would be the possibility that he might not have enough fuel for the landing. There were some nights when the tanks were all but empty by the time he got back. Just as well in one way, with so many naked flames around, but dangerous too. If he crashed, the whole world would know about them.

'Now,' Bob said, bending to light the first flare.

The two of them sprinted back up the field, knowing by now exactly when to bend to the jars of oil. They were a real risk when the weather was like this, with the grass ready to flare up and volatile petrol vapour hanging about all over the place. Months ago, when they'd first made their plans, they'd decided that electric landing lights would be too noticeable by day. This dangerous, primitive alternative was better by far. Each man had a small extinguisher hanging from his belt, ready to blast out any flames before they could spread.

The plane was already down by the time they reached the end of the strip and they ran back, putting out the little flames as fast as they'd lit them. Tim killed the engine and swung himself down from the pilot's seat.

As soon as Ron had driven the van away, Tim and Bob turned the plane full circle and pushed it towards the old shed that served as its hangar.

'Just the flares now,' Bob said when they were safely inside and could talk normally. The pilot nodded, rubbing dirty hands across his face. He looked like shit. 'What's stopping you, Tim? Get a move on.'

'Give me a minute. It's been a long night. I couldn't make them understand on the other side how important it is to keep the plane stable. The cargo was sliding about all over the place on the way back. I thought I was going to have to dump it in the Channel.'

'But you didn't. So we'll get our money. Come on. We need to get the jars back.'

Tim stripped off his flying jacket at last, and dumped it by the plane. 'Let's get it done then; I need a bloody big drink.'

They had this part down to a fine routine. Bob collected the can and a big plastic funnel so he could pour the oil back into it out in the field. Tim picked the wicks out of the jars, stuffed them in a bag, and brought the jars to Bob for emptying. Tim was bending for the last one when Bob's head jerked up.

'What?' whispered Tim.

'There's someone in the trees.'

'Don't be stupid.'

'Shut the fuck up. Wait.'

The two of them stood, silent, holding their breath. Nothing moved. The last of the wind had dropped. Then Tim heard it too, the unmistakable sound of human panting and a kind of sliding rustle no animal would ever make. The body producing it was too big for anything but a cow and no cow slid over dry grass and leaves like that. Bob dropped the can and funnel and sprinted for the trees.

Tim followed much more slowly. In the moonlight he could see the shape of their quarry from yards away and recognized the ungainly scramble as the man tried to get to his feet. There was something metallic in his hands as he brought them up to his chest. Bob flung himself on the man, bringing him crashing to the ground. His head banged against a tree root and his breath burst out in a gasping cry. Bob swore as he stood up and started to kick.

Tim froze. Bob's rages had always terrified him, and he didn't want to get in the way of this one. Then the man screamed like a stoat in the grip of a weasel, and Tim knew he had to intervene. He drove himself forwards, feeling as if he was wading through treacle. His mouth was full of saliva and his hands were shaking. He didn't know what to do.

Bob was working on his victim's head. Blood was flooding out of the man's nose. He was trying to protect his skull and wipe his face at the same time.

Blood was everywhere, pouring into his mouth and choking him. His red-edged teeth scrabbled over his split lips, and his hands smeared the blood over his eyes and up into his hair as he clutched his head to guard it from the rhythmically pounding boots. He groaned. He was gasping as he begged for the agony to stop.

'Bastard,' Bob hissed. 'I knew something was wrong tonight. Bastard. Shut up.'

'For Christ's sake, Bob, stop it.'

At the suggestion of a rescue, the man looked up. Bob's boot landed right in his face. It cracked like an egg. He screamed and rolled himself into a defensive ball, with his ruined face pressed against his knees, but not before Tim had seen the damage to his nose, his eyes, his teeth.

Gagging, Tim put out his right hand, wanting to touch Bob and remind him that he was human. But he couldn't force himself to make contact. Bob's left boot crashed into the man's spine. And again. Just beside the kidneys.

'Stop it!' Tim said, brave enough at last to make a grab at Bob's arm. 'You'll kill him. Bob! Stop it!'

But Bob was out of reach of any words. His hands were clenched into fists, although he wasn't using them. All he needed were his booted feet. One after the other, they thudded into the man's body. Bob's face was set with concentration now; all the hatred gone. His eyes were back to normal. He looked like a man with a job and the determination to get on with it until there was nothing left to do.

Soon, the thuds gave way to crunching sounds as bigger bones cracked under the assault. Yet more blood poured out over Bob's boots and on to the hard-baked ground. It didn't soak in; it pooled, red and glossy, on the dusty surface. At last the kicking stopped.

In the silence, Tim's ears were ringing. He could barely breathe and didn't think his mind would ever work again. Bob looked down at the battered, bloody thing that had once been a man, then up at Tim, as though measuring him, deciding whether he needed kicking into silence too.

Tim knew he had only one chance to save his own life. Forcing himself to forget the man on the ground, fighting the nausea that threatened to choke him, the ringing in his ears and the fierce wish that he'd never met either of the appalling Flesker brothers or fallen in with their plans, he said, 'We'll have to bury him. I'll get the shovels.'

'No,' Bob said at once, then softened it by adding, 'but I'm glad you're on side. They always find buried bodies in the end. And if it's on your land they'll start asking you questions. You'll never stand up to interrogation. We all know that.'

'What then?' Tim didn't risk challenging the insult. 'There aren't any quarries round here to drop him in.'

'We'll take him to the meat works.'

'That's disgusting.' The words were out before Tim could stop them, and he could feel his whole body tense. He clenched his hands behind his back, and dug his top teeth into his lip to stop himself whimpering.

'Don't be stupid.' Bob laughed, which gave Tim the confidence to let his lip go. 'We'll put him under one of the lorries going to Smithfield in the morning. Eighteen wheels and God-knows how many tons of refrigerated container driving over him will make enough marks to hide everything we've done. Safer than trying to hide the body.'

'But what about the blood? It hasn't started to soak in yet, the ground's so dry. Even when it does, the evidence will last for months in the soil. Years maybe. Scientists can find tiny traces anywhere these days.'

'Can't you stop whining for a minute? Get Boney over here and he'll soon lick it up. There's no one going to bother to test soil samples unless they've seen some blood.'

Tim couldn't speak, but he managed to shake his head. There

was no way he was going to let his spaniel anywhere near this killing ground if he could help it.

'You called him after Napoleon, didn't you, so why d'you always treat him like a poodle? You're happy enough to see him eat anything he kills. What's the difference?'

'How are you going to get the body to the meat works?' Tim asked, because that was safer than saying nothing or trying to explain. 'Ron's got the van, and we can't put it in my car. It would leave evidence. That'd be far more dangerous than burying him on my own land.'

'You've been watching too much telly. We'll use his car. He must have one round here somewhere.' Bob uncoiled the battered body, straightening the legs and torso so that he could feel in the trouser pockets. It looked like a man again, in spite of all the damage Bob had done. Tim couldn't face it. Then he heard a chink and risked a quick glance. Bob was withdrawing a bloody hand from one pocket, and there was a bunch of keys dangling from his fingers.

'See. Now we've just got to find the car. The lock bleeper'll help. And we've got to find out why he was here. What was it he put in his front pocket? Get it out, will you, while I . . .'

Tim shook his head. He'd never be able to make himself touch the body. Bob looked at him, his hands twitching. Tim knew how near the danger was, but he still couldn't move. He felt himself swaying as the blood drained from his brain. Bob muttered a filthy insult, then jammed his hand into the big pocket of the dead man's parka. The seams ripped apart like Velcro.

'A camera! A sodding video camera!'

'Who the hell is he?'

Chapter 2

July, Plough Court, The Temple, London

Trish Maguire was waiting for her head of chambers on Monday morning, and looking over her gown to make sure there were no tears. There had been more than one moment last week when the fabric had snagged on a sharp edge and had to be pulled free. She'd been too busy to do anything about it at the time and didn't want to look like a scruff this morning as they walked side by side into the Royal Courts of Justice. Hearing the unmistakable sound of his step in the passage outside, she let the gown slip out of her hands to make a puddle of black cloth on her desk.

When he'd first taken an interest in her career a few years ago and used her as his junior on some big cases, she'd been flattered but scared of his notoriously demanding standards and excoriating tongue. Then she'd got to know him better and found her fear overtaken by disapproval of tactics that could seem perilously close to bullying. Only now, when she'd apparently passed some invisible test, had he begun to reveal a much lighter side to his character. She was enjoying it.

'Hi,' she said, smiling as he came into her room. 'Good weekend, Antony?'

'Tetchy. How was yours?'

'Not bad. It felt a bit weird, seeing the family go off to Australia without me, but I'm OK. Raring to go.'

'Good. I want you to take the re-examination of Will Applewood today. Are you up for it?'

She nodded, hiding her pleasure, then said, 'But are you sure? He's the most important of all the claimants, *and* the most wobbly.'

'Exactly.' Antony Shelley laid his hand on her black tin wig box. The ends of his long fingers just curled over the edge of the lid. 'And I spook him, which makes him mumble and look shifty whenever I ask him anything. You must have noticed.'

'Of course. But I didn't think twice. Most people are frightened of you.'

'Not you, though, Trish.'

'What makes you think that?' she asked, suppressing the words 'not any more'.

The smile that lifted his eyebrows into triangles and tweaked the corners of his lips was full of all the cynical self-awareness she was coming to expect from him.

'Because I never fancy frightened women, and I fancy you something rotten.'

'Yeah, yeah,' she said, laughing at him. 'I've heard enough gossip about your taste in luscious blondes to know that I could never be your type.'

'Luckily Applewood's got the hots for you, too,' he said, getting back to what mattered. 'No surprise of course, but convenient.'

Trish had never heard Antony talk so frivolously about a case, but everything about this one was turning out to be extraordinary.

Lots of people had told her she was mad to take it on when they'd heard it was to be run on a no-win no-fee basis. Antony, who'd been earning well over a million pounds a year for ages, could easily take the hit if he had to, but she needed the money. Even so, she hadn't hesitated for a minute when he'd invited her to be his junior.

Their clients were a group of small food producers, who were claiming damages for breach of contract against Furbishers Foods, one of the biggest and most ruthless of the supermarket chains. Trish had always hated corporate bullies quite as much as any other kind, and Furbishers had come to symbolize every single one of them for her. Antony had teased her for her passionate loathing from the start, while refusing to answer any questions about his own motives for accepting the brief.

'Applewood's subconscious will push him to make himself attractive,' he went on. 'Even though you'll be the target, it'll have a good effect on the judge.'

Trish felt her skin prickle with energy. 'Machiavelli had nothing on you, did he?'

Antony's face changed into the expression she privately called his 'wicked seducer look'. It had always made her laugh so much that she couldn't imagine anyone succumbing to it. But then he probably used different tactics when he wanted a result.

'I keep telling you it's mad to waste the way people feel about each other,' he said, moving towards her. At just over six feet, he was three inches taller than she, so she had to look up to meet his eyes. She could smell the faint cologne-ish scent of the soap he always used. 'When will you admit I'm right?'

'*Never*,' she said, stepping back and slapping her arm across her chest like a Victorian hero refusing to surrender the colours, even though all his comrades lay slaughtered at his feet.

Antony's eyes warmed with amusement, which did much more for her than their earlier seductive glint. They were a curious greenish-blue that could look turquoise in the sun or dull grey in the artificial light of a windowless court, and they were the one remarkable feature in a face far more ordinary than the mind it concealed.

No one outside the law would have had a clue who he was; within the tight, competitive world they inhabited, he was instantly recognizable. But there weren't many people who would have dared to accost him, which was one reason why Trish liked flirting with him so much.

'We'll be late if we don't get going,' he said, watching her as though he couldn't quite decide what she was thinking. Then he pushed one hand through his thick blond hair, shrugging himself back into professional seriousness, adding: 'Oh, and don't raise any objections during the cross-examination. I'll deal with anything that needs to be said. OK?'

Trish nodded as she swung her bag over her shoulder, enjoying the soft bump as it bounced off her spine. She followed him, clattering down the stone stairs. To cap everything else, the air outside was hot and yet without any of the usual late-July mugginess. Even the dust smelled of spice rather than dirt.

There were few other people to be seen as they walked up through the Temple, matching each other stride for stride. Trish hardly noticed the beautiful buildings with their fountains and gardens because she knew them so well. But she did register the emptiness of the place. Most of the courts had closed for the summer. She and Antony were still at work only because their case had overrun its expected length when their opponents had launched a long procedural argument. It had failed, but it had messed up the timetable. The judge, who was on vacation duty anyway, had elected to carry on until the case was over.

This wasn't unprecedented, but it was rare, as well as inconvenient for everyone involved. The Lord Chancellor's department had been agitating for years about the slowness of the judicial process and kept urging everyone involved to speed it up. Mr Justice Jeremy Husking had chosen this way. Once he had spoken, no one had any option but to obey.

Antony had packed his wife and teenage children off to their Tuscan palazzo without him, and Trish had had to cancel her share of a long-awaited trip to Sydney with her partner, George, and her ten-year-old half-brother, David. The thought of how they'd get on without her to mediate between them had been keeping her awake at night.

David had arrived in Trish's life two years ago, on the night his mother was murdered. She had been so frightened of a man who had been stalking her that she'd sent her only child halfway across London for sanctuary with his unknown half-sister. Until then Trish had known nothing of his existence either, but once it had become clear who he was and that no one else could look after him, she'd taken him in and done her best to give him the security he needed. He'd spent the first eighteen months with her apologizing every two minutes, as though afraid she'd throw him into the street if he offended her. That had stopped now, and he'd even begun to answer back. She'd been glad enough to see it, but it did mean his fights with George had got worse.

Still, for a whole month she wouldn't have to deal with either of them. She could swan around her big art-filled flat, doing precisely what she wanted, eating or not eating as she chose, without ever worrying about anyone else's feelings. She'd hate to be on her own like this for long, but the novelty was adding an unexpected sparkle to her life.

There was a bounce in her step as she and Antony emerged through the shade of Temple Lane into the dazzle of Fleet Street. The twisting road was narrow here at its junction with the Strand, and choked with traffic. Puzzled tourists clogged the pavements, cars hooted and everyone in sight seemed to be shouting. The pounding clangour of a pneumatic drill ripped through the rest.

Sodding roadworks, she thought, as she stepped round a row of orange and white traffic cones and tried not to breathe in the dust thrown up by the drill. Even without it, the air would have been worse out here. The heat haze that shimmered on the cars and around the muscular dragon on top of Temple Bar was already acrid with exhaust fumes.

Her pupil had gone on ahead with all the bundles of paperwork the team would need in court today, which was a relief. Tugging a trolley full of files and cases through this lot would have been a nightmare.

Breathing as shallowly as possible, she and Antony made their way to the stony coolness of the Royal Courts of Justice. For once there were no television cameras to record the arrival of celebrities. Theirs was the only case being heard.

Trish shoved her bag on the X-ray machine's rollers for the usual security checks and walked unchallenged through the metal detector.

'There's Applewood,' Antony said as their eyes adjusted to the gloom indoors. 'Get on over to him and sort him out before you go to the robing room. He looks far too twitchy. I'll keep out of your way so you can make him feel truly loved.'

Trish felt his hand flat on her back, pushing her forwards through the small rabble of lawyers, claimants, defendants and ushers. She didn't need the encouragement, but she enjoyed the moment of physical contact. Looking back over her shoulder, she could see that he knew. She flashed him a wicked smile and faced forwards again.

Will had seen her and was beckoning. He'd shaved carefully this morning, in preparation for his long-awaited stint in the witness box, and his springy hair was as smooth as the dark City suit he'd put on. When she'd first met him, he'd been wearing tweed, apparently chosen to look as much like a muddy field as possible, and well-polished brown brogues. Today his cheekbones were a lot sharper than they'd been then, and there were big grey smudges under his eyes.

'You didn't have a good night, did you?' Trish said, putting all her pent-up sympathy into her smile.

'Not exactly.' He laughed, and the cheerless sound made her scalp tighten. 'When I wasn't rehearsing my answers to

Antony's questions, I was telling myself we *can* still win, even after the way they savaged us last week.'

'It's good to have confidence in the outcome of the case,' Trish said, picking her words with care, 'but all you need to think about now is giving your evidence as clearly and accurately as you can. So long as you do that, you'll be fine.'

Will grinned. His teeth were clenched, and the muscles around his mouth quivered. Trish laid her left hand gently on his forearm. She could feel his tendons, hard as steel hawsers.

The case would never have come to court if it hadn't been for him. When Furbishers' machinations had driven his business into liquidation, he'd collected twenty-nine other victims and taken their case to solicitor after solicitor until he'd found one prepared to take them on without any guaranteed payment.

Trish had always liked Will's passion for the employees who'd lost their jobs as much as she admired the strength of his conviction that justice would be available to them all if he could only find the right words to explain exactly what Furbishers had done. Unfortunately the right ones rarely came to him. He'd try mouthfuls of new ones to tell her all over again, in quite different but still furious sentences, which threatened to tip him over into hysterical rage. Neither habit was likely to impress the court.

At their first meeting Trish had summed up five minutes' worth of his muddled ranting in two crisp sentences. His relief had been all the reward she'd wanted for the headache-inducing concentration needed to pick out what he had actually been saying from the maelstrom of outrage and irrelevance he had produced. Antony's half-mocking approval had been an unexpected extra and had set the tone for all their work on the case since.

In the old days, Will had had a small business on the Hampshire-Sussex Border, making traditional meat products for the upper end of the delicatessen and mail-order trade. He had never intended to expand; the company had made him a good living, and provided ten jobs in a rural area of high unemployment. Everything had gone well until he'd had the first, highly flattering letter from Furbishers.

'It was a fantastic moment,' he'd said at that first meeting in chambers, 'even though I'd never had any ambitions to trade on such a huge scale.'

In order to fulfil Furbishers' requirements, he'd bought more machines, taken on more staff and committed himself to ordering vastly increased supplies of raw materials, financing it all with a bank loan guaranteed against his house and all the business assets. Then, three months after he'd started to make his deliveries to Furbishers, they'd at last sent through the written contracts with an infinitely lower price per unit than he'd agreed.

Having committed himself to the expansion, Will had struggled to make the deal work, and stuck with it for far too long, losing money every day. Eventually the bank had called in the loan. He'd lost everything.

Some of the more comprehensible parts of his original diatribe came back to Trish, full of the emotion that had made him gobble and gag on the words. 'I did everything I was supposed to do and half-killed myself to get Furbishers what they said they wanted, then they screwed me royally and didn't give a shit.

'People like that *have* to take responsibility for the damage they do to the suckers they trick into believing in them. What they did to me would have made it impossible for anyone to fulfil their contract.

'It's not the money. I mean, it's not only the money. It's my marriage, my self-respect, my home, my faith in the basic decency of other human beings, my—' Tears of fury had filled his eyes, and he'd had to fight for control. Trish had considered explaining the law on consequential loss, but had decided to wait for a better time. The effort Will had made to keep his voice steady deepened it into a rolling bass. 'Everything. Then they made me believe it was *my* fault.'

That had been the killer accusation for her. In the past she'd seen plenty of rapists and paedophiles who'd made themselves feel better by blaming their victims. Furbishers' crime might not have been as bad as theirs, but the tactic was the same. She'd always thought it was vicious. This time it had ratcheted up her already powerful sympathy for her client.

'By the way,' she said to him, 'it won't be Antony asking the questions today. It'll be me.'

Will shook off her hand so that he could grab her by the shoulders, turning her so that the light from the high leaded windows fell on her face.

'Honestly?' he said. 'Oh, Trish, thank God. I wish I'd known. I'd have slept much better.'

Over Will's shoulder she could see Antony, raising his thumb like a merciful spectator of gladiatorial games. She let one eyelid droop in acknowledgement, hoping Will wouldn't notice.

'I've got to go to the robing room now,' she said. 'I'll see you in a bit. OK?'

He produced a quivery smile and nodded her away.

Chapter 3

Tim Hayleigh stood in the garage forecourt, feeling sick. The smell of petrol stuck in his throat and made it worse. It had taken him weeks to summon up the courage for this encounter and it wasn't going the way he'd planned.

'What are you so scared of?' Ron said. He had at least half his attention on the clicking figures on the pump, as he filled up his battered blue van. 'If there was going to be trouble about the body it would've happened ages ago, and definitely before the inquest. You're safe, the pair of you. Stupid, but safe. No one's going to go back on a suicide verdict now.'

'But the man had a camera.' Tim's voice was shaking. He was pleading as abjectly as if he'd fallen on his knees in front of everyone, but it didn't have any effect on Ron. 'There *must* be other people out there who knew what he was doing. They'll have been watching us ever since. It's a miracle we haven't been caught yet, but it'll happen one day. I know it will.'

'I doubt it. Not now. But if you're that worried, just tell my big brother you won't fly for a bit. There's nothing he can do to you.'

'You didn't see what he did to that snooper,' Tim whispered, wiping his hand over his mouth and feeling his lips mash against his palm. 'I keep thinking of the way the poor bugger's cheek-bone went. It kind of split and things burst out. He was still alive then.'

'Bob's not going to do anything like that to you.' Ron looked into Tim's face, as though searching for something he needed. 'He knows you're the only one of us who can fly. Just say no. It's easy enough.'

'What about the people on the other side?'

'What about them? There's nothing they can do to you if you're not there.'

'W-will you tell Bob for me?'

Ron shook the petrol nozzle, like a man in a urinal determined to make sure the last drop doesn't fall on his trousers, and stuffed it back into the side of the pump. Then he looked Tim full in the face.

'Can't you even do that much for yourself?'

'You didn't see him that night.'

'I know what he's like.' A faint smile softened Ron's expression. 'I was five when I worked out that the only people he never hurt, even when he got into one of his rages, were the ones who could give him things he couldn't get for himself. You can, with the flying, so you should be OK so long as you don't cringe. That always gets him going.'

'Oh, God.'

'And don't forget to take the plane up sometimes. You need to keep your neighbours remembering the noise is normal for when you find the guts to start again.'

Ron hoisted himself into the van and slid the door shut with a decisive crunch. Tim was left on the forecourt, still sick and wishing he'd brought Boney with him.

Trish paused for a moment in front of the mirror to make sure her wig was straight. The voluminous black gown made her seem even taller than usual and accentuated her pallor. Luckily her dark eyes and high-bridged nose were dramatic enough to stop her looking washed out. As she left the robing room, she saw that she'd have to run the whole length of the nave-like hall to catch up the rest of the team.

The sound of her heels clacking against the marble floor echoed up in the stone vaulting of the roof. The building was more like a vast church than anything else. Dating from the height of the Victorian passion for Gothic architecture, it provided a suitably awe-inspiring setting for the administration of justice.

She reached Antony's side just as he was making his silk gown swish with extra vigour as he passed Sir Matthew Grant-Furbisher, the chairman of Furbishers Foods. Sir Matthew didn't react, but when he caught sight of Will the two of them flashed such hatred at each other that Trish flinched.

Why had Grant-Furbisher come to court today, when he wasn't likely to be called to give his evidence for a long time yet? Was he trying to spook Will into even more of a turmoil than usual?

Belatedly Trish noticed a young redheaded woman in the corner watching Grant-Furbisher with fear in her eyes. Maybe he was stalking the halls to remind his employees of what he wanted them to say when they came to answer for their actions on his behalf.

'Bully,' Trish muttered as she settled the wig even more firmly on her smooth black hair, tucking it behind her ears to avoid muddling it with the grey horsehair curls. Some of her old-fashioned colleagues of both sexes looked like pantomime charladies wearing mops on their shaggy heads.

'Don't worry about it,' Antony whispered over his shoulder as she slid into the bench behind his. 'You look great.'

'Not like a moulting eagle then,' she whispered back, quoting one of their old clients, who had disapproved of her severe professional style.

Antony's eyebrows lifted again. Once the judge was in court, he would be all seriousness and devotion to duty. But there were still a few moments to go, and his expression told her he was planning to make the most of them.

'Not these days. If it's got to be any kind of bird, I'd say a cormorant, with black feathers sleek and body sinuous as it dives for its kill.'

'Steady on,' Trish said, trying not to laugh out loud. In the old days, she'd never have believed her abrupt and tyrannical head of chambers could be capable of this kind of cheerful silliness. 'I know you spin words for a living, but that's way over the top.'

As he turned away, she couldn't help thinking about the kind of bird that might best represent him. He had peacock qualities, obviously, and a tendency to overbear anyone who irritated him, but he had too much cleverness and wit for any creature as small-brained as a peacock. And he was capable – occasionally – of the most surprising kindness.

An usher appeared from the door behind the bench. Antony straightened his back. Everyone in court stood and bowed in silence, as Mr Justice Husking followed the usher. The judge was nearly as plump as Grant-Furbisher but a lot taller and more dignified in his black robes and neat wig.

Trish was too old a hand to feel nervous at this stage. Later, after the defence had had their chance to rip into Will's story, it would be different. Then she'd need some fear to get enough adrenaline pumping through her system to make her perform at her best.

Will was called and made his way to the witness box. The sight of his shaking hands and visibly heaving chest made her add even more confidence to her smile.

'Is your name William Applewood?' she asked him.

'Yes.' He coughed to clear his croaking voice, then said it again.

She established his address and occupation, before asking him to turn to page one of the witness statement in front of him, then the last page, which he had signed.

'Could you please tell the court if this is your signature?'

'Yes, it is.'

'Have you had an opportunity to re-read the statement since you signed it?'

'Yes.'

'Do you invite the court to accept that statement as your evidence in this case?'

'Yes.'

Trish had done all she had to do for the moment. She bowed to the judge and sat down, thinking of all the discussion that had gone into drafting the statement so that Will would come over as the careful but spirited entrepreneur she knew him to be, with the wildly emotional victim kept well in the background.

Ferdinand Aldham, QC, Furbishers' leading counsel, didn't deign to acknowledge her. He paused for long enough to make everyone aware of his importance, then rose, barely even nodding to the judge, and directed a beetling glower at Will Applewood.

'This statement is, of course, an unconscionable tissue of misinformation, isn't it?'

'No, it bl—' Will caught himself up, nodded apologetically to the judge, then said moderately, 'No. It is the absolute, unvarnished truth.'

'Are you sure it is not the case that you were so over-excited by the idea of being able to expand your little empire that you completely misinterpreted Furbishers' mild expression of interest in your, er –' He looked deliberately down at his notes – 'your pheasant, pork and, um, *pis*tachio terrines?'

Trish knew perfectly well that he was trying to instil in the judge's mind the idea that the magnificent and enormous Furbishers empire was far too important to bother to do anything intentionally to harm a pissant little rural business. After all, Furbishers made a huge and well-known contribution to the United Kingdom's economic, political and cultural life. They believed they were untouchable.

The judge's minute smile suggested that he knew what Aldham was doing, too. He made a note and turned his head away from the silk, whose poker face did not change.

'No one takes six weeks to prepare estimates of costs, income and profits in a frenzy of excitement,' Applewood said firmly, directing his responses to the judge as Trish had advised. 'I went into every possible eventuality and decided that the deal Furbishers had offered me was a good one.'

'But they hadn't at that stage offered you the deal, had they?'

'Of course they had. Arthur Chancer, the buyer, and I shook on it. He told me the men in suits took for ever to produce the paper contracts and he didn't want to wait for them before putting such a potentially popular product on the shelves. He said that actually signing the papers would be no more than a formality, and we should get going straight away.'

'That's not quite accurate, is it?' Aldham shuffled through his papers, presumably looking for the buyer's witness statement. 'Didn't Mr Chancer actually say that the men in suits took for ever to get out the paperwork and so he would like to offer you a trial agreement for two deliveries a week for three months, while they worked out the terms of the deal they would eventually offer you?'

'No.' Will shot Trish a small triumphant glance, inviting her to notice his unemotional rebuttal. She wasn't allowed to make any kind of signal, so she couldn't nod her approval.

'Didn't he add that those three months would give him time to assess the popularity of the product, so that he could work out the best price he could offer you for a long-term supply?'

This was, of course, the crux of the case, and given that there were no incontrovertible documents to prove it either way, the verdict would depend on the judge's assessment of the balance of probabilities, and of the characters involved.

'No, he didn't,' said Will, still firm and polite.

'Did anyone ever advise you not to buy the new machines until you had a signed contract?' Aldham asked, sounding dangerously casual.

'No.'

'Are you sure?'

'Yes.'

'No one at all ever said anything like: "be careful to get something on paper before you spend all this money"?'

There was a pause. Trish felt her heart thudding. Aldham might be fishing, but she had a feeling he had some documentary evidence somewhere to support this. She and Antony had, of course, seen the skeleton arguments Ferdy was going to use, just as he had seen theirs. But there could still be surprises in the detail.

'Only my wife. My ex-wife. And she didn't understand that I *had* a firm contract,' Will said. 'She was ignorant enough to believe that a contract has to be written down, and you know as well as I, Mr Aldham, that is not the case.'

'But she still warned you, didn't she?'

'It is true that she once wrote to me in those terms from her mother's, where she was staying at the time, but she knew nothing about the details of this particular deal, so I threw the letter in the bin.'

Will looked at Aldham as though he suspected the flamboyant silk of fossicking through dustbins in search of documentary evidence.

' "She knew nothing," ' Aldham quoted. 'And yet she put her finger on the very point that subsequently caused your problems, did she not? Could this have been because she knew your unbusiness-like and over-emotional habits?'

Will said nothing.

'Had she ever had cause to comment on what might be called your grandiosity before this?'

'Sometimes,' he said, looking injured. 'But she's never run a business. She thinks in terms of someone budgeting for a week's food shopping for a small family. You can't equate the two. Running a business like mine needs much more long-term and strategic planning.'

'Her housekeeping instinct means that, unlike you, she has never been in debt in her life or developed an irrational hatred of supermarkets, whereas you have, have you not?'

'No. I don't hate supermarkets,' Will said in the tones of one about to add a fiery insult. He managed to choke it down, looking as though it gave him burning indigestion.

'No?' Aldham's voice was heavy with satisfaction. 'Then could you please tell the court about the two reports you sent to the Food Standards Agency about meat you falsely claimed was contaminated by dangerous chemicals when it was offered for sale by my clients and some of their competitors?'

Trish might not have noticed the tiny stiffening of Antony's back if she hadn't been so worried herself. This was the most dangerous part of the evidence against Will. He stuttered and stumbled over his belief that substandard meat, brought in from foreign countries with much lower standards of animal husbandry, was being passed off as prime British meat in many outlets. Trish winced. She'd heard this was a common misconception in the farming world.

'They may use drugs that aren't allowed in the UK, and chemical fertilizers we're banned from using to produce the feed crops.' Will's voice was gobbling again, as the old anger seized his throat and made his tongue swell in his mouth. 'So their yields are greater than our farmers' and their prices lower. British consumers buy their garbage instead of the real thing. No one knows what the chemical residues are doing to the health of the people who eat it or their unborn children.'

If Antony hadn't forbidden her to raise objections, Trish would have been on her feet by now. Will was already in a tangle and clearly had no idea that the way he'd phrased his outburst suggested people were eating their unborn children. She dreaded to think what he'd come up with next.

'And you can't blame them. They don't know any better.'

There was the faintest quiver at the corner of the judge's mouth again. He'd noticed Will's gaffe even if no one else had. Trish could understand why Ferdy Aldham wasn't trying to choke off the rant, but why was Antony letting it run? She had to wait for three more questions before he got to his feet and with casual but deadly skill put Ferdy in his place.

By the time the court rose for the day, Trish was hoarse with the effort of putting her questions to Will in precisely the right form to elicit the answers she needed and choke off any extraneous information he might feel like offering. She longed more than anything to submerge herself in cold water. The airless atmosphere of the room, with its dark panelling and artificial light, the endless repetitive questions, and the need to concentrate on every word spoken made her feel as though her head was filled with popcorn. But there was plenty more to come before she could go home. The whole team would have to walk back to chambers now to analyse everything that had happened during the day, then plan tomorrow's campaign. After that, she was due to go to friends for dinner.

Her empty flat beckoned seductively, but she'd made the arrangements with Caro Lyalt and her partner more than a week ago. She couldn't back out now.

Chapter 4

Caro Lyalt had never felt so hated. Her suspect's eyes were like chunks of torn steel, and she knew he wanted to hit her. She didn't look away for a moment, even though his wife was standing only a few feet from his side. He'd terrified young PC Hartland into submission yesterday. Someone had to show him he could be beaten.

'There's not a mark on Kim, Inspector.' Daniel Crossman's voice had not yet lost the hectoring bark he must have worked for in his years as an army sergeant. 'And there's nothing wrong with her, except homesickness and you lot. All that poking and prying! It's no wonder she's frightened. The sooner she's back here, the better.'

No, it's not, Caro thought, remembering the last time she'd seen Crossman's stepdaughter. Six years old, bolt upright, and with so much maturity and suffering in her expression that Caro would have done anything to keep her safe.

It was going to be hard, though. Other members of the Child Protection Unit were already wavering, and Pete Hartland had shown how easily they might give in. As Crossman had said, there was no physical evidence of assault or abuse anywhere on Kim's small body, but that didn't mean she was unharmed. To Caro, the child's refusal to speak had been as eloquent as the flaring of her nostrils and the clenching of the small muscles around her eyes as she'd tried not to cry. Someone had terrorized Kim Bowlby into silence, and the obvious candidate was this man.

The flat smelled of bleach and silicone polish. Every surface was bare and clean. There were no books, no ornaments, no cushions, and nowhere to hide. The floor was covered with ice-grey vinyl so shiny it looked dangerous. The uncurtained windows looked out only on to a heavily shaded wall. There was no softness anywhere.

'Not all wounds leave marks, Mr Crossman, you should know that.' Caro spoke with the detached coolness that was the only thing she'd ever found that would hide her hatred of what men like this did to the people in their power. She put her empty teacup on a small white table.

He marched forwards, hands by his sides, until his nose was only inches from hers. She didn't flinch, but his fury clawed at her.

'No one here has done anything to Kim.' He jabbed his index finger sideways. Caro didn't let her eyes move. 'Ask her.'

At last she looked away and tried to decode the expression in his wife's lined face. There was fear there, certainly, and misery, and a dozen other things. The clearest was resentment. Between them, these two were tormenting Kim. There was no doubt about it. The only questions were exactly how they were doing it and what Caro would have to do to get the evidence she needed to prove it.

'Why won't you leave us alone?' Mrs Crossman said, in a whining voice that set Caro's teeth on edge. She looked at the woman's hands, red and flaking from using too much cleaning fluid, and tried to feel sorry for her. 'You've no right to come here like this, upsetting everyone.'

'I have every right to find out why Kim has run away twice and why she's been exhibiting so many of the signs of serious abuse. Her safety is my only concern.'

A baby wailed in the next room. Mo Crossman was across

the shiny floor and out of the door before Caro had taken two breaths. She looked straight at Crossman and said with stony deliberation, 'Apart from the baby's, that is. We are watching you, Daniel. And we won't stop until we find out what you've been doing.'

He stared at her, not bothering to answer.

Caro still hadn't got him out of her mind when she staggered home with two heavy plastic bags of shopping at the end of the day. It was a relief to find Jess happily sharing a drink with a friend of theirs. Her partner had failed to get yet another possible part in a television series last week and had been very glum since. Tonight it looked as though Cynthia Flag had managed to cheer her up. Caro kissed them both, then invited Cynthia to stay for supper, adding, 'You'll like Trish. She has all the right ideas, even though she doesn't do family law any more. I mean she hasn't sold out or anything. I'm doing sausages and mash for her and me, but I'm sure Jess would let you share her cheese-and-potato pie. And we can all have the same salad and pudding. Do stay.'

'I wish I could,' Cynthia said, looping her slippery dark-gold hair back into the combs she used to keep it up. 'But I'm on my way to meet someone. In fact, I ought to get going.'

'Not yet. Stay and talk to Jess while I get started on the cooking.'

'Why don't we do that for you?' Jess said. 'You look as though you could use a shower.'

Glad to see her in such high spirits, Caro left the kitchen to the two of them. It was good to be able to take time under the hard jets of water and feel the day's tensions being washed away. She emerged, cool and a bit calmer, to dress in loose linen trousers and a T-shirt. She would have kept her feet bare, except that it was dustbin day tomorrow and she'd have to take the rubbish out later.

Cynthia and Jess were still talking amid the potato peelings and onion skins, while savoury smells wafted out of the oven. When Caro joined them, Jess looked her up and down and said, 'Couldn't you have made a bit more effort? Those trousers make you look like the back end of an elephant. Even you must have noticed that pure linen only works when it's new.'

'Oh, Jess! What does it matter? They're comfortable, and Trish won't mind what I look like.'

'I mind.'

Caro couldn't stop herself snapping, which made Jess rush out of the kitchen.

'You're a bit hard on her,' Cynthia said gently, laying a hand on Caro's shoulder. 'Couldn't you cut her some slack while she's having such a tough time?'

'She's not the only one.'

'Don't, Caro.'

'Don't what?'

'Talk like an angry police officer. I know you don't mean to do it, but I don't think you've got any idea how hard it must be for Jess to deal with after she's spent an almost silent day on her own, worrying about whether she's ever going to get another job.'

Caro shook her head, not sure whether she was offering an apology or expressing disbelief. Cynthia just smiled. Later, when she'd gone and Jess was taking her turn in the shower, Caro cleared up the kitchen as a penance and distracted herself by thinking about Daniel Crossman.

She had seen far too many men like him to mistake the cold watchfulness in his eyes or miss the violence hidden behind his superficial stillness. He was a control freak; he had an obsession with cleanliness that, to her at least, meant there were things about himself he could not bear to acknowledge; and he ruled his unhappy little household with tyrannical rigidity.

The only problem was that no one knew what else he had

been doing. Unless they found out within the next fourteen days, Kim was going to have to go back and face it all over again. Getting the interim care order had been hard enough. If the chief social worker hadn't been so much on Caro's side, Kim would probably have been sent back already.

Caro lifted the heavy plastic rubbish bag and carried it out of the flat. As she turned into the side alley, where the bins were kept, she heard a familiar voice calling her name from the street, and adding, 'D'you want a hand with that?'

'It's fine, thanks, Trish,' she said, turning to greet her friend. 'How are you? Not that I need to ask. You look fantastic. But you must be sweltering in that black suit.'

'It's cooler than it looks,' Trish said, flapping the sides of her jacket over the white muslin shirt. 'Although I envy you your trousers. I wish I'd had time to go home to change. We had a heavy session today.'

'Poor you.'

'But you look as though you haven't had too easy a day either. A tough case?'

'Awful.' Caro had learned not to talk to Jess about the children she was fighting to protect, but Trish was different. She wouldn't mind listening to the whole story and it would be a relief to share some of it. Trish might even have some ideas about how they could persuade Kim to break her silence. Still talking twenty minutes later, they went upstairs to rescue the sausages and to see how Jess was getting on with her cheese-and-potato pie.

Three hours later, Trish at last reached her own flat and let herself in with the feeling of a traveller returning from the most arduous trek across unforgiving terrain. She had always found Jess hard to like, but this evening had been worse than usual. Knowing how worried Caro was, Trish thought Jess might have shown some sympathy for her – even a little practical help – but she'd been mulish in the extreme. It had been Trish who'd got up to carry the dirty plates out to the kitchen and help Caro with the washing up. Jess had stayed in the sitting room, lying on the sofa in her svelte clothes and listening to music turned up so loud it had been painful even in the kitchen. Trish had often wondered why Caro had fallen in love with Jess in the first place, and why she stuck with the relationship when it was obviously so difficult.

The big Southwark flat was quiet, and it smelled wonderful. The smoky scent of dried lavender from a bowl in the middle of the table mixed with the smell of oil paint from the latest abstract Trish had bought, and the beeswax polish her cleaner liked to use. Revelling in the glorious absence of food cooking, she double-locked the door, stretched out one arm to turn off the external light and headed up the spiral staircase to her bedroom under the eaves.

Later, wrapped in a scarlet towel after a long self-indulgent shower, she checked that the radio-alarm beside her bed was set for six o'clock. Tomorrow was going to be an important day with the opening of Furbishers' defence. She would need all her faculties to pick up the real evidential points Ferdy Aldham made as well as the subliminal messages he was generating.

She opened *The Plague* by Albert Camus, which Antony had recommended and prepared to read herself to sleep. The novel was said to be a seminal work, but so far it had left her unsatisfied. Only some sorts of fiction managed both to drag her deep into its particular world and tell her something new about herself. This had done neither yet, and she found it cold. She thought she might go on with it for a little longer, but if it didn't perk up soon, she'd bin it, however clever and important it might be.

The book falling on her nose woke her. She took off her glasses and turned out the light.

Later it was a griping spasm that wrenched her out of sleep.

Her whole bed felt full of pain; her mind wouldn't work. The room was very dark and very hot. Another spasm forced a groan out from between her clenched teeth. She knew she had to get out of bed. Bending over the ache, holding both hands round her body, she ran for the bathroom.

Next morning Trish felt as though a ten-ton truck had been driving back and forth over her body all night. When she staggered back into the bathroom in search of another Imodium, she saw her reflection in the mirror over the basin and flinched. Her skin was greyish and made her look old enough to be her own grandmother. Great dark circles under her eyes showed how little sleep she'd had. Her throat felt raw, the pain in her gut was nearly as bad as it had been in the night, but the pills she'd swallowed had been doing their work. She managed to clean her teeth and rinse out her mouth, but she didn't risk anything more than milkless tea for breakfast.

Antony took one look at her as they met outside chambers and said, 'What the hell d'you think you're doing, giving yourself a hangover on a court day?'

Trish shook her head. This was Antony back to his old acerbic self. 'Don't! I was up all night. NHS Direct say it sounds like food poisoning, but I think I'm on the mend now.'

'Sorry,' he said, as the affection relaxed his face again. 'I should have known you'd never be so irresponsible. What were you eating? Shellfish? That can be a bugger in this weather.'

'No. I went to friends. It was only sausages, and pretty well-cooked at that. Overcooked in fact.'

'Sounds remarkably unsuitable for such a hot evening. Are you up to a day in court?' She'd never heard his voice so gentle, or seen his eyes so soft.

'So long as I don't try to eat anything.'

'Good. Warn me if you need to go out, won't you?'

She was touched by the way he made Colin carry all her

paraphernalia as well as the day's files and gave him strict instructions to take notes for her of every point the defence made. But she was determined to do her job properly.

The first person she saw when she walked into court was Will Applewood, sitting alone on the claimants' bench. She wished he hadn't come. There was nothing for him to do except listen to interminable arguments about contract law or evidence from Furbishers' employees impugning his brains and business sense. His face lit up as it always did when he smiled at her, and she forced herself to smile back.

All day, she had to fight waves of pain, concentrating as hard as she'd ever done. There were one or two scary moments, but she held on, took painkillers and another Imodium at lunchtime instead of food, and kept going.

Antony sent her straight home when the judge rose, telling her that he and Colin would take her stuff back to chambers and he'd see her in the morning.

'And think about whether you want to sue the people who poisoned you,' he called after her.

Trish waved him off, but the comment did make her think. Jess, who had eaten quite different food, couldn't be affected, but if the damage really had been done by the sausages, Caro must be suffering too.

Jess answered the phone, sounding tearful. 'She's in hospital,' she said, as soon as Trish had said who she was.

'Food poisoning?'

'How did you know?'

'Because I had it too,' Trish said crossly, thinking no one could be that stupid. 'But nothing like badly enough for a trip to hospital. How is Caro?'

'I don't know. Barely conscious.' Jess gulped. 'I didn't know what to do when she started throwing up in the night. I made her mint tea, which nearly always helps, but she couldn't even keep that down. It got worse and worse and it was hurting her so much that in the end I called an ambulance. She was furious. But I was so frightened.'

'I'm sure,' Trish said, in her most professionally soothing voice, although she disliked Jess's familiar habit of exaggerating everything.

'And I've been sitting with her in casualty all day long, trying to help. They took her up to a ward about an hour ago and said there wasn't anything more I could do. So I came back here.'

'It sounds as though she's really ill,' Trish said, with more than a twinge of guilt.

'Of course she is. She could die,' Jess wailed. 'And they won't even let me stay with her.'

'It *can't* be that bad. Which hospital is she in?'

'Dowting's. It's the nearest. But they say they won't have any news until tomorrow at the earliest. And by then she may be . . .'

'They'll look after her, Jess. She'll be all right. But what about you? Do you need anything?'

Jess sniffed, then said, 'I'm fine, but I stuck to veg. I've been telling her for weeks that meat is poison, but she didn't believe me, you see. Oh, Trish, what's going to happen?'

How the hell do I know? Trish thought, while she murmured the kind of soothing reassurances she knew Caro would have wanted her to offer.

Bob had refused to go to Ron's pub, which had seemed like a bad omen. Now he was sitting opposite Tim in one just outside Stubb's Cross, where no one knew either of them. They'd got pints of the local bitter in front of them. Bob had barely started on his, but Tim had drained the lot. He'd hoped it would give him enough courage to embark on an explanation of why he wouldn't fly again until he could be sure no one was going to ask questions about the man Bob had kicked to death.

'Got any idea how long I'll have to wait till you feel safe

again?' Bob said at last, in a voice so casual that Tim was deceived.

He started to say that he wouldn't know till it happened, when he saw Bob's eyes bulging, as they always did when he was about to let his temper rip. Tim grabbed his tankard as though to drink, but there was nothing left in it. Feeling like a fool as well as a coward, he said, 'Don't you think it would be mad to take such a risk?' He hated the way his voice quivered. He coughed, but it didn't help. 'It'll probably only be a month or two. Till we're sure no one's going to come looking for us. By then there'll be much less evidence anyway. So we should be all right even if they did come nosing around. You must see that, Bob.'

Waiting for the usual explosion, Tim found himself staring at the scars on Bob's hands. As he watched, they curled into fists, then slowly relaxed again until they lay flat against his powerful thighs. They looked as if they belonged to a man fighting every instinct to hit out. When Bob finally spoke, his voice was tight with suppressed fury.

'We *can't* stop now. It's taken too long to set this up and get it working to throw it away. I'm paying all the pet-food people to keep quiet. If I stop their money, they're going to be tempted to grass you up, and I can't afford to bung them without the profits from your flights. You wouldn't want them knowing how you killed that man, now would you?'

Tim's mouth opened, but he couldn't produce any sound. All he'd done that night had been to watch as Bob had kicked the snooper to death. Tim would have called the police straight off, if he hadn't been terrified for his own life. No one could pin any of the blame on him. He considered pointing that out, then saw Bob's face and thought better of it.

'I suppose if you won't fly, you won't,' Bob said, as though he hadn't noticed Tim's shock. 'But I'll have to look around for someone else who will. There's bound to be someone.'

Tim forgot everything in the glorious sensation that

enveloped him. It was as though someone had lifted him off his uncomfortable chair and wrapped him in the softest duvet. Bob could get another pilot. It was so simple. Why the hell hadn't he thought of it for himself? Trying to hide his relief, he produced a noncommittal shrug.

'I couldn't quarrel with that.'

'Good.' Bob got up and leaned over him, holding him down with one heavy, scarred hand on his shoulder. His grip was tight enough to hurt. 'But that doesn't mean you're off the hook. If I ever hear so much as a whisper that you might've talked to anyone, I'll be round your place to make sure you never talk again. Got that?'

Tim nodded. He knew it was true. Bob let him go at last and shoved his way out of the little pub. When Tim could move again, he cranked himself to his feet and got another pint from the bar. He needed it to take the taste of fear out of his mouth and give him the illusion of control over his life.

When he got home again, he fed Boney, made himself a pot of tea and settled down to do his accounts. He'd been putting them off for weeks, but even they weren't as scary as Bob.

An hour later, sweating, Tim reset the calculator and added up each column all over again. The totals came out the same. He couldn't believe it. All his relief drained away. He'd been right up against the overdraft limit for months, but he hadn't realized he had only six pounds fifty left. He'd started to grow cherries on some of his land years ago, when he'd first understood how the price of lamb was collapsing, and the fruit had made just enough difference to keep the farm going. But this year's harvest had netted the smallest profit he'd ever made. Bills were flooding in every day. Without the money Bob paid him for the weekly flights to France, he'd never be able to settle any of them. He'd always had a legitimate sideline, taking aerial photographs for local landowners and estate agents, but that was never going to plug this kind of gap. No legal business could.

Could he make himself crawl back to Bob now? Having had that one fantastic glimpse of freedom, it would be like slamming the door in his own face. And Bob would make him pay for his weakness.

Caro was in a general admission ward, full of mainly elderly patients who had been brought in after falls at home or in the street. Some were unconscious, but several beds had two or three nurses shouting supposedly soothing explanations at the confused and frightened occupant.

Trish found Caro eventually in the furthest bay from the door. She was asleep, which seemed astonishing in the middle of this cacophony. Her complexion looked even worse than Trish's had in the night, and already her cheeks were sunken. Her nose jutted up under the skin like a spike. A drip was attached to her right arm. Trish leaned towards it to read the name of the drug they were pumping into Caro.

'Can I help?' asked a heavily accented voice behind her.

Trish turned to see a tall blond nurse hurrying towards her. There was a harassed expression on his pale, chiselled face. His accent suggested he came from Eastern Europe, or possibly even Russia.

'It's OK. She's a friend of mine and I just wanted to see what you're giving her.'

'Only saline to keep up fluids,' he said. 'At this stage.'

'Do you know what kind of food poisoning it is?'

'Not yet. The results are not back from the lab. Why do you ask?'

'Because I was eating with her yesterday, and I've been affected too, though not like this.'

'Ah. The doctor thinks E. coli maybe, but the lab will say for sure in a day or two.'

'E. coli? Is that enough to make her as ill as this?'

'Oh, yes. If resistance is lowered, E. coli can be . . . severe. The infection is able to spread, maybe affecting the blood, too. This is known as septicaemia.'

The last thing Trish wanted now was a lesson in medical terminology. Horrified at the thought of what could be happening inside Caro's body, she said, 'What are you doing about the source of the infection?'

'Is nothing we can do. We think it will have come from the sausages she ate, but no one knows what brand they have been. Often it will be poor hygiene, not the food itself, that infects.'

'Even so, it should be checked out. And Caro's partner must have the wrappings in their flat. I could go now and—'

The nurse put his hand on Trish's arm to hold her back. 'All the packagings have been thrown out, and garbage removed this morning. We have asked this already. Miss Jess says often her friend will buy food when she is at work and it will be out of the refrigerator all day. Is enough to allow bacteria to multiply. How are *you* treating this?'

Trish told him and was relieved to hear that the advice she'd been given over the phone by NHS Direct had been correct. But that did nothing to change the fact that her best friend was lying in front of her, unconscious, perhaps dying. Could it be true? Trish gripped the metal bedstead and tried to think sensibly. The only ideas her mind threw up were like a child crying 'it's not fair'. Caro was too rare a person – and too *necessary* – to die. It couldn't happen if there were any kind of justice.

Trish pushed the thought away. She'd learned years ago that no one could guarantee justice.

Chapter 5

Pain was everywhere, absorbing all Caro's brain cells and tearing at every part of her body. She moved to ease it and something tugged at her arm. Her eyelids felt too heavy to lift, but she had to know what it was. Trying to focus on the transparent worm that was burrowing into her flesh, she heard someone calling her name.

'Inspector Lyalt! Inspector! *Inspector Lyalt*!'

At last, she managed to force her eyes fully open. Someone with short dark hair was hanging over her. The picture fizzled at the edges and bent out of shape, then reformed.

'Guv,' he said, still urgently. 'Can you hear me?'

'Yes.' She ran her tongue around her mouth. It felt as dry as sandpaper and tasted horrible. No wonder her voice hardly worked. Her mind swooped. She tried to talk. This time the sound was better. 'Yes?'

'You're in hospital.'

She began to remember. The worm must be part of a drip. This was serious, then. 'What happened?'

'They think you've been poisoned.'

Memories of a night with Jess and buckets and panic came back. Then there were the ambulance paramedics, whose certainty and kindness had blessedly soothed Jess. They had wrapped red blankets around Caro and strapped her into a stretcher. The sensation of security had been unlike anything she'd ever felt.

'Who are you?' she asked now, feeling as though her tongue was the size and texture of a steak.

The face hanging over her moved back. It looked hurt.

'Pete,' said its owner. 'PC Peter Hartland.'

'Of course. Sorry.' Caro lifted her hand to rub her eyes. 'Not myself. Why are you here, Pete?'

'To see you. And to ask whether you ate or drank anything when you were interviewing Daniel Crossman.'

Concentrating was hard. Like lifting the biggest weights in the gym. The time before the pain seemed dim and unreal. Trish was there. And a leaky rubbish bag. Jess was upset.

'Crossman?'

'Think back.' Pete's voice was panicky. 'You went to see him and his wife. Don't you remember?'

'About Kim?'

'That's right.'

She could feel his breath on her hot face as he exhaled. He was much too close. He'd been eating cheese and pickle.

'Well done,' he said, blowing into her nostrils again. She blinked. 'Did you go into their flat, guv?'

'Yes. It was cold. The sun doesn't reach it. Very clean. The baby was crying.'

'Did you eat anything, or drink anything while you were there? A cup of tea maybe?'

'Tea?' It had been strong, and the darkest, hottest thing in the flat. The tannin had scraped at her tongue. She hadn't known what to do with the cup, holding on to it while Crossman tried to frighten her out of his flat and his life, just like he'd done to this boy, and to everyone else who'd tried to help the child. 'Yes. Why? Did he do this?' Her hand moved protectively to her stomach.

Pete Hartland disappeared. There were voices, quiet but

furious. Caro tried to lift her head to see what was happening. Someone in a strange uniform – white with buttons down the front – took his place.

'How are you feeling?' The voice was male and foreign but kind.

'Horrible.'

'Are you in pain?'

Caro felt a laugh forming, but it was too much effort to let it out, so she just tried to explain about the grinding in her back and the clenching in her gut, and the way all her muscles felt as though she had been racked.

The nurse started tidying her up, smoothing the sheet that had rucked up under her and flattening the pillows. Then he did something to the transparent bag at the end of her drip and added a note to the card at the end of her bed.

'What happened to Hartland?'

'He is gone. He should not have been here, disturbing you with questions. He was told not to.'

'He said I'd been poisoned.'

'You have *food* poisoning. That is all. We think it was the sausages you cooked the night you were brought in here.'

'Why?'

'Because you had a friend eating with you, who has also suffered.'

'Trish? Is she here?'

'No. Her case was less serious.'

The world was swimming around Caro again. She was being sucked under. As she went down, she heard herself say, 'Tell Pete.'

It was so urgent that he should know Daniel Crossman hadn't done this to her that she fought to stay above the surface. But she couldn't make the nurse understand. He didn't know how passionately Pete hated Daniel Crossman.

With his past, Pete should never have been let anywhere near

Child Protection, but the powers that be hadn't listened to her when she'd warned them. It wasn't that he'd been physically or sexually abused himself as a child; they'd have understood that and kept him right away. But he had been emotionally terrorized by the grandfather who'd brought him up. Any male authority figure could make him suddenly behave weirdly. He'd responded well to Caro when they'd put him on her team, and she liked him. He was a demon for work, too, but he was driven by forces he didn't properly understand, and that made him dangerous.

He had to be stopped now, before he took the law into his own hands and screwed up every chance they had of rescuing Kim. What was it Pete had said after Crossman had thrown him out of the flat? 'Someone needs to teach that bastard a lesson. I hope I get the chance.' Caro tried to call out. No one answered.

The white blob of the nurse's uniform had dwindled to nothing and Caro's voice didn't seem to work any more.

Trish spent the following day listening to Ferdy Aldham and Antony as they tried to elicit from Furbishers' witnesses sufficient evidence to persuade the judge one way or the other. It was hard to concentrate because it was all so familiar. Still, she had to keep her mind on the job, noting down each point the witnesses made and mentally ticking them off against the lists she and Antony had prepared. Then they had to go back to chambers for the usual post-mortem, so it was after eight by the time she was free to go back to Dowting's to find out how Caro was getting on.

The news wasn't good. At the front desk they told her that Caro had been moved into a proper bed. Trish made her way up to the tenth floor and found herself in a bay that was a lot quieter than the admissions ward. The view was good, too, straight over the Thames to the Houses of Parliament. If this had been a private hospital, such a position would have commanded a big premium, but it wasn't. It was the National Health Service at its best.

Trish went from bed to bed in the bay, apologizing to occupants and visitors as she peered at them. At last she found Caro, lying with her eyes closed and mumbling. She looked awful.

There was a man standing beside her, looking down at her ravaged face. He was wearing loose grey-blue trousers and a collarless natural linen shirt. As Trish approached, he looked up. She recognized his smooth-skinned roundish face at once, even though she could not put a name to him.

'Trish!' he said in a light voice that teased her memory. 'How wonderful! It's Andrew. Andrew Stane.'

'Of course,' Trish said, identifying him as the social worker she'd met over one of the worst cases of child cruelty she'd ever been involved with. She'd admired his devotion to the job from the start and she'd come to like him as they fought to protect the child whose parents had systematically tormented him for years. Starvation and cigarette burns had been the least of it. 'How are you?' They shook hands. 'It must be a good five years since I saw you.'

'More, I should think. But I've never forgotten the way you worked with little Dean Welkins when no one else could get through to him. We'd never have won without you.'

'Thank you.' Trish tried not to let her memory yield any details of the boy's agonizing story, but she couldn't keep them all down. She'd never forgotten her first sight of his heart-shaped white face and piteous black eyes, and the story she'd helped him to tell had shaken her more than any other.

'How's he doing?'

'Not well, I'm afraid. But with that kind of start, how could he?' Andrew's smile was so sad it made Trish's teeth ache. 'I tell myself that at least he's alive, and safe, warm and fed. That's a lot more than he could have been sure of before we intervened.'

'Not enough, though, is it?' she said, remembering all over again why she had moved away from work with brutalized children. 'Are you involved with Caro in this business of the girl with the terrifying stepfather?'

'Yes. And I came tonight because I'd heard she was better, making sense again. But look at her!'

Trish edged closer to Caro, who was still lying with her eyes closed, but talking all the time. Nothing made sense. There was just a jumble of sounds.

'What's she saying?'

'I've been here twenty minutes and it's been a complete mishmash. Sometimes she talks about Kim – the child – sometimes Jess. Sometimes you. One of her colleagues features occasionally; he was in here today, so that may be why. But mostly it's nonsense. Occasionally there's a whole sentence. They think she may be able to hear us; then again she may not.'

'Do they know why she's so ill?'

His face hardened. 'No. The bacteria involved have been confirmed as E. coli 0157. But it doesn't usually have this effect.'

'Although it can be serious,' Trish said, remembering the nurse's warnings, as well as old news reports. 'People have died from it, haven't they? Vulnerable people.'

'That hardly applies to Caro,' Andrew said. 'She's the fittest of the fit and in the gym at least three times a week.'

'Yes, but stress can go for the immune system, and this case seemed to be stressing her more than usual.'

'She's not the only one.' He rubbed both hands over his smooth face, and stopped with them steepled against the end of his nose. He looked at Trish over the top. 'We've only got two weeks left. If we don't get any evidence, Kim is going to have to go back to her stepfather. Caro was the driving force. Without her, I don't know what we're going to do. Even the psychiatrist has admitted defeat. That's why I came this evening. I mean, I'd have come anyway to see Caro, but we need her firing on all cylinders. And look at her. There's no way she can help now.'

A nurse appeared behind him, leading an elderly woman on a Zimmer frame, and urging her on with a stream of gentle encouragement. The woman's skin was almost transparent, and white wisps of hair kept blowing in her foggy eyes. Her fingers were gnarled with arthritis and the skin discoloured with pale-brown spots.

She's the kind of patient who should be at risk of food poisoning, Trish thought, not a tough police officer in her thirties. She looked back at Andrew, who'd let his arms drop to his sides again.

'So the child still won't talk?' she said, remembering everything Caro had told her.

'That's right. There were signs Caro was beginning to get through to her during their last interview. Now we're stuck.'

'I'm so sorry,' Trish said. There wasn't anything else to say.

Andrew must have recognized that for he asked about her work. She gave him a quick sketch of the case against Furbishers.

'I hope you win,' he said politely. 'Are you still living in Southwark?'

'Yes. I love the flat too much to move. What about you?'

'I have moved. I'm in Muswell Hill now. It's not ideal, but it'll do.'

Trish looked at Caro's twitching face. It seemed all wrong to be making this sort of trivial conversation while she was so ill. Telling Andrew Stane she had to go, Trish hurried out of the ward. At the nurses' station, she stopped and scribbled a note to be given to Caro when she was well enough to read it.

'I'll see she gets it,' said the young Filipina nurse who took the envelope.

'She is going to get better, isn't she?'

'We hope so.'

With that cold comfort, Trish went back to her flat to spend what was left of the evening picking at a bowl of cottage cheese and trying not to think any more about the possibility that Caro might die.

When the phone rang, she grabbed it, more than ready to talk to George, who had promised to ring from Australia tonight. Then she saw that it was still too early for him, so she gave her name much more cautiously.

'Trish, it's Andrew. I'm sorry to phone you at home. I just thought it would be easier to ask this if I could be sure we wouldn't be overheard.'

'To ask what?' she said, puzzled.

'For your help interviewing Kim Bowlby, the child in Caro's case.'

'I couldn't,' Trish said at once, without even thinking about it. 'I'm up to my neck in my own work. Besides, I'd have no standing. I don't do family law any more.'

'I could swing it, having you as an expert, I mean, given your experience. Please, Trish. You helped Dean to speak and probably saved his life. If anyone could work the same kind of miracle with Kim it would be you.'

'I can't, Andrew. I'm sorry, desperately sorry, for the child, but I can't help. It's just not possible.'

'Even to save Caro's reputation?'

'What?'

'The buzz is that she's not half as ill as she seems, that she's faking this near-death condition,' Andrew said.

'Who could possibly believe anything so idiotic?' The snap in Trish's voice echoed back at her down the line.

'Her colleagues in the Child Protection Unit,' Andrew said with all the mildness of a man trained to avoid reacting to aggression. 'The suggestion is that she's come to realize that she's overreacted to the Kim Bowlby case for some unknown reason of her own. Projection probably. And now she's staked so much of her reputation on the outcome, she can't back down. Being ill will let her off. They think she'll carry on like this until the interim care order has expired and then make a miraculous recovery, when it's too late to do anything for Kim.'

'That's ludicrous. And unbelievably offensive. Caro is far too self-aware and experienced to do anything like that. She'd never be so irresponsible,' Trish said, adding silently to herself: or make the people who care about her go through this kind of terror.

'Misreading what goes on in families and relationships does happen. To all of us. You know that. But this is another reason why I'd do anything to get Kim to talk. She's important – any child in that kind of state would be – but Caro matters more. She's in a position to save a hundred Kims, so long as she doesn't lose her confidence and standing over this. You *have* to help.'

Blackmail, Trish thought. Sodding blackmail. 'How do you know that's what her colleagues are saying?'

'There's a young PC there, Pete Hartland, who's devoted to Caro and passionately determined that Kim should be saved from her stepfather. Hartland has been keeping me up to speed. It was he who told me Caro was better, which is why I rushed straight round to Dowting's this evening. I told you: we've got less than fourteen days to deal with this. You know what I found. She's not in a position to help anyone now.'

'Look,' Trish said, feeling her resolution crack, 'whatever happens, however urgent it is, I couldn't do anything until the weekend. I have to be in chambers for pre-court preparation by seven every morning; we're in court all day; then there's the post-mortem conference and plenty more after that.'

'The weekend may be the best we could do. But if I got permission, would you talk to Kim then? Please, Trish. The child needs you. We all need you.'

She thought of her empty flat and the sense of freedom that

rushed towards her each time she opened the door now, knowing there would be no one else there. Usually at the end of the day, she'd find George in her kitchen, cooking an elaborate and terribly filling dinner as a way of dealing with the frustrations of his day, while David would want help with his homework and then a chance to talk or play Scrabble. Shuttling between the two of them, she sometimes felt as though she'd never had any time to herself since she'd taken David to live with her. She didn't regret that decision, but it seemed hard to have to sacrifice the rare luxury of being on her own. Then she thought of the child Caro had described. Anything could happen if Kim were sent back home. Trish knew she'd never forgive herself for refusing help if the child were hurt – or killed.

'Oh, all right,' she said. 'But make it Sunday so that I can read the files first. I'll need all the background you've got, if I'm to have any hope of getting through to her in such a short time.'

'Great. I'll get back to you as soon as I can.'

When they'd said goodbye, Trish tried to remember what she knew about Caro's own childhood that might explain Andrew's comments about projection. It was a familiar enough syndrome, in which adults who had themselves been damaged in childhood assumed they could see evidence of their own suffering in the children with whom they worked. Every adult Trish had ever met had shown some signs of unresolved pain left over from a family trauma. Most admitted to it when questioned; she'd often thought the rest were liars. But she couldn't remember Caro's saying anything except that she had never known her father. Jess might know more.

Trish rang Jess's number. It was clear from the hoarseness of Jess's voice that she had been crying.

'She *is* getting better,' Trish said. 'I heard at the hospital today that she'd come round for a while this afternoon.'

'Yes, but it didn't last, so she's *not* getting better. Don't try and comfort me, Trish. She looks terrible. She didn't even recognize me when she opened her eyes. The staff won't talk to me. Or even look straight at me. That's because they think she's going to die. I know it is.'

'Jess, don't. She's running a high temperature because of the infection. It happens. And that's what leads to the confusion. But they're working to lower the fever. Now, listen, how much has she told you about this child she's working to protect?'

'Trish, I've got to go.' Jess sounded unlike herself: efficient to the point of brusqueness. 'I've got someone here.'

She cut the connection. Trish tried to work out what could be going on. In that last comment Jess had sounded completely different from the hoarse, tearful woman who had answered the phone. Who could be there in the flat to make her sound so different, so tough? And why hadn't Jess mentioned the presence of a third party straight away? What the hell was going on?

Disliking her suspicions, Trish put the receiver back on its cradle. Her mobile started to ring almost at once.

'Trish Maguire,' she said coolly, knowing it couldn't be George. He'd never call her mobile from Australia.

'Trish. It's me. Will Applewood.'

'Oh, hello,' she said. Now that he had finished giving his evidence, there was no reason why she couldn't talk to him, but she'd have preferred to get on with the case without any more personal contact than she had to have. She wasn't going to encourage him.

'I say, are you all right, Trish? You didn't look as awful in court today as you did yesterday, but you're still not yourself. I had to phone to find out what's the matter. I thought yesterday might have been a hangover, but they don't last this long. Are you ill?'

She suppressed a sigh. It was kind of him to bother, but she could have done without the interruption. She explained.

'E. coli 0157?' he said. 'God, you must be careful. It can be really dangerous. Have you seen the quack?'

'No need. I stopped throwing up twenty-four hours ago, and I've even managed to eat some cottage cheese today.' She looked at the bowl and saw that she hadn't made much of a hole in the mound of soft white particles.

'Even so, you ought to get checked out. It can go for the kidneys, you know. How did you get it?'

Trish told him the story of the sausages and the disappearance of their packaging, adding, 'And I was so angry at the idea that anyone could sell such dangerous food that I thought for a mad moment I might go chasing off after Caro's dustbin men. I wanted to find the wrappings so that I could identify the suppliers and get something done about them. Then I remembered all those TV news shots of landfill sites, you know with tractors flattening the stuff and wild dogs eating it and seagulls pecking at it.'

'I know what you mean. The kind of place where you could lose a dozen bodies. You'd never be able to find and identify one bit of packaging. But someone should find out where the sausages came from and get wherever it is cleaned up,' Will said, his voice positively throbbing with sincerity.

Trish forgot about not encouraging him and asked why he was so het up. After all, he hadn't been poisoned.

'Because I hate the bastards who peddle filthy meat products. Have you really no idea where these came from?'

'None,' Trish said, thinking of a way Andrew Stane might give her a quid pro quo for her help with his case. 'Although I'm told my hostess used to pick up food for supper when she was out visiting people she had to interview. I could probably find out where she was on Monday afternoon, and then go into all the nearest shops to— Except that I haven't got time.'

'But I have. More time than I can fill.' Will sounded eager. 'If you find out roughly where she was, I can do the legwork.'

'D'you really mean that?'

'Sure. I haven't got anything else to do now I've given my

evidence. And it'll stop me trying to decide whether it would be better to jump out of the window now or wait till we've lost the case.' He laughed to show that he wasn't serious.

'Oh, Will,' Trish said, knowing that he was and longing to comfort him. 'Whatever happens, it's not going to be that bad. You'll get back on your feet again, and . . .'

'If you tell me what the sausages tasted like,' he said briskly, as though he hated overt sympathy as much as he wanted it, 'I'll have a fair chance of identifying them when I see them.'

'They were spicy; really spicy, I mean, not that over-peppery nastiness you get in some mass-produced ones. And the meat was chunky not smooth. I thought they were good, and I don't usually like sausages at all. Especially not when the weather's boiling like this.'

'Spice can be used to cover every kind of disgustingness,' he said. 'Get me the relevant routes your friend might have walked and I'll see what I can find.'

If he were out hunting for contaminated sausages, he couldn't be sitting in court, listening to evidence designed to show him up as a greedy fool. That had to be a good thing.

'Would you?' Trish said. 'That would be terrific, Will. I know I could never do it on my own even if I had time.'

She heard him breathe more deeply, as though he was already expanding into a bigger space than the one he'd been inhabiting for the past few months.

Tim Hayleigh was sitting in his pyjamas, with Boney in his lap and an opened bottle of wine by his side, trying to concentrate on the sitcom he was watching. A character in it shouted at someone and threw a glass against the wall. With the crash ringing in his ears, Tim was whisked back to the night Bob had smashed the snooper's face with his boot.

At first he'd been terrified of the police coming to arrest him. Now he thought it might not be so bad. After all, if he were convicted he could forget about his financial disaster for as long as the sentence lasted. He'd be fed and housed in prison. But then he might not survive long enough to be sent there. Bob would definitely try to kill him long before either of them got to court.

'So why are you even thinking of going back to work for him?' he asked himself out loud.

Boney winced at the sound of his voice, then moved closer to provide a little comfort. Boney was the only one he could talk to now, apart from Ron, who didn't count.

Tim's teeth chattered, even though it was so hot. Boney looked up, as if to say something useful, but there was nothing anyone could say. If he wasn't going to prison, Tim had to get some money fast. Flying for Bob was the only way he knew. Somehow he had to find the courage to go back.

He rubbed his shoulder, where Bob had gripped it as he'd made his threats. Could he do it? Could he go back, knowing how much he risked?

Chapter 6

Five grey concrete tower blocks reared up from a space the architect had intended to be a spirit-nurturing garden. Now it was a mixture of rubbish-strewn tarmac and straggling grass decorated with condoms and drug addicts' leavings. Wind tore through it, making the swings jangle at the end of their rusty chains. A young woman with rough peroxided hair was desultorily pushing a toddler in one of them. Three other pre-school children were kicking a ball towards the apology for a lawn.

Will watched one of them trip and smack down on the tarmac. That was probably safer than the grass. At least it couldn't conceal dirty syringes or dog shit. The boy lifted himself a little off the ground to reveal a forehead pouring with blood. He screamed. The woman at the swing ignored him. Will moved forwards; someone had to help. He picked up the child, who looked and felt the same size as his nephew and must have been no more than about four. Will stood him on his feet and squatted down to ask where he lived.

'You leave him alone.' The hoarse shriek made him turn. Another woman was running towards him, black hair flying behind her. 'Let him go or I'll have the law on you.'

Will stood up to explain. The woman grabbed the boy and hurried him off. The other children who'd been playing with him looked after her but didn't move. Squeaking chains told him that the mother at the swing was still pushing her toddler. No one said anything. When Will looked around, none of them would meet his gaze.

That's what you get for trying to help, he thought, wanting to shout out that any parent should be grateful a stranger bothered to pick up her bleeding child, and that if the law were to be used against anyone it should be her.

She'd meant the police, of course. Once Will would have agreed. These days he knew that 'the law' was something quite different, a matter of interminable arguments over minutiae fought out between two clever barristers hoping to please a third. None of the triumvirate would have any direct experience of the lives they debated, and none would care a toss about what happened to the people concerned.

That's not fair, he told himself. Trish cares.

A nasty little imaginary voice he hadn't heard for a long time asked him if he was sure of that. He smothered it and set about what he had come to do.

He was here to walk in the steps of her friend so that he could identify the source of the poison that might yet kill her. He abandoned the children and headed off towards the block he needed. There were so many exits from this estate that he wanted to know exactly where this Inspector Caroline Lyalt had been, in order to match her journey. It probably wasn't necessary to go to the very flat, but he'd made Trish get the full address, so he'd do it anyway. He'd found out the hard way that detail mattered.

Ten minutes later he was standing with his back to the shining front door of flat 36B, nine floors up from the ground in South Tower, and trying to decide whether his guide would have taken the lift or the stairs. Trish had said her friend was very fit, and the lift was absolutely disgusting, so the stairs were a distinct possibility. He looked left towards them, then right again to where the lift was creaking towards a stop.

Its doors jerked open to reveal a man about Will's height but a few years older, dressed in tight blue jeans and a pristine white T-shirt. He was carrying two Furbishers plastic bags. When he saw Will, he dumped them both on the ground.

'What're you looking at?' he barked.

'Nothing,' Will said. 'I was just trying to decide whether to take the lift or the stairs.'

The man's arms didn't move, but all the muscles in his chest rippled. Will could see them bunching and flattening under his shirt.

'You must think I was born yesterday,' he said, so wired he didn't even notice he was spitting with every word. 'I don't like people hanging around my flat. I want you out of here. Now. Or else . . .'

Will had had enough of threats so he turned his back and went for the stairs. When he heard the grating of a key as it turned inside its lock, he risked a look back. The man was letting himself into 36B, so he must have been the target of Trish's friend. Running down flight after flight, Will sympathized with her. No woman should have to face a man like that, even if she was a police officer. He hoped she'd had plenty of back-up. He wondered what the man had done, and who was dealing with him now.

On the ground floor, Will pushed his way out of the swing doors and had to make another decision about where to go. He picked the nearest exit and walked out between broken concrete bollards into the main road, where juggernauts and buses jostled the bicycles and little cars into all the biggest potholes. The pavements were cracked, there was litter blowing everywhere in the humid wind, and there wasn't a single food shop in sight.

How do they bear it? he wondered, then shivered. Soon it might not be a question of 'they' but 'we'. If Furbishers won the case, Will thought he'd probably be lucky to end up in a place like this. He wouldn't be able to go on living with his sister and her husband much longer, and he'd never be able to get a job that would fund a mortgage, or even much rent. In fact, he couldn't think of a single job he was qualified to do, except farming or running a food business. No one was going to employ him for either now. Since he'd rather die than work for a supermarket, his only option would be unskilled labouring somewhere. A building site probably.

'At least that'd be in the open air,' he muttered.

There was a newsagent's down the road. They might know where the nearest food shop could be found. This was going to take a long time.

'So, Trish,' Antony said as they left court at lunchtime, 'you must be feeling better.'

'I am. How did you know?'

He narrowed his eyes into the seducer's glint and whispered, 'Because you look divine, dearest.'

Usually she'd have been as likely to spit as to giggle in the august corridors of the Royal Courts of Justice, but she couldn't help it now. She wondered what their disapproving clerk would say if he could hear her, or witness the great man's frivolity.

'Antony, for heaven's sake! I think I'd rather be a slimy fish-eating cormorant than "divine, dearest".'

He laughed. 'You're such a monster of rectitude, Trish, you can't blame me for trying every technique that might just conceivably work.'

'Maybe not, but you'd better put a cork in it now, or you'll shock poor Colin when he brings the sandwiches, and he's got enough to put up with. Oh, did you give him any money for our lunch today?'

'Sod it. I forgot. And I haven't any cash on me.'

'Don't worry,' Trish said, glad to see Antony was back on

track as her pupil brought the laden tray to their usual corner table. 'I have.'

She leaned down for the handbag she'd dumped on the floor and fished out a twenty-pound note. Colin looked relieved, even though he made a whole string of polite protests about taking her money.

'I don't remember,' Jess said, keeping well away from the three plastic trays of sausages. She sounded sullen.

Will thought he'd like to take her for a forced march, pretty and fragile though she was, down all the miserable streets he'd trodden today.

'Come on, Jess,' Trish said. 'You did see the packet Caro brought, didn't you? I'm sure she said you'd helped her cook dinner.'

Jess looked towards the friend who had been with her when Trish and Will arrived. She had a sad, elegant face and strands of dark-gold hair falling in sexy dishevelment from a loose knot at the back of her head. She was leaning against the Smeg fridge-freezer Jess had bought after her last television series was repeated. Was this the person who'd been in the flat when Jess had sounded so unlike herself on the phone?

'Could it be those ones with the leaves on the label, Jess?' she said. She had a remarkable voice, very deep for someone as slight as she, and beautiful. 'They do look familiar.'

The sausages to which she was pointing weren't the plain pink sort, detestable for their smoothness and claggy taste, but a speckled mixture of dark-red meat and white fat, with dots of spice and flecks of herbs. Will ripped off the shrink-wrapping. A strong smell of gamy meat, mace, bayleaves and allspice was familiar enough to make Trish recoil. Jess backed right against the wall to get away from the contamination of her nostrils.

'I suppose so,' Jess said, sounding like a child forced to tell the truth after a long struggle. Her gaze slid away.

'Sure?' Will Applewood asked, tempting Jess with the other two brands he had brought with him.

All three were attractively packaged and, Trish saw from their labels, almost equally expensive.

'Yes. The box-thing was green. And Cynthia's right: I do remember the leaves on the label.'

Above the price, weight and sell-by date was a charming watercolour of a typically English country scene, with the word 'Ivyleaf' in elegantly austere roman lettering, and a border of dark-green ivy leaves around the edge.

'Do you know anything about the makers, Will?' Trish asked.

'Not a thing. And that's interesting in itself. I thought I knew all the meat processors in the country.'

'How could you possibly?' asked Jess's friend from her refuge between the sink and the fridge.

She was wearing a close-fitting cotton cardigan in a harebell blue that matched her eyes. It had a deep V-neck, which showed off her well-tanned cleavage, but she kept her arms tightly crossed over her body in an extraordinary mixture of come-on and defence.

Will launched in with a résumé of his case, adding, 'So I phoned every single meat processor I could track down to find out whether they'd been screwed by Furbishers too.'

A tingle of alarm kept Trish silent. She'd always known Will had been the originator of the action, but this was evidence of an obsession she hadn't quite understood. She thought of the exchange of glares she'd seen in the hall of the Royal Courts of Justice. What could there be between him and Matthew Grant-Furbisher to explain such hatred?

'I've known the other two makers for years,' he went on, jabbing at one of the packages, 'but not these people. I'll look into it. How's your friend doing?'

Jess's big eyes filled with tears. Her visitor moved away from the fridge to offer support. Jess swayed so that her shoulder just touched the other woman's.

'They've taken her into Intensive Care.'

'Why?'

'The infection's in her blood now. You know – septicaemia. And both kidneys are affected. And they can't control her temperature. She's been catheterized, she's being fed with drips, and they're giving her intravenous antibiotics, but the infection isn't responding.'

Trish winced. She wanted to ask a question, but Jess was still talking.

'And you know what they say about penicillin-resistant bacteria and hospital-acquired infections. There are more and more of them all the time. In the state she's in, she could pick up any one of them. And even if she doesn't, her kidneys could be destroyed. The infection could infect her heart valves, too. And if she gets necrotizing fasciitis or MRSA as well as septicaemia, she'll—'

'Stop it, Jess.' Her friend's voice had the effect of a slap. Jess gasped and fell silent, moving away so that the two of them were no longer touching. 'It always takes time for them to find the right antibiotic. They have to give each one time to work before they give up and try a different one. You won't help Caro by panicking. But your friends are right: they may be able to give the hospital useful information if they can work out exactly what food carried the infection.'

'I don't think it was the sausages at all,' Jess said, looking resentfully at Trish. 'You weren't nearly so ill.'

'Maybe I was just lucky or have some kind of partial immunity. Will, what do we do now?'

He was putting the sausages back into the bag the delicatessen had provided. 'I get them tested for E. coli. And I find out more about this Ivyleaf company.'

'Just like that?'

'I've still got a lot of friends in the business,' Will said, very much on his dignity. 'And there's a writer I know who specializes in every aspect of the meat trade. If there's anything iffy about Ivyleaf, he'll know all about it.'

'Who is he?' Trish asked, surprised by Will's unusual certainty.

'Jamie Maxden. He's an investigative journalist. We haven't been in touch for a while, but I'm sure I can get hold of him. Here, Jess, you keep the other sausages, put them in your fridge,' he said. 'You don't want to waste them. They cost a fortune.'

She shuddered, closing her eyes and spreading her lips in disgust. Trish quickly explained that Jess was a vegetarian, frowning at Will to stop him making any unsuitable meat processor's jokes about lentil-wearing sandal-eating freaks.

'Why don't you take them to your sister?' Trish added. 'I'm sure she could use them.'

'Good idea. It's time I made a contribution to the housekeeping.'

'It's a perfectly sensible life choice, you know,' Jess's friend said from the far end of the kitchen.

All three of the others looked up. There was an expression of relief on Jess's face, as though she'd expected to have to fight this battle on her own. But Will was puzzled.

'What is?'

'Vegetarianism,' said the friend. 'There are all kinds of health benefits, quite apart from the moral objection of rearing sentient animals simply in order to kill and eat them.'

Will opened his mouth, then looked sideways at Trish, and shut it again. After a moment, he shrugged. 'Each to his own. We'll never agree, so there's not much point making each other angry.'

'You're right there.' The woman smiled and crossed the room to shake his hand. 'My name's Cynthia Flag. I've got a card somewhere. Will you let me know if you do find the source of the contamination?'

'Sure,' he said, taking the rectangle of cream cardboard and sliding it into the back pocket of his jeans. They had such sharp creases down the front he must have been keeping them in a trouser press. 'If it's OK with Trish.'

'Of course,' she said, to forestall any protest. 'Look, Jess, we ought to be going. Will you be OK?'

Jess nodded. 'I'll be fine. Cynthia's staying with me at the moment.'

Trish told her hackles to calm down. Just because Cynthia was ravishing, her presence in the flat did not mean that she and Jess were having an affair. Surely even Jess wouldn't do that while Caro was so ill.

Outside the flat, Will thrust a hand through his hair, scratching his scalp.

'What's up?' Trish asked.

'I can't take all those intense female emotions.' He shuddered. 'You could've cut the atmosphere in there with a knife. Give me a rotten sausage hunt any day. I'll phone you as soon as I get anywhere. How was it in court today?'

'Dullish. They just brought witness after witness to testify to Furbishers' probity, good business and fair contracts. There wasn't anything for us to do, no point trying to shake them. You didn't miss anything.'

Trish heard no more of him until she dialled her voicemail for messages during the lunch adjournment on Friday. First there was one from Andrew Stane, telling her he had got permission for her to interview Kim Bowlby and would therefore like to make arrangements to drop off the files that evening. Then came Will's voice, sounding much more cautious than usual.

'Ivyleaf don't actually make anything. They're just a kind of packaging operation in Kent, and fairly new, which must explain why I didn't find them in my trawl for Furbisher victims. I haven't been able to get hold of my journalist yet, but I asked a mate of mine in the business who Ivyleaf are and where they buy their meat. He didn't know much, but said he was fairly sure they get some direct from the nearest abattoir, which is called Smarden Meats. They're only about twenty miles away, so it makes sense. Anyway, I thought I'd go and talk to the Smarden people, find out what they know about Ivyleaf. We're more likely to get useful information from someone a bit detached than if we go baldheaded into the place itself. Will you come with me? They work on Saturdays.'

Trish phoned him back, concerned that he might be spending more than he could afford on the hunt for the sausages that had made her and Caro ill. She wondered what he would say if she offered to pay his expenses.

'I don't think I can come with you,' she said, thinking of her professional ethics as much as all the work she had to do. 'In any case, wouldn't you do better just phoning the abattoir to ask for information?'

'You don't know the meat trade, Trish. It's so wrapped up in secrecy that getting anything out of anyone involved is like cutting through ten strands of razor wire. The only way to get anything is to trick it out of them. We'll need to go there on a good pretext and get pally with whoever is showing us around, then slip in the important question when we've lulled them.'

'I know nothing about meat in the raw. There's no way I'm going to be able to get pally with anyone involved. Will, I really don't think I can help here.'

'Please come.' He sounded desperate enough to remind her of his frequent jokes about jumping out of windows. 'I can do all the meat-talk bit. But I need you as a witness to anything I see – or hear. No one ever believes anything I tell them, but everyone accepts whatever you say. You'd be ideal, even if you weren't a lawyer. You can spot a bullshitter a mile off. Plus, you know how to ask questions in a way that makes people talk. I need you, Trish.'

Andrew Stane had already used that lever to persuade her to involve herself with Kim Bowlby. She had the case against Furbishers, too. Even without George and David to keep happy, she had nothing to spare for anyone else's needs, and she wanted some time to herself. The prospect of having much of that was dwindling.

'Please, Trish.'

'How far is it from London? I've a lot of work to do over the weekend, and I've promised to see someone on Sunday.'

'Only about an hour and a half's drive. I'm sure I can borrow Susannah's car to take you. You will come, won't you?'

'I've got a car. If you'll map read, I can drive.'

'Oh. All right.' He didn't sound too pleased at the prospect of being a passenger, but for Trish the thought of borrowing someone else's car was absurd when her own soft-top Audi was sitting quietly in its expensive parking space near her flat. 'I hope you don't share my ex-wife's habit of redoing her make-up whenever she gets bored with looking at the road.'

'I can promise you that,' Trish said, surprised he hadn't noticed how rarely she put anything on her face. 'Could we start quite early? That way I can get back to my files in good time.'

'Sure. If you give me your address, I'll be there at six.'

'Not quite as early as that,' she said, laughing. 'I keep forgetting you were once a farmer. Make it eight, and I'll be ready for you.'

Trish wasn't sure how Antony would react to the idea that she would be cavorting around the countryside with one of their clients, but there was something about Will that made it impossible to disappoint him. Maybe it was just that he'd had a tough enough time already.

Colin had already finished his sandwiches and gone, but

Antony was still in the café when she got there. His eyes popped as he glanced at her tray, which held a yoghurt and a packet of shortbread, as well as the usual cheese-salad sandwich and raspberry smoothie.

'Your brush with E. coli seems to have transformed you,' he said. 'I've never seen you eat so much. You'll get delectably plump if you go on like this.'

'Plump? Yuk!'

'Oh, I don't know. George would love it, and I've always rather fancied a few gentle curves myself. A little bit of padding improves sex no end. Grating hipbones are such a turn-off. Heard anything from him lately?'

She felt her whole face easing, as if a tight rubber mask had been pulled off. 'Yes. He phoned last night. The flight was OK, though boringly long, and now they're having a whale of a time. There's a huge pool, three dogs, and every possible kind of bicycle, Rollerblades and so on. David and his cousins spend the whole day charging about outside. And apparently his aunt's a real charmer.'

'Sounds as though you haven't drawn such a short straw, after all,' Antony said with a grimace. 'I know that kind of family holiday. Wonderful for the children, but a nightmare for any adult who wants to relax. How's George bearing up?'

Trish peeled the top off her yoghurt. 'D'you know, it sounded to me as though he was enjoying himself almost as much as David. No clients, no colleagues, no worries about his practice. I think he's letting go for once.'

'But no you either.' The skin around Antony's greeny-blue eyes crinkled as he smiled his best smile. 'In his place, I'd dump the boy with his perfect relations and come haring straight back to Southwark. How much are you missing him?'

'A lot,' Trish said, scraping out the yoghurt from the bottom of the pot. She licked the spoon and watched Antony's face over it. 'But I quite like it, too.'

He laughed. 'You always were too honest for your own good, let alone his. But you make me—'

She never heard what she did for him, because Ferdinand Aldham pulled back one of the other chairs just then, dumping a cup of coffee on the table.

'You don't mind if I join you, Antony, do you? This place is like a morgue.'

Trish put down her spoon. When she looked up again, she saw Antony still watching her. He forced his gaze away.

'Not at all, Ferdy,' he said, drawling so much it was clear he meant the opposite. 'You know you're going to have to speed up a bit with your witnesses or else bore Husking into finding against you.'

Trish murmured something about having a look at her papers and pushed herself up from her chair.

'Was I interrupting something?' Ferdy asked with a lascivious smile, looking from Antony to Trish and back again. 'Sorry about that, old boy. While the cat's away and all that. What *is* the news from Tuscany?'

'Oh, grow up!' Antony said, sounding seriously put out.

That afternoon, he punished his adversary by making the last of Ferdy's witnesses look weak and ignorant enough to be manipulated into doing almost anything to anyone his bosses might target.

Trish was only just ready when Will banged on her door on Saturday morning. She had slept better than she had for years and hadn't woken until after seven. It was a relief, too, to be able to ignore all the black suits in her wardrobe and put on cotton trousers and a loose pink shirt.

Will looked as though he'd had a better night too. The red moleskin trousers and checked shirt he was wearing made him look like a City banker on holiday, instead of the conventional countryman up in town for the day she'd been expecting. His eyes were lighter and happier than she'd yet seen them. He kissed her cheek, as though they were setting off on a date.

'Would you like some coffee before we start?' she asked, pulling away. 'I'm sure there's time for that.'

'I've had some, thanks. If we go now, we'll miss the traffic. Come on, Trish. I thought you wanted to be there and back in time to work this afternoon.'

The car nosed through the narrow, crowded streets towards the South Circular and on out of London, as Trish followed Will's efficient directions. As the suburbs were beginning to give way to country and the green patches grew bigger with every mile, he said, 'You're not scared, are you?'

'I'm not scared of anything,' Trish said, lying. 'Although I must say I'm not too keen on the idea of watching screaming animals have their heads chopped off.'

'It's not like that. And it's not like you to be so silly. You sound nearly as idiotic as that Jess-woman. Go right here.'

Trish checked her mirror and braked sharply, just in time to position herself for the turn across the oncoming traffic.

'God, isn't England gorgeous at this time of year?' Will said, his voice luxuriously warm.

Trish, who rarely drove out into the countryside, had to agree with him. If anyone had asked her what was most beautiful about England, she would have talked of the view east along the Thames from the south side of Lambeth Bridge. She loved the look of the pale stacked-up buildings of the City when they were dyed pink by the evening sun against a steel-blue sky, with the grey river between them. Now, she wasn't so sure. Here the hedges looked very green against the golden fields, and the sky was the blue of an old-fashioned striped milk jug. Every so often the excessively brilliant yellow of another crop shrieked against the subtler tapestry of barley, hedge and grass, but nothing could destroy the glory all round them.

A sigh like an explosion distracted her. She looked at Will and saw a glimpse of something quite different from his usual misery.

'I hate living in London,' he said. 'Grubby streets, filthy air and slutty crowds. How do you bear it?'

'Easily. I love it. But I have lots of space and work I like and my own place. I can see how hard it is for you, having to be a lodger in someone else's house.'

'It's not that. I'm lucky to be a lodger. It's knowing that if I hadn't screwed up, I'd still be living in the most ravishing bit of the British Isles, on land that fed my family for generations. Instead of that, I'm hanging about doing nothing but breathe air so polluted it leaves black marks on everything. I mean, do you ever blow your nose, Trish?'

'Only when I have to,' she said crisply, not wanting to explore the subject in any detail.

'And it's not just that. The filth gets everywhere: into all my clothes and my skin, and under my nails. I can't keep them clean for more than two minutes before the grime oozes back. It's like my mind. The black thoughts seep in, however hard I try to keep them out.'

'Will . . .' she began, her voice soft.

'Don't be kind to me, Trish. It'll only make me feel like snivelling. I screwed up. Nothing you can say will change that. I thought I could do better than my father, but I couldn't, so I lost the lot. Even the house. His ghost is probably fulminating at me right now. I'd have been able to hang on if I hadn't trusted sodding Furbishers. But I did. So that's my fault, too. Everything's my fault. Just like he always said it was.'

Out of the corner of her eye, Trish could see him squaring his shoulders, as he tried to force himself out of the slump into which he'd sagged. He glanced at her.

'Don't look so worried,' he said. 'I'm fighting back in every way I can. And I don't believe in ghosts anyway.'

'Good for you, Will. Look, there's a roundabout coming up. Which way?'

'Second exit,' he said, like a driving instructor.

As they swung out of the roundabout, he told her what she could expect to see in the abattoir, which had once supplied some of the pork he had used in his famous terrines.

'But you were right on the far side of Sussex, weren't you, almost into Hampshire?' Trish said. 'That's miles away'

'I know. Part of the typical sodding mess the last few sodding governments have made of food production in this country.' His anger reminded her of the kind of sticky foam hairdressers had used in the days before gel, expanding to fill all the available space as soon as it was let out of its pressurized container.

'There used to be neighbourhood slaughterhouses all over the country, producing really good, tender meat,' he went on. 'Most have gone out of business now, so instead of having animals gently moved across a few fields and despatched by someone familiar, you have them loaded into vast lorries. They thunder down the motorways, with the animals getting more and more stressed with every mile, until they can be unloaded to join queues of other poor beasts, squealing and terrified, in some ghastly big impersonal killing factory. Not surprisingly the meat is so tough it's barely edible and it often tastes vile, too.'

Trish swallowed a mouthful of hot saliva and told herself she was tough enough to witness a big impersonal killing factory if she had to.

'But Smarden Meats is a good one, isn't it?' she asked hopefully.

'As they go, yes. They provided OK pork for us, anyway. I mean, we weren't going to pay for hand-reared Gloucestershire Old Spot premium-grade meat as the filling in a terrine.'

'Not for pâtés. I can see that.'

'Smarden have various grades,' he went on, unaware of her struggles to control her heaving stomach.

He could have had no idea of the battles she'd had with food in the past. Whenever life had threatened to overtake her, or stress to turn from a spur into a straitjacket, she'd stopped eating. Looking back, she could see that at such times her intake of food was just about the only thing she could still control. She was long past that stage, but even now anxiety – or rage – could make it hard to swallow anything more than a fruit smoothie. It worried George, whose need for food rose in parallel with his stress level.

'And we had to go quite far down in order to meet Furbishers' price,' Will was saying cheerfully. 'We decided we could do that so long as we kept on with big, good-looking chunks of pheasant to make the layers.'

'I'm sure,' Trish said, trying not to look at a radiantly gleaming cock pheasant that was stalking along in the neighbouring field. She didn't know enough about country sports to know when shooting was likely to start, but she couldn't imagine this bird lasting much longer.

'I was always tempted to go that little bit lower and try MRM,' Will said. 'It would have doubled our profits.'

'MRM? What's that?'

He turned his head to stare at her. Keeping her gaze on the road ahead, she asked what was so surprising.

'You must know. Mechanically recovered meat: a kind of slurry got from blasting the last shreds of raw flesh from a butchered carcass with high-pressure hoses.'

'Oh, gross!'

'It is. But it's cheap, which is why it was always a temptation. I kept having to shave a bit off the cost of my stuff here and another bit there. We had to halve the number of pistachios at one stage, as well as lower the proportion of pheasant. But it still went like a bomb until Furbishers . . .' He bit his lip.

'You never did succumb to the temptation of MRM, though, did you?' Trish asked, to distract him.

'No. Filthy stuff. But we could have. It's still legal to use it from pigs and chickens, so long as you include it on the label's list of ingredients.'

Trish felt as though she were in a meat-products seminar as he told her about changing attitudes and legislation. The details didn't interest her, but she was intrigued to see how well authority sat on Will, as he talked about a subject he knew backwards.

'But who could bear to use it?' she said when he'd told her everything he knew.

'Funny you should ask that,' he said airily enough to put her on alert. 'Furbishers put it in their cheapest own-brand pâtés. And I happen to know they get their supplies from Smarden. If I could prove that the supply might be contaminated, I'd have something on Matthew Grant-Furbisher, which could be bloody useful if things don't work out.'

Trish lifted her foot from the accelerator so that she wasn't tempted to ram the car into the nearest hedge. She'd been feeling so protective of Will that the discovery of his secret agenda for this trip was like getting his fist in her face. What else hadn't he told her?

When her fury was under some sort of control, she said, 'Is that why we're here? To get ammunition for some post-trial campaign you're planning to run against Furbishers if they win the case?'

'Not exactly.' He managed to sound hurt, but shiftiness echoed in his voice too.

'Then what? Another general assault on supermarkets' meat-buying policies?'

'Someone has to do it.'

Trish bit down hard on what she wanted to say about men who pretend to be pathetic and needy in order to trick you into doing things for them you'd never have contemplated in any other circumstances.

'But, honestly, that's not the only reason why we're here, Trish. We've come primarily to find out what's killing your friend. I thought you wanted to know that as much as I do.'

She pressed down hard on the accelerator again. The hedges blurred in her peripheral vision. This trip was beginning to seem like a worse idea by the minute.

'By the way,' Will added. 'I've told them at the abattoir that you're advising me on starting up again in business. That seemed like the safest cover story. You're not going to be cross with me, are you?'

'Don't play the wounded child,' she said with a distinct snap. 'It doesn't suit you. I loathe being lied to – and about. You should have told me what you were up to when you asked me to come today.'

'I thought you'd know. You're so clever at working out what I mean when I get muddled that I—'

'Oh, come on, Will. Don't pretend to be a country bumpkin. You're a businessman, not a cowhand,' she said, adding to herself, even if you do own a slurry-coloured tweed suit and clumping great brown shoes.

He grunted. 'I may have been once. Not any more. So many people have told me how hopeless I am that I can't trust my judgement unless you're there to support it, Trish. That's why I needed you with me today.'

'Well, we're here now,' she said coldly as they reached a big pair of open gates.

There was a discreet sign identifying the place as Smarden Meats, and plenty of security cameras trained on the forecourt. When she'd parked and locked the car, she looked straight at Will, hoping to see in his expression some clue about what he was really up to.

'Don't lie to me again. I don't like it in anyone, and in you it makes me nervous. Don't forget I still have to argue the rest of your case in court. That'll be harder than it needs to be if I can't trust you. OK?'

He shuffled his feet, raising dust that blew up around their ankles. 'I'm sorry, Trish. It's just that I *needed* you today and I thought you wouldn't come if . . .' He let his voice tail off. She sent him a freezing glance and stalked towards the unimposing entrance of the abattoir.

Almost everyone they saw looked hostile. The only people who offered smiles were the officiating vets from the Meat Hygiene Service. They were there, Trish learned, to check the living animals for signs of disease, enforce the legislation that protected their welfare at slaughter, and inspect and health-mark the carcasses as fit for human consumption.

It seemed impossible that with so much supervision any contaminated meat could ever leave an abattoir of this kind to get into the sausages she and Caro had eaten. She stopped to ask one of the vets what would happen to the pig's carcass he'd just refused to stamp.

'It's easier here than in many places,' he said. 'The managers almost never challenge our decisions, so we don't have to go to the magistrates for a destruction order. This one will go into the condemned meat chiller until it can be destroyed by the abattoir staff under our supervision. Sometimes they go for pet food.'

'I see. Thank you.'

He looked curiously at her, but turned back to his work without any of the dislike apparent in every gesture and every glance from the plant's own staff. Mr Flyte, the manager who had eventually agreed to show them round, didn't look as aggressive as the rest, but even he seemed twitchy.

Will had told Trish about the secrecy of every part of the meat trade, but she hadn't expected this. They moved on through the abattoir to a completely different section, which dealt not with the pigs she'd already seen, but bullocks. They were first stunned, then killed, skinned and eviscerated.

Trish wasn't usually squeamish or sentimental about animals, but there were processes here she couldn't force herself to watch. She knew the smells were going to remain with her for ever. It wasn't just the blood, but also the half-digested food – and worse – that made the air almost impossible to breathe. She could see now how bacteria might be transferred from an animal's digestive system to the muscle tissue that would provide food for humans, but she was still surprised at the idea that any of the watching vets could miss that sort of contamination.

In a strange way, the skinning was the worst of all, more terrible even than the killing. The sight of the hides being ripped down the bodies made her own skin prickle and sweat. And the tearing sound hurt. She knew she would never be able to describe what she'd seen and heard to anyone else.

'And this,' Mr Flyte said, pushing open a door for them, 'is the boning room.'

Headless, skinned and gutted carcasses hung on hooks along one wall, while men dressed in blood-spattered white overalls and short white gumboots stripped out the spinal cords. Relieved the heads were off, Trish followed Mr Flyte to watch the easier sight of other men removing usable chunks of meat from the carcasses before the remnants were whisked off to a different area. Two long rows of steel tables held the smaller pieces, as skilled boners reduced them to the kind of joints familiar from high-street shops.

Trish would never forget the sound of knives hitting first bone then steel. There wasn't as much blood here as there'd been in the room where the pork carcasses had been gutted. There, oceans of it had been washed away by hissing hoses as the edible offal had been separated from the rest, to be flung into deep once-white plastic tubs. Jess's vegetarianism seemed the most rational life choice in the world.

'Mind your backs,' said a stentorian voice from behind them. Will moved too fast and knocked into a stocky man who was in the process of separating chunks of meat from a bullock's foreleg.

The man whirled round, his wickedly sharp knife barely missing the left arm of his neighbour at the boning table and pointing straight at Will's stomach. Trish gasped. If he'd been six inches closer, the knife would have gone in. She'd seen how easily it could slide through muscle and sinew.

'You stupid c—' The boner choked on the word, substituting: 'Afternoon, Mr Flyte.' His face was spotted with blood and little chunks of meat, but it wasn't that which made Trish move even further back: it was the way his nostrils flared and his eyes bulged. After a tense moment he put the knife back on the table. She saw the scars on his hands and the strong, blunt fingers, and tried not to shudder.

To her relief, they moved on again and were soon watching nicely familiar joints of beef chugging along on a conveyor belt, monitored by a man in a pristine white coat and mesh hat. He even held a reassuring clipboard. Trish got her breath back and asked about the man with the knife in the boning room.

'Bob Flesker?' said Mr Flyte, nodding. 'You mustn't take that too seriously. He was just startled. It happens. He's a good worker and he's never hurt anyone.'

'I'm glad to hear it,' Trish said, surprised at the casual way he'd offered his reassurance.

'That's not what I meant. There's always a risk of fingers being cut in the boning room. It's impossible to prevent it completely with the pace at which the men have to work. But Bob has never let his knife slip or stray in all the three years he's been with us.'

'He must be good,' she said politely, fighting queasiness again.

'He is, but then he's had more experience than most,' Flyte said.

'His family had their own craft slaughterhouse for generations.'

'What happened to it?'

There was a hint of a smile on Flyte's face, as though something in the butcher's past appealed to him. 'Uneconomic these days, like most of the others of that size.'

'Trish, I think we ought to be getting on,' Will said, very brisk and stern.

She took the hint and kept the rest of her questions to herself, leaving Will to open the subject of Ivyleaf and their sausages. As she listened to him getting absolutely nowhere, she still couldn't forget the sight of the razor-sharp knife pointing at his stomach. Or the sense of fury only just held in.

Emerging into the clean air outside was like being born again. The ordinary sounds of traffic and aeroplanes were as reassuring as the beat of the sea.

'We need lunch,' Will said, apparently unaffected by anything they had seen or heard. 'There's a really good pub I know about ten miles away. OK?'

'Sure.' Trish felt sick, and her ears were still ringing with the screams and the sounds of tearing, the clang of metal on metal and the swish of gumboots through viscous liquid. She didn't think she'd be able to eat again for a week, but she wanted to sit somewhere dark and comfortable for a while.

The sight of the gold-and-green countryside washed across her eyes, and she gradually let her hands quieten against the steering wheel. But when she'd parked behind a small old brick and tile inn and tried to get out of the car, she found her legs were shaky. She leaned against the car door for a moment, breathing in the medicinal smell of the cow parsley that laced the hedges, and getting her mind and stomach in order.

Later, consuming half a pint of classic bitter and even nibbling at a little cheese, in a pub as dark as she'd wanted, Trish found her brain working again.

'You were amazingly cool with that bloke who nearly stabbed you. I was impressed.'

Will looked at her with an unreadable expression. She searched for the usual fear and anger and couldn't find either.

'Enough to forgive me?' he asked.

For a moment she couldn't think what he was talking about. Her own rage seemed to have belonged to someone else, as though she really had been born again.

'Yes,' she said, remembering now. 'But don't lie to me again.'

'OK. Then I'd better tell you that I didn't feel at all cool,' he said, smiling like a boy caught out. 'More like a rabbit in the headlights. And a terrible coward for not doing anything to protect you. I thought you might be cross about that too.'

'Don't be silly. *I* wasn't in any danger.' Trish drank and felt the thin, bitter liquid cleaning her tastebuds. 'But you were and you didn't flinch. You're more of a dark horse than I'd realized, Will.'

'I learned how to hide fear when I had to a long time ago.'

'What happened, Will?' she asked gently.

His eyes were changing as she watched. There was no pleading in them now, and no boyishness either. His jaw clicked, with a sound audible even over the pinging and squeaking of the one-armed bandit in the corner. She was about to ask her question again in a different form when she remembered a piece of advice from her first instructing solicitor, in the old family law days, 'Never push an angry man. That's what tips them over. They hate it from anyone, but from a women it's like a match in a box of fireworks.'

Chapter 7

The children's interview room at the local psychiatric unit was a cheerful yellow colour, although the paint was beginning to flake and there were the marks of small grubby hands in a dado around the walls. Above it, at right angles to the window, was a huge one-way mirror, which hid the observers with their video camera and recording machine. Anatomically correct dolls were kept in one of the cupboards and other less carefully designed toys were strewn carelessly about the room so that a roaming child could pick them up and use them to tell unbearable stories. There were paints and crayons and a generous supply of paper piled casually in one corner.

Having read Kim Bowlby's file yesterday evening, Trish had known she must choose clothes that would look unthreatening. She'd picked a pair of faded jeans and an old droopy cotton sweater, which George disliked for its dishcloth colour and texture. She was sitting in a low chair and had crammed her long legs under the child-sized table so that she would not seem overpoweringly tall when Kim Bowlby first saw her. She wished the interview were already over.

This place was better than many of the rooms in which she had waited to unravel the secrets of brutalized children. A few had come with one parent or the other, but most of the escorts had been social workers, under-funded, under-supported and protecting themselves in the only ways they knew from too much horror. No one could give the children what they most needed: one-to-one care in an atmosphere of unstinting and unconditional love. In many cases they couldn't even guarantee the basics of decent nutrition, physical safety and adequate education.

They were not holding hands, the child and her foster mother, when they eventually appeared. Kim walked with an unnaturally stiff gait and straight back. Trish didn't stand up to introduce herself because of wanting to stay as small as possible. Instead, she smiled, hoping it would make her black eyes look soft, and said that her name was Trish Maguire.

'I'm Kim,' said the child, holding out her right hand with stiff formality, while the woman who'd brought her moved quietly back to the other end of the room. 'My surname is Bowlby.'

'May I just call you Kim?' Trish waited a long time for an answer, but eventually the child felt safe enough to nod. 'Thank you.'

Name, rank and serial number, she thought, wondering whether the ex-army stepfather had coached Kim in what to say during interrogations. It seemed better to ask nothing difficult now. Kim had already been questioned into exhaustion. Instead Trish waited, interested to see which toy would attract her attention. None did. She simply stood where her foster mother had left her, waiting in silence. In spite of the stuffy heat, her skin was quite dry and her hair so tidy it looked like a wig.

'Would you like to sit down?' Trish asked, and saw Kim's eyelids lift briefly. The eyes themselves were a wonderful blue, but they held no signs of either warmth or pleasure.

Trish knew from the file that the first symptom that had worried Kim's teachers had been her sleepiness. At one time they had thought she must suffer from narcolepsy because she kept drifting off in lessons and during school dinners and even at play time. Now there was no sign of it, and she did not look especially tired, either, only tightly watchful, as though waiting for the test she was sure would come.

It was an expression Trish had seen too often in David's face to misunderstand. When he'd first come to live with her, it had been almost constant. Now, to her intense relief, it was rarer. But it had taken her months to shift it at all. Could she, in the tiny amount of time available, give Kim some of the same reassurance?

'Do you like playing with dolls?' she asked. Kim's blonde head shook. 'What about painting?'

She sighed a little and then nodded, as though it seemed more sensible to humour this strange woman by agreeing to something than to go on resisting. Trish fetched paper, paints, brushes and a jam jar of water, moving as quietly as she could to avoid imposing her size and strength on the child. She brought the painting materials to the table. Kim didn't touch them.

'Have a go,' Trish said.

Kim bit her lips. Her eyes crumpled. Trish waited for the burst of tears she was sure must come, but Kim fought it, swallowed, then said in a thread of a voice. 'What do you want me to paint?'

'Anything.' Trish kept her voice as warm as she could. 'Whatever you like.'

Carefully, Kim selected a small brush, dipped it in water, wiped the excess off on the edge of the jar and dabbled it gently in a jar of pink paint, again cleaning off any bits that might drip. Then she painted a diagonal from the top left of the page down to the bottom right, without once lifting her brush from the paper. The line might almost have been drawn with a ruler. Trish waited, without a word.

Kim sighed again, washed her brush in the water, reloaded it with lime green and drew another line, only about two centimetres from the first. A third line, in pale yellow, completed her painting. She washed the brush, looked in vain for a paint rag and then shook as much water as possible off the bristles before laying the brush down on the table beside the water jar.

'I have finished,' she said. 'Thank you.'

Trish wished she had some expertise in interpreting children's art. To her this said nothing except that Kim was unbelievably neat, over-controlled and doing her best to provide whatever the adult in charge of her wanted.

'You work very tidily,' Trish commented. 'I always make sploshes and drop bits. I couldn't do anything like that without a ruler.'

The child's eyelids lifted again. Now Trish thought she could see the faintest sign of pleasure. Or maybe it was just relief that Kim had passed a test.

'Do you always paint in lines?'

Kim nodded.

'Always the same colours?'

'They're my favourites,' she whispered. Trish wanted to celebrate. This was the first unsolicited comment.

'What other things do you like?' she asked, hoping she wasn't pushing too far. 'Toys and TV programmes and food and things like that?'

The interview progressed for the next thirty minutes, during which Trish failed to elicit any facts at all. At the end of the session, Kim's foster mother came back to the table from her seat in the corner. Kim didn't look at her or move.

'Thank you for talking to me,' Trish said. 'I hope I get a chance to see you again.'

The child continued to sit. Her foster mother held out a hand. 'Come on, Kim. It's time to go home.'

Kim continued to look at Trish, who eventually nodded. At once Kim slid off the chair and pushed it neatly, and without any sound at all, under the table.

Trish watched them go and waited for Andrew Stane. She

knew he'd been observing the whole session with the psychiatrist who had been working on the case, and who had given up her Sunday afternoon for this unusual meeting. When Andrew came in, his round face was tight and his voice was much higher than usual.

'What were you doing? We haven't time for a lengthy therapeutic acquaintance, Trish. If we don't get her to talk about her stepfather before next weekend, she's going back.'

'I know,' Trish said, pressing her fingers against the ache between her eyebrows. 'But it was clear from the file that questions about him weren't going to get us anywhere. Did you notice how quiet she was?'

'Most frightened children are quiet.'

'It was more than that. When you run the video, watch the way she washes her brush. Most children slosh the bristles in the water and the shaft of the brush rattles against the glass. Kim made absolutely no sound at all. And it was the same when she tidied the chair.'

'And what does that tell you?'

'I'm not going to speculate. But there's more to this than simply being told not to talk about what's been done to her. I need to see her again. And quite often if I'm to get anywhere.'

'Like I said, we haven't time for a lengthy therapeutic association.'

'I know.' Trish fought for patience. Andrew was the gatekeeper. She needed to make him understand. 'And I'm not a therapist anyway. But she's so frightened of getting it wrong that I can't do anything that might suggest the answers I want. She'd agree to anything I said, and it's not going to help you or her to build a case on that kind of falsity.'

'You're right there.'

'So, I'll need to see her often if I'm to tease out what has been happening. The bugger of it is that I never know when I'm going to be free of court. Look, would it possible to have her here at half past four every day so that I could have half an hour with her before I go back to chambers?'

The judge nearly always rose by four, and Trish thought she could fend off Antony for an hour after that. He was in such a good mood these days that she might not have to tell him about Kim to explain why she needed the time.

'I'll do my best,' Andrew said.

All the way to the hospital, Trish thought about the child and her quietness, playing scene after scene of what might have happened through her imagination. She wished she could have talked the case through with Caro, but that was too much to hope for. Trish thought she'd settle for finding Caro even a little better than she'd been on Friday.

Will woke at five on Monday morning, and lay in bed hating his life. In adolescence he would have been able to sleep for England if his father hadn't always been there, hoiking him out from under the duvet at dawn. Now he could barely manage four hours, and he couldn't bear to get up until he'd heard his brother-in-law leave for the City. Rupert's contempt was less vocal than the old man's, but somehow worse.

At last a heavy door banged downstairs. That must be him going out. Will hauled his aching body up off the unnaturally squishy mattress to shave and dress. But he'd misjudged it. The bang must have been the newspapers arriving. He heard Rupert's voice from halfway down the stairs.

'The suspense is killing me. Do we have any idea when his bloody case is going to end?'

'No,' Susannah said wearily. 'All Will's said is "not more than a week or two now". But I don't think he really knows. Poor man.'

'I suppose it must be worse for him.'

'Of course it is.' Susannah's voice was acid. 'I haven't seen him this bad since Dad died. It's far worse than when Fiona left him.'

Rupert laughed his rich banker's laugh. 'I'm not surprised. He was probably glad to be rid of her. She'd have driven me barking in five minutes. How could anybody that pretty be so stupid?'

'I think she was just unhappy and bored. And she hated country life.'

'She should've thought of that before she married him. Why was he so cut up about your father's death? I thought they hated each other.'

Will's jaw clicked, sending pain shooting up into both his ears. It was none of his brother-in-law's business what he'd thought about his father. And the last thing he wanted now was anyone so sodding clever asking questions about the time the old man died. He pressed fingers to the hinges of his jaw to soothe the ache.

'I know.' Amazingly Susannah sounded as though she was on the brink of tears. 'It used to worry me. But I've come to think it must have been because they never had a chance to make peace. They fought all the time and with Dad just dropping dead on the spot like that, Will must have been beating himself up for everything he'd ever said.'

Stop there, he thought, willing her to come to her senses. She didn't know anything, but that didn't mean it was safe to chatter on like this. The sooner everyone forgot the day his father died, the better.

'I've been trying to get him to go and see Annabel, you know the one I was at school with who trained as a counsellor, because—'

'No therapy's going to help a man in Will's position. Winning damages might, and getting back to work, but nothing else.' Rupert's voice had softened a little, but it crisped up again as he added, 'Except getting out of our house. From the look in his eye whenever he can't avoid catching mine, he'll be as glad to go as I'll be to see the back of him. I hope to God it's soon.'

'Rupert, that's unkind.'

Uncoiling his fingers, forcing himself to keep calm and not burst into the kitchen to tell his brother-in-law what he thought of him, Will turned to creep back upstairs. He might be a charity case, but he had his dignity. There was no way he could bear to be caught eavesdropping on this particular conversation.

An hour later it seemed safe to go down again. His niece and nephew had finished reducing the kitchen to the usual battleground and were chasing each other around their rooms in search of their swimming things. As he opened the kitchen door, Susannah looked up from her shopping list to ask whether he'd be in this evening.

'I think so,' he said, safe in the knowledge that if she'd wanted him to babysit again she'd have given him a bit more warning. 'Why don't I take those sausages out of the freezer and cook them? Give you a chance to put your feet up for a change.'

She made the face that had been familiar all his life, a screwed-up expression of pitying disgust.

'I don't like sausages, and I've promised Rupe shepherd's pie in any case. It's his favourite.'

'Well, don't go and buy supermarket mince, whatever you do.'

She sighed. 'Will, I wish you'd drop it. I've been feeding the family mince since I got married and it hasn't done any of us any harm.'

'You have no idea what kind of rubbish may have been mixed in with the meat. Susannah, you must—'

'Leave it, Will.'

He felt like a puppy that had to be trained not to chew her best shoes.

'Are you going to court again today?' she asked a moment

later, smiling brightly, as though the little episode had never happened.

Susannah found Will's drooping around the house more than she could bear. If it went on much longer, she'd have to rent a cottage somewhere and take the children away for the rest of the school holidays.

Her pity for her brother was infinite; and her gratitude for the way he'd divided the proceeds of the land sale, immense. Their father had left everything to their mother, except for the farm itself and the stock, which had gone to Will. Hating farming as he always had, he'd sold the land straight away and split the money equally between the three of them. Their mother's share was funding most of her nursing home fees, and Susannah had bought this house outright just before the property-price explosion of the late nineties, so she was well in profit. Unlike poor Will, who'd blown all his on the failed pâté business.

But that didn't make his presence in the house any easier. She didn't know why Rupert was making such a fuss: he was out all day.

In the first months after the collapse of Will's business and the forced sale of his house, he'd been buoyed up by his need to bring a legal case against Furbishers. The phone bill had quadrupled as he'd searched for fellow sufferers, but the bill would have been cheap at twice the price for the way the campaign had kept him busy. Then had come his battle to find a solicitor to represent them all, and then, best of all, the preparation of the case itself. The conferences with important lawyers in the Temple had positively excited him. Now that he had nothing to do except go over and over everything he'd said in the witness box and castigate himself for not saying it better, his distress filled the whole house.

'I'll probably look in later,' he said. 'But there's a mate I've got to phone first.'

She ruffled his hair, fighting for the affection she wanted to feel, and said, 'Well, for heaven's sake use the house phone this time and don't go wasting your own money on the mobile. A few calls here or there won't make any difference to our bill.'

Will kept the smile on his face and felt his fillings grate against each other. When she'd gone, he smoothed his hair down again, then cleared the table and stacked the crockery carefully in the dishwasher. Susannah had her own weird rules for what should go where. It had taken him an age to learn them, but she kicked up such a fuss if they were broken that it seemed worth the effort of getting it right.

Something sticky on his fingers made him look down and he saw a piece of wet, chewed toast rejected by one of the children, which must have stuck to the edge of his plate. He ran the hot tap over his hands. He wouldn't have minded raw meat or mud, but this saliva-soaked reject from a pampered infant's mouth felt disgusting. Even cow dung would have been preferable, and that was saying something. This small domestic life was burying him alive.

Drying his hands, he looked at the phone. He'd have given anything to use his own mobile, but it was a pay-as-you go one and he'd run out of credit. With the old-fashioned receiver clamped against his ear, he rang the number of the lab to which he'd sent the Ivyleaf sausages for testing.

'Will, I was going to phone this morning,' said Mark Jones, the director. Will's heart sank. 'There's nothing much to tell you, I'm afraid. Certainly no trace of E. coli in any of the samples we've tested.'

'What? There must be.'

'Nope. But that doesn't mean much. The batch your friend ate could have been contaminated locally. It's not hard to do, after all. Happens all the time. There's been no news of a major outbreak – I checked – so that seems the likeliest answer.'

Will could feel his shoulders slump. 'I was so sure . . .' His voice died. What was the point? He'd made enough of a fool of himself already, failing to get anything useful out of anyone at the abattoir. How was he going to tell Trish?

'Listen, old boy,' Mark said with enough kindness to do a lot more damage to Will's fillings, 'you've got to get over this obsession with other people's meat products. I can see where you're coming from, believe me, but it's—'

'This has nothing to do with the past,' Will said. At that moment he even believed it. 'One woman is in Intensive Care, another has been through a bad time after eating sausages with the same label as the ones you're testing.'

'But I've just told you—'

'I know. But there's more. Listen, will you? No one will tell me where the sausages are made. Why? What's the point of keeping that secret, unless there's something to hide?'

'Are you absolutely sure they're not just trying to stop you running another hare? I mean, everyone in the business must know what happened the last time you were sure you'd uncovered a food scandal.' Mark's voice wasn't aggressive, just matter-of-fact. 'Or the time before.'

'Didn't you find *anything* in the samples?' Will was begging now, and he hated that too.

'Only the ingredients properly mentioned on the label, and the faintest trace of clenbuterol.'

'Ah! I knew there had to be something. Angel Dust, by God. I didn't know anyone was still using it in this country.'

'It's not that significant, Will,' said the scientist with even more pity in his voice. 'It was only a trace. All it means is that some of the meat in the sausage mix came from animals fed an illegal muscle-promoting drug. It's irrelevant to your friend in hospital; it's a beta-agonist, not a food-poisoning bacterium.'

'I know. But it adds weight to the suspicion that the sausages come from an iffy source. What else did you find? Come on: I can tell from your voice that there's more.'

'Nothing but a trace of bleach,' he said casually, 'which probably came from some piece of equipment that hadn't been properly rinsed.'

'Bleach?'

'Now don't get excited, Will.'

'But you know as well as I do what that could mean. Remember all those poultry cases?'

'You're grasping at straws, Will.' Mark sounded headmasterly now. 'Just because there have been a few cases in which people with pet-food licences have cleaned up unfit poultry meat with bleach and sold it on for human consumption doesn't mean every hint of chlorine in a food product is sinister.'

'No. But it makes you think, doesn't it? Combined with the secrecy and the clenbuterol, anyway.'

'Will, you've got to watch the paranoia,' Mark said, still kindly. 'You really have. And I've got to get back to work. Listen, old boy, I wish I'd never agreed to run these tests for you, but since I did that gives me the right to say: drop it. You'll only land yourself in even deeper shit. And with your case due to end soon, you have a real chance to start again. Don't screw that up by charging off on another mad crusade.'

'Thanks for the advice,' Will said coldly, knowing he couldn't take it. Then he let his mind and voice warm up again. 'And for the tests. It was good of you to run them so fast. You'd better send me a bill.' He had no idea how he'd pay it.

'Have this one on the house. See you.'

Will needed to think. He felt as though the washing-up and the babysitting and the being polite to Susannah and Rupert had dried out all kinds of important bits of his brain. He made himself some instant coffee, piling the granules into the cup until it was strong enough, then drank, wincing at the bitterness.

He was going to need help with this. As he'd said to Trish, the obvious person to give him a hand was Jamie Maxden, whose suspicions of the bottom end of the meat industry had always been as great as his own. But so far Jamie hadn't answered any of the messages Will had left on the answering machine.

Was Jamie still pissed off? He probably had the right to be, even though Will thought they'd made peace long ago. They'd agreed then that they ought to keep their distance for a while, and it had never seemed quite the right moment to re-establish contact. But if Jamie had wanted to, he could always have taken the first step and phoned. In fact, Will rather wished he had. A bit of sympathy would have been welcome as the world came crashing down around his ears.

'No, it wouldn't,' he said aloud, much more honestly. Maybe Jamie had understood that and stayed away in case it looked as if he were crowing.

Of course, he could be away on a job and unable to access messages left on the machine in his flat. Will knew he must have the number of Jamie's mobile somewhere. He charged back to the top of the house to ransack the boxes of papers under his bed, where he kept his old diaries.

This time he didn't mind using Susannah's phone so much. He dialled Jamie's mobile. But he only got a recorded voice telling him the number he'd called was no longer in use.

Had Jamie binned his old phone in favour of something newer and slicker and smaller in the years since they'd last been in touch? For a moment, Will felt helpless. Then he told himself there had to be other ways of tracking down any journalist.

Susannah must have some phone books somewhere, but he had no idea where. He started searching, pulling open cupboard doors he'd never touched in all the months he'd lived here and looking behind and under tables all over the house, even in her bedroom. She'd got a lot tidier since she married Rupert.

Eventually he found a stack of directories in the cupboard

under the stairs with the Dyson. Two minutes later he was phoning the *Daily Mercury*'s main switchboard and asking to speak to Jamie Maxden.

'There's no one of that name listed,' the receptionist said after a short pause. 'Can anyone else help?'

'But he writes for you. He must be there.'

'He isn't. I've looked. Maybe he's freelance.'

'Maybe he is. Who would know?'

'I can put you through to Features. They might help.'

'No. Features won't be any good. Put me through to News. He's an investigative journalist. You must have heard of him.'

'No. Sorry.'

Don't you ever read your own newspaper? Will wanted to shout at her in exasperation. But it wasn't her fault he was on such a short fuse these days, so he kept quiet.

'News desk,' said a bored male voice, which sounded too young to belong to anyone in work.

'I'm trying to contact Jamie Maxden.'

'Who?'

Will repeated the name with as much patience as he could muster. 'He's a journalist. He writes for you.'

'Not for us he doesn't.'

'But I've seen his name at the top of articles.'

'A byline? Not on this paper. You could try the press agencies. Oh, hang on; here's my boss. He's been here since the Dark Ages; he might know more.'

The phone went silent. Will couldn't believe he'd been cut off. Then he realized he'd only been put on hold.

Trish saw Will the minute she emerged from court. He looked awful, but he didn't move, not even to beckon her. He just stood, leaning against one of the pillars as though he hadn't enough strength left to hold himself upright.

'I'll catch you up, Antony,' she said and thrust her red bag at

Colin, who was already manoeuvring the trolley full of documents. She crossed the floor, hugely relieved after all that Andrew had texted her at lunchtime to say that she wouldn't be able to see Kim today. When she'd read his message, she'd gone straight outside the building to phone him and remind him of the urgency. He'd tried to pacify her, which had made her frustration worse. Now, with Antony wanting to discuss the day's proceedings and Will looking needier than ever, it was just as well she wasn't having to rush away.

'Thank you, Trish,' he said, swallowing. 'I knew you'd come over here. I need help.'

'I know. I can see that much. Will, I promise I'll do whatever I can, but first I've got to go back to chambers to thrash out what we're going to do tomorrow.' He looked even worse, so she reminded him that it was his case she and Antony were killing themselves to win.

'I know. Sorry.' Will looked at the floor. His big shoulders were slumped. 'And I can't tell you any of it here, but I *have* to talk to you.'

'OK. Look, I'll phone you the minute I'm free. Where will you be this evening?'

His eyes looked harder suddenly. But she was too busy and too preoccupied to work out what it might mean. Then his eyelids dropped and there was only skin to be seen, with a few tiny capillaries pulsating under it.

'At my sister's. I'm not going out much these days.'

'Give me the number and I'll phone as soon as I can.' She waited, barely controlling her urge to tell him to hurry, while he found an old envelope in his pocket, scribbled the phone number on a corner and tore it off. 'Thanks. Don't let it get to you, whatever it is. Bye, Will.'

She was panting when she caught up with Antony and his small party. They were already at the door of Plough Court.

'Such eagerness,' Antony said, putting a hand on her hot

forehead. Colin looked surprised, then hurried on ahead with the solicitor.

'It's dead flattering, Trish. But don't give yourself a heart attack. I'm going to need you on top form tonight.'

'I hope "tonight" is an exaggeration, you old slave driver,' she said. 'I've got things to do. And there wasn't anything particularly startling in today's evidence.'

'Pedant! This afternoon, then. But talking of tonight, Trish,' he said, putting on his wicked seducer's look, 'we could . . .'

'No we couldn't,' she said firmly. Then she laughed. 'Oh, Antony, if you knew what a turn-off that leer is!'

'*Leer*?' he said in outrage. 'I don't leer.'

'Sure of that, are you?'

'Monster! Oh, all right; if you won't play, I suppose we'd better go and work.'

He was laughing too, as he led the way up to his room. Naturally it was the best in chambers, with a spectacular view and ravishing old mahogany furniture.

Caro knew that Jess was sitting by her bed, wanting something, but she couldn't provide it. She tried, through the pain and the weakness that kept her sewn to the mattress, but all she could do was force up her eyelids and mumble something. Instantly Jess was there, holding a cool, damp cloth to her forehead.

'It's all right, Caro. I'm here. They're doing everything they can, and soon the antibiotics will work. D'you want me to call a nurse?'

Caro didn't want anyone else. She couldn't do anything for anyone now, not even Jess. The pain dug deeper into her back and she groaned. The damp cloth was removed and Jess tiptoed away from the bed. Caro didn't even have the energy to beg her to come back. Two hot tears slid out of her eyes.

Chapter 8

'It's not late, Trish,' Antony said when they'd got rid of Colin and the solicitor. 'If I promise not to leer, will you have dinner with me?'

She couldn't resist an invitation like that and said so.

'Great. At this time of year we could probably get in anywhere. What would you like? The Ivy? The Ritz?'

'Nowhere grand. Or smart. Somewhere we can sit with our elbows on the table and not have our ears burned out with noise.' She fanned her face with her legal pad. 'With air conditioning.'

He nodded. 'I know just the place. It hasn't been trendy for forty years, but the food is good and it's always quiet. Cool, too.'

'Sounds perfect, but I have to phone someone first.'

'Fine. I'll make sure there's a table. Meet you outside in ten minutes?'

'OK.'

She still hadn't got used to her new room in chambers. The old one had been poky and dark, but she'd had it for years and it had become a kind of refuge, even though she'd usually had to have a pupil in it with her. Colin would have been fine, but some of his predecessors had been a lot less likeable and she'd have done anything to get rid of them if she could. Luckily they only stayed with each pupil master for six months.

This room was much lighter than her old one, and nearly twice the size. It also cost her twice as much. At first she hadn't been sure she would ever fill it, but that hadn't taken long, and now she found it comfortable. It was good, too, to have a window that opened onto a reasonable view, instead of the grimy walls of the lightwell at the back of the building. Of course, if they didn't win this case against Furbishers, she'd get no fees and might have to retreat to her old room – and lose all the face she'd gained in the last couple of years.

The phone rang and rang; at last a woman answered.

'Hello,' Trish said. 'Is that Susannah? Look, I'm really sorry but I don't know your surname. Will always talks about you as Susannah. My name's Trish Maguire.'

'His barrister?'

'One of them. Might I speak to him?' she said, unable to understand the hostility in the other woman's voice. Surely she didn't think Trish was contravening her professional ethics. If Susannah knew anything about them, she'd know that now Will had finished giving his evidence they were free to talk whenever they wanted.

'He'll be sick to have missed you,' Susannah said. 'I made him go for a walk because he was driving us all mad jiggling about waiting for your call. Can you give me a number where he can reach you? He's determined to talk to you tonight.'

Trish thought of the unsmart, quiet restaurant and knew she couldn't have that disturbed by phone calls. She gave Susannah her mobile number, adding, 'But don't let him waste money phoning until after eleven.'

'Thank you.'

'That's fine,' Trish said. 'Please tell him I'm sorry I missed him.'

Twenty minutes later she and Antony were sitting in a small dark-red room lined with portraits. It would have been old-fashioned even when she was born. The menu read more like the record of a banquet from the fin de siècle than anything from the twenty-first century. Trish had never eaten classic French dishes of this kind and chose the simplest-sounding ones, hoping for the best. Antony insisted on ordering her a glass of champagne as an aperitif.

If anyone had told her at the beginning of her career that she would ever sit at ease in a place like this, let alone with a man like Antony, she would have laughed. She'd chosen the Bar as a career only because her stepfather had told her patronizingly that it wasn't suitable for 'a girl with your background'. He'd added that, being quite clever, she might well make a useful solicitor one day and he would talk to friends of his about getting her a training place in a reasonable firm somewhere in the provinces. She could still remember her fury and the determination it had given her.

It made her think of Kim and acknowledge her own luck. Trish's stepfather had merely gingered up her ambition; Kim's had traumatized her. Would Kim ever find a way to fight back against the damage Daniel Crossman had done?

Trish's rage had taken her a long way, but it hadn't helped when she'd come out of Bar school with excellent results and a massive chip on her shoulder. It had taken years for her to stop resenting the smoothly confident people she saw all around her. Now, she supposed, she was one of them. It was an odd thought.

The only other diners in the restaurant were a party of four in the far corner. They must have all been in their seventies, and they had a kind of civilized elegance that suited the place. Far too dignified to whisper, like people in most half-empty restaurants, they were talking easily about architecture with the authority of those who knew a lot and had nothing to prove.

'So, Trish,' Antony said when the champagne had been

poured, 'with George and David away, who are you looking after now?'

'Why should I be looking after anyone?'

'With a heart that's open to all comers and the social conscience of a Fabian, you're never happy unless you are. And you're so sexy these days, you have to be happy.'

She laughed, even though the thought of Kim was anything but funny. One day she'd tell Antony about Kim, but not now.

'I just hope it's not that poor tight-arse Will Applewood,' he said, ripping his roll in two with a great explosion of brittle crust.

'Why?'

'Because he'd swallow you whole.'

She frowned. Nothing she had seen in Will had suggested any kind of greed, even if he had shown himself to be capable of lies and manipulation.

'He needs too much,' Antony added, raising his glass to her. 'You'd do better with someone more secure, who wants only a little piece of you. Good. Here are my coquilles Saint Jacques.'

A smile made her lips twitch, but she didn't say anything. Antony was looking towards the kitchen door to make sure her starter was coming too, but he didn't miss her amusement.

'I know,' he said, holding her gaze. His lips softened into a smile of such self-conscious wickedness that she had to laugh. It was much better than the supposedly seductive version. 'I should be eating oysters to make this scene all it could have been. But not while there's no "r" in the month.'

'In any case, oysters might have been a little too obvious.'

'What about your asparagus?'

After that, it was hard to eat with any kind of dignity, but they were soon laughing too much for it to matter.

Later, he pressed her again about what was preoccupying her and she told him the truth. 'It's a child, damaged and terrified. And silent. The only person who might have been able to get her to talk is incommunicado in hospital and someone's got to get through to her before the weekend. The social workers have failed, and so has the psychiatrist in the case. So they've asked me to have a go. It's a last-ditch thing. I thought I might nip out after court tomorrow. They couldn't set it up in time for today. You don't mind, do you? It shouldn't take too long and I'd come straight back to chambers.'

'As I thought, you have the social conscience of a Fabian,' he said seriously, giving her story its due, then he pushed it away, adding a lighthearted reprise: 'and a heart that's open to all comers.'

'Not quite all,' she said, taking her tone from him.

'No?'

'No,' she said more definitely.

'Now that really is rather a pity. I'd been making plans for it.' Antony picked up his fork and started to talk about the latest Covent Garden production of *Tosca*. Only his eyes told her that they hadn't finished the other conversation yet. A frisson she hadn't felt in years raised all the hairs on her arms. As though he'd felt it too, he suddenly interrupted himself to say, 'You know you'll never experience everything life can offer if you go on cutting off the highs and lows like this. You're wasting yourself in this perpetual struggle for dreary balance.'

'Only someone who's never known the lows could think that balance is dreary,' she said with feeling, and turned the conversation back to *Tosca*.

'Did you know there's someone waiting for you?' the taxi driver asked Trish as she handed over her fare.

'Where?'

'On them iron stairs behind you. He's just stood up. He's been reading the paper.'

'In this light?' Trish didn't turn immediately. It wouldn't be the first time that someone had been waiting to accost her outside the flat. But tonight it seemed unfair: she was too relaxed to deal with anything difficult. 'What does he look like?'

'Handsome bloke with lots of dark hair and a square chin. Check shirt.' The driver gave her some change.

'Oh, him.' Trish shook the coins in her hand until two pounds were between her fingers and thumb. She gave them back to him and nodded. 'I know him.'

'That's all right, then.' The taxi wheezed into life again and the driver made a U-turn, leaving her to Will. Antony's warning echoed in her mind, displacing all the other things he'd said to her later.

'Hi. Have you been waiting long?'

'Not much more than a hour,' he said. 'It was good to sit after the walk. And it's the first time I've felt cool in weeks. Susannah's house is stifling, however many windows I open.'

'You *walked*? From Fulham? But why?'

'I always walk. It's the only exercise I get these days, and moving stops me thinking too much and sending myself mad with regrets. Besides, I can't afford the fares.'

'But why not phone? Never mind. You'd better come on in and have a drink and tell me what the problem is.' As she unlocked the door and switched on the lights she saw his face. The unhappiness in it shocked her into guilt over the way she'd abandoned him to joke and flirt with Antony.

'You know the journalist I told you about?' Will said abruptly. 'He died outside Smarden Meats only a few weeks before we went there.'

'*What*?'

'It's true. Didn't I tell you that if there was a story, he'd know all about it?'

'But there hasn't been anything in the news,' Trish said.

'In fact there has, but it was only a few tiny paragraphs here and there. None of the papers gave any details. Even I missed it and I knew his name, so I'm not surprised you didn't pick it up.'

'No wonder they were so jumpy at the abattoir.' Trish remembered the hostility she'd seen in every face. She remembered the sounds, too, and the smells and tried to force her brain to shut them out. 'They probably thought we were spying for the press. I'm surprised they let us in at all. What happened to him?'

'The official line is that he committed suicide, as a protest against cruelty to animals, by lying down under the wheels of a meat lorry destined for Smithfield Market.'

'That's ridiculous. No one would do that. He can't have meant to die. He must have been trying to stop the lorry leaving. How awful! And for the driver.'

Trish retreated to the kitchen to fetch glasses. She knew from something Will had said casually when they first met that he was a whisky drinker and she had a bottle of Glenlivet at the back of one of the cupboards. She poured him a stiff one. For herself, queasy with her memories of the abattoir, she took a bottle of Badoit out of the fridge.

'You don't believe it was suicide either,' she said as she watched Will add a splash of water to the heavy tumbler. 'Do you?'

'No. They said his pockets were stuffed with animal rights and vegetarian leaflets and he even had a placard with him about pig pens. But that wasn't Jamie's style. I mean, it was never the animals he fought for; it was the people who had to eat them.'

'Maybe he had a sudden conversion.' Trish thought of Jess. 'It happens.'

'Not to Jamie. I told you, he was a hard-nosed investigative journalist, used to working undercover. He must've been at the abattoir to report on something they're doing there.'

'Who was he working for?'

'It used to be the *Daily Mercury*. They denied all knowledge of him when I phoned. Then I got on to someone who knew a bit more. He told me Jamie hadn't had anything much published in the last few years.'

Will put the glass to his lips and breathed in the fumes, but he didn't drink. His Adam's apple, usually well hidden, moved as though he had swallowed. He looked up at her, and she saw that his eyes were dark with misery.

'He was a good bloke, you know, Trish. He would have been furious about what happened to you and your police friend.' This time he did drink, holding the liquid in his mouth, moving it back and forth across his tongue. At last he swallowed it down in one, like bitter-tasting medicine. 'He did a terrific story once about dangerous chemicals and the additives that screw up children's mental health.'

'Then why hasn't he had anything published recently?'

'I asked the man at the *Mercury*, and he just said a big story Jamie had written went down in flames.' Will was sitting with his knees wide apart, leaning forwards. His elbows were propped on his knees and he held his glass loosely between his big hands. Suddenly he stiffened and turned one of his feet on its side so that he could look at the sole. 'I've been treading muck on your floor, Trish. I'm sorry.'

'That's OK.' She looked back towards the door. It was true there was a line of dusty footprints across the pale polished wood, but they were hardly 'muck'. Her cleaner would whisk them away in minutes.

'Will, I'm really sorry you've had this awful news about your friend, and I wish there was something I could say that might help, but—'

'That's not why I came, Trish. Don't you see? Jamie's death means that there is something seriously wrong at Smarden Meats.'

'Oh, come on, Will. There's no—'

'Listen. There's too much coincidence in all this if he wasn't there to get evidence to back up a big story. Someone must have caught him and drugged him or forced him to lie under the wheels. It could even have been that bloke who nearly stabbed me.'

'Will! That's absurd.'

He pushed back his chair. Hearing the screech of its legs against her polished wooden floor, Trish winced.

'I thought *you'd* believe me. Christ! You were there too. You must have seen the aggression in him. You even said you were scared by it.'

'I know, but—'

'Don't worry. I'm sorry to have bothered you. Goodnight.'

'Will, don't be like that. Sit down again. Have some more to drink.'

'No. It's late. And you've got to be in court tomorrow.' He was already at her front door, tugging at the latch.

She followed him and put her hand on top of his on the lock. 'Will . . . You're right: it is late, and I'm not surprised you're upset about your friend's death, but—'

He slid his hand out from under hers.

'I'm not upset, as you call it.' His dark eyes were steady now. 'I'm fucking angry. Goodnight.'

He was halfway down the iron steps, making much more noise than he had to, when she called after him, 'Will!'

He turned. The moonlight fell across his face, accentuating his cheekbones. Surely they were even sharper than they'd been last week. Was he starving himself now?

'I can understand the anger, too, Will, but that's no reason to make wild leaps of logic into dangerous fantasies like this.'

'What makes you think it's a fantasy? I was looking for Jamie because I hoped he'd be able to tell me something about the meat used in the sausages that poisoned you. Now it looks as though he could have – if someone hadn't killed him first.'

He ran on down the stairs, taking two at a time and never missing his footing. That was an exit even Jess would have admired, Trish thought as she shut the door and locked it. She went up the spiral staircase to shower and try to get back the pleasure of her dinner with Antony.

It didn't work. All through the night, memories of the hate in the slaughterman's eyes kept dragging her up out of the sleep she needed. If anything could have persuaded her that Will wasn't wallowing in paranoia, it would have been the thought of those eyes, and that knife hovering inches from Will's stomach. But if the coroner had come to a verdict of suicide, he must have had good reason.

It was after two o'clock. Trish turned over and tried to forget about the abattoir and everyone connected with it. But she'd never slept well on her front, so she turned again, pushing the hot duvet to one side. After a while she drifted into sleep, but it didn't last. She woke with a jerk and saw that the clock's hands had barely moved. This time the eyes she could see in her mind were not Bob Flesker's, but Kim's.

She had looked terrified, as though she knew that the slightest mistake or noise could set off some appalling punishment. Trish *had* to persuade her to talk. No child could live in that much fear without permanent damage.

Next morning's session in court was so dull it took all Trish's determination to stay awake and concentrate on the evidence of Furbishers' delicatessen buyer, Arthur Chancer, instead of thinking about Kim and how best to set about interviewing her that afternoon.

Trish wasn't the only one to find it hard to avoid dropping off. It was another boiling day and the air-conditioning didn't make much difference. More than one of the ushers were nodding.

Chancer produced very little of interest in his answers as he explained the company's policy when looking for new suppliers, trying out their products and negotiating prices with them. He was insistent that the supermarket had always offered new suppliers a very limited contract before making a longer-term deal with them. He claimed that he had always made it clear, and that it wasn't his fault if some of the naive over-excited producers like Will Applewood had misunderstood him.

'*Thirty* of them?' Antony asked, in tones of a man invited to believe that not only is the moon made of green cheese but that the earth consists of gingerbread. 'Do you not think it is asking too much to expect his lordship to believe in so many coincidences?'

Chancer turned an appealing smile on the judge. 'In my experience, my lord, there's nothing like need and excitement to deafen any small trader when he's faced with big new opportunities.'

'It is true, is it not, that in several cases you have followed a quite different line when negotiating with suppliers?'

'Occasionally, yes.'

As Chancer launched into a long explanation of the way he carried out his job, Colin began to slide down the bench beside Trish. She poked him to make sure he wasn't falling asleep, and he pulled himself upright. She had actually drifted off in court once during her pupillage and she'd hate anyone she liked to suffer the humiliation she'd felt then.

Antony's taut shoulders showed that he was listening to every word and taking in every nuance, as usual. It was partly his ferocious attention to detail that had made him so successful. Trish nudged Colin again and pointed to the notes he had been writing. He blushed and picked up his pen.

She hoped Antony wasn't going to stop her leaving for her interview with Kim Bowlby at the end of the session. He hadn't made any objections last night, but it would be pretty eccentric for the junior on a case as big as this to abandon her leader halfway through the day's work.

When the judge rose, Antony turned sideways on his bench,

smiling at her over the pristine gathers at the back of his gown.

'If you're going to talk to this child, you'd better run.'

She almost reached out to touch his cheek and saw from the affection in his eyes that he knew it.

Kim was already sitting at the table when Trish rushed into the interview room, wishing she were fitter. The foster mother was at her seat in the corner, ready to intervene if Trish's questions alarmed her charge, and Andrew would be in the observation room.

'Hello, Kim.' Trish worked to calm her breathing. 'I'm sorry I'm late.'

The greyish eyelids lifted to reveal the child's eyes. For once there was an expression in them: surprise. Maybe she had no experience of adults apologizing to her.

'How are you?'

'Very well, thank you.'

'Good. Tell me about your baby,' Trish said, launching straight into what she was sure had to be the crux of the tension between Kim and her stepfather.

'I haven't got a baby.'

'No. I meant the one at home, in the flat. Your brother.'

'That's my mother's baby.'

'When was he born?'

'After Easter.'

'That must have made quite a change in your life.'

'Yes,' Kim whispered after a pause to make sure it was safe to answer.

'Do you like babies?'

'Sometimes.'

'Do you play with your brother?'

'He doesn't play. He sleeps.' Her eyelids closed for a second, then lifted to reveal the old blankness.

The baby has to be the key, Trish thought, even though she knew from the file that the Child Protection Team had failed to find any signs of abuse on his small body either. Kim had only started falling asleep at school after he'd been born. It would have been too much of a coincidence if there were no link. Maybe it was just that his crying had kept her awake all night, so that she'd snatched what sleep she could during the day.

'What about feeding? Who gives him his milk?'

A tiny smile produced a relaxation of all the muscles just under Kim's skin.

'He has a bottle now, so sometimes I sit with him and I hold the bottle.'

'How does that make you feel?'

'I like it.'

'And what about your mum: how does she feel when you help?'

Kim whispered that her mother liked it too. She looked less certain now. The questions went on, with Trish striving to keep out of her mind the answers she hoped to hear. Any hint in her wording, her manner or her voice might trigger Kim's need to provide what the adult in charge of her wanted.

Once again she sat quite still throughout the session, even when Trish suggested that she might like to play, or paint again. At last, Trish said, 'Is there anything you want to ask me?'

Kim's eyes flickered. For a moment Trish thought she might speak, but she didn't even open her lips. In the past, even the most traumatized children had given Trish the feeling they were desperate to talk, but had no idea how to start without setting off a trail of catastrophe they couldn't control. Only Kim had ever held on as tightly as this.

'Do you remember Caro?' Trish asked, hoping for more of a reaction. 'Inspector Lyalt?'

The smooth head nodded.

'She's in hospital. I'm going to see her tomorrow after work. Do you want me to give her any sort of message?'

There was a long pause before Kim whispered that she hoped Caro would get better soon. Then she waited passively in her chair until her foster mother came to her side and Trish gave her permission to move.

Andrew burst into the room as soon as they had gone. 'Trish, I know you haven't time to stop now, but what was all that about the brother?'

'It's clear that Kim has been threatened. I'm not sure how or with what, or even why, but I think the baby has to be involved in it somewhere. She's such a responsible child that I think it could be she's not talking because she feels she's got to protect *him*.'

'I've told you: there's not a mark on him either.'

'There are plenty of things that don't leave marks, as you very well know,' Trish said sadly. 'I once heard of a nanny in the days before North Sea gas, who used to dope noisy children in her charge by holding them over the cooker with all the gas taps full on. That didn't leave marks. A pillow over the face wouldn't either. You don't get petechial haemorrhages much short of death. And there must be plenty else Crossman could be doing that wouldn't scar their bodies: threatening them with violence he's never actually carried out – knife cuts, or burns, or ropes, anything. Fear can be almost as effective a punishment as actual bodily harm; you must know that.'

'God! It's so frustrating.'

'I know, but we will get there, Andrew. Look, I've got to run now. I'll phone you.'

Tim Hayleigh stooped to pick up a stick to throw for Boney and saw that the earth was still discoloured with blood. He'd come this way because he'd hoped it would have faded by now and wanted to be sure.

If only it would rain! Nothing else would drive this evidence right out of sight. In spite of the coroner's verdict, he still couldn't believe that no one had come looking for it yet. Had no one cared enough for the journalist Bob had murdered to try to find out what had happened to him?

The thought of the dead man still haunted Tim. He would find himself massaging his cheekbones, as if it had been himself cringing and squealing under Bob's boots. He tried not to think about what would happen to *his* mangled body if Bob left it lying somewhere in the countryside. No one would come looking for him. It would be weeks before he'd be missed.

He'd hardly seen any of his cousins since his parents died. He'd never been able to persuade a woman to stay with him once she'd seen the state of the farmhouse and found out how hard he had to work, so love affairs were a thing of the past, too. Sometimes he felt as though his only friends were Ron and Bob. That seemed like the saddest failure of the lot.

Boney brought the stick and dropped it so that he could start nosing around the contaminated patch of ground. Tim shuddered and flung the stick again, running after it himself when Boney didn't move.

'Come on, boy. Come on, Boney.' He slapped his thigh. '*Come on.*'

But Boney was far too interested in where he was digging to obey. Tim promised himself that he wouldn't bring Boney back here to the edge of the wood ever again. Not even when the bloodstain had faded into nothing.

He ran on, tripped and went sprawling over the ground. He heard something crack as he fell and felt a sharp pain in his kneecap. For a moment he thought it must have shattered, but it was only the branch he'd thrown, splintering under his weight as the journalist's bones had done under Bob's boots.

Oh, God! Would he ever forget what Bob had done? Or the way he'd hung back, too terrified to intervene?

Tim laid his face on the tough dry grass and tried to empty his mind of everything that had happened that night.

Chapter 9

The beer in the pub nearest the abattoir was good: yeasty and barely fizzy, not like the gassy continental lagers Will was always being offered in London. He was halfway down his first pint and tucking into home-made bread and nutty Cheddar.

The whole place was honest, he thought, even better than the pub he'd been to with Trish. Its small windows meant that the interior was nicely shaded from the blinding sun. There were even some men whose boots looked as though they sometimes had muck on them. It shouldn't be too long before it was possible to get into conversation and find out all the gossip there was on Smarden Meats and Jamie's so-called suicide.

Will chewed a mouthful of cheese. It had just the right degree of sharpness and the texture was good, too: dry but not crumbly. He realized he was thinking like a food producer once more, testing everything he ate against his own taste and his own products. That had to be a good sign, as if his sanity might be returning at last. But would he ever get to do it for real again?

'Sorry, mate,' a man said, as he collapsed on to the hard wooden bench next to Will.

He looked up, wondering what the apology could be for. Damp soaking through the knee of his trousers told him, just as the man pointed to a spreading stain on the cloth.

'That's OK.' Will smiled and dug a handkerchief out of his

pocket to mop the unabsorbed spillage. 'It happens. I was miles away.'

The other man didn't answer.

'You from round here?' Will asked and watched him nod. 'D'you farm?'

'Not any more.' The man took a long pull at his beer.

'Like me. When did you sell up?'

'Wasn't me that sold. I was a tenant. Gave up nearly a year ago.' The man looked at Will, considering him. Whatever he saw seemed to reassure him. 'There didn't seem much point going on when everything that went to market cost more than it made. We were pouring money down the drain as fast as over-quota milk. Luckily we'd had a chance to buy the house in the good years. Some of it still belongs to the building society, but enough is ours to make life possible.'

'So what d'you do now?'

'Bed and breakfast. My wife always did it, and we're just about making do. Thank God the mortgage rate's as low as it is. When I think what we've paid in interest over the years, I could . . .' He drowned what he'd been going to say in beer. When he raised his face from the tankard again, there was a faint foam moustache above his lips. 'What about you?'

Will sketched his reasons for selling the farm he'd inherited. As he spoke, he edited his loathing of the years of servitude to his father, and what it had made him do. He thought of the day when Trish had poured out her fury about people who lied to her. What would she do if she ever found out that he hadn't always told her the truth? How could he make her understand?

After everything that had happened, he could see that the awfulness of the life hadn't all been his father's fault; it had been imposed on him, too, and his father, and his father's father, which made everything worse.

Familiar guilt made his body squeeze in on itself. He tried to ease it by remembering all the reasons he'd had to hate his father. One particular episode still burned in his memory. He'd been working for his mock 'O' level exams, so it must have been after his fifteenth birthday, more than twenty years ago.

The noise of his father coming into his room woke him, but he wasn't going to show it. He always slept on his back so he hardly had to move his head to see the illuminated figures on the alarm clock by his bed. Half-past five. His stillness didn't save him. Nor his schoolwork. A callused hand dragged back the duvet.

'Come on, son. Stop faking. There are cows out there that need milking.'

Will could feel his own hands even without moving them, chapped and swollen from yesterday and the day before that. It wasn't the actual milking he hated; even at this time of the morning in the raw darkness and with his head hollow with the endless need for sleep and his eyes smarting, he didn't mind dealing with the cows. Sometimes he felt sorry for them, rounded up and hustled into the milking parlour, their huge, heavy udders clamped into the machines. Occasionally he'd give the poor beasts an extra stroke and think he could see gratitude in their big brown eyes. It was the cleaning up afterwards that he hated. The smell of cow dung clung to his hair and every crevice of his body, in spite of all the scrubbing that only added to the soreness of his skin. He could still smell it now, just as he could see the greeny-brown slime in his mind's eye, swirling away from the jet of the power hose. It was no wonder Suze's friends turned their backs on him.

'Let me sleep, Dad. I've got exams today.'

'Don't give me that.' He felt his father's calluses against his forehead as he grabbed a clump of Will's hair and tugged. 'Wake up! The cows need milking. On your feet, boy.'

'Susannah doesn't have to help around the place.' He shut his eyes so that he wouldn't have to see his father's expression. He knew he'd have to get up, but he didn't see why he should make it easy for the old bastard. 'So why should I?'

The hand wound tighter in his hair and pulled. Will let his head follow to lessen the tug. In a minute he was on his feet just like the old bastard wanted. His toes curled up from the hard coldness of the floor and his lanky body shivered. He reached for his work trousers and the rough heavy jersey he'd put on over his pyjamas.

'She's younger than you and she helps her mother. Who d'you think would have a hot breakfast for you when you get in from milking if it wasn't for them? Hurry up. I haven't time to waste on this performance every day. Come *on*, Will. If you left your cock alone when you went to bed, you wouldn't be this wiped out. Come on.'

'Then I lost my food business, too,' he said at the end of his story, having cut out all the really painful bits, like the beating he'd had from his father when they heard he'd failed his exams. He still felt the injustice of that, even after all these years. 'But it looks as though I'm going to get enough damages to start up again. I thought I might try this part of the country. I couldn't bear to go back to the Hampshire border. Anyway, it's too expensive now. What's it like round here?'

The bed-and-breakfast man shrugged. Levering himself to his feet, he asked if he could get Will another drink to make up for the stain on his trousers.

'Thanks. It was a pint of Special.'

'Ron!' the other man called as he shoved himself off the bench, which rocked again. 'Two pints of Special.' He ambled over to the bar, exchanging laconic courtesies with some of the other drinkers on the way, and handed the barman some money.

They drank in companionable silence for a while. The taste of the beer was still right, bigger and meatier than anything Will had had in months. It was good, too, to be back in the company of men like these. He wiped his mouth as he put down his tankard, and asked again about conditions here in Kent.

'It's not so bad,' said the other man with a bitter edge to his voice, 'if you're a City commuter with a bonus and a fast car. Tough though if you belong here and have no chance of earning a decent living, with a wife who thinks you're a useless lump, and a houseful of strangers who treat you like a moron. Thank God for this place. I'd go mad without it.'

'But some people are still farming,' Will protested. 'The land's well kept round here. There's money being spent on it, too. They can't all be merchant bankers building up Petits Trianons for the weekend.'

'Petty Whats?' asked a third man, putting a pint down on the table in front of Will's new friend. 'How are you, Gus?'

'Got balled out by Jeanie this morning for leaving skin on the breakfast hot milk. It's no life for a man, running round after a bunch of townees.'

'At least you've got money coming in. Think of poor Tim: no wife, so no bed and breakfast. Not even egg money.' The newcomer leaned across the table, hand outstretched, saying: 'Jack Morgan. How are you?'

'Will Applewood. Good to see you. Who's Tim?'

'Ex sheep farmer on the edge of the Marsh. He switched to cherries a few years ago,' said Gus. 'Tim's OK. He may not do B and B, but he brings in a bit extra taking aerial photographs for surveyors during his off-season. Sometimes the bankers pay him to take pictures for their Christmas cards. He said the other day that he just about earns enough from it to make the plane pay for itself. So his one hobby is free. Good thinking.'

'So long as petrol prices don't go up. That would screw his sums,' Jack said. 'Like the price of cherries must be doing these days. No one wants proper Kentish white-heart cherries like

Tim's. They're after those great glossy black ones that look good, but taste of sod all. Dunno how much longer he can go on, even with the photography. He probably should've kept to sheep. Now that lambs are being held back from slaughter to restock the foot-and-mouth-hit farms, you can get a decent price again. So he's missed out all ways round.'

'Maybe he'd be open to offers for some of the buildings then,' Will said, fighting to forget his sympathy for these men and complete what he'd come here to do.

He'd decided to be a property buyer because that let you ask anything you wanted, even the most unbelievably offensive questions.

'Where can I find him?' he asked.

'Don't even try. His place isn't much more than eight miles from here. But I don't want him thinking I said he'd be likely to sell up. He's on a short fuse these days. Anything sets him off. I'd likely get an earful, if nothing worse.'

'Does he drink in here? Maybe I'll run into him. It could be easier that way.'

'Doesn't drink anywhere except at home, as far as I know. No spare cash.'

'Oh. OK.' Will caught the barman looking at him and quickly raised his voice. 'Then is there anyone you know of who *is* trying to sell?' He tried to look like someone with the millions necessary to buy any substantial piece of land in the area. All he could see were his fraying cuffs. He could feel the slope of his heels, too, where he'd worn away the rubber with his long walks on London's pavements. At least his hands were like a rich man's now, soft from lack of work.

As he listened to the discussion of which struggling local farmers might want to sell, Will mentally rehearsed the other questions he'd come to ask, the ones about Smarden Meats and the men who worked there.

*

'Yesterday, Mr Chancer, you told my learned friend that you cannot be held responsible for some naive suppliers misunderstanding the type of contract you were offering them.' Ferdy Aldham paused, as though to make sure everyone was awake.

Several people moved their heads and one or two rubbed their eyes. Colin turned to smile at Trish, as though to assure her that he'd never succumb to heat and boredom again.

'That's right,' Chancer said in his slightly nasal voice.

'What exactly did you say to them to make it clear?'

'I can't tell you exactly because I didn't keep any record. But in every case, I explained that we'd be taking their products at the price agreed for three months and then, when we were sure there was a market for them and our contracts people had looked at everything, we'd be offering them a long-term deal.'

'And how did they react to that?'

'Well, my lord,' Chancer said, turning his head to address the judge, 'they mostly just grabbed the offer with both hands. There was only one of them who didn't.'

'And who was that?' Ferdy asked, looking so satisfied that Trish began to worry.

'Mr Applewood. When I ran through the details with him, he said he wasn't in the business of doing trial runs, and that I'd had samples of all his products already and that if I couldn't tell which ones would sell, then I shouldn't be doing the job I was.'

Trish kept an expression of mild interest on her face and willed Colin not to show any of the dismay he must feel. Thank God Will wasn't in court this morning. He'd have been jumping up and down by now.

'And have you any evidence to support this statement?' Ferdy asked.

'Yes,' Chancer said. 'It's in the letter I wrote him after our meeting, the one about the timing of his deliveries.'

'That is document 5063, my lord,' Ferdy said, riffling through his own bundle to place one plump finger on the page.

Trish looked down at the relevant passage. Chancer had written:

'As to your dislike of our need to assure ourselves of the quality and marketability of your product, I have to say that if there is anything in our terms you consider too onerous, now is the moment say so, before either of us is committed.'

Surely there wasn't enough in this ambiguous sentence to sway the judge in Furbishers' favour. It was no wonder they hadn't picked it up as they prepared the case; in itself it was far too vague to prove Chancer's assertion. If only he hadn't claimed to have spelled everything out to Will in a face to face meeting!

She said as much after the judge had risen for the lunch adjournment. Colin had gone ahead to buy the sandwiches, so she and Antony were alone with Will's solicitor, Neil Stanton.

'I don't know,' Antony said, pulling off his wig and scratching his scalp. 'On its own the letter wouldn't cause us much of a problem, but old Husking might believe Chancer's oral testimony and take this as confirmation of it. You know Applewood better than either of us, Neil,' he added to the solicitor. 'Could he have lied about what Chancer said to him at the meeting?'

'I wouldn't have thought so, but I can't be sure.' He bit his lip. 'That's not helpful, Antony, I know. But it's the best I can do. He's probably not above the odd fib. Are any of us? But he's so full of righteous outrage about what Furbishers did that I'd find it hard to believe.'

'Good. Now, we'd better get on with lunch.'

Colin had their sandwiches waiting, along with Trish's raspberry and cranberry smoothie and some yoghurt. The four of them plunged straight into work, chewing as they discussed the implications of what had happened this morning, and how best to deal with it in the closing speech.

When Antony and Neil strolled off to the gents together,

Trish pulled her mobile out of her pocket and switched it on to collect her messages. There was one from Andrew Stane, asking her to phone.

'Andrew,' she said as soon as she'd got through. 'What's up?'

'Kim has a raging temperature, and the doctor insists she stays in bed, so you won't be able to see her this afternoon.'

'Shit! We've only got till Saturday. It's not enough time anyway, but if we lose a whole day, I—'

'You don't have to tell me, Trish,' he said, and she could tell from the tightness of his voice that he shared all her fears. 'But if she's that ill, we're not going to get anything out of her by dragging her out of bed, or by invading her sickroom.'

'I suppose not. D'you think you might be able to get an extension of the interim care order because of this?'

'I don't know. I could certainly try. But let's see how she does over the next twenty-four hours. I'd rather not even apply unless we absolutely have to. We'll be lucky to get one more chance, and I can't use it up lightly. My other phone's ringing. I've got to go.'

The prospect of spending the rest of the day in the stuffy court, listening to Ferdy encouraging more damaging bits of evidence out of Furbishers' buyer, when a child's life and sanity were hanging in the balance was awful.

'Trish?' Colin was looking anxiously at her. 'Are you OK?'

She blinked, then smiled, reminding herself of her real job. If Kim couldn't be interviewed today, she couldn't. It would be mad to let frustration fog her brain.

'Sure. Just a bit of tiresome news,' she said. 'By the way, Colin, if you have a spare moment, you might look something up for me.'

'Of course,' he said, surprised that her request was so tentative. His job was to look up anything she wanted.

They walked out of the coffee shop side by side and waited outside court for Antony and Neil to catch them up.

'It's about the death of a journalist,' she said, taking advantage of the short freedom, 'a man called Jamie Maxden. I gather there was an inquest a few weeks ago. You might see what you can find out. But it's not a priority.'

'Sure? I'm due to play squash this evening, but I could cancel it.'

'No, it's fine.'

'Great. Thanks. I'll get what I can. Why are you interested in him?'

'He had a history of writing exposés of the food industry,' she began, hoping he was still too nervous of her to ask many questions. She thought of her own days of running errands for her various pupil masters and knew she'd never have dared ask them to justify any of their requests. 'And I think he was once quite successful.'

Colin simply nodded, just as she'd have done in the old days.

Unaware of his legal team's problems, Will had spent the whole of the fifty quid he'd borrowed from his brother-in-law along with the expensive red trousers from Hacketts. Still, he had a fair amount of information to show for the money. He waved at his new-found mates and the barman and went to sit in Susannah's car outside the pub. Wanting to be sure he was sober enough to avoid scraping her long Volvo against any of the hedges, he wrote up notes of what he'd heard.

As he scribbled, he kept thinking of other questions he should have asked, but he knew he couldn't go back. Not today, anyway. It was strange that both the men he'd talked to had only good things to say about Smarden Meats. The manager was helpful and not extortionate when it came to slaughtering the odd animal for home consumption. And there was no local gossip of anything nefarious going on. As far as the men in the pub knew, Smarden Meats was squeaky clean and obeyed every single one of the EU's absurdly stringent laws.

Neither of the drinkers had much sympathy with Jamie. They knew all about the discovery of his body outside the abattoir and didn't seem to think it particularly odd. In their view, anyone who chose to involve someone else in his suicide deserved anything that happened to him.

'Not fair on the driver,' had been Jack's comment. 'He couldn't get back in the cab for hours. Shaking like a catkin in a hurricane, they say. Thought it was his fault, poor bugger.'

The most interesting thing Will had learned was that neither of his fellow drinkers knew anything at all about Ivyleaf, which had produced or packaged the sausages Trish and her friend had eaten, even though their plant was only twenty miles to the east of Smarden.

Since he was so close, he thought he'd better drive there, try to blag his way in and see what he could find out about the origin of the sausages. He'd have more chance of getting his questions answered face to face than any other way. But it wouldn't be easy.

Meat – entirely respectable meat – had often been sold on by several dealers before it reached any retailer or food processor. The people working at Ivyleaf probably had no idea where the contents of their sausages came from, even if they knew who the actual makers were. And, in any case, they'd be unlikely to let out that information to anyone.

Failure folded itself around Will again like the shabbiest of overcoats. Once he'd been a player, in charge, making money and plans, with other men working for him and a wife who thought he was wonderful. Now there was nothing.

'What'll become of me?' he muttered as he felt in his pockets for the keys he'd put back while he sobered up. He was only thirty-five. There might be fifty more years to get through.

He thought of the guns that had been sold, along with everything else. They'd been his father's and his grandfather's before that. They weren't Purdeys or anything smart, just workaday, undecorated twelve-bore shotguns, carefully maintained and used to rid the land of vermin.

'Quite,' Will said aloud in Antony Shelley's snootiest voice.

A bunch of ducks waddling towards a pond beside the car park stopped and stared at him. He did the rest of it in silence: You've fucked up big time, over and over again, but you don't have to make it worse. You are not vermin, whatever you've done. Don't give in. Don't. Trish is right: you may yet win the case, then there'll be damages. You can start something else. In the meantime you can do something useful by finding out more about the E. coli sausages. She'll be grateful if you do. She would have done it herself if she'd had time; she said so. And if you find out why Jamie died, you might stop feeling so guilty about the rest of it.

The hugeness of his debts made him feel helpless. It was all he could do to put the key in the ignition. But he knew by now that the feebleness would only feed on itself until even the effort of breathing would be painful. It wouldn't take any real energy to drive to Ivyleaf Packaging. He reached behind him for the map Susannah kept on the back seat to check the directions the barman had given him.

His muscles were so tight that he wrenched his shoulder as he turned. It seemed incredible that he'd once been able to heave hay bales around with one hand and push cows out of the way with no more than a nudge. He'd even let himself off the thirty press-ups he'd once done every morning. He ought to start again. Being fit stopped you feeling like a complete blob.

At last he forced himself to turn on the engine and get the car moving. It purred expensively. All the way to the packaging plant, he tried on one story after another to justify the questions he wanted to ask. In the end he decided to be a man in search of a bargain. The story built up as he drove. There would be a vast barbecue to celebrate something, a wedding perhaps. Yes, a sister's wedding barbecue, for which he would need huge quantities of impeccable sausages. He would present himself as a man obsessed with hygiene because of everything he'd read about food poisoning in barbecued meat and equally obsessed with value for money.

'You're just like every other consumer,' said the young receptionist from Ivyleaf much later in the afternoon, as Will gave her a lift home to her house in the next village, 'you want top-quality food for rock-bottom prices. It's no wonder supermarkets have to put the squeeze on producers.'

'I am *not* like all the rest,' Will said, suppressing his instinct to pour out his own story and get at the sympathy he could sense lying behind her bubbly laugh and kind eyes.

'No?' she said, rearranging her frilled cotton skirt across her neat round little knees. Bare as they were, they showed faint white lines of childhood scars like cobwebs spun through the smooth tan. It was hard to keep his eyes on the road.

'No,' he said firmly. There was a tractor ahead, cranking slowly up the hill. Clods of dried grass and mud fell from the deep tread of the tyres. Overtaking it would fix his mind on something other than her naked knees. 'Because I don't want to add to their profits. I'd much rather pay you a bit more than the wholesale price you'd get from them. That is, if I could be sure of what I was getting. I mean, if you could let me know exactly what it is I'd be buying.'

'I can't tell you any more about the sausages because I'm not on the buying side. All I know is that most of our meat is French. So maybe they are too.'

'Aha,' said Will, as he plastered a sickly smile on his face, 'that must be why they taste so bloody good.'

'We're here,' she said, touching his leg with a hand as neat and brown as her round knees. He noticed that she bit her nails. 'It's that little pink house with the blue door. You are kind to bring me home. There's no one else here right now. D'you want to come in and have a cup of tea?'

It had been so long since anyone had been prepared to have sex with him, let alone invited it, that it took Will much too long to understand her reluctance to put on the kettle once they were inside the tidy little house.

As he followed her up the narrow wooden staircase, he wished he'd said no. How could he risk it? The last few ghastly times with Fiona had made him feel as though someone had cut right through his spinal cord.

Much later, he found out that her name was Mandy, which seemed perfect. She knew nothing about his past, or his failures, or what anyone else thought of him. She'd taken him as he was and given him back the certainty that there were still some things he could do well.

Lying with the evening sun painting gold bars across her cosy body, she looked fantastic. She turned and snuggled her face against his arm.

'You're lovely, you know, Will.'

He felt like a world beater.

Chapter 10

Andrew Stane was coming out of the hospital at a run. Trish put out her hand to get his attention.

'Sorry, Trish.' He was panting. 'There's an emergency. I've got to go.'

'Kim? Is she worse?'

'No. The doctor says she should be fine tomorrow, so I've asked Mrs Critch to bring her back to the unit at five o'clock then. Can you be there?'

'Yes.'

Andrew was already past her. 'Good. Don't forget it could be your only chance to get anything out of her.'

'Why d'you think I asked you to get an extension?'

'That's not looking hopeful, so you'd better assume we can't. Which means you'll have no time left for niceties like making friends or feeling your way. You'll have to plan your questions carefully.'

'That would be easier if I knew more about the stepfather,' Trish said, willing Andrew to slow down. 'There's almost nothing in the files.'

'He was in the army.'

'I know.' She was holding on to her patience as though it was something slippery and alive, like an eel. 'So, there must be people there who know a fair amount about him. Have you talked to anyone in his old regiment?'

'Nope.' He was moving backwards and forwards, as though someone had him on the end of a rubber band and was tugging him away all the time.

'Well, try to get someone; but do it informally. The official line is likely to be that he was a frightfully good chap – brave and all that. Men who knew him, served with him, will have the real story. The best would probably be a junior officer. Not so likely to be frightened of talking as a squaddie and with less invested in his own dignity than a general.'

'You don't ask much, do you? Trish, I've told you: I have to go.'

This time she didn't try to hold him back.

There was a crowd outside the four lifts near the entrance and a lot of impatient shuffling. Everyone was standing looking at the illuminated numbers on the fascia above the lifts, muttering. Trish decided to take the stairs. The Intensive Care unit was only on the fifth floor.

Jess was already sitting at Caro's bedside. Still panting from her rushed climb, Trish was about to turn away when she saw Jess beckoning at her through the glass. Surprised, she went in and said quietly. 'I thought they only allowed one visitor at a time in here.'

'Caro needs to ask you something,' Jess said.

Trish saw that Jess was holding one of Caro's hands as she lay, eyes closed, against the heaped pillows.

'Trish is here now,' Jess said, using her other hand to stroke Caro's forehead.

Caro's eyelids rose and her lips widened a little, as though the effort of producing a full smile was far too much.

'You're helping Andrew with Kim, aren't you?' she said, breathing carefully. She licked her dry lips.

'Yes. Trying, anyway. There's not much time left.'

'So you know all about them now. You've got to stop Pete Hartland.' Her eyelids fluttered down.

'Caro, hold on,' Trish said urgently. 'Who is Hartland?'

Caro's eyebrows twitched. The eyes themselves looked frightened as well as puzzled. 'Constable in the unit. He thinks Dan Crossman – you know, Kim's stepfather – poisoned me and wants to punish him. You must stop it. Tell him you were ill too.'

'Ah, yes.' Now Trish understood. Unfortunately that didn't mean she knew what to do about Hartland. 'Who's his boss?'

'Me.'

Trish looked at Jess, whose shrug showed how little help she could offer.

'Then who should I talk to?'

'Pete.' Caro turned her head on the pillow, reaching towards Jess, as though only she had what Caro needed now.

'OK,' Trish said. 'I'll do my best. But I'll need the number.'

Jess grabbed a pen from the bedside table and pulled an old envelope from the wastepaper basket. Deep furrows appeared in Caro's face as she concentrated. She swore.

'Don't force it, darling,' Jess said with the utmost gentleness. 'Let it come. It will. You'll remember, if you just trust yourself.'

Caro sank back against the pillows, smiling at Jess. After a moment she nodded and dictated the number to Jess, who tore off part of the envelope and handed it to Trish.

'Don't worry too much, Caro. I'm glad you're getting . . .' Trish could see that Caro wasn't listening. Her eyes were still open, but they were fixed on Jess. On her feet now, she was hanging over Caro, stroking her hair, murmuring something too private for anyone else to hear.

Trish had no part in this scene. She walked quietly backwards. For an instant Jess looked up. There was no satisfaction in her clear gaze, only depths of generosity and gratitude. Then Jess gave all her attention back to Caro, leaving Trish to retire, shaken at the sight of a love she'd never believed Jess capable of giving anyone. What else had she misunderstood?

Outside the hospital, she saw Cynthia Flag parking a battered Renault. She waved. Cynthia locked the door and walked across the hot, squidgy tarmac, reknotting her ravishing hair. There were tiny bubbles of sweat on her upper lip and in her cleavage. They did nothing to destroy her allure.

'Have you seen Caro?' she asked when she'd reached Trish.

'Yes. She seems to be making progress. And Jess is with her. They looked as if everything is . . . fine.'

Cynthia smiled. 'I think it is now. But they've been through a lot to get here.'

'What—' Trish stopped herself. However close a friend Cynthia might be to Jess, she was still a stranger. Trish had no business discussing Caro's relationship with her. In any case, still reeling from the love she'd witnessed, she wouldn't know how to explain herself. Her old dislike of Jess was beginning to look horribly like jealousy, which shocked her.

'I think,' Cynthia said, producing a luxurious smile, 'that they were both putting so much energy into holding each other up that that's precisely what they did.'

'That sounds clever,' Trish said, still fighting herself, 'but I don't understand what it means.'

'No? Never mind.' She laid a long smooth hand on Trish's. 'Good to run into you.'

Dismissed and remembering that she'd paid for only twenty minutes' parking time, Trish hurried to her car.

Back in the flat, she took out the piece of paper on which Jess had scribbled the number of Pete Hartland's phone. A truculent voice answered her call.

'Hi,' she said. 'My name's Trish Maguire. You don't know me, but I'm helping the social worker with Kim Bowlby, and Caro Lyalt asked me to phone you.'

'Yeah? How is she?'

'Better. Much better. But she's really worried, Pete.'

'She's not the only one. Kim's going to have to go back to that bastard if they don't get anywhere with her by the weekend, and this time he'll kill her. I know he will.'

'Hang on a minute. And calm down.'

'You don't know him.'

'That's true.' Trish worked for the confidence and quietness that were the only weapons she had in this battle. 'I've never met him. But I've seen Kim's fear. And so—'

'Then you ought to realize what he's like. He's a devil. He's got to be stopped. If—'

'Pete, listen to me a moment. Stop talking and listen.' She paused and heard nothing but heavy breathing from him. Good. 'Caro is worried about you. She thinks you might try to do something to him.'

'She's right. If I could think of something that would save Kim, I'd do it like a shot.'

'Good. Me, too. But the only way to make sure she's safe for ever, is to work within and through the proper channels. If you start—'

'What the fuck are you accusing me of?'

No wonder Caro was worried, Trish thought, with this much aggression so near the surface of Pete Hartland's psyche.

'Nothing. I'm just passing on a message from Caro. She wants you to hold back and wait. Don't contact Dan Crossman. Whatever you do, you—'

She stopped talking because it was a waste of effort: Hartland had cut the connection. And she hadn't even had the chance to tell him that Crossman hadn't poisoned Caro. She dialled his number again and was diverted to his voicemail.

'Pete, you didn't give me a chance to get to the meat of what Caro wanted me to tell you, which is that I also had food poisoning. Not as badly as she has it, but definitely caused by the same food. We'd eaten together that night. She could not possibly have been poisoned by Daniel Crossman. You have to accept this as fact.' Trish paused for a moment, then added that if he wanted to know any more, he'd better ring her. Hoping he wouldn't, she nevertheless left her number.

'Have you really got to go?' Mandy asked, watching Will pull on his trousers.

'I really have. It's my sister's car and she needs it to take the children somewhere in the morning.' He leaned over to kiss her. 'But . . .'

'You'll come again, won't you?' He nodded. How could he resist her? 'Great. And you can email me, which is better than phoning when I'm at work. It's easy. I'm "Mandy at Ivyleaf dot com". You won't forget that, will you?'

Her hands were sliding up inside the sleeves of his shirt. He should have done up the cuffs before he'd leaned over her again. Now he wasn't sure he'd be able to leave her. She twisted against the bright whiteness of her sheet, rubbing her back against it and inviting him back into bed. She was the most gorgeous creature he'd ever seen. Her hands reached up to his armpits.

'Come back, Will. It won't be light for hours.'

'I can't. She'll worry. I have to get back to London. I'll email you as soon as I get there.'

She pulled on a thin flowery dressing gown and pattered downstairs, barefooted, to let him out of the front door. So many women looked awful after making love, tangled and frowsty, that he wanted to say something about her minty neatness, but he couldn't think how to put it, so he just kissed her again and left. She stood on her doorstep, waving him off with her free hand, while the other clutched the sides of her dressing gown together just under her amazing breasts. He wondered what her neighbours would think.

Driving back towards London in a daze of pleasure, he tried to work out where his laptop might be. It hadn't been sold with all the rest. He couldn't quite think why not, unless it had been considered to be his personal property and not part of the business. He hadn't touched it for months.

Would his email account still operate? He'd had one of the free ones for his own affairs, and he had a feeling that the server dropped you if you didn't use it for ninety days. He couldn't remember when he'd last logged on.

As soon as he got back to the house, he ran as quietly as possible up the stairs to his little attic room and started foraging in the boxes he'd never bothered to unpack.

'Will, what on earth's the matter?'

He looked up to see Susannah glaring at him.

'Nothing. Sorry. Was I making a noise?'

'It's four in the morning, for Christ's sake.' Her hand was shaking as she pushed her hair out of her red face. He'd never seen her lose her temper, but the warning signs were obvious. He took a step backwards, but it didn't help. She shouted, 'Have you gone mad?'

'No. Go back to bed. I just had to find something. Ah. Great. Sorry, Suze.'

He hardly ever called her that these days and saw the effect of the nickname breaking through her anger. She shrugged and tossed her head, looking just like their mother and making him feel about four years old. Then she told him more kindly not to tear himself up and to get some sleep, for God's sake.

When she had gone, he waited until he heard the door of her big bedroom close. There was a faint rumble of voices. He must have woken Rupert, too. There'd be hell to pay for that. Any City mogul like his brother-in-law needed what little sleep his deal-making permitted.

Giving them ten more minutes for luck, Will took off his shoes and crept downstairs to the kitchen, where there was a spare phone socket.

He set up his laptop on the kitchen table, ran the modem

cable along the floor to the socket, then booted up the machine. Two minutes later the familiar screen welcomed him into the cyberworld that had once been his second home. He clicked on Outlook Express, typed a brief affectionate message to Mandy, and then clicked on 'Send and Receive'.

His eyes widened as he saw that there were over two hundred emails to download. Watching the numbers clicking through, he thought guiltily about Rupert's phone bill. But at least he was doing this at night when the cheap rate must operate.

One hundred and ninety-six emails had come through and something seemed to have seized up inside the machine. Nothing moved. He clicked again on 'Send and Receive' to remind it of what it was supposed to be doing. Then he saw the little incoming arrow icon still pulsating.

With the pace of an arthritic sloth, email number one hundred and ninety-seven eased its way into his inbox. Nearly five minutes later, it was done. It was from someone called JAY, all in capitals, and had a huge attachment. The subject line simply read: 'Important message'. Whoever JAY were, they'd probably sent it to him by mistake, unless it was a taster for a porn site, inciting him to give his credit-card details for more. They'd be lucky. He hadn't had a credit card since Furbishers had ruined him.

The remaining messages whizzed through in no time. Will clicked off line, and settled down to read.

Dozens of them were advertisements for things he'd never want; some were indeed invitations to porn sites or stock market tips or newsgroups. The advertisements for penis extensions and Viagra made him laugh. With Mandy, who could ever need either?

He was deleting almost as fast as the messages had arrived. But there were lots from old friends and acquaintances, who had heard about his disaster and the case. Almost all of them were sympathetic and offered help of every kind. He couldn't think why he'd never bothered to look at them.

Heat slid through his skin like an oil slick as he thought how their senders must have reacted to his silence. An elderly widow, who had been one of his father's oldest friends, had written of her faith in him and of his father's pride and told him not to let himself be too cast down by a single reverse like this, but to fight on. She knew, she had written, that his next venture would be a success.

'Your father's pride'. Will shivered and had to wipe the back of his hand across his eyes as he read that. He hurried to type in a reply and an apologetic explanation of why he hadn't been reading any of his emails. Hers was the most touching, but it wasn't the only one that needed an answer, so it was after six o'clock before he got to the JAY email with the huge attachment. As he opened it his heart jolted, as though someone had hit him hard in the chest.

> Keep this for me, Will, just in case something happens to my copy. I'll explain later. Whatever you do, don't delete it. More to follow asap. And don't tell anyone, or send it on. I just want you to keep it in case of disaster, while I collect the rest of the evidence. I've been watching them for months. At first I was distracted by the decoy flights. The real ones go out once a week, regular as clockwork, like tonight's. Jamie.

There was only one man called Jamie who could have sent an email like this, and he was dead. Even so, the message made Will sag in relief. It showed that Jamie hadn't died hating him. That was something saved from the wreck he'd made of his life.

When he could think of anything except his friend, he read the email again and wondered what it meant. What 'more' had Jamie planned to send? And why hadn't he? When exactly had he died? And why?

Will's fingers felt huge and clumsy as he tried to click on the attachment, but at last he made the mouse work. A film, dark and difficult to see, began to unfold in front of him. He fiddled with the monitor's control buttons, but they didn't help much.

When he'd watched it all the way through five times, he knew that Trish had to see it. Now that Jamie was dead, his request for confidentiality could be set aside. Will duplicated the video, filing the copy in a specially created folder and saving the original email attachment separately. He thought of forwarding it to Trish, then remembered the time it had taken to download. If she were in a hurry to deal with her messages before court this morning, that kind of delay could cause her a real problem. It would be much better to go in person and show it to her on his own laptop.

Guilty about the use of Rupert's electricity, he set the computer battery to charge up and took himself off to shower and shave. There must be nothing about his appearance or presentation to make Trish doubt him today.

Chapter 11

For once Trish slid into consciousness instead of waking with her head full of angst and the inside of her mouth clamped between her teeth. As she came to awareness that she was no longer asleep, she found herself thinking about Kim.

The phone rang. She reached for the receiver.

'Trish Maguire.'

'Trish. Have I woken you?' It was Andrew Stane's voice.

'No, I'm up, and concentrating on Kim.'

'Great because I'm about to have breakfast with a young captain who knew Daniel Crossman in the army. If you get your skates on, you could join us in the pub in Smithfield.'

'I'll be there. When?'

'Seven-thirty.' He gave her the precise address, adding: 'You should still have time to be in chambers for most of your pre-court warm-up session.'

Grateful and bursting with energy, Trish thanked him and put down the phone. She grabbed the nearest black linen suit out of the wardrobe and pulled it on over a plain white cotton shirt. A new packet of tights fell into her hands like a piece of ripe fruit, and the tights practically unrolled themselves up her long legs, instead of sticking and snagging, as they usually did when she was in a hurry.

The air outside felt thicker than in the last few days, and the sun was just as bright. She wished she hadn't needed the tights.

A clinging mixture of nylon and Lycra was the last thing to wear on a day when the heat made you feel you were inside a boiler, but no barrister had ever gone bare-legged into court.

Andrew's talk of getting her skates on had made her think she would have to rush, but as she reached the far side of the bridge and looked round the great curve of the river towards Big Ben, she saw that it was still only a few minutes past seven. The walk up to Smithfield and through the market would take fifteen minutes at the most, so she could linger on the bridge and indulge herself with her favourite view.

The dome of St Paul's was golden in the morning sun and the river sparkled. One day, she hoped, the cranes that disfigured the cityscape would be gone. Now they stuck up like thorns all round the cathedral, reminding her that nothing could be perfect. If she ever let herself expect that, she would be in for another crash.

'Don't ask for too much and you'll end up with more,' she told herself as a welcome puff of wind touched her face. She breathed deeply, then turned her back on the cranes.

Twenty minutes later, she found the two men in the upstairs room of the pub, surrounded by traders from the meat market. She was the only woman in the place, and the air was fuggy with steam, and loud with hoarse east London accents. Andrew Stane, who looked comfortable but out of place in his softly crumpled linen, was sipping coffee. The man opposite him was tucking into a vast plateful of meat and offal, like most of the other customers. Trish gagged and decided on coffee, then changed her mind and ordered tea.

'I've just taken my platoon for a ten-mile run,' the man explained, pointing to his half-eaten plateful as though he had to excuse his appetite.

He was good looking, probably no more than twenty-nine, with smooth golden-tanned skin and fine dark hair, cut very short. His colouring suggested a Mediterranean ancestry, but his voice was as English as could be. It also had all the drawling confidence of a public-school upbringing.

'No one of your shape needs to apologize for what he's eating,' Trish said, not minding his voice nearly as much as she would have done when she'd first come to London as a lonely, spiky law student with a degree from Lancaster and an impoverished Buckinghamshire childhood behind her. 'Now, neither of you has any more time than I have, so let's get down to it. What can you tell me about Daniel Crossman?'

'You know I wouldn't be here at all if he was still serving with the regiment, don't you?'

A waiter picked his way between the tables, carrying four huge plates of eggs, steak, bacon, kidneys, sausages and black pudding.

'We'll take that as read,' Trish said, encouraged. No one made protestations of loyalty if he had nothing dangerous to say. 'Look, I don't know your name. I can't just call you "you".'

'Charles. Hi. OK, well, there'd always been rumours about Crossman,' the captain said, rushing out his words in case she pressed him for his surname, 'but never anything substantial.'

'Rumours of what?'

'Bullying.' He'd produced the word as though it had no more than one syllable, like the cough of a silenced pistol, but Trish heard it all right. She nodded to urge him on.

'That doesn't mean it was true,' Charles said, painstakingly decent and determined to do the right thing by everyone. 'Sergeants have to be tough on recruits, you know. And men who've never been subject to any kind of discipline see harassment where their grandfathers wouldn't have noticed anything out of the ordinary.'

'Really?'

'Absolutely. I mean, you should see the riff-raff we're getting in now. No one's ever told them what to do: they're scruffy and unfit; they've never learned how to sit still for more than two minutes or concentrate on anything. They've never even known what it is to be part of a team. They have to be licked into shape. It's the duty of sergeants, in particular, to—'

'Go back a minute,' Trish said, gripping her cup so tightly that the handle bit into her finger. 'You said something about having to learn to be part of a team.'

'Yes.' His expression was puzzled, as though he couldn't imagine why anyone would question it. 'Everyone in the forces has to learn that. You can't let the others down under any circumstances whatever. You have to accept that your life is far less important than keeping the platoon – or brigade, or regiment – going. It's obvious.'

'Yes,' she said, thinking of her early-morning ideas about Kim. 'But what I want to know is how Crossman taught them to feel that they were part of a team.'

'I don't understand.' There was enough stillness in Charles's body now to tell Trish she was on the right track.

'I've heard of people who force a sense of collective responsibility by using scapegoats,' she said warily, determined not to scare him off. 'Is that what Crossman did?'

'How d'you mean?'

'Say one of his men broke a rule. Did he punish the individual, or did he take someone else – someone weaker; maybe a friend – and make the offender watch him being punished instead?'

Andrew Stane stiffened, but Trish wasn't looking at him. The captain's face gave her all the confirmation she needed. But she wanted him to say it too, so that Andrew could hear. There was a pause, long enough to stretch anyone's nerves. Deliberately defusing her own impatience, Trish drank some of the cooling tea. She'd left it so long that there was scum on the surface and around the side of the cup.

The waiter shouldered his way through the crowd to bring Charles a rack of toast and about half a pound of butter.

'If you knew that,' Charles said at last, shifting from buttock to buttock in his chair, 'why did you make me come here?'

'I didn't *know*,' she answered. Andrew Stane re-crossed his legs. Still Trish wouldn't look away from the young officer. 'But I—'

'Why isn't there anything on his record?' Andrew burst out, as though he couldn't bear to keep quiet any longer. 'If you knew what he was doing, your senior officers must have known, too. We should've been warned as soon as we asked questions about him. A man like that isn't fit to be alone with little children.'

'Oh, for God's sake,' said the captain. 'We're not interested in whether our men will make good baby-sitters. We're training them to fight side by side with each other and to be strong enough to see their best friend killed in front of them and still go on fighting.' He dropped his knife and fork, greasy with egg yolk and dripping with tomato ketchup. Trish had to look away.

'Don't forget it's men like Dan Crossman who kill for people like you,' he went on. 'When the next war comes . . . you'll be damn grateful for men who've been trained by the likes of him.'

'I understand what you're saying,' Trish said, meaning it. She hated the whole system he'd defended so uncomfortably, but she could see that he had to believe in it while he did the job for which he'd signed on. 'Is there anything else that might help us? Do you know anything about Crossman's private life? His family?'

'No. I mean, he didn't have any. He never spoke about his past or had any friends outside the regiment. It happens, specially with some of the long-serving non-commissioned officers.'

'Why did you get rid of him in the end?' Andrew asked nastily. 'Did he do something so particularly brutal even your lot couldn't contain him any longer?'

The captain tidied his knife and fork and stood up, pushing

his thumb and forefinger into the back pocket of his tight jeans. Trish could see the outline of all his muscles.

'He'd done twenty-five years,' he said, pulling out a battered brown-leather wallet. It looked as if it could have been his grandfather's. He extracted a twenty-pound note. 'I've got to go.'

Trish stood, too, and gave him back his money. 'This is on me. I'm so grateful that you came. You've almost certainly helped us save at least one child, probably two.'

His eyes opened a little wider. Suddenly he looked very young. Then he nodded crisply, fighting for the impervious mask he needed to cope with the life he'd chosen.

'Listen,' he said, leaning closer to her and sounding far more intimate than he had before, 'you need to know where Crossman was coming from. He'd seen service in the first Gulf War. D'you know what that means?'

'Only what I read in the newspapers.'

'Then look at them again, and think what it must have been like. He had to watch men he'd trained since they were boys stuck in range of the enemy's guns when their tank seized up in the sand. They burned. Do you know what that means? What the temperature is inside a tank that's on fire?'

Trish shook her head.

He told her, adding, 'Six of them died in that inferno. *They* were his family then. Doesn't that make a difference? Don't you think that kind of experience would make any man impatient with a whining little girl?'

'We don't know she whined.'

'I bet she did.' His full lips twisted in an unhappy grimace. 'I've got sisters. I know what they do to get what they want.'

'Are you really saying that killing and seeing other people killed excuses terrorizing a child?' Andrew's voice was hostile.

The captain's mouth twisted even more. 'No. But that kind of experience does things to you.'

Trish was only a couple of inches shorter than him. She took a step back so she could look him straight in the eye.

'So does growing up in terror.'

He opened his mouth, shook his head and turned away. After two steps he came back. Trish wanted him to give in, to admit the humanity she knew existed in him. All he said was: 'Andy Stane promised me absolute discretion. You'll abide by that, too.' There was no question in his voice; he was giving her orders, just as he'd been trained to do.

'I won't pass any of this on to anyone else,' she said, thinking: Andy? Where did these two meet? How did Andrew get him here so promptly? If he knew about this captain before, why didn't he consult him until now?

'I can't be quoted in court or made to appear as a witness. Or anything like that. Andy promised me.'

'I understand. That's fine. Don't worry. We just needed the information to help us help the child to talk. You go on. We won't get in your way.'

He nodded again, seemed to be on the verge of saying something else, then turned on his heel and marched himself out of the hot, friendly pub.

'How did you know that?' Andrew asked when she'd got herself back under control and was sitting down again.

'What?' She looked at him and saw unusual resentment in his nice round face.

'The way Crossman punished his men.'

'It was something that came to me overnight. I'd been thinking about Kim and the baby again. But it wasn't only that. I can't explain.'

'You think he punishes the baby when she does something wrong?'

'Or vice versa.'

'What could either of them do that's so bad?'

'I don't know, but I'd guess it has something to do with

making too much noise. Anyway, thanks to your friend Charles, I'll know what questions to ask her this afternoon.' She pushed her tea away to the far side of the table. 'You know Crossman must have had a hellish time when he came out of the army if he really had as little real life as Charles said.'

'He certainly married Mo pretty quickly, which suggests there was a huge gap to fill.'

All round them, men were pushing back their chairs and paying their bills. Breakfast was over.

'God! I feel sorry for her.'

'Your trouble is you feel sorry for everyone, Trish. Even a brute like Crossman.'

'Only a bit.' She picked up a napkin and wiped her face. The steam from the coffee machine and the heat of the bodies around them were making the atmosphere like a sauna. She thought of Crossman's wife and the two children.

'What must it be like in that flat? Crossman can't have any idea how he feels, or what his emotions are making him do, let alone what drives Mo, or what the kids need.' She put down the napkin and stood up. 'I've got to—'

'Run,' Andrew supplied, smiling for the first time that morning. 'I know. On your way.'

'Oh,' she said, coming back to the table a second later, 'did you manage to sort your crisis? The one that dragged you away from Caro's bedside?'

The smile deepened. 'I did. Thanks for remembering it.'

The compliment triggered another memory just in time, and she left him with enough money to settle the bill for all of them. One day she would ask him how he'd found the perfect source of information on Crossman's army career so quickly, but there wasn't time now.

'I'll have your change waiting when you come to talk to Kim,' he called after her.

Trish waved from the doorway and hurried through the

market, towards Fleet Street, dodging men dressed in white mesh hats and blood-stained white coats, who were carrying bare carcasses over their shoulders.

Trish had seen him when she first came into court. Will knew that, even though she hadn't waved or smiled. And he watched her closely all morning. The whole legal performance still seemed absurdly over-complicated, and idiotically long-drawn-out, but he was prepared to go along with it.

Today they had Sally Trent, a junior from Furbishers contracts department, in the witness box, and the Furbishers silk was asking her to confirm the truth of her statement. She looked far too innocent – and too young – to have been part of the conspiracy. Will wondered how Antony Shelley would make her confess.

But even that wasn't enough to stop him thinking about Jamie Maxden's video clip and hoping Trish would see in it what he had seen and understand how it proved everything he'd been saying. He tried to get hold of her at lunchtime, but he wasn't quick enough. By the time he'd got out from behind the crowd, there was no sign of any of the lawyers.

He had to go off to eat an expensive, pappy sandwich from a coffee shop in the Strand and fight for patience. Gulping it down, sucking in air with every rushed mouthful, and burning his tongue on the weedy coffee, he gave himself severe indigestion. But he was back outside court fifteen minutes before the time the judge had stipulated.

'Trish!' he called, seeing her approach from the far end of the corridor. He saw her turn and murmur something to Antony Shelly, then come towards him making an effort to smile. He'd hoped never to see that deliberate gentleness again. She was obviously angry with him.

'How are you doing?' she asked. She sounded cool.

'Fine. I've got something you have to see. It's a—'

'Will,' she said, laying her long white fingers on his sleeve, 'I'd love to see it, but we have to go back into court now. This afternoon's cross-examination is immensely important after Arthur Chancer's evidence that he *had* spelled out the terms of the two deals to you—'

'That's a sodding lie!' he said, and couldn't understand why she looked suddenly happier.

'So I don't want to water down my concentration,' she said, without explaining herself. 'OK? Let's talk afterwards.'

He had to breathe carefully to get a grip on his fury.

'Will, it matters that I do well this afternoon. To you more than to me.'

His head rocked with the violence of his nodding. 'I'll wait here afterwards. It's important that you see this today. It's about the sausages.'

'I'll be here.'

She turned tail, her gown flicking him as it flew out behind her, and said something dismissively curt to her boss. Then the two of them swaggered into court. Will had to tell himself several times that Trish was on his side before he could make his mind and thumping heart calm down.

Trish wished she'd never involved Will in the hunt for the organism that had poisoned Caro. She also wished that he'd stayed away today. She shouldn't have mentioned Chancer, but Will's sudden appearance had jolted her, and she was concentrating too hard on this afternoon's witness to think straight. Over lunch just now Antony had asked her to take Sally Trent's cross-examination.

'She's the one, I'm sure. We can get to her. And I want you to do it. Get matey with her. She's resentful. Did you see her hating Ferdy this morning? Get her to talk about her loathly boss. Lead her into her sympathies. I'll bet you there's someone she cares about, likes to protect. She's that kind. Just make sure it's you today. Get her to want to help you. You can do that, Trish.'

All these people needing different things, she thought. Kim and Will and Antony and the rest of the clients. And now the defence's witnesses too.

It was a bit like the first months after David had come to live with her, when he and George had competed – probably unwittingly and in their quite different ways – for every ounce of her attention. David had been so needy then, so frightened and so determined to do what he thought she wanted, that he'd been her priority.

Even he hadn't needed as much as Kim. Would they ever find out what was behind her silent terror? And what if they didn't? What if she were sent back, and her stepfather did kill her, as Pete Hartland was so sure he would? How would it be possible to live with the knowledge that she could have saved Kim with a bit more care, a bit more intelligence?

Trish pushed the thought away and felt like Sisyphus condemned eternally to roll the same boulder uphill. Concentrate, she told herself. Don't split yourself and your attention or you'll short change them all. Do one thing at a time. It's not disloyal to forget the rest while you're at it. She smiled at the woman in the witness box.

Will settled down to watch what his lawyers were going to do for him. He wished he knew exactly what sodding Arthur Chancer had told the court. He was such a twisting weasel, who never quite said what he meant, that he might have tricked them into believing him. Bastard. He'd have to ask Neil, even if it was too late to do anything about it now.

Two of the other claimants were sitting on the same hard bench. If they'd been here yesterday, they might be able to tell him what had happened. Will nodded to them. It didn't surprise him they were keeping an eye on the proceedings. The only odd thing was that so many stayed away. Or maybe they were the ones whose businesses had not gone down the tubes and who were still capable of making a living.

Trish was getting to her feet. Will was glad to see Antony giving up the limelight again. Leaning forwards, propping his chin on his clasped hands, Will waited.

The young contracts assistant was in the witness box again. She looked a bit like Mandy, with the same snub nose and cheery eyes, although this girl's hair was red and she was better dressed. He didn't think she could have a tenth of Mandy's warmth. No one could.

Memories of Mandy's sexy body and all the generosity she'd shown in bed were the only things likely to keep him from going mad. He wished he could see her every day. If it weren't for emails, he didn't think he could wait. Thank God for the Internet! He wanted to be with her all the time, and touch her. And . . . He felt his cock stir and thought he'd better start concentrating on Trish before anyone else noticed what he was up to.

'And so, Ms Trent,' she was saying in a smiley kind of voice, 'could you tell the court how you come to be working in Furbishers' contracts department?'

Will wished he could see Trish's face, but all he had to give him a clue about her attitude to the witness was the sound of her voice and the back of her ludicrous wig and ugly black stuff gown.

'I was a secretary there originally, and I gradually got promoted.'

'Do many secretaries get to take on quasi-legal roles or management responsibilities?'

Trish saw the intelligence gleaming in Sally's eyes.

'It's hardly management,' she said. 'I just look after the staff in the department and organize the changes to the boiler-plate contract.'

'Does that allow you to know all the department's wrinkles? And the strengths of your managers?' Trish smiled in sympathy.

'Oh, sure.'

'Sketch them in for us. Who's the best negotiator?'

And so it went on until Sally trusted her. The atmosphere in court was warm and very female. Trish could feel Antony's approval. Sally grew in confidence with every bit of information that pleased Trish. And Trish took care not to ask or say anything that might make Ferdy leap to his feet and break open the cocoon she was spinning around herself and the witness.

It wasn't long before she found herself liking Sally. They might never meet again, but for the moment they could have been best friends. Trish had no thought for the judge or Antony or Will or anyone else. There might have been only Sally and herself in the court, as she drew out the story, word by word and smile by smile.

And then at last Trish got it. She had to work hard not to let her mouth drop open in amazement.

Sally simply said, 'It was one day in March when my line manager, Martin Watson, told me I had to spin it out. I'd been settling the questions too easily, he said. He liked a good fight and I was spoiling it for him by negotiating all the difficulties out of the way so soon. Like all women, he said, I wanted to keep things sweet and it was bad for business and for morale. I'd never progress until I stopped being so afraid of people being angry with me. I had to be like him and learn to enjoy conquering them. It would be good practice for the next rung up the ladder to get used to fighting, he said, so I'd better generate some good long battles now to show management that I could cope. He wanted me to spin out all the negotiations I was handling for a minimum of three months.'

Could she possibly not know the significance of what she'd said? Trish wondered.

This was the first half of the evidence she and Antony had

been angling for, the admission that Furbishers had deliberately lengthened the negotiating period. Without that, Will and the other clients would never have been forced to commit themselves to the huge expenses that had locked them in by the time the real, and much less satisfactory, deals were offered. Now, all Trish and Antony needed was someone to contradict Arthur Chancer's damaging evidence. That would be a lot harder to get.

'That was brilliant, Trish,' Will said as she stopped to speak to him when the judge had risen for the day. 'Amazing.'

'Thank you. She was a good witness. And honest. Look, Will, I'm not trying to stall, but I will have to go now. What is it you want to show me?'

'It's a video clip I was emailed by Jamie Maxden,' he said, flushing. 'I haven't been checking my emails for months, so I didn't know it was there. I think you ought to see it, but it's long and takes time to download, so I didn't want to clog up your system, and—'

'That was thoughtful. Thank you. But in fact it would be easier if you sent it through, so that I don't keep Antony waiting now. I'll check my emails as soon as I get home tonight. I promise. OK?'

'Well, yes,' he said, flushing an even deeper crimson, 'only I don't have your email address.'

Trish grabbed a pen and scribbled it down for him. As she handed it over, she touched his arm and said, 'Today made a difference, Will. You should be able to let yourself sleep tonight.'

'It's not enough, though, is it? Specially not if the judge believed Arthur Chancer. If this is the best we're going to get, maybe all the doubters were right and there was no point even starting the case.'

'You're right: there's still a long way to go. But today *was* good. Don't underestimate it. There *is* still hope. Honestly.'

He didn't look convinced.

'You've got to hang on, Will.'

'It's easy for you to say. OK. I know . . . you've got to go.'

Antony had sent Colin ahead to take the solicitor to his room, and he was waiting for Trish in hers. She shrugged off her gown and hung it on the peg behind the door. She felt his hand on her back, and turned.

'The conqueror returns,' he said, kissing her cheek. 'Well done.'

'It wasn't that much.' She walked round to the other side of her desk to remind him there was work to be done yet. Two people were waiting for him only a few yards away and she had to see Kim.

His eyebrows tweaked up as he produced his best smile. 'Maybe not, but it gives us a terrific excuse for a celebration. The Ritz has some very glamorous bedrooms. Or we could go to the Rookery. You'd love it there, Trish. The sexiest hotel in London.'

'Maybe,' she said, wondering if he could possibly be serious, 'but I'm not up for that kind of celebration. We're in the middle of a case, anyway. What are you thinking of?'

The smile turned wicked. 'Do you really want me to tell you? Now? Here?'

'Certainly not,' she said quickly, knowing that in this mood he was capable of saying anything. 'You and I are too much married to celebrate with anything but food, wine, and good stories.'

'*You're* not married, Trish.'

'In every way except the strictest legal sense, I am.'

'In that case, you're the most shocking flirt I've ever met.'

Laughter bubbled up in her. She leaned across the space she'd fought to keep between them and kissed his cheek. The day's stubble rasped her lips.

'So, you vile seducer, are you. The others are waiting for you and I've promised to see the traumatized child again. I told you that.'

'True enough,' Antony said. 'OK. *Vamos*.'

Chapter 12

Andrew Stane greeted Trish at the door of the psychiatric unit.

'She's here,' he said, 'waiting for you.'

'Great. Has she said anything so far?'

'She hasn't, but her foster mother reported that she had some kind of nightmare last night and woke the whole house, screaming. In fact Kim was the only person who didn't wake, until she was prodded. Mrs Critch says she's never seen such fear on any child's face as she saw then, but Kim wouldn't tell her what she'd been dreaming about; she just shook and apologized over and over until it was unbearable.'

With that warning, Trish had a fair idea of what she was going to see. Even so, the sight of Kim's face shocked her. Trying to block out everything else, particularly the need to get somewhere today, she concentrated on making her face and body as small and gentle as possible.

'You must have been very frightened last night, Kim,' she said. 'But it's over now. No one is going to be punished because of you. No one at all.'

A tear swelled in the corner of each of the child's eyes, and trembled on the edge of the lid before bursting. She pressed the backs of her hands against her eyes, saying nothing and making no sound. Tears poured around the edges of her hands and dripped off her pointed chin.

Trish was terrified that Kim was going to choke. She longed

to pick the child up and hug her and promise that nothing terrible would ever happen again; but one was against all the rules, and the other impossible. All she could do was provide paper handkerchiefs and hope the waves of unexpressed sympathy would reach her.

'Thank you,' Kim whispered, pressing the tissue to her eyes, instead of her fists. Eventually she blew her nose, too, and looked round for somewhere to put the soggy mess. Trish fetched a wastepaper bin and was rewarded by a faint smile.

'Kim,' she said, feeling as though she was stepping out on to ice so thin it crackled under foot, 'I don't want to make you unhappy or frightened, but if I'm to help you properly I have to ask some questions. Is that all right?'

There was no answer. Kim let her eyelids and her whole head droop, hiding herself all over again.

'Kim?' This time Trish allowed a little authority into her voice.

'Yes?'

'Kim, try to look at me. If you can.'

The smooth blonde head shook.

'All right. Don't worry about that then. Just try to tell me what happened at home if you screamed when you had a nightmare like last night's.'

There was a gasp then a gulping swallow from the child, but no words. Trish tried again.

'Kim, I think someone has told you that you mustn't ever tell. But they won't know about anything you say here in this room. No one will tell them. You are safe with us. And it's safe to tell us what happened.'

Still looking down at the table, Kim spoke very quietly, but the words were absolutely clear and distinct from one another: 'If I had a bad dream, I had to take off my nightie and stand on the box.'

Trish felt her head jerk up as though someone had pulled a string attached to her scalp. She caught the foster mother's eye and knew she was as surprised as Trish herself.

'What box?' Trish asked gently.

'At the end of his bed.'

'The baby's bed?' Trish could feel the frown dragging her eyebrows together.

Kim looked up, surprised and a little pitying. 'No,' she explained, as quiet and matter of fact as ever. 'At the end of Daniel's side of the big bed.'

'Ah.' This could be enough on its own to extend the interim care order. 'Have I got this right, Kim? When you had a nightmare, you had to stand, without any clothes on, at the end of your stepfather's bed in the night? Is that right?'

'Yes.' There were no tears now, but Kim started shaking. Her hands gripped the edge of the table as though vertigo was making the chair rock under her. Blood was driven out of her finger ends as she held on, until the tips of her fingers were like a corpse's. Trish knew she couldn't be made to answer any more questions today.

'Try not to worry, Kim. You'll be all right now,' she said, standing up very slowly so that the child could be sure she was not going to be touched in either anger or perverted desire. 'I have to go out of the room for a moment, but Mrs Critch will be here. And I'll be back soon. All right?'

There was the usual long pause, then Kim nodded and whispered, 'Yes. That is all right.'

Andrew met Trish in the corridor and hugged her. 'You've cracked it, you wonder.'

'It's only the beginning, but I don't see how we can put her through any more now. Did you see how precarious she feels? She was hanging on to the table as if it were the only thing that would stop her falling to her death. Have you got enough to keep her safe for the present?'

'I think so. And I agree, she has to be let off now. Are you going to tell her?'

'I'd better; it'll only confuse her if she's faced with another adult now.'

'OK. And will you tell Caro? It was your breakthrough, so you have the right.'

'You could get to the hospital sooner than I could because I've got to go back to chambers now.' Trish smiled at him, glad that he'd remembered how much Caro minded about this child. 'So why don't you tell her? I'll call in this evening on my way home and answer any questions she may have.'

'Great. Thank you, Trish. I *knew* we could count on you. We can take it from here. You've done great, even if you were wrong about Crossman punishing her for the baby's noise or vice versa. I never did find that very convincing, I must say.'

Trish nodded and went back into the interview room. Kim was still sitting with her small hands gripping the edge of the table. Trish gave her a wide berth before coming face to face with her, smiling.

'I haven't got any more questions now.'

The tight hands relaxed and blood rushed back up under the nailbeds, making the pale-yellow flesh dark red.

'And you will be safe with Mrs Critch.'

The foster mother caught Trish's eye and nodded. Andrew had said she was one of their most experienced emergency carers, with an unblemished record and huge reserves of kindness and warmth. If anyone could make Kim feel safe in her bed at night, it would be Mrs Critch.

'I hope I'll see you again soon, Kim,' Trish went on, 'but I have to say goodbye now. Thank you for being so brave.'

More tears hung on the edge of her eyelids and Trish cursed herself for the choice of words. Terms like bravery, courage, grit would have been part of any retired sergeant's lexicon, along with their opposites. Had Kim's stepfather shouted at her for being such a little coward, a noisy snivelling little coward, for crying in her nightmares, before he'd forced her to strip and stand on the box at the end of his bed?

Trish understood just how DC Pete Hartland felt. She wanted Daniel Crossman to pay for what he'd done. Even more, she wanted to whisk Kim away to safety. For a dangerous moment, Trish thought of the sense of security she'd managed to give David and longed to take on Kim, too. But she knew she couldn't. She had to smile with the easy, uninvolved affection that was all she could safely offer, and back away.

'Oh, Trish!' Colin's voice caught at her two hours later, just as she reached the last of the stone steps out of chambers. She paused and looked back.

'Yes?'

'You know you asked me to look up that journalist who died at the slaughterhouse? Jamie Maxden.'

She walked back up the steps to stand with him in the doorway. It wasn't his fault she was feeling wrung out and longing to be on her own, or that she still had to deal with the video clip Will wanted her to look at tonight.

'Have you discovered something?' she asked, trying to sound excited.

'A bit. You're right: he was once quite famous for his work on the meat trade. Then he turned in a story that could have landed his paper with a vast libel claim and everything went pear shaped. The editor demanded proof. Maxden refused to name his source or provide any back-up evidence, and—'

'Why?'

'He said it was because the whole thing had been given to him off the record. He'd guaranteed anonymity, and he claimed the documents he had would identify the man – or woman, I suppose – who'd given him the information, so he refused to hand them over.'

'Brave man.'

'Or foolhardy. The editor promised he'd be backed to the hilt, so long as he could convince the lawyers the story would stand up. When he couldn't provide a single shred of evidence, the editor decided he'd fabricated the whole thing, including the source. After that he couldn't sell a report of a local flower show to a parish mag under his own name – hence his despair.'

'So they really do think he killed himself, do they?'

'Oh, absolutely. One last stand and a kind of "you'll be sorry when I'm dead". Apparently they'd been calling him Mad-Jamie-the-Meat for years. All the editors in London looked away when his name popped up in their email inboxes.'

'I'm impressed. How on earth did you find all this out?'

'A mate of mine, who's a bit ahead of me at the Bar, is already reading *The Times* overnight for libel, so he's well placed to ask these sorts of questions.'

'Handy! D'you think he'd be able to find out why Maxden's death wasn't reported? It sounds like a pretty good story to me: crusading anti-meat journalist's dramatic suicide outside abattoir.'

'There's nothing sinister,' Colin said, looking pleased. 'I've already asked about it.'

Trish could remember the first time she'd done something more than her pupil master had expected. She gave Colin all the approval that had been withheld from her then. He took it with admirable coolness. She was surprised and rather impressed.

'Apparently,' he said, 'the discovery of the body was well reported in the relevant local paper, but none of the nationals picked it up from the press agencies. It was the same day as the Peckham cyanide scare, and that grabbed all the space.'

'Cyanide?' Trish felt as though bits of her mind were scattering in all directions, like rabbits startled by the sound of shooting.

'You must remember,' Colin said. 'When they found a minilab, brewing up some ghastly poison-bomb thing for the tube.'

'Oh yes. Of course.' The reports had come out just as Trish was embroiled in all the last-minute work for the case. She'd barely had time to listen to the radio and hadn't read a paper for days.

'And it happened on a Tuesday.' Colin looked as though he was enjoying himself now. 'Apparently that makes a real difference. If it had been a Friday, they'd probably have run the story. For some reason there's never much news to print on Saturdays.' He grinned. 'The whole system sounds weird to me.'

'Even weirder than the Bar?' she asked, thinking of the puzzled concentration with which he usually listened to older members of chambers.

'Maybe not quite.' He laughed. 'But what could be?'

'Not a lot. You've been really helpful. Keep that channel open. It could be seriously useful.'

'To you or to me?' Colin asked, showing unusual cockiness.

'Both,' she said with a smile. 'I take it you won at squash yesterday.'

'Yeah. Thrashed the bastard. Made up for my last four defeats.'

Trish laughed. So it was that and not her compliments that had given him this new confidence. 'Well done.'

'Thanks. Anything else I can do for you while I'm at it?'

'I don't think so. Not at the moment.'

Trish wasn't accustomed to watching shaky video film, and this had been shot in a peculiar kind of monochrome, with odd shadows and strange gleams. It was a while before she realized it must have been filmed in the dark with some kind of infra-red camera. She could see a small plane standing in the middle of the field. That wasn't at all hard to decode. The rest was trickier.

There were men running. It took two replayings for her to

work out that there were only three of them going backwards and forwards. They didn't look very different and the camera jumped about so much that they could have been a small army. At one moment the lens would point towards the plane, then sweep around a huddle of buildings, before catching the line of men or focusing on one at a time.

Luckily the tallest had a distinctive gait, lurching sideways with every step, which identified him in each of the six journeys in the film. Another had a tear in the back of his dark shirt. The third moved differently from the other two, as though he'd once been a sprinter. The others leaned forwards, hunched over as they ran, whereas he kept his head up, aiming his body and the force of his running at a fixed point. Someone had once trained him to race.

On every journey towards the plane the men carried something big and heavy. She couldn't see what it was beyond the fact that each package was slithery. Sometimes one of the men would stop to push his load back, to rebalance it on his shoulder, before tucking his chin over the edge of it. It was hard to judge the length of the packages because of the foreshortening effect of distance. The bundles were wrapped in dark, shiny material. It could be black plastic, like a bin liner, but it was hard to see for certain. All the textures were fuzzy in the film, like the colours. There were really only light or dark. The men's faces, which would definitely have been categorized as 'white', must have been different shades of pink or tan in reality. On the film they were a uniform silvery grey.

Something about the man with the tear in his shirt nagged at Trish and she played the film again and again, pausing at the point when he was running, unladen, towards the camera. Her face was almost touching the screen as she peered into it, trying to see his features more clearly. Only as the static sizzled between her nose and the screen did she remember that she had some kind of photographic program in the computer. It had been pre-loaded when she bought the system, and she'd never considered using it until now.

She tried the help key, but couldn't get any help she could understand. The manuals that had come with the package were stacked in the bottom drawer of her desk. She fumbled around until she'd discarded the ones that explained the computer itself, the printer, the operating system, and the word-processing program. At last she found something that referred to the rest of the software.

The weirdly phrased instructions had her so frustrated that she was whacking her fists on the edge of her desk before she'd learned how to freeze one particular section of the video and then enlarge it. Tapping the keys again and again until the man's face filled the whole screen, she found she'd gone too far. As she reduced the image, click by click, the face became distinct enough for her to recognize the features – and the aggression.

Without moving her gaze from the screen, she felt for her phone. Then she did have to look away from the man's face; the number of Will's sister's house in Fulham wasn't familiar enough to dial from memory. She must have it written down somewhere.

'Oh, hello,' she said when a woman had answered, brusquely reciting her number. 'Is that Susannah? It's Trish Maguire here.'

'I'll get him,' the frosty voice said without any kind of greeting. Trish heard faint voices and the clanging of a heavy pan.

'I seem to have upset your sister,' she said when Will eventually came on the line.

'It's not you, Trish; it's me. I woke her in the middle of last night and then today I ran her car dry of petrol, so when she tried to fetch one of the children this evening it wouldn't start.'

'Poor woman.'

'Yes. And then she went to a lot of trouble to cook a special dinner tonight, and we're only just eating it because her husband was late home from work, and now I've left the table in the middle of the main course. She's pissed off with everyone. But it's not your problem. Have you looked at the film?'

'Yes. And I can see why you wanted me to see it. It's that man from the abattoir, isn't it? The one with the knife, who nearly stabbed you.'

'*What*?' The sound ripped into her ear and she moved the receiver a little way away. When Will's voice sounded again, it was tinny with distance. She brought the receiver closer again. 'Which man?'

'The one with the rip in the back of his clothes in the video. Wasn't that why you wanted me to see it?'

'No. I just wanted you to see that Jamie Maxden had been filming people carrying carcasses to a plane in the middle of the night.'

'Carcasses?' she said, feeling sick. She'd managed to bury most of her memories of the slaughterhouse. Now they came rushing back.

'Yes. Pork, I think, judging from the size.'

Trish started the film again, peering at the screen and using only one hand to hit the proper keys because the other still held the phone clamped to her ear. 'Are you sure you're not seeing what you want to see? They're just long wrapped packages. You can't possibly tell what's inside them. Couldn't they be chemicals of some kind?' She thought of everything she'd learned during the background research for his case. 'Illegal farm chemicals? There are a lot that have been banned but are so useful to farmers that they do sometimes buy them on the black market.'

Will laughed with a sound so harsh it reminded her that he'd once been a farmer himself and given up because of the conditions that had made it impossible to make a living from the land.

'In theory I suppose they could,' he said, 'but it's the shape and the weight that say these are carcasses. Look at the way the men are holding them. And at the way the packages bounce that little bit whenever the men's right feet hit the ground.'

Maybe Will was right and the mysterious packages were sides of pork. The stance of these men was the same as the ones she'd seen at Smithfield this morning, with their right hands lying on the front of the animal, balancing the load. And the weight did look similar; she recognized the small bounce he'd pointed out too.

'They're sides of meat,' he said. 'I was always sure of it and now you've recognized the slaughterman, that makes it even clearer. He must be stealing from the abattoir and having the meat flown out in the plane you can see in the video. No wonder he looked as if he hated us. He must have thought we were on to him.'

'Will . . .'

'It's bigger than just a few sausages, Trish. It must be. If Jamie was interested, it's got to be a proper scam. They're probably working with slaughterhouses all over the south of England. God, who'd have thought a poxy little sausage hunt would turn into something like this?'

'Steady on, Will.' Trish had to stop this fantasy before it did any damage. 'There's no evidence of anything like that.'

'I know. That's why—' He broke off. Trish could hear a rumble of voices in the distance. 'Trish, I'm going to have to go back to eat. But I need . . . I mean . . . Listen, you once said you'd do anything you could to help me. I don't suppose you could lend me some money, could you? I hate asking, but I . . . Call it a kind of advance against the damages.'

If we get them, she thought. Most no-win no-fee cases involved the clients taking out insurance against losing. Not this one. No insurance company had been prepared to take the risk. If she and Antony didn't win, she'd have earned nothing for months of work. There'd be no more flights to Australia for

David. Even his school fees could be an embarrassment if she didn't get another paying client quickly.

'How much do you need?'

There was the hiss of indrawn breath, then Will said, mumbling over the figure, 'Two hundred pounds, maybe. Is that . . .? I mean, I know it's cheeky, but it's urgent.

'No. That's OK.' It was a fleabite compared to what she'd thought he might ask. 'I'll leave it for you at chambers. Just ask the chief clerk. His name's Steven Clay. But what—?'

'I have to go. I'll report when I get back. Don't tell anyone about the video, will you?'

'No. Will, what are you going to do?'

'I'll tell you later. Don't worry, Trish. I know what I'm doing.'

The phone went dead in her hand. If past experiences with matrimonial finance cases hadn't made her hate people who used money as a weapon, she'd have made her loan conditional on his telling her how he was going to spend it.

There might not be time to get it in the morning, she thought, if the first cash machine she tried had run out of funds. That happened sometimes. She collected her car keys and went out to get the car. There was no way she was going to walk around Southwark in the middle of the night with a couple of hundred pounds in her pocket.

When she got back she could hear the phone ringing from the top of her iron staircase as soon as she opened the door. She slammed it shut behind her and sprinted for the phone.

'George?'

'Yes. How are you? You're panting. Have you been running? You must've been working very late.'

'Yes, and no. Don't worry about me at the moment. How are you? Is it going all right?'

'Brilliantly! The weather's OK, even though it's winter down here. David's happy. I don't know when I last slept so well. In fact, Trish, if it weren't for missing you, it'd be perfect. This is a wonderful place. We must make time to come out again together one day.'

She stretched out on her soft black sofa, with a scarlet cushion under her head and a purple one under her feet, and listened to his voice pouring out enthusiasm. Her breathing slowed and her whole body softened.

After they'd shared all the news, he asked if she had yet had Sir Matthew Grant-Furbisher in the witness box.

'No. Why?'

'Just that I ran into someone in Sydney, who used to work for him years ago. She said she'd always wanted to play poker with him because it was so easy to tell when he was lying: he'd scratch around his right nostril; not picking his nose, you understand, just scratching away at the skin outside the nostril as though something had got stuck there. She said that if the lies were big enough, he could even draw blood.'

'That's exceedingly helpful, George. Thank you.'

'Thought it might be. Now, David's here. He wants a word.'

'Trish? Is that you?' His voice was light and jaunty, with a distinct Australian twang.

'Hi, David.' She squealed in pleasure at the sound of his perkiness. 'How are you?'

'Excellent. It's really great here, Trish. The cousins are great. I like them all. And they like me.' He sounded surprised.

'Of course they do. Everyone does. I really miss you, you know.'

'Me too. But are you all right?'

'Just about surviving without you,' she said. He laughed and said they were calling him, so he had to go.

As she put down the receiver, echoes of his new confidence made her think of Colin. Would he mind such a late call? She dialled his number.

He sounded quite wide awake, and untroubled by the interruption.

'Colin, you know you asked if there was anything else you could find out for me?'

'Yes. Have you changed your mind?'

'Actually, yes. That is, if you're really volunteering.'

'Of course.'

'Great. There used to be a craft abattoir in Kent, somewhere near Smarden, run by a family called Flesker. I think it went phut about five years ago. You wouldn't like to see if you could find out what the problem was, would you?'

'Sure.'

'You're a star.'

Chapter 13

Friday was another glorious day. Trish took her time walking through the Temple. There was still no one about and hardly any cars parked between the eighteenth-century buildings. She'd rarely seen the place look so good. Only the leprous bark of the plane trees held any ugliness and even that diminished as she thought of the Gerard Manley Hopkins poem about his delight in 'dappled things'.

In the old days, poetry hadn't formed any part of her interior life. George often used the verses he'd learned in adolescence as a vehicle for thoughts he couldn't otherwise express, much as some of her teenage clients used to tell her 'it's like in *East-Enders*, know what I mean?' when explaining some otherwise incomprehensible emotion or relationship. For a long time she'd found George's habit irritating, but lately she had started to read some of the poets he'd quoted most often, and she was beginning to understand what he took from them. His devotion to Hopkins alone told her that he, too, must once have had to climb up out of despair. She might wish that he'd told her directly, but it was better to find out this way than never to know it at all.

What she still didn't know was what had flung him into the depths and whether it was something more than the bizarre upper-middle-class way he'd been brought up. Sent away to boarding school at eight, beaten for poor exam results or breaking rules, taught that the most important thing in life was the suppression of tears and all obvious emotion, he hadn't had much chance to learn to be at ease with himself and his feelings. Even so, there had to be more. But she'd never wanted to rip off his defences by probing for it.

Pushing George to the back of her mind, along with all Hopkins's dappled things, she wondered what there might have been in Will's past to make him at once so needy and so angry; why he so often felt he had to hide his intelligence. And what was really driving him in this investigation of Smarden Meats.

Why on earth hadn't she asked more questions before she'd promised to lend him the money?

She fumbled in her bag for the envelope to give her clerk, hearing Colin's voice behind her.

'You know you asked me about that abattoir?' he said.

'Yes. Have you discovered something?'

'A bit. It was run by a man called Thomas Flesker and his two sons, Robert and Ronald. They fought to keep it open as long they could, but they were badly stretched by funding all the improvements required by the new EU regulations. For some weird reason, the big so-called industrial abattoirs got government grants to subsidize the upgrading of their premises, but the smaller ones didn't.'

'What? Why not?'

'I don't know. Policy. And pressure from the industrial ones, I think. Then, on top of making the improvements, they all had to pay for vets to invigilate what they were doing.'

'That I did know,' Trish said, thinking of the helpful one she'd met at Smarden.

'It was a vet who caused Robert Flesker to explode. Because there weren't enough British ones available at the time to do this kind of work, they were having to use a French one. He cost them ten times what the old local authority chap had charged to check their carcasses. And that pissed them off in itself.'

'I can imagine.'

'Then he made a whole slew of demands for new practices in barely comprehensible English, couldn't understand what they said in response or answer any of their questions. So he got angry and threatened to close them down there and then for non-compliance. Robert let fly with some racist insults about the vet's compatriots' attitude to food safety and hit him. Laid him out in fact; tore up all his forms and threw them over him.'

'Was he was arrested?'

'Yup. He did three months in prison.' Colin grinned. 'I can't say I blame him, but it was a stupid thing to do. I'm afraid that's all I've found out so far.'

'It's brilliant. I'm really grateful. How did you do it?'

'A mixture of the Internet last night and a few phone calls this morning. Luckily everyone I needed was at work as early as me. You will let me know as soon as there's anything else you want, won't you? I'm enjoying this.'

'I will,' she said, impressed. If you're really offering, I'd love to meet your mate with the press contacts. Maybe we could all get together for a drink in El Vino.'

'Sure.' Colin's green eyes looked eager. 'When?'

Trish had taken him to the quintessential legal winebar for a drink when he'd first become her pupil. She'd watched him identifying the famous faces all round them, and revelling in the wild stories of amazing feats of advocacy, which anyone could overhear if he stopped talking for a moment. It wouldn't be half as exciting this time, with all the famous faces sheltering from the rain abroad, but she needed information fast, and it sounded as though his friend had access to most of it.

'Tonight?'

'I can try. But he lives with his girlfriend and she gets antsy if he's out too often without her. Have you got more questions for him about that journalist who died?'

Trish grinned. 'You know me too well. I have, but we can't stop to talk about them now or we'll be late.'

'Not that late,' he said, glancing at the clock on the wall of her room. 'And Antony hasn't appeared yet. Why don't you write me a list? That way I can get Angus on to checking them out straight away, so you'd get something tonight, even if he can't get away from his girlfriend.'

'Great. Thank you.' She dropped into the chair by her desk and flipped open her laptop. After years of doing most of her work on computer, her handwriting had degenerated into something that looked as though a drunken spider had waded through an inkwell. Ten minutes later, the questions she wanted to ask were printing out.

Colin caught the sheet as it was spat out. He looked up.

'You've got a question here about the journalist's next of kin. I told you: he didn't have any family.'

'I know you did, but I don't believe it. No siblings, parents, cousins, uncles, girlfriends, boyfriends? Everyone has someone. A next of kin must be recorded somewhere.'

'Fair enough. I'll go and phone Angus now. If he wants the list emailed, can I use your laptop?'

'Sure. That way he can email me straight back.' She heard the familiar sliding strut that heralded their head of chambers. 'Here's Antony.'

Colin moved fast to get to a phone where he could talk discreetly. She wondered how much he knew or had guessed about her interest in the journalist.

Antony was moody on the walk between chambers and court. Trish thought about cajoling him out of the sullens, then decided he was a grown-up and ought to be able to manage it himself.

'Have you heard from George recently?' he asked as they hit Fleet Street.

'Yes. They're having a great time. What about your lot?'

He hunched his shoulders. 'There was a message from Liz when I got back last night. She's furious that I didn't have my mobile on. She's furious that I'm not there to help amuse the children. She's furious that it's raining all the time in Italy, while London is hotter than it's ever been. And she's furious that I'm on the loose here, while she's bored out of her skull with nothing to do and no one to talk to.'

He grabbed Trish's wrist to hold her back from the zebra crossing as a pair of motorcycles zoomed across it like maddened hornets. 'She's coming home on Saturday. It's like the end of half term. I can't bear it. Let me come and have dinner in your flat tonight, Trish.'

'Antony, I . . .'

Swinging round to face her, he said, 'You must know that I won't lay a finger on you. Just let me—'

'I can't. I've got things to do.'

'Put them off. We're never going to have this kind of opportunity again, with both Liz and George away. What could be more important than that?'

She didn't want to tell him about Will Applewood or Jamie Maxden and his film, or even about the quest for the source of the meat that had half-killed Caro Lyalt. Nor did she particularly want Antony in her flat.

'Why are you looking so worried, Trish?'

'Because we've had fun flirting, but this sounds like something else. I told you, I can't . . .'

'Oh, don't be so bloody sensible!' He whirled away and was across the road before she'd moved, missing another motorbike by inches. When she caught up with him, he stalked on in silence for a while, then relented. 'You may be right, but that doesn't make it any better.'

His smile did, though, and they walked up the stone steps side by side.

*

Will bought his ticket at Waterloo, wishing he'd asked Trish for more than two hundred quid. He hadn't realized that the walk-on price of a seat on Eurostar in high season was so much more than a pre-booked special-offer day-return ticket in winter. The only other time he'd taken the train to France had been a trip to Paris with Fiona just after they'd got engaged. She'd told him what she wanted, so he'd phoned ahead to book a table at the Tour d'Argent as well as arranging the rail tickets. The fares had been a lot cheaper than the meal they'd eaten, but it had been worth it. Fiona had loved it. At that moment, her pleasure had been all that mattered.

He thought of her as she'd been then, sleek and fascinatingly strange and hanging on his every word. Her life had been spent entirely in London, and she'd worked first at Christie's, then for an art publisher. She'd never got up in the raw dawn to manhandle cows; the mention of silage didn't conjure up for her the sweet, rotting smell he'd always hated; and slurry was just a word that sounded amusingly sloshy. She'd used it for all sorts of things, always with the gurgling laugh that had been the first thing he'd noticed about her when they were introduced at a party.

It had been exciting to be with her, so smooth and different from all the women he'd grown up with. His mother and her friends had had faces reddened by wind and rain, and hair that was furry round the edges. Even Susannah's had been like that before she'd become a Londoner. Now, with Rupert's bonuses to spend and his status to protect, she had all the gloss anyone could want, in spite of living with the children all day.

Trish Maguire had it too, although her version was more sober. He wondered whether Trish ever looked messy. Even in the loose trousers and crisp pink linen shirt she'd worn when they went to the abattoir, she had seemed unrufflable, unlike bubbly little Mandy.

Will felt a smile untying the tension in his neck at the thought of Mandy. Her neat white bedroom, with its frilled muslin curtains and its flowery smells, was the nearest thing he knew to heaven. She seemed to think sex had been invented for fun. She laughed and twined herself around him and encouraged him until he laughed too. Fiona had had a tendency to shout and then weep, even in their better days, and some of her predecessors had behaved as though they were enduring a tough exercise session in a punitive gym, going for the burn. Only Mandy had fun, and gave it. Bundles of it.

French and English voices broke into his memories, announcing that the train would be entering the Channel Tunnel any moment now. There was something so official in their tones that Will braced himself and tried to forget the uncomfortable little thought that kept insinuating itself into his memories of Mandy.

He'd taken advantage of her; no question about it. When she was lying, half-asleep and happily post-orgasmic, he had asked her again about the origin of the sausages her company sold to retailers like the deli he'd found in Vauxhall. She had snuggled up even closer and told him cosily that she didn't know where they were made, honestly, but that lots of Ivyleaf's meat came from a farm near a little village in Normandy called Sainte Marie-le-Vair. It was owned by an Englishman and no one was supposed to know anything about it.

Even then it might have been all right if Will hadn't tensed and reached behind him for pencil and paper to write down the name before he forgot it. Looking up from his note, he'd caught her watching him with so much disappointment, he could have cut out his tongue. Instead, he'd made jokes and tea and teased her back into cuddliness. But he couldn't forget the look in her eye. It had made him push down all the other questions, about Smarden Meats and whether Jamie Maxden had ever come to Ivyleaf Packaging in search of the same information.

A boy of about twelve slopped along the corridor, eating a *croque monsieur*, dropping crumbs and molten cheese on the carpet. Will bit down on his hunger. He had barely enough money left to hire the most basic of cars to get himself to Sainte Marie. There was nothing to spare for luxuries like food.

Antony hogged the cross-examination all day. Trish sat behind him, tracking his every move, so that if he needed anything from the bundles she would be able to hand it to him without fumbling, but it was hard to keep her mind away from all her anxieties. Now that Kim was safe, they were mostly about Will. What on earth could he be doing with the money?

Will found Sainte Marie-le-Vair without difficulty, parked his hired Deux Chevaux under the straggly trees in the square and decided he had just enough Euros for a cooling *pression* at one of the tables outside the bar. Waiting for someone to take his order, he looked around the scrubby village and wondered why it made him feel so glum.

There were a few grey stone houses strung along the road, which divided around a dusty, gravelled oval, where the café-bar had its outdoor tables. A row of lime trees provided some shade, but they'd made the chairs and tables sticky. All there was to look at were rusting metal signs, advertising beer or soap, screwed to the walls of a few of the houses. Some thin pigeons pecked about in the gravel until a mangy cat slunk towards them, scattering them like dusty grey confetti.

It could only be twenty-odd miles to the coast, and yet this place looked as though no tourist had ever been here. There was nothing to draw them. Not that there was all that much on the coast itself, as far as Will could remember.

Years ago, the whole family had come to stay in a big white hotel not far from here, and it had been hell. His mother had been nagging for years about needing a proper foreign holiday but his father had always refused to contemplate the expense. No farmer could happily take two weeks off in high summer, but in the end he'd given in for the sake of peace and hauled them off to France for a week at the beginning of July. Everything that could have gone wrong had done: it had rained every single day; the food in the hotel hadn't been excitingly foreign, just dull and tough; there'd been no one to talk to except each other, and nothing to do except go for rainy walks along the beach or play bar football in a leaky outhouse.

Will would probably have been happy enough dreaming of the girl he'd chatted up at the school's end of term dance, except that Susannah, bad tempered as ever, had spent the whole time telling him no girl with a working brain would ever fancy a lout like him.

Someone crunched over the gravel. Will looked up, glad to be relieved of the memories, and smiled at the waiter who dumped his beer on the thin green table. He summoned up his schoolboy French to thank the man and ask whether there were many English people in the area. For extra verisimilitude, he added the usual excuse that he was thinking of moving over here himself.

The waiter sneered, shrugged like the hammiest English amateur actor playing a French rake, then said, 'Only at Jeannot le Fou's farm off the Rouen road. They say some English fools bought it for *gîtes*. Even if they get planning permission, which they will not, Jeannot was a terrible farmer and the place is one vast pile of *merde*. *Merde des cochons, des vaches, et des hommes*. The smell that comes from there when the wind is from the south! *Affreux*!' He shuddered with the artistry of long practice.

That's definitely the place I want, Will thought.

He hadn't understood all the waiter's words, but the general drift was easy to grasp. He said clumsily in French that it sounded terrible and not at all the sort of place a man like him would want to go. Then he asked where it was, to make sure he avoided finding himself in such a stinking heap of ordure. The waiter, no longer sneering, told him, then added that there were said to be some nice châteaux being built further along the coast. His mother-in-law's cousin was the estate agent and could no doubt furnish monsieur with the necessary details.

In the interests of cover, Will took down the address of the estate agency, paid for his beer and drank it slowly. It was the last he was going to get until he was on his way back to the train and sure that his funds would see him safely home, so he made the most of it.

Not as good as the brew in the Smarden pub, he decided, and altogether too cold and too thin, but it slipped down easily enough. A quick trip to the gents came next, then he was back in his rattly little tortoise of a car, bucketing out of the village towards the piles of steaming *merde* the waiter had so graphically described.

Could the story of Mad Jeannot's legacy be no more than a cover to keep nosy locals and interested visitors out of the way?

Trish half expected to have to fight Antony for time to go to El Vino with Colin and his friend, but he said nothing more about a final private dinner before his wife returned; he didn't want even the usual post-mortem of the day's evidence. When they emerged from court at half past four, he asked Colin to drop his wig and gown back in chambers with the documents, and said he'd see them both at eight o'clock on Monday morning. Trish felt surprisingly short-changed.

'The treat's well and truly over now, isn't it, Trish?'

She turned to see Ferdy Aldham leering at her from the shadows thrown by the pointed stone arch over the door to the street.

'Sorry?'

'So you should be, playing around with a man like Antony. I'd thought better of you.'

'Oh, grow up,' she said, forgetting that it had been Antony who had first thrown that insult at their opponent. 'Coming, Colin?'

'Sure.' He walked beside her in silence as Ferdy's giggles echoed after them. Once they were striding down between the plane trees towards Plough Court, he asked if he'd been missing something.

'Only some idiotic, sub-primary-school joke of Ferdy's, that isn't at all funny.'

'No. Right.' Colin's face split into a cheerful smile. 'It's so damn hard to decode all the legalese, let alone the in-jokes, that I usually feel particularly dim when I'm around you and Antony.'

'No need,' Trish said. They reached the door to chambers and swept in past the cream-coloured board with all the tenants' names in black. 'You're shaping up a treat, Colin. You'll be there soon enough; don't worry about it.'

'Unless I piss Antony off and he votes against me when the time comes for you all to decide which pupils get tenancies,' he said. 'That's why I watch him all the time to work out what he's thinking. By the way, have you seen how he *loathes* Ferdy Aldham? Far more than you do.'

'Does he?' Trish wasn't very interested. 'Look, I want to check my emails, Colin, in case your mate has responded. Then once we've had our drink, I ought to visit a friend in hospital. Will you be OK for a few minutes?'

'Sure,' he said, but he didn't leave her room. She looked up, puzzled, from the laptop. This time his smile was more tentative, almost pleading.

'I just thought it might be useful for you to know that I asked someone whether there was any history between them, and he said they've hated each other since Bar school, when Ferdy got the top marks and Antony only came second. Then Antony got pupillage first, started winning cases first and took silk first.

Even so, it's not thought to be enough to make up for the exam rage.'

Trish stared at him, fitting the news into the jigsaw in her mind. Might this at last explain why Antony had accepted the brief? And why he hadn't challenged Ferdy when he was leading Will to make a fool of himself in the witness box?

'Where did you get this choice titbit, Colin?'

He flushed. 'My godfather was there with them. I asked him.'

Trish looked at him with new respect. It would have taken more confidence than she'd had at his age to avoid dropping names that might be useful, particularly in a world like theirs, where so much old-boy stuff still went on. She couldn't remember ever having heard Colin mention that he had a godfather at the Bar, and she was certain it hadn't come up at any of his interviews before he was offered a pupillage at Plough Court.

'Who is he?' she asked and was even more impressed when he just shook his head.

'There's an email here with all the answers from your friend because he says he can't meet us tonight,' she said. 'Why don't we go and have a quick drink anyway?'

'I'd love it.' He was blushing. 'But what about your hospital visit?'

'There'll be time for both. Dump that lot and let's go.'

She came back to chambers to read the email properly after she'd despatched Colin to his basement flat in Tooting. His friend had done an admirably thorough job. He'd found out that Jamie Maxden's next of kin was a sister, Clare Blake, with whom he'd had no contact for years. She lived in Twickenham. Colin's friend had even provided a phone number.

In answering the rest of her questions, he'd also offered the interesting fact that the police had found a suicide note in Maxden's car. Apart from the note, they'd found nothing except his mobile phone and his laptop computer, which had slid under the passenger seat as he drove. The police had obviously checked that and found copies of letters and emails to editors all over the country, begging for work. Some of them went back years and they'd have shown evidence of suicidal depression even without the note. The lack of luggage had been thought to confirm that he hadn't been planning to live out the night. The last three emails he'd sent on the night he'd died had been despatched to suicide websites on the Internet.

He'd had £33.67 in his pockets, along with two credit cards and his driving licence, which was how they'd identified him, but nothing else. He had enormous debts and the mortgage company was about to throw him out of his flat. The inquest verdict was no surprise to anyone.

'You might be interested to know,' the email ended, 'that Maxden's sister arranged to have the body cremated.'

As soon as she had printed out the email, Trish raced to the hospital.

There was no sign of Jess in the Intensive Care unit, but Caro was looking more alert. There was even a trace of colour in her cheeks. At the sight of Trish treading carefully across the polished floor, Caro stretched out her hand. There was still a drip trailing from it.

'Thank you, Trish,' she said. 'Andrew told me what you've done for Kim. What a triumph!'

'It all seems to be coming right, doesn't it? You look better, too. That must mean they've found the right antibiotic at last.'

'They have, and my temperature's coming down. My kidneys aren't quite sorted yet, which is why I'm still up here.' Caro's light voice was at odds with her face, which was as blank as a mask before she forced the smile back. Even then it didn't touch her eyes.

Trish knew that Caro had to be facing the possibility that her kidneys would never recover fully. She was far too well informed not to know what that meant: a lifetime of dialysis until her veins were so damaged by needles that even that ceased to be possible. Then a transplant would be the only way of saving her life, and there was a terrible shortage of kidneys, now that road accidents were rarer and victims cared for more efficiently.

Roll on the day when transgenic pigs can be bred to provide organs for transplant, Trish thought. At least until stem-cell research gets to the point where they can be grown in a lab rather than in another body. Anything would be better than the destruction of a life like Caro's.

Her frightened brown eyes warned Trish not to say anything sympathetic, so she smiled instead, and asked whether Caro had had many visitors.

'Jess.' Her face softened. 'She comes every day with clean pyjamas and tiny amounts of pristine food I can eat.'

'Meat?' Trish couldn't stop the question, in spite of her new appreciation of Jess.

'Of course. She'd never impose her own diet on me. And Cynthia comes sometimes, and Pete Hartland.'

'Has he accepted that Crossman didn't poison you? I couldn't make him talk to me for long enough to find out whether I'd convinced him.'

'I think he does believe it now. Luckily. He could have caused a lot of trouble. By the way, is your friend still trying to track down the source of the E. coli? Jess told me he'd found the deli where I bought the sausages. She's dead grateful for all the work he's putting in.'

Trish remembered the antipathy that had burgeoned between the two of them and said lightly, 'Even though she didn't like him?'

Caro laughed, which was all the acknowledgement Trish needed.

'His charms are a little unusual,' she added, 'but once you get to know him you realize they're real. There isn't much I can tell you. He's borrowed some money off me and gone to ground.'

'Why does that worry you?' Caro sounded so much stronger, and so like her usual self, that for a moment Trish was tempted to ask for the advice she needed. But until she knew for certain what Will was doing, she couldn't risk bringing the police anywhere near him.

'No reason,' she said and hoped she sounded confident. 'I was just thinking about the sausages and wondering whether anyone else suffered from them. Have you heard of any other cases?'

'No. And each time I ask, the nurses tell me not to worry, love. If there'd been a big outbreak, the authorities would have made enquiries, but there hasn't. So you just lie back and relax. We're looking after you.' Caro said this in a deliberately syrupy voice. Reverting to her own astringent tones she added, 'It's enough to send my temperature back to the top of the scale without any infection whatsoever. If your friend does find anything out, you will bring him to see me, won't you?'

'Of course,' Trish said, then added in silence to herself: if it's safe.

On her way out of the unit later, Trish felt a tap on her shoulder. She turned, expecting to see one of the nurses. In fact it was a man almost as young as Andrew Stane's captain, but much less sturdy. She looked enquiringly at him.

'Are you Inspector Lyalt's friend who was ill, too?' he asked. 'The one who's been talking to Kim?'

'Yes, Trish Maguire.'

'I work with her. My name's Pete Hartland. You phoned me. Can I talk to you? Outside, I mean. I don't want to disturb her.'

'Sure.'

Beyond the swing doors to the ward there was a dingy cream-painted corridor with a bench about halfway along. Trish led the way there and sat down.

'How can I help?'

'When are you going to see Kim again?'

'I'm not. I did the last interview yesterday, and she said enough to enable the social workers to extend the care order. They're going to take it from here. Haven't they told you?'

Hartland leaped up from the bench, then came back, looming over her. Trish blinked and leaned back.

'Yeah, but it's not enough, is it?' The words burst out of him. 'We can't do him for cruelty on what you've got. OK, Kim may be taken safely into care. But nothing will happen to Dan Crossman. He'll be glad to be rid of her. It'll look like winning to him, and he's got to be made to see he didn't win. Otherwise he'll do the same sort of thing again and again.'

Trish watched him pacing about like an animal in too small a cage. Anyone who had ever seen Kim would have been driven to help her, but this passion seemed excessive.

'What's your particular interest in him?' she asked.

'He doesn't remind me of my dad, if that's what you're thinking.' He spat out the words. 'I wasn't abused by anyone else either. I had a great family life.'

'It never occurred to me to suggest otherwise. Has someone else said you were?' she said, remembering Andrew Stane's idea that Caro could have been projecting some emotional damage of her own on to Kim. What had happened to this man to make him so keen on punishing Dan Crossman?

Pete's shoulders lifted up round his ears. 'Of course. These days you can't show any interest in little children without being called a paedophile yourself, or a victim of abuse. I hate the bastards who mess about with little children, just like I hate the other ones who beat up old ladies for their electric money. There's no difference. And I hate seeing the bastards that hurt them get away with it just because they've got clever lawyers.'

'I'm a lawyer.'

'I know.' At last he smiled and showed her a glimpse of the eager boy Caro liked so much. 'But you've never defended bastards like that. I checked.'

'Did you indeed? Still, I don't see what I can do to help you.'

The smile wavered, then returned. He came back to sit beside her on the bench, laying both his hands palm upwards on his right knee. 'The people I checked with say you can tell what's going on in someone's head just by looking at them.' He waited for a comment.

'Then they're flattering me, whoever they are. It's not true.'

If it were, she thought, I'd know what Will's doing now, and why. And why he hates Grant-Furbisher so much. Could that be projection too?

No, she told herself, wondering why she'd never seen the obvious truth before. It's not projection in Will's case. It's substitution. He must see Grant-Furbisher as doing to him what his father did. Both of them made him feel like an irresponsible, greedy failure. He can't dump enough hatred on his father now that he's dead, so Grant-Furbisher's getting a double dose.

'It *must* be true,' Pete said, looking so disappointed that Trish tried to comfort him.

'Sometimes experience gives me a clue about what's behind the mask someone's wearing, but that's all it is. A clue. And I've done all I can with Kim.'

'It's not her I'm thinking of. I want you to see Crossman. I want you to find out what he's been doing, because it's not just making Kim stand naked on a box. I know that much.'

'Oh, Pete,' she said, touching his supplicant's hands with one of her own. 'I can't do that.'

'You could. Not officially or anything. But I know the pub where he drinks. The Black Eagle, near Vauxhall Station. Even though it's mainly ex-army men that go there, it's a public place, and it's only a short walk from here. I could take you, just going for a drink see, and you could have a look at him. Watch what he does and how he interacts with people, and see if you can see anything.'

'It doesn't work like that.'

Disappointment smeared itself across his face again. 'Please. I know there's more been going on. Just come and have a pint with me there and look at him. You could do that, couldn't you? For Kim. And for Inspector Lyalt? Before she was taken ill she was just as keen as me to get him sent down for what he's been doing. She'd want you to come with me.'

Trish didn't think Caro would want anything of the sort, but on the other hand she thought she might do it. She'd never seen Crossman and she was curious about him.

Chapter 14

The smell was terrible. But it was not the smell of any muck heap Will had ever known. There was a rank sweetness to it and an acrid edge as well. This was putrefying flesh just as he'd expected once he'd tied together Jamie Maxden's film and Mandy's stories of a secret source for meat coming into Ivyleaf Packaging from abroad.

It wouldn't be dark for ages, and Will didn't want to risk encountering anyone who worked here. Scouting around, giving the buildings a wide berth, he saw a kind of coppice to the east of the farm. He made his way there, stepping sideways as a watchdog caught his scent down in the farm and started barking its head off.

Surprised that any animal could smell anything above the stink of rotting meat, Will dropped his head and sprinted for the copse, keeping as low to the ground as possible. He could vaguely hear men's voices, but not what they said. There was an interrogatory shout, then a mumble. He thought they must be speaking English because the intonation was so familiar, but he wouldn't have sworn to it.

The copse wasn't big, but it would give him enough shelter. His combat trousers and sweatshirt, both dull olive green, would blend nicely with the local scenery. The worst problem was going to be boredom. He didn't smoke and, anyway, it would have revealed his hiding place. He hadn't brought a book because books bored him even more than doing nothing. He would just have to lie up here and dream of being back in Mandy's bed, or handing over to Trish all the information she could possibly need to make her believe what he now knew was going on.

He could just imagine her, standing there with her eagle's nose and her sparky black eyes, a little wary and disdainful at first, as she so often was, then melting into astonishment at his achievement, and admiration, and . . .

Will told himself to stop being such a fool. His idiotic imagination had suddenly rolled Trish up with Mandy. However much he admired Trish, relied on her good opinion and her professional skills, he didn't fancy her. She wasn't his type at all. Far too long and thin, and much too clever. Although there was something about the way her lips could curve when she smiled, and the way her black eyes turned soft instead of glittering when she was trying to comfort people. Still, she would never curl round him like an affectionate hedgehog, protecting both of them with her own vulnerable back, or giggle as he made love to her and tell him that he was the best she'd ever had and she was going to give him the best time *he'd* ever had. Women like Trish didn't do that sort of thing.

The hours dragged themselves out in a mixture of memory and fear. The bumps in the ground grew harder and harder. As the sun dropped over the horizon, Will began to feel cold. Why on earth hadn't he had the wit to bring something thicker than a sweatshirt?

The day eventually gave way to grey dusk, then real darkness. Tonight the moon was only the faintest sickle and wouldn't betray anyone, but there were still the dogs with their supersensitive noses. Will inched forwards towards the edge of the trees, trying to work out which way the newly gusty wind was blowing so that he could check whether it would carry his scent down to the farm buildings or away from them.

Before he could get very far, he caught the sound of an engine on the wind. It became louder and louder, but it wasn't until it was almost on top of him that he let himself believe it was the aeroplane. Other sounds, of men running, panting like the ones in the video, and dogs snuffling and pulling against their chains, sent Will squirming back into the coppice.

Lights sprang up like flowers in the grass ahead of him. Unlike flowers, they were in two straight lines with another joining them together at the top. An unmistakable runway. Will couldn't believe his luck. Jamie had said in his email that the flights happened once a week, and today was exactly ten weeks since he had sent it, but there'd been nothing except Will's own investigations to suggest that the flights from Kent landed up here, just outside Sainte Marie-le-Vair. And he had cocked up far too often to have much faith in his own deductive powers. Or anything else.

Then it hit him, like an ice pick between the eyes. He hadn't got it right. Unlike Jamie, he did not have any means of recording what was happening. There would be no evidence of this flight, nothing to persuade anyone, except his own words, and he'd seen how highly those were valued.

Why the hell hadn't he asked Trish to come with him? A barrister of her standing would have been able to support him and make people listen to him, even without actual evidence. No one would push her away, as the authorities had done whenever he'd tried to alert them to the food scandals he knew lay behind supermarket profits all over England. No one would tell a lawyer like Trish that she was an over-emotional fantasist and had no judgement and brought all her troubles on herself.

Will wished he could see more from the sparse lights of the makeshift runway. He thought there were several men and at least four big dogs. There were mutterings in English, but some in another language, too. Not French, unless it was a strange dialect he'd never heard. It sounded too guttural.

The plane took another sweep over the field. Another light, held at about waist height flashed three times, then after a pause, three times more. Two minutes later, the plane was down and the voices were much more urgent and a good bit louder. Will inched forwards to see better, crinkling up his eyes and craning his neck.

Some time later, he heard it: unmistakable footsteps coming towards him across the dry grass. One of them must have seen him. He was about to get up and run. Then he swore silently to himself. All that would do was ensure that he was seen and caught and probably killed, like Jamie. Keeping still was the only possible way of protecting himself. It might not work. But the alternative definitely wouldn't.

The man stopped only feet away from him. His breathing was short and sharp, like someone facing danger. The snuffling grumble of one of the dogs was close by too. Will could just see the man as a slightly darker blodge against the darkness of the backdrop, with two small points of glitter where his eyes must be. They disappeared and the blodge shifted and twisted.

Eyes, Will thought. That must be what gave me away.

He should have shut them. But he couldn't bear to have no warning of whatever was going to happen to him. The man took a few more steps forward. Will ducked his head towards the ground and nearly screamed as his face landed in a nettle patch. His skin burned as the poison bit into it. Shifting sideways as quietly as possible, he kept his eyes down to stop them from sparkling. The other man's sharp, shallow breathing showed he knew he wasn't alone.

'Keep those fucking Dobermanns out of my way,' he shouted over his shoulder, in such unmistakably middle-class English that Will nearly rolled back into the nettles.

'I need a slash and I don't want them chewing my plonker,' the man went on, using slang Will hadn't heard since school.

The man unbuttoned his trousers and Will put a hand over

his head. But the man aimed in the opposite direction. As the stream dwindled, he said quietly in clumsy, British-accented French, '*Restez la. Ne bouge pas. Ne parle pas. Compris*?'

Will's mouth was dry and his throat felt tighter than a hangman's noose. Who was this Englishman? He produced a hoarse, muttered '*Oui*', thanking God the man thought he was French.

'*Bien.*'

He shook himself and buttoned his fly, before trampling noisily away and leaving Will with about a million questions crashing about in his head. There was only one that mattered. Why on earth had he been protected?

There were clanking noises whenever the wind dropped, and other sounds, too, human and furtive. Something heavy was being dragged over hard surfaces.

At last the plane took off again and the lights were put out. Several journeys were made on foot to and from the field. Those sounds told Will that whoever was making them was carrying heavy weights. He was sure this was the equivalent of the journeys made to and from the plane in Jamie Maxden's video. When they stopped, he was going to have to find enough courage to go down the fields after them and find out exactly what they were doing in their stinking dog-protected buildings.

He tried to tell himself that he'd done enough to convince Trish at least. His nettle-savaged face still stung. He had bruises all over his stiff body from lying on the ground for so many hours. But there was too much he still didn't understand. He didn't even know for sure whether tonight's plane was the same one Jamie had filmed. Maybe when he watched Jamie's video again he'd be able to get everything he needed.

And maybe you won't, stupid, he told himself in his father's voice. No, he had to go down to the farm.

One of the dogs howled in the darkness, then fell silent. Someone must have thrown it some meat. Would the food be enough to keep the animals so sated they'd miss a stranger creeping around them?

No, of course it won't, stupid. It was his father's voice in his head again. They're guard dogs.

Will pushed himself to his feet, shaking his arms and lifting one shoulder after the other, before wagging his head from side to side to ease the aches. At least he could pee now.

Even that was only a distraction. He had to go down to the buildings and deal with whatever happened to him there. If he flunked this, he might as well give up everything for ever.

The Black Eagle was as full of men as the pub in Smithfield, but the atmosphere was entirely different. The meat porters had been a cheerful lot, hungry and bustling. These men were tense and still. An acrid haze of cold cigarette smoke hung over their heads. One or two women sat among the drinkers, but they were mostly grey haired and looked as held-in as the men. Some lively sounds banged around at the far end of the building, where Trish could see glimpses of green baize and pool balls. In the main bar the crowd was quiet.

'What'll you have?' Pete Hartland asked.

Trish had no wish for beer, but it wasn't hard to see that a request for wine in a place like this would make the two of them stand out even more clearly than her haircut and tidy black suit. Already there had been some aggressively curious glares. She wished she still had her old gelled spikes; at least they hadn't marked her out as anything but an eccentric.

'Scotch, please,' she said, discreetly pulling a ten-pound note out of the top pocket of her jacket and offering it to him. She couldn't make a young constable pay for such an expensive drink for her.

'OK.' He looked surprised but took the cash and shouldered his way through the crowd at the bar.

Trish looked behind her and saw two thickset men with very

short hair get up from a microscopic table. She shot between the crowd and perched on one empty stool, ignoring the waves of fury she could feel at her back. If she sat still, she thought, and didn't make any noise or thrust her femaleness at any of them, they might forget she was here. Pete would just have to find her. The last thing she was going to do was wave at him or call his name.

It took a while, but that could have been because the crowd at the bar held back his order. He'd brought her a double and himself a pint in the kind of straight glass with a bicep-like bulge at the top that had long ago replaced the old-fashioned dimpled tankards she'd liked as a child.

'Cheers,' he said, raising the glass but keeping his wrist between her and the drink as though she might grab it.

She nodded and wet her lips with the whisky. It was raw and burned her tongue as she licked them.

'Is he here?'

'Yeah. Two tables over to the right, back to the wall. Always sits like that. He's the one with the red polo shirt.' Hartland flicked open a packet of cigarettes and shook one forward to offer to her.

'No thanks.'

He struck a match and she looked casually away, as though protecting her eyes from the spark or the smoke. Daniel Crossman wasn't hard to identify. There was only one red shirt. He wasn't looking in her direction so it seemed safe to study him.

Above the open shirt collar was a face no different from any of the others in the pub: watchful and lined about the eyes and mouth. He must have been in his early forties. From what she could see through the fug, his eyes were grey, his lips were thin and dry, and he carried his shoulders high and tight. He looked as though he had just sat down for a moment and was ready to spring into action any second, and yet there were three pint glasses in front of him, messy with foam. One had an inch or two of beer in the bottom.

There was no one on the stool opposite him, and neither of the drinkers beside him looked at him or spoke.

One of the barmen was collecting glasses, going from table to table with orderly efficiency. Trish watched Crossman watching him, picking up whole bunches of glasses between the fingers and thumb of one hand and lifting them on to the tray he held on the other. The tray was full before he reached Crossman's table, so he turned away. Trish saw Crossman's gaze following him resentfully. He pushed his empty glasses to one side, before wiping his hand on a very white handkerchief. Then he stood, uncoiling his body with neat control.

He was wearing the ubiquitous jeans, but they were much cleaner than Trish thought anyone's jeans had a right to be, and ironed into savage creases. He stepped out through a narrow gap between the tables and walked straight over to her.

'What are you looking at?' he said, bending down to speak straight into Trish's ear. The buzz and clatter of the rest of the pub receded. She could feel his breath on her ear.

'Hey!' Pete said. 'What d'you think you're doing?'

'And you, keep your sodding mouth shut.' He turned back to Trish. 'I asked you a question.'

She gathered her wits and said carefully. 'I was looking at the barman and wondering how he balanced that heavy tray, even when he had to bend down for the glasses.'

'Hah!' Crossman straightened up. 'You must think I'm stupid. You're another of Inspector Lyalt's dyke policewomen, aren't you? He work for you?' He jutted his chin towards Pete. 'Too wet behind the ears to be out on his own? That it?'

Trish could see Pete longing to be up and at him. No wonder Caro had been afraid he might attack Crossman. Trish had never seen anyone wanting a fight so much.

'No, he doesn't,' she said, trying to copy Andrew Stane's

refusal to react to aggression. 'And I am not a police officer. Why should you think I was?'

'Because your boyfriend here is. So who are you then?'

'Hey, mate, leave the lady alone.' It was the barman back for another trayful of dirty glasses. 'She's done you no harm.'

'That's all you know.' He still hadn't stopped looking at Trish. 'This is harassment. I'll be making a complaint. You can depend on that.'

Trish looked at the barman and was glad to see he was older than she'd first thought, and quite as tough-looking as any of the drinkers. Maybe he'd been in the army with them. He nodded to her, then squared up to Crossman.

'Go on. You've had enough. Time to go home.'

Trish watched Crossman's hands bunch and sat very still indeed. She wished she'd never agreed to come here. She didn't think she was in any danger, but she'd probably made life a lot harder for Caro, and she'd learned nothing she hadn't already known or guessed. Crossman was an angry man, probably unhappy, who was prepared to pick on anyone he perceived as weaker than himself. She hated the thought of Kim in his power, but there was nothing she could do here to help keep the child out of it.

'Go on. Leave her alone,' said the barman, pushing his way towards them.

A bigger, older man, called out, 'Hey, Dan! Come and settle an argument for us. John here thinks the AK47 is a brilliant weapon. I think that's bullshit. Come on. I'll buy you a drink.'

Crossman hesitated, then moved towards him. The barman leant over Trish's table to grab some glasses from the other side of her.

'This isn't a good place for you,' he said.

'Why not?'

'Can't you see?' He looked around the crowd, then across the table at Pete Hartland. 'You: take her somewhere else. Whether you meant it or not, it's provocation. He doesn't need that. Nor do his family. And nor do I. OK?'

Pete drained his pint, then wiped his mouth on the back of his hand. Trish abandoned her Scotch. They waited just long enough to satisfy Hartland's self-respect, then oozed as unobtrusively as possible towards the door. The men shifted to let them out. No one said anything.

The exhaust-laden air outside tasted very sweet. Trish knew the whole uncomfortable episode had been her fault. She should never have listened to Hartland. He was too young to know any better.

'You see what he's like?' he said before they were more than twenty yards from the pub's front door. 'What did you think of him?'

'Nothing I hadn't expected. And nothing to give me any clues to whatever else he's been doing or threatening to do. That barman was right: we shouldn't have gone in there. Crossman recognized you, even if he got me wrong; my presence with you will just have complicated your job. I hate to think what Caro will say when she hears about it. And Andrew Stane.'

'But you must have been able to see something else.' Hartland was nearly crying with the effort of thinking the situation into something it could never be.

They had reached the river now. On the opposite side was the disciplined bulk of Tate Britain, sitting in the thin early moonlight amid its cloak of trees. Trish stopped with her back to it, leaning against the cool stone balustrade. She wanted to comfort him, but there was nothing she could say that would help.

'What about his body language? That must've told you something.'

'What do you want me to say that you don't already know, Pete? Crossman's body language was both aggressive and defensive. It shows that he's wary and on a short fuse. He's probably paranoid, too. But then he'd have a right to be, wouldn't he? We *were* there to spy on him. He looks fit and tough, but then so did ninety per cent of the rest of them.'

Hartland took a step away from her, then came back. She wanted to tell him that all evening his own body language had been expressing indecision and petulance, both of which betrayed a childish need to get his own way.

'Caro thinks you're brilliant,' he said at last, his face crumpling at the unfairness of her failure.

'I can't help that. Nothing about Daniel Crossman's behaviour gave me any new information. I must go.'

'Yeah.' He walked away.

Now it was her turn for indecision. Should she let him go without trying to help? Or should she pass on what she'd taken such an unforgivably long time to learn for herself? She hurried after him. 'Pete.' He paused but didn't turn. 'Pete, it's good to be personally involved with what you're doing,' she said, 'but you'll only fog your own perceptions if you can't learn to keep your distance.'

He did turn then. The street light turned his pink face orange, but it didn't disguise the cold anger, which showed a lot more in common with the drinkers than he'd probably guessed. 'Keeping your distance didn't do much for your perceptions just now, did it?'

He was as tense and watchful as the battle-stressed men in the pub. Was it his work that had done that to him?

'That's true,' Trish said. 'But don't take it as a reason to go after Crossman yourself. Please.'

'Nothing else is going to stop him torturing little children.'

'Pete, think of what Caro would say. She's been terrified of what you might do because anything outside the law is going to screw up any chance there is of nailing Crossman one day.'

His face set in concrete obstinacy.

'Think about it. If you go after him, you'll ruin your own career, probably Caro's as well, and whatever satisfaction you get will be at the cost of never having Crossman properly punished and his family made safe.'

Still he didn't respond. But he hadn't moved away either. Trish felt like Sisyphus all over again.

'Pete! Come on. Concentrate.'

'I'll try. But I can't wait for ever. If nothing's done, I'd rather get him and be sacked than know he's never going to pay for his crimes.'

Will turned his face this way and that to work out where the wind was coming from. The gusts made it harder than ever. His father would have been able to tell without a moment's thought. He'd have forecast tomorrow's weather too, more accurately than any computer-assisted weather man.

Forget him, Will told himself. You don't have to measure yourself against him. And even if you did, now wouldn't be the time.

Tonight's wind was coming from the south, he decided. He worked his way back round the farm buildings, pausing now and then to make sure he could feel the gusts blowing straight against his face. Now he came to think about it, it wasn't that difficult. All he had to do was make sure he was breathing in the stink from the buildings.

In the distance he could hear the faint chink of chains. The dogs must still be there, but so far they hadn't noticed him. He crept closer, bending at the knees as though that would make him less obvious to them.

His eyes were well adjusted now and in the faint blue-grey starlight he could make out the bulk of the buildings and see the gleam of unshuttered windows here and there in the long low facade. He'd go for one of those. Speeding up, he stopped crouching and ran upright and fast towards the gleam. Only when he was within about ten feet of it did he drop again and crawl forwards. No lights showed inside the windows.

At last he was right up against the sides of the building. He could feel the roughness of the wood against his cheek and smell the creosote with which it had been treated. A much better smell than the rest; cleaner, even if it was chemical. There was no sound nearer than the wind in the trees now.

He craned his neck forwards, then turned his head. With his neck at full stretch, he lifted his lids just a little.

At first he could see nothing but vague heaps in the greater darkness inside. Soon he made out windows on the opposite side of the long room into which he was looking. The building formed one side of a courtyard. Through the further windows he could see the dark slinking shapes of the dogs. They were restless, but maybe that was no surprise with the smell of old raw meat all around them.

Will had a torch in his pocket, a slim pencil-like thing. When he was sure that there were no men awake with the dogs, he switched it on, cupping it in his hand, then directed it through the dusty window. At first all he could see clearly were the cobwebs that had been spun from frame to frame. Then, moving the narrow beam systematically, he made out a heap of carcasses, some still in their black wrappings; others ripped open. There was a series of metal baths, leading to a bigger table with great butcher's boards on it and rows of knives. Sliding the beam around, peering to get a view of the nearest side of the room, he thought he could see piles of polystyrene trays and there was definitely an industrial-sized shrink-wrapping machine.

One of the dogs barked, then the others took it up. Will snapped off his torch and ran. He hadn't seen everything he needed, but there'd been enough to confirm the suspicion that had been with him for days now. Whether or not this place had anything to do with the infected sausages, it was definitely an illicit meat factory. And it dealt with far more carcasses than could be brought here in one small plane once a week. Like he'd said to Trish, this was a major scam.

His only concern though was with the meat the plane did bring in. All he had to find out now was where it had come from. It could be anywhere. But he was convinced some at least originated at Smarden Meats. Why else would the furious slaughterman who worked there be starring in Jamie's film?

Through the ragged, furious barking of the dogs, Will could hear men's voices. He didn't stop to listen to what they were shouting. It was only a few more yards to the road and therefore the car. Would it still be there?

He was at the hedge. The gate had to be somewhere here. He couldn't use the torch now without bringing the men straight to him. They probably had guns too. His only hope was to keep himself as dark as the hedge and find a way through it. Running his hands along the bushes, ripping his skin on their vicious thorns, he felt for an opening. More shouts sounded as though the men were closing in on him. He couldn't breathe properly. Fighting to get oxygen further into his body than the base of his throat, he fumbled on.

Clanking chains, then running feet and panting told him they'd loosed the dogs. He gave up all thought of the gate and flung himself up the hedge, clawing at the sharpest of the branches until he was perched on top, then over it and dropping on to the road. His ankle slipped under him, sending pain shooting up his leg. He put his weight on it as an experiment. Thank God, it wasn't a sprain or a torn tendon. He could cope with the pain so long as he knew the joint would hold him up. Blood was making his hands sticky. He raised his palms one after the other to lick them before wiping them on the back of his combats.

They weren't too bad. They wouldn't slip on the steering wheel. But the key. Where was the car key? He felt in both main pockets. Nothing. He bent further down as he ran towards the dusty little Deux Chevaux, feeling in the knee pockets of the combats. Still nothing. Only when he put one sore hand to his chest to hold down the leaping of his heart did he feel the comforting hardness of metal.

Of course. He'd hung the key on a thong around his neck.

The dogs were at the hedge now. He could hear them snuffling and tearing at the lower branches. They must have found his blood.

He had the key in the lock and turned it. However pathetic the car, he thought absurdly, at least they'd kept the locks oiled. Then he was in, crunching the back of his thighs on the exposed metal edge of the seat. What did that matter? The engine fired straight away. He stalled, trying to move the car on. But a second later he was away.

When he reached the crossroads that would take him back to Sainte Marie-le-Vair he began to laugh. Who'd have thought anyone could make a getaway in a car like this?

By the time he was the other side of the village, he was singing, belting out all the old songs his mother had liked: sea chanties, ancient British marching songs, and a few plaintive folk tunes like 'Oh Waley, Waley'. When he couldn't remember the words, he added his own and pressed down harder on the accelerator.

A vast meat lorry thundered past him, bringing back all the memories he'd managed to forget and cutting off any urge to sing. Resentment ate into him like acid, as he thought of all the trouble he'd taken to source his meat properly, rejecting anything that didn't have a clear traceable line from farm to abattoir to his factory, or via a wholesaler, sometimes paying far more than he'd had to. They'd come to respect him in the end, those meat traders. His own customers had liked him, too. And sodding Furbishers had taken it all away.

The last of the songs died in his head as he asked himself what on earth he thought he'd been doing, running about the French countryside, like a schoolboy playing escaped prisoners, when his life was still up for grabs. And it wasn't really an escape in any case. If they'd wanted to catch him, they'd have driven after him. Pretty much anything could have caught a Deux Chevaux. Maybe that's why they hadn't even tried to come after him. Once they'd seen his car, they'd probably half-killed themselves laughing at it. They must have decided he was a harmless local, brought by curiosity and running away because he'd been frightened by the dogs.

He drove on more slowly. Would Trish and the terrifying Antony Shelley ever manage to swing the case and get him enough damages to make any difference?

The car lurched under him, as though it had suddenly gone lame. A bloody puncture, he thought.

The last thing he needed. And if the state of the car was anything to go by, the spare wouldn't be much good. But he couldn't drive like this. The verge was quite shallow here, so he nudged the car up on to it and set about finding out how to open the boot. Thank God he had the little torch with him. There was no other light, except the thin gleam from the stars and the mean slice of moon. Holding the torch between his teeth to shine straight in front of him, he felt around in the boot for the tool and spares.

Some bastard had done up the wheel nuts far too tightly and it was ages before he could get them to shift. The tears in his hands opened again before the old wheel was off and he had to shake them at intervals to make the pain bearable. But he had it done at last and was back on the road and driving towards the port again. He was hungry and cross, so he stopped for another *pression* and a *jambon au beurre* sandwich. It wasn't enough, but it was something.

There was a phone in the bar, too. He thought he'd better ring Trish. If something were to happen to him now – and it still might – she had to know what he'd found. Stuffing his hand in his trouser pocket, he brought out the last of the money she'd lent him. There wasn't much left and he might need coffee to stay awake long enough to drive back to the car rental place. He wondered whether she would accept a reverse-charges call.

Chapter 15

There had been nothing more Trish could do, so she had let Pete Hartland go. Watching him speed off towards Vauxhall Station, she had felt a lot more than her fifteen years' seniority. After a while, she turned the other way and set off towards Southwark and her own flat. She decided to phone Andrew Stane and warn him about Pete, and then leave it at that. He, at least, wasn't her responsibility.

Lots of taxis passed with their lights on, but it was a fine evening and her shoes were flat so she ignored them. She was glad of the exercise, and of the chance to walk off the fear that she'd screwed up by going to the pub.

Ahead, all her favourite buildings glowed palely in the mixture of moon- and lamplight. She settled down to enjoy the walk. The distances were deceptive, and it took her a good half-hour to walk round the curve of the river, skirting the old red-brick wall of Lambeth Palace and then the hospital to get to Waterloo Station. Turning right at the roundabout, she plunged under the station's bridges and hurried through the scary emptiness so that she could reach The Cut.

She hadn't realized how late it was until she saw theatre-goers pouring out of the Old Vic, but it was good to have the streets full of people again. So far she had never even had her bag snatched, but her flat had been invaded more than once and she would never feel completely safe on her own in London after dark.

There was a savoury smell of roasting meat, as though one of the restaurants had just opened its kitchen door. She pushed through the crowds streaming up towards Waterloo Bridge and saw two men huddled over a brazier on the little square opposite the theatre. They were wearing old overcoats and were surrounded by plastic and canvas bags. The smell of meat was stronger here. One man turned his dirty bearded face towards her, and she saw he was tearing a roasted pigeon in half to eat.

It was like a scene out of a medieval judgement painting. His round, startled eyes and straggly beard, as much as the charred meat in his hands, made him look just like one of the minor devils in the bottom corner of the painted hell she'd once seen on the west wall of a small country church.

Sobered, she walked on. What had happened to her city that homeless men were reduced to cooking and eating vermin on the streets, inches away from people who had just paid upwards of thirty pounds each to sit and watch a play?

Plunging into darker, emptier streets after she'd crossed Blackfriars Bridge Road, she walked under more railway bridges and past the bulk of more rough sleepers. She hurried on, looking straight ahead. At last, she was at her own iron staircase and a moment later inside the flat and double-locking the door.

The phone was ringing. She reached for it.

'Allo? Allo?' said an unmistakably French female voice, before asking whether she would accept the charge of a call from Calais.

Curious to know who could possibly be phoning her from France, she agreed to pay for the call and a moment later heard Will's voice, breathless with gratitude.

It took some time before she could understand what he was trying to tell her, but then she grasped his need to give someone all the information he'd collected in case something prevented him getting home with it.

'If I could've found an Internet café I'd have emailed you, Trish,' he said. 'But I can't. The only one I've seen is shut, and I haven't got a mobile with me to text with. Can I tell you?'

'Fire away.'

To pacify him, as well as to get the facts clear, she switched on her laptop and, with the phone between her ear and her shoulder, quickly typed up everything he was saying, without thinking very much about any of it. Even so, she had plenty of questions to ask. They would have to wait until he was calmer and she wasn't having to type with the phone clamped between her chin and her neck, sending pain shooting through her.

'I've got all that down,' she assured him.

'On your computer?'

'Yes, Will, on my computer.' What did it matter how she'd recorded it?

'Will you run Jamie's video again then, and see if you can make out any markings on the plane?'

'What, now?' She tried not to feel like an impatient nanny.

'God, no. The call must be costing you a fortune anyway. But as soon as I'm off the line. And if there are some markings, will you find out what they mean? Where it's registered or whatever little aeroplanes have to be. There must be a number on it somewhere.'

'OK. Now, are you all right, Will, after all those adventures?'

'Sure. A bit hacked about the hands, and I've got nettle rash all over my face, and a wrenched ankle. Otherwise I'm fine.' He laughed and she hoped he was telling the truth. 'Can I come and see you tomorrow? There are things we need to talk about.'

She felt tired at the prospect, but there was no good reason why he shouldn't. Ashamed of her reluctance, she told him to meet her at the flat at eight in the evening.

'I'll feed you,' she added, out of some obscure impulse to make up for his torn hands and nettled face. And maybe to make up a bit for disappointing Pete Hartland. And definitely out of conscience for London men so poor they had to catch and cook a street pigeon.

'Great, so long as it's not sausages from the local deli. Bye, Trish. You've been fantastic. I'll pay you back for all of it as soon as I can.'

He clicked off the phone. It rang again almost at once.

'Trish?'

'Hello, Antony. What's up?'

'You've been out.' He paused, waiting for her to tell him where.

'I told you: I had things to do.'

'So you did. Well, I've been dining at the Oxo Tower with friends,' he said. 'They've gone off now, so I thought I might come and take a cup of coffee off you. You're only about five minutes' walk from here, aren't you?'

'I am, but I'm on my way to bed.'

'Perfect. I could join—'

'I'm sure they can get you a cab at the restaurant,' she said cheerfully.

'Let me come and talk to you, Trish. I'm not going to ravish you.' There was enough mockery in his voice to make believing him a matter of pride. 'You must know that.'

'All right. I'll put some coffee on. See you in five minutes.'

When she'd filled the kettle, she flung cold water over her face and rubbed it dry on the nearest tea towel. No one could walk along the streets where she'd been this evening and keep her face clean. Seeing the grime on the tea towel, she was glad she'd thought of it. There wasn't time to brush her hair, so she pushed it behind her ears, and left the tarting up at that.

The kettle boiled. She poured it over the coffee grounds, breathing in the scent with pleasure, and looked for biscuits. She never ate them, but she couldn't believe George would have left himself without any emergency rations, even in a part-time abode. No, here they were: delicious-looking foreign ones covered in thick dark chocolate. She put them on a tray, added coffee cups and the pot. There was no need to bother with milk or sugar. She knew Antony's tastes as well as her own.

He arrived just as she was putting the tray in the middle of one of the black sofas by the huge open fireplace that divided the eating from the sitting ends of her main room. When she opened the door, she saw he was wearing much less formal clothes than usual: a loose buff-coloured linen suit and no tie. The light over the door sparkled on his blond hair, and the shadows it cast took away the ordinariness of his square face. She couldn't see much of his eyes.

'Come in,' she said, standing aside.

He kissed her cheek, then tugged gently at one of the muddled strands of her hair. 'What on earth have you been doing to yourself?'

'Nothing. I walked a long way this evening and it got tousled.' She led the way to the sofa, telling him about the men and their pigeon.

'Ugh, don't, Trish. It's hardly the most romantic subject. And I had pigeon breast for dinner.' He touched his throat. His long fingers were tanned, but the skin of his neck, which hardly ever saw the sun, was very pale.

'Sorry.' She poured coffee into both cups and offered him one. He took it but didn't drink.

'And this isn't very romantic either, Trish. You must know I didn't really come for coffee.'

'No, I don't. You said you weren't going to ravish me.'

He laughed. 'True, but that doesn't mean I wasn't hoping you might ravish me. The prospect has been haunting my dreams these last few weeks.'

'Antony, we need to get something straight. I don't think you can have believed me when I told you that in all respects except the straightforwardly legal, I'm married to George.'

'So?' The wicked seducer's glint was in his eyes, making them brighter than ever, and his eyebrows were peaking. That reassured her.

'What d'you mean, "so"?'

'Trish,' he said, putting his cup down on the tray and peering into her eyes. 'You're not telling me you've never made love with anyone else, are you?'

'Since George and I got together?' she said, leaning away from his scrutiny and the significance of the surprise in his voice. 'Of course I haven't. That's what I meant. I didn't think you could have believed me.'

'Then why have you never married the poor brute?'

'He's not a poor brute, Antony,' she said, summoning up all her hard-learned advocacy skills. Now, if ever, was the time to use them; she had to make him understand. 'Although if we'd married, either he or I would probably have become one by now.'

'Oh, come on, Trish. That's taking cynicism too far.'

'I don't think so. I've never seen a marriage in which both parties were completely equal. George and I are. We're like free sovereigns of independent states. And that's why it's safe.'

Antony didn't say anything, but she was glad to see no sign of a sneer on his broad-cheeked face. He looked around the big room, as though searching for clues to her character.

'If you feel like that,' he said at last, 'why do you always give the impression that you could walk away tomorrow?'

'I didn't know I did.'

'You do. Take it from me.'

She smiled. How to explain her reality to someone for whom commitment clearly didn't meant what it meant to her?

'I couldn't walk away,' she said, surprising herself, 'but if George did, I would survive.'

'Is that what you're afraid of?' Suddenly he was gentle. She had to look away, knowing her face would be naked. 'Trish? Are you so unable to believe in yourself that you think George might leave you? By God, you are, aren't you?'

'I suppose so.' She frowned. No one else had ever made her explain her philosophy and so she'd never had to think it through. 'But even that would be better than being trapped in the kind of marriage so many people have, where they spend their whole time finding devious ways to punish each other.'

'Come on, Trish! There aren't many that are that bad.'

'Of course there are.' Now it was her turn to be surprised. 'Have you never listened to couples sniping? Or seen the hurt that makes the victims' eyes go dead? And then, later, watched how they take revenge? I see them everywhere and wonder how anyone could bear it.'

He seized the coffee tray and carried it over to the table, then came back to pull her to her feet. He put both arms around her and she felt one of his hands cradling the back of her head. She was too tall to tuck her head under his chin.

'You're nuts, you know. George is besotted with you. It's written all over him. And you're more than tough enough to deal with anything he or anyone else could do to you.' He rubbed her back, then let her go. However clumsily she'd expressed herself, she could see that she'd done what was necessary.

'This explains a lot. You know, if you learned to trust yourself, you'd be able to trust other people more easily. I'll see you in chambers on Monday. Take care of yourself, Trish.'

When he'd gone, she took four of George's chocolate biscuits up to bed and ate them there, hoping he might phone.

Back in the house, Tim watched Boney wipe his long purple tongue round the empty bowl then look up for more.

'You've had enough,' he said. 'You'd hate it if I let you get fat. Here, have some water.'

The sounds of Boney's tongue lapping and the water sloshing over the edge of the bowl were so familiar they helped a bit. But not enough. Tim had always known the journalist Bob had kicked to death couldn't have been working alone. Now he knew there'd been at least one colleague in France.

Thank God he'd seen the man hiding in the coppice before the thugs who loaded the return cargo on to his plane had, and warned him to keep quiet. And thank God the man had obeyed. If the thugs had spotted him, he'd probably be dead too. His survival was the one thing Tim could pride himself on in all this ghastly mess. It couldn't be long now before the whole thing unravelled. In some ways, the sooner the better; he couldn't take the suspense much longer. But he dreaded the moment of discovery.

He knew he'd never be able to resist interrogation for long. But he'd have to try or Bob would kill him.

Tim felt as though he were on a seesaw, bouncing from one impossibility to another. He had to have money. But if he went on earning it like this, he'd end up in prison. Or dead. Bob still owed him the cash for the last two flights. If he backed away again, he'd never get it, and his creditors' threats were getting worse. The money he was owed would keep most of them quiet. Somehow he had to get it. He was sure he could; just as he could find a reason not to fly that even Bob could accept.

Boney looked up, water dripping from either side of his mouth. Tim put his hand under the dog's chin and stared deep into his eyes. They looked kind. And they gave him an idea.

'Wish me luck, old friend,' he said.

He passed the shelf of oil jars and wicks, ignoring them. This time he didn't need a runway. He wasn't going anywhere.

Ten minutes later, he had the plane out of its shed and ready to go. He fired the engine and felt it begin to bounce over the grass. It wasn't much of a risk. Not really. Just a question of gauging the speed and the likely damage. And getting out fast in case the whole thing went up in flames.

He pressed harder on the throttle and let the plane begin to taxi.

Chapter 16

Will put down the phone. Now all he had to do was get the car back to the rental place in Calais and then find a quiet spot to sleep in until the train was ready. But he was itchy with the coolness of Trish's reception of his news. There was also a residue of fear at the bottom of his mind, like a kind of sludge, which would stop him getting much rest. He jiggled the coins in his pocket, then took a risk and dialled the operator to ask for another reverse-charges call.

'Will?' Mandy's squeak was as excited as ever.

So, he thought, she doesn't bear any malice. It may still be OK.

'Where are you, Will? What are you doing in France? And why have you reversed the charges?'

To lie or not to lie? That wasn't even a question. He knew he had to do it, if he wasn't to spoil everything with her. He just hoped he could make her believe him.

'I came over here to see a mate. He's marrying a French girl. They were all over each other in the bar, and they've gone home now. It made me miss you, Mandy. And I've run out of dosh. I wanted . . .' He hesitated.

'What? Don't make me guess, Will. I'm all stupid with sleep. I've been in bed for hours. I have to get up at six, you know.'

He thought of her, downy and sweet in her big white bed, with the dawn light breaking through the muslin curtains. He wished he were there, instead of stuck in this dim café in the middle of Normandy, far too hungry to bear the smell of *steak-frites* that had just been brought to the table nearest the phone. He turned his back on it.

'Listen, Mandy, I'm booked on the first Eurostar tomorrow morning. You're not all that far from Ashford. I could get off there. Then if you came and met me, we could . . .'

'What could we do, Will?' Her voice sounded much more awake now, and dancing on the edge of a laugh. 'Tell me. Exactly.'

He leaned against the side of the phone box and told her exactly, listening to her slide between breathlessness and a giggle.

'I work on Saturdays, but I suppose I could have a migraine,' she said after a while, 'if you really can spend the whole day with me.'

'All day, sweetie,' he said, his eyes closing as he thought about it. He had to get to Trish's flat in time for dinner. 'Till about half-past six anyway.'

'I'll be on the platform. Promise you won't go to sleep and miss the stop? I'll never forgive you, if you do.'

'I promise.'

Even when she'd gone, he hung on to the receiver to keep the moment with him a little longer. Someone rapped on his shoulder. Half dazed, he looked round and saw an angry man in a shabby dark-blue jacket, his finger jabbing towards the cradle. Will nodded, said an elaborate English farewell to the empty receiver, then put it back on the phone. As he moved away to make room for the man, he murmured a '*je m'excuse*'. The man grunted and hunched his shoulders around the phone to guarantee his privacy.

Will had some uncharitable thoughts about unnecessary aggression, then paid his tiny bill and went out to the car. As he was opening the door, he heard the rumble of an enormous lorry and looked round. Either there were a lot of English meat lorries in this particular part of Normandy, or the one he'd seen before had turned round and come back. He set off after it, trying to believe it would be too much of a coincidence for the driver to have been heading to the farm outside Sainte Marie-le-Vair. Will wished he'd had the guts to wait a bit longer and see everything, in spite of the dogs.

Just in case it was relevant, he took a pen out of his pocket and scrawled the registration number and the carrier's name on the back of his other hand.

Trish had brought her coffee and bacon sandwich back upstairs to bed and piled all four pillows behind her. She should have felt like purring. She had no work to do today and no David to amuse or take to his rowing club. She could stay in bed as long as she liked and wallow in her lovely solitude. And she could eat the bacon sandwich in peace. It was just about the only kind of food George truly detested, so it was a treat she kept for his absences.

But with her head full of Will and what he had been doing, she couldn't even begin to relax. There was Kim too. She might be safe now, but would she ever feel secure? And with this kind of start in life, how would she ever achieve any sort of happy relationship in the future? It was hard enough with a normal childhood behind you.

Trish finished her coffee, and brushed crumbs off the front of her T-shirt. She put the tray on the floor and shook out the news section of the paper, hoping to fend off her thoughts.

'Leave comfort root room,' she muttered, quoting Hopkins as easily as if he'd been her favourite poet in the first place.

She forced her head further back into the pillows and felt their softness rise up around her. As she started to read, she made herself take in every word of the article, until the familiar discipline had pushed her uncomfortable ideas to one side. Most of them anyway.

The shriek of the doorbell startled her out of a piece about floods and starvation in Bangladesh. It took moments before her head was clear. The bell rang again. She looked at the clock. Who on earth could be trying to get into her flat at half past eleven on a Saturday morning?

The bell rang a third time, on and on, as though someone was leaning on it. Trish dropped the paper and slid out of bed, pulling down her outsize T-shirt. The long mirror by the door told her it covered a fair amount of her thighs, so she pattered down the spiral staircase to protest at the interruption.

She opened the door and found herself staring at Antony's wife.

'Good lord! Liz!' Trish brushed her hair out of her eyes, trying to forget that Antony had come to the flat last night and revealed himself as someone quite different from the brilliant, witty cynic she'd thought she knew.

Even though Elizabeth Shelley must have come almost straight from the airport, she looked as though she'd just emerged from a three-hour session in the hairdresser's and been given a professional makeup. Her light summer dress was pale and fluttery and her bare legs were silken smooth above the Jimmy Choo sandals.

'You'd better come in. Sorry I'm not dressed, but I wasn't expecting—'

'No, I'm sure you weren't, Trish. But I'd like to talk to you.'

'Sure,' Trish said, wishing she'd had some warning of this.

Elizabeth wasn't the kind of drama-queen to rant or howl about other women trying to steal her husband, but Antony was the only reason she would have come uninvited like this. Trish tugged the T-shirt even further down her long, thin thighs.

'Look, Liz, I was asleep. I'm a bit fuddled still. Could I leave you for a moment while I put some clothes on? Then I'll make us some coffee.'

Liz looked at Trish's chest, then up again with an expression of the clearest contempt she had seen in anyone except opposing counsel. Suddenly she remembered the slogan on her T-shirt and felt as if she'd been dipped in hot wax. It read: 'So many men. So little time.'

'It's a joke of my father's,' she said quickly. 'He sent it to me as a peace offering after he came here and caused trouble between George and David one day.'

Liz didn't comment, so Trish ran back upstairs, trying to decide how much to say and how much to withhold when Liz started to ask questions.

Five minutes later, Trish was back, with cleaned teeth and brushed hair. Her blue jeans were firm and tight enough to feel like armour. The pink silk shirt with its deep V-neck might send out another wrong message, but it was the first clean one she'd found. She waved to Liz and headed for the kitchen, saying that she'd make some coffee.

'Not for me,' Liz said. 'I had too much for breakfast, so I'm already buzzing.'

'What about tea, then?' Trish called from the kitchen. She needed the support of caffeine. 'Or some mineral water or something?'

'I'm fine.'

Trish put two large cups on the tray anyway, with a jug of milk. There were still some of George's glamorous chocolate biscuits left, so she added them. The kettle boiled and she filled the cafetière.

The sofa was big enough for both women, with about four feet of space between them. Trish put the tray down in the gap, trying not to remember last night, and poured a cup of coffee.

'Help yourself if you change your mind,' she said, tucking her bare feet up under her bum. She'd decided to broach the subject of Antony herself, rather than wait for Liz to do it.

'Did you come back because of the weather? Antony said you

were having the most ghastly rain. It seems very unfair that Tuscany should be wet while London basks in the sun.'

'So he talked about me, did he?'

'Only about the holiday. Just as I talked to him about George and David, who are in Australia. Liz, what's the matter?'

She opened her quilted leather handbag and took from it a folded sheet of paper.

'Go on,' she said, handing the paper to Trish. 'Read it. It was sent Special Delivery, which is why I got it in Italy only about a week after it was sent.'

Trish felt a frown bunching the muscles between her eyes. She opened the letter and read:

Dear Liz,

I know it's a while since we've been in touch, but I couldn't let this pass without warning you. Antony is swanning all over London at the moment with Trish Maguire, his junior on the case we're doing. He can barely keep his hands off her and she looks like the cat that's got the cream. They can be seen eating together most nights and, as for the rest . . . well, I won't sully your eyes with a full description of what's going on.

You'd be well advised to come back and put a stop to it. Quite apart from the damage it's doing to Antony's reputation, it's going to make it very hard for you to come back into a world in which everyone knows he'd rather hang out with his girlfriend than holiday with you and the children.

Yours ever

Ferdy Aldham.

Trish wanted to wash. She refolded the letter and handed it back.

'I'm surprised he signed it,' she said. 'That kind of slime is usually anonymous.'

'Is it?' Liz raised her beautifully arched eyebrows. 'I wouldn't know. But then I have never been the target of anything like this before.'

Trish uncurled her legs and let her bare feet lie flat on the polished wood floor. They looked huge beside Liz's delicate sandals. 'Come off it, Liz. You don't really think it's true, do you?'

'Isn't it? I can always tell when Antony's after someone new. He was like a peacock with a new tail when he refused to let me postpone the journey to Tuscany. That bloody judge has a lot to answer for.' She poured an inch of coffee into the bottom of the white bowl-like cup and sipped it, shuddering at the strength.

This was horrible. Trish couldn't honestly say that she hadn't been flirting with Antony, but it wasn't going to help Liz to know that he'd propositioned her and been turned down.

'I know we're not exactly soulmates, Trish.'

Liz was also looking down at their contrasting feet. Then she glanced up and Trish felt her breath stop for an instant. Liz's expression showed that this was no matter of wounded dignity. She had been hurt in just the way Trish would have been if George had said he wanted someone else.

'But I'd never have thought you capable of something like this.'

Trish wondered whether Antony knew how much his wife cared. How could the man who'd shown such sensitivity last night not have noticed something as obvious as this? But if he knew how much he hurt his wife, how could he carry on as he did?

'Liz,' she said, trying to hide her pity because she had a feeling it would come across as the worst kind of insult, 'Ferdy knows nothing about me or my life. I don't have affairs with anyone, but even if I did I wouldn't sleep with my head of chambers. It would be madness.'

Liz's face looked as if she'd just had a dozen Botox injections, stiffened into immobility.

'It's true that we've had dinner while you've been away,' Trish added, 'but have you ever known a case in which counsel didn't eat together?'

Do I confess to the flirtation, she wondered, or is that just going to make it harder for her to believe me?

The first signs of doubt were reducing the Botox-effect a little. Liz's skin even showed a few wrinkles as her eyes and mouth moved.

Watching them, Trish felt an even bigger surge of sympathy. What must it be like to keep finding yourself face to face with women who had reason to think they knew more about your husband than you did? You'd feel as though you'd been rolled out with the garbage. You'd have to wonder, too, how much he'd said to them about your failings and your private fears about yourself.

'Why do you suppose,' Trish said slowly, 'a man like Ferdy Aldham would send this kind of truly revolting letter?'

Liz shook her head. The immaculate blonde hair didn't move, but her grey-blue eyes showed all the vulnerability she wanted to hide.

'I heard the other day that he and Antony have hated each other since Bar school,' Trish went on, trying to protect Liz as well as she could. 'I think this could be part of their long-running fight for supremacy.'

Unless, Trish thought in fiercer anger, it's just a tactic to throw Antony's concentration and distract him from the case. If so, I want Ferdy reported to the Bar Council. How could he do this much damage to a woman like Liz for career advantage or private satisfaction? What a bastard!

'Have you talked to Antony about it?'

'What's the point?' Liz put the letter back in her bag and clicked it shut. The gilt chain rattled as it fell back on the sofa.

'He's the best liar in Christendom. And he'd only make me feel stupid for asking. And rather disgusting. "Prurient" is the word he always uses.'

That didn't sound anything like the man who'd sat on the same sofa only about twelve hours ago. Trish thought of his eventual acceptance of her description of mutually punishing marriages and wondered just how much he might have recognized in it.

Will rolled over and lay on his back, gazing at the ceiling. Mandy kissed his shoulder. He breathed in the heady mixture of sex and clean sheets and the little herby pillow she kept tucked under the real ones. He slid his arm under her and pulled her right up against his side, twisting his head so that he could kiss her hair.

'You're lovely,' he said.

'And you're the first man that's ever talked to me after.'

'D'you mind?'

'Don't be daft. I love it. But you're allowed to go to sleep, too. You must be knackered after getting the early train like that.'

'Oh, Mandy, you're a woman in a million.' His eyelids did feel a bit heavy. And his mind was working at half its usual speed. It turned up a memory he'd meant to deal with sooner. 'Did they make any trouble for you at work?'

'No. I made it sound as if I was really ill. They didn't question it for a second. I'm a really good actress, you know.'

'I'll bet you are.' He kissed her again, then let her go, to give himself up to the rolling waves of sleep he could feel rushing towards him. Something held it up for an instant, some faint worry, but it wasn't enough to keep it back for long.

Liz left eventually, but the miasma of her distress and Ferdy's malice hung over the flat. So did the memory of the fun Trish and Antony had had flirting. Trish flung the last of the coffee down the sink and put the cups into the dishwasher, noticing the thick smear of Liz's lipstick on one.

Trish had to get out of the flat. Outside, she hailed the first free cab she saw and asked the driver to take her to the Black Eagle in Vauxhall. He looked a bit doubtful, but she assured him she knew what she was doing.

The pub was closed after the lunchtime rush, but there were all the sounds of cleaning she'd expected when she reached its front door. No one answered her knock there, and she wasn't going to try to summon anyone through the double cover of the pavement hatch that must lead down to the cellars. There had to be a back door somewhere for the kitchen staff and supplies. She walked round the sides of the big brick building until she found it. There were a couple of bells beside the newly painted door. She pressed the top one. There was no answer to that either, so she tried the one below.

A young woman, barely out of her teens, opened the door. She was wearing a neat mesh hairnet, the female equivalent of the Smithfield meat porters' hats, and a clean white overall.

'Yes?'

'Hi. My name's Trish Maguire. I was wondering if I could speak to someone.'

'What about?'

'I was in the pub yesterday and there was a bit of a barney. One of the barmen came to my rescue, and I'd like to thank him. I've got a couple of questions for him, too.'

'A barman?' She sounded half-witted.

'What is it, Jo?' asked a male voice from the darkness behind her.

Trish recognized the man she wanted. She smiled and held out her right hand, saying her name again, and went on, 'I'd very much like to talk to you.'

'This is the landlord,' Jo said, 'not one of the barmen.'

'All the better. Great. Might I come in?'

'I'll deal with this, Jo. You go back to the kitchen. Sure,' he said, turning to Trish. 'Come on through.'

He led her through the pool room and on into the big bar at the front. Two fit young men were busy with vacuum cleaners and a third was polishing the bar. All the windows were open. Even so, the air was heavy with old cigarettes, hard to breathe and thoroughly unpleasant. Trish made sure she wasn't wrinkling her nose.

'Can I get you something?' he asked.

'That's kind. Umm, tomato juice?'

'Sure.' He was back a moment later with a glass and a small bottle of juice for her. He had a Coke for himself. 'What can I do for you?'

'I wanted to ask you about Daniel Crossman. That's the man you saved me from last night.'

'I know who he is. But who are you? Last night you said you weren't the police. You don't look like any social worker I've ever met. So what's your interest in this?'

'I'm a barrister. I used to work in family law. I've been a kind of consultant in the case.'

'Been?'

'Yes.' Liking the look of this man, and still grateful for last night's intervention, she wasn't going to lie to him. 'Any formal involvement is over now.'

'So you're just poking your nose in?'

Trish smiled. 'That's right. But if a few more people poked their noses into this sort of thing, fewer children would be killed by their stepfathers. You must know that.'

He drank some Coke, then put down the glass. 'I'm Mick Thompson by the way.'

'Hi. How long have you had the pub?'

'A while now.' He hesitated, then added, 'I'm one of the lucky ones. I have work that's worth doing, an income, and a wife who isn't afraid of me.'

'Unlike Crossman?'

He confirmed it with a crisp nod.

'What's his problem?' Trish asked. 'In particular, I mean.'

'He lost everything when he lost the army. Most of the blokes who come here did.' He wasn't looking at her.

'The job and income, you mean?' she asked, remembering her own views of how hard Crossman must have found the real world after he'd been pushed out of the army.

'More than that. Don't you see? Everything about you that's valued in the service is wrong when you come out. You've learned to be tough. You've worked for self-discipline and the right to discipline other people. You're trained to fight and endure. And to kill. Then you find yourself in a few poky little rooms, penned up with kids yowling and a woman who nags on at you to talk about bits of yourself you don't even want to know you've got. And your only exercise is shopping – which you always get wrong – or changing the kids' nappies. And woe betide you if you lay a finger on anyone, or even slam your fist into the wall.'

'So, you're not talking about post-traumatic stress or anything like that?'

'No.' He did look up then. There was a faint smile around his lips. 'There's plenty of that, too, of course. We've blokes come in here who've been in Afghanistan, which was an almighty fuck-up; Bosnia; the Gulf. And Ireland, of course – always Ireland. Most of us have done several tours there. We even get some from the Falklands. None of them have forgotten. But in most cases that's not it.'

'So what is, apart from what you've already said?'

'Isn't it enough?'

'You look like a man with more to say,' she said, and was relieved to hear him laugh, even though there wasn't much pleasure in the sound.

'It took me a long time to understand, but you get used to

having an enemy,' he said at last, his gaze now on one of his helpers, neatly coiling the long flex of the cleaner with as much care as though it was the fuse of an incendiary device. 'Losing that leaves a big empty space in your life.'

Trish didn't take long to decode Thompson's last comment. 'Are you saying the families get put there?'

'Yup. And it takes a strong woman to get you out of the habit. My wife did it for me, but she's exceptional. I went through all the usual stuff: you know, silence, anger, non-cooperation; violence, even. She didn't let me get away with any of it. We've made it this far because of her.'

'And Crossman hasn't got anyone like that?' As she spoke, Trish thought of Will, and the wife who'd left him.

'Doesn't seem like it.'

'You've never met his wife?'

'Nope. Not many of the women come in here. Not the young ones, anyway. They don't like it. And the lads need to be with their own kind once in a while to sit quiet or talk about things like the AK47 so they don't have to think about the mess inside their heads. Otherwise, they blow.'

'I can see how it must help, but it's tough on the families.'

'The whole thing's tough on them.'

'What about Crossman's stepdaughter?' Trish asked, which was what she'd come to do. 'You obviously know what's going on in his household – the police suspicions and so on. Have you any idea what he could have been doing to her?'

'No.' Thompson's voice deepened. 'But he wouldn't be the first to put a child in the space he keeps for his enemy.'

He cares, Trish thought, he really cares. Aloud she said, 'A fragile, six-year-old girl? Are you sure?'

'Anyone can get put there if they threaten something you need.' His expression hardened into something much more like the faces she'd seen last night. 'You don't have to look at me like that. It's not only blokes who do it. Haven't you ever seen a young mother trying to feed a child who won't eat? Mouth clamped shut, spoon pushed away, mess all over the bib, bowl on the floor. That baby's the woman's enemy and they both know it. It may not often be a fight to the death, but it's always a trial of strength.'

Trish considered some of her friends who'd had children. Then she thought of Estella Welldon's terrifying book *Madonna, Mother, Whore*, which she'd turned to for enlightenment when she'd had a case in which it had been the mother who'd abused her child.

'What do you think Kim threatened in Crossman's life?' she asked, trying to forget.

'I don't know. But whatever it was will be why he went for her – if he did. They say no one's ever found a mark on her.'

Always that same phrase, Trish thought, as though the only cruelty that mattered was the kind that left physical marks on the body. And this time it had come from a man who must know all about modern techniques of breaking the will of a captured enemy. No one needed ropes and electrodes these days to get information out of anyone; not when they had sleep deprivation and drugs and all sorts of other ways of disorientating their victims.

Chapter 17

Will shook the blood out of his eyes and tried to make them work better. He could hear that Mandy was still breathing, but he wanted to see her. The gurgling sound told him her throat and lungs had to be full of blood. It wouldn't be long now.

He had his hands round the slaughterman's throat and thought for a bare second that he was winning. Then the man somehow got his hands up between Will's arms and forced them apart with such speed and power that he lost his grip. A fist like a hammer crashed into the side of his head. He tried to hit back. Seconds later something happened to his legs. They started to quiver. His balance was going and his vision with it. His knees buckled and he was down.

'Come on then.' A taunting voice broke through the dizziness and pain. 'On your feet, arsehole. Or have you had enough?'

Will fought himself and his fury and his knowledge that the gurgling from Mandy's throat had stopped. He dared not look towards her, for fear of what the man would do to him. He got as far as his knees. Now he could see the bastard's feet, never still for a moment. He thought of launching himself in a kind of rugby tackle. Then the man danced sideways. Will knew he'd be flat on his face if he tried. Blinking the last blur from his eyes and feeling blood pouring over his face, he pushed himself up. He could see again, even though a cut near one of his eyes was leaking blood into it.

The slaughterman was silhouetted against the white muslin curtains. His fists were up. Will couldn't make out his expression because of the dazzle.

'Come on, then. You think you're so tough you can mess about with a girl like Mandy, but you're nothing.' He wasn't even panting, in spite of the non-stop movement. 'A tosser who doesn't know his arse from his elbow or what you're meant to do with either. Come on then. It's different when you're facing a real man, i'n't it?'

He danced again from side to side. Then the miracle happened. One dancing sidestep took him into a puddle of Mandy's blood. His foot skidded and he fell. As he went down, his head caught on the open drawer of Mandy's dressing table. The crack was like a pistol shot in the little room and it galvanized Will.

An instant later he was sitting on the man's chest, ready to ride him like a bucking horse if he came round again. At last Will could look at Mandy, lying in a pool of her own blood under the window.

Her face was a pulpy red mass. Only her eyes were untouched. There was no light in them, no movement, no hint of anything happening in the brain behind them. But they seemed to be staring at him in accusation. He had to look away.

The pretty dressing gown was rucked up around her knees. He couldn't tell which red blobs were the roses printed on it and which the blood splatters. Her ghastly head was bent at a terrible angle.

She had to be dead. Even from where he sat, Will could tell that. You didn't grow up on a farm without recognizing death when you saw it. Not from this close anyway.

Had she known the man from the slaughterhouse was coming? Had she been involved in the whole scam all along? Was that why he'd found it so easy to get into her bed? And to make her tell him about the farm at Sainte Marie?

He groaned. What was it Mandy had said this morning? 'I'm a really good actress, you know.'

Had she set him up?

A siren whooped nearby. Then another. Someone must have called the police. No surprise really. They'd been making enough noise to worry a whole neighbourhood, what with him roaring like a bull, the man from the slaughterhouse shouting obscenities and Mandy screaming.

They were both quiet now. There was no urgency left anywhere in Will any longer. Not with Mandy dead and the man out cold between his thighs. Will eased himself off the man's chest.

Will struggled to his feet, and limped towards the door, heading for the stairs. His left arm dangled in a weird way, and the hand wouldn't do what he wanted. He tried to waggle the wrist and the grating of bone against bone told him he'd broken the arm. His head wasn't right either. There was a kind of swooping sensation in it and a buzzing in his ears.

The siren had stopped. Men were shouting and running up the pavement outside the house. Will was halfway downstairs, ready to let them in, forgetting the lock had already been burst open. A blur of blue and silver erupted towards him, bellowing. He couldn't tell if they were shouting questions or orders. The noise came in barks, sounding like the dogs in France. He leaned against the wall and let it support most of his weight as he slid down into a crouch at the side of the stairs.

One of the shouting men paused long enough to say, 'What's upstairs?'

'One dead girl and an unconscious man. At least, I left him unconscious.' His eyelids drooped and he thought he was going to fall. He put out a hand to steady himself, and a leaden foot trod it into the wood beneath. He couldn't help screaming as his knuckles cracked. Other hands pulled him upright and lugged him downstairs. Someone was talking about an ambulance.

Someone else was asking him questions about what he'd done. The voice rose until it was yelling like the rest, crashing into his head like the slaughterman's fists. Will hadn't the energy to answer anything. He didn't know what to say. He just wanted to pass out. A moment later, he got his wish.

Trish walked into a huge supermarket, trying to decide what to give Will to eat. Everything she saw seemed to hold catastrophe under its neat plastic wrappings. Even the plastic wrappings themselves had been involved in one of the endless food-scare stories she'd read. Someone had written about them contaminating food with cancer-causing chemicals.

As she leaned down to pick up two corn cobs, she saw that the box was littered with small black mouse droppings. Revolted, she went in search of a member of staff. A uniformed man was unpacking fruit a little further along the display case. She told him what she'd seen and watched a pleased smile widen his mouth.

'Is that what they are?' he said. 'I didn't know. But it makes sense because when I opened the box last week, a mouse jumped out.'

Eventually she left the vast store with a corn-fed chicken she proposed to roast to death, which ought to deal with any microbes lurking in its flesh. There were also a couple of potatoes in her bag, which she would bake, and some purple-sprouting broccoli. That could swim in a bath of boiling water for long enough to deal with anything except rogue prions (which she assumed vegetables couldn't have) or chemical contamination.

Thoughts of chemicals were still with her after she'd deposited her purchases in the fridge and sat down at her computer to make sense of Will's outpourings from last night.

Obedient to his instructions, she watched Jamie Maxden's video again. There were markings of some kind on the plane, but the film wasn't clear enough to distinguish them. Even when she used the enhancing programme, she couldn't see more than a blur. And there were no obvious landmarks around either. The roofs and trees and grass she could make out might be anywhere.

She peered again at the screen, trying to see more of the wrapped packages the men carried. It was still hard to tell exactly how long they were, but it was true that they looked pretty much the same size as the split carcasses she'd seen on the shoulders of men walking through Smithfield. If they had been sacks of chemicals, wouldn't the packages have flopped more than these? Maybe not, if they were packed tight enough. But then they wouldn't have that little bounce at the end with each stride.

Looking wasn't going to tell her any more, so she clicked off the video and brought up a screenful of Will's hurried information. She smiled as she thought of their first meeting and his flood of anger and explanation of what Furbishers had done to him and the others. That diatribe had been a lot harder to deal with than this. Then she'd had to listen and remember in order to pick the story out of the unnecessary detail. Now all she had to do was highlight each piece of real information and copy it to a new file.

Coffee became necessary towards the end of the afternoon and she brewed herself a whole pot. Then she abandoned the computer in favour of pencil and paper. Doodling had always brought her thoughts to order in the past and usually led her on to the questions that would open up the still hidden facts she needed.

Little pictures of aeroplanes crossing the Channel made her wonder why Will had felt it necessary to go to France and how he'd landed on any particular place there. Looking again at the video, she couldn't see anything to identify the field as belonging to any particular country, let alone a precise spot.

They'd assumed it had to be somewhere near the abattoir, where Jamie's body had been discovered. How had Will found the derelict farm in France?

She drank more coffee and was momentarily distracted. This wasn't just a hot wet drink with enough caffeine to make her brain cells jump. It was a rich, slightly powdery liquid with chocolate notes and just a hint of bitter caramel. Wonderful.

Refreshed, she remembered something about an aerial photographer in the notes she'd made of Will's story. Her eyes were drying out and her head was dizzy before she found it: a tiny comment in his description of a conversation he'd had in the pub near Smarden Meats, where he'd gone for information on the knife-happy slaughterman. Her notes were full enough to bring back memories of what he'd said last night.

'What I think is happening is that the slaughterman is stealing carcasses, or maybe just hijacking the ones that have been condemned and are supposed to be destroyed, although I don't know how he stops the Meat Hygiene Service people noticing they've gone from the condemned chiller. The pilot is flying them over to an illegal meat-processing plant in France, where they're butchered in the French way – which is quite different from the way we cut up meat. I imagine some must be sold locally, but I'm convinced that a sizeable proportion is brought back into this country through the Channel tunnel, probably in apparently respectable meat lorries but with faked documents, to sell at premium prices.'

Trish grabbed her pen to scrawl in the middle of her doodles, 'Why would anyone bother?'

At the beginning of her career at the Bar, she'd done a six-month pupillage with one of the criminal specialists in chambers. He'd become a judge years ago and she rarely saw him now. But he'd taught her that wherever there was money to be made legitimately, there was more to be made by criminals.

Even so, could transporting slabs of meat like this ever pay enough to justify the risk? She wished she knew more about the economics of the legitimate trade. It would be something to ask Will this evening. She added to her short list of questions.

'That's why no one's suspected them so far,' she read in the notes she'd made of his long explanation last night. 'Usually stolen or uncertified meat is flogged off very cheap in markets in little out-of-the-way towns, or sold at the back door of scruffy restaurants and takeaways. But if you make your stuff expensive enough and offer it through glamorous shops, people are much less likely to doubt it.'

But why does the meat have to go anywhere near France? If it's having faked documentation anyway, why not just take it from the abattoir to Ivyleaf Packaging? And if it has to go to France, why isn't it sold on there?

Maybe money wasn't Flesker's only motive, she thought, remembering Colin's account of the episode that had closed the family slaughterhouse. It had been EU regulations that had started their difficulties and a French vet who had compounded them. Maybe Flesker was taking revenge on the authorities by flying dodgy British meat to France and bringing it back under their noses to sell at a huge premium. But could even the combination of some cash and the satisfaction gained from revenge make this kind of exercise worthwhile?

She couldn't make sense of any of it, so she took herself off for a mind-clearing shower. As the water beat down on her head, she ran through her summing up of Will's story, still looking for the profit. Surely the pilot and his mates would earn enough from whatever they were doing only if the plane brought something back from France, after they'd delivered the meat. She thought of the email that had accompanied the video. 'I'll send you the rest later,' Jamie Maxden had promised.

Both she and Will had assumed that 'the rest' would be more shots of the men, their burdens and the plane. Or possibly something happening at Smarden Meats itself. What if it had been a record of the return journey with a revelation of its cargo? Her teeth clamped around her lip and frustration made her bite.

The chicken wasn't only cooked to death now; it was in danger of incineration. Trish turned down the oven. Where on earth was Will? She checked her watch for the fifth time, trying not to feel irritated. She told him to come at eight and he'd agreed. It was well after half past nine now. No wonder his sister had been so angry when her husband had been late home the other night. To have something cooked at an agreed time and then watch it spoil while you were left hanging, not able to eat yourself, or do anything else, because you didn't know when you were going to be called upon to serve up the food! Exasperating. And insulting. The message that came over loud and clear was 'your time is worth far less than mine'.

The phone rang. If this were Will, she thought, in a pub or caught up with a mate, she would be tempted to tell him to go straight home and then eat whatever remained edible beneath the charcoal on the chicken carcass by herself.

'Trish?' Antony's voice was neither languorously seductive nor sharply irritated. He sounded concerned and brisk. She hoped he wasn't going to say anything about Liz's visit. 'Sorry to interrupt your dinner.'

'No problem. What's up?'

'Will Applewood has got himself in trouble.'

'Oh, shit! What's he done?'

'No one's quite sure. He's in hospital in Kent after a fight. It's bad. There's a young woman dead, and another man with severe injuries. The fight took place in the woman's bedroom. No one yet knows which man was the aggressor, but Will got off more lightly, so it looks like him.'

Antony waited, as though for a comment, but Trish had nothing to say through the swirling mixture of anxiety and rage that was choking her.

'The other bloke isn't conscious yet,' he went on after a moment. 'They're both in hospital, under police guard. In due course one of them will almost certainly be charged with the woman's murder.'

There was no expletive fierce enough to deal with this. Trish waited for more.

'The last thing we need in the middle of the case is one of our clients getting himself charged with something like this, so I've got Petra to agree to act for Applewood.'

Petra Knighton was a legend in legal circles. At more than sixty, she was still known to be one of the toughest solicitors working in crime. She was almost equally dreaded and admired. There was a famous, possibly apocryphal, story of an ill-prepared barrister actually fainting when he saw her swinging towards him outside court one morning.

'She knows it'll have to be Legal Aid, and she's ready to go down to the hospital now to take instructions. Are you still there, Trish?'

'Yes. So Will's conscious, is he?' It was funny how you could talk even when your head was boiling and your throat clenched as though someone had his hands round it.

'Apparently. But before Petra talks to him, I thought you might brief her. I get the feeling you know rather more about Applewood and his recent activities than I.' There was a pause, as though Antony was waiting for a confession. 'You do, don't you, Trish?'

'Some. OK, I'll see her. When do you want us to meet?'

'Right away. She's here now and could be with you in ten minutes. OK?'

The grip on Trish's throat was easing as her mind began to work again. 'Antony, how do *you* know about this?'

'Applewood asked the police to inform chambers, rather than his family, or you, interestingly. I happened to be here and took the call.'

Yes, thought Trish, I can see why you might want to take refuge in chambers today. But it's rough on Liz.

'I see,' she said aloud. 'OK. Yes, do send Petra round.'

Petra Knighton had short straight white hair cut very blunt, round brown eyes, and a complexion any twenty-year-old would envy. She was shorter than Trish, but just as slight, and she was wearing casually elegant dark-grey silk trousers and a loose collarless jacket the colour and texture of old-fashioned string. Her narrow feet were bare inside flat taupe-leather loafers.

'So let me get this right,' she said, putting down her whisky. 'This over-emotional, virtually destitute man, whose professional and economic life is hanging in the balance until the end of the action against Furbishers Foods, took time off court to track down the source of some sausages that made you and a friend of yours ill?'

'That's right.' Trish was drinking yet more coffee. She needed a clear head to deal with her own confusion as much as the questions. 'After he'd given all his evidence. I mean, obviously I didn't see him outside court while he was doing that.'

Petra just looked at her with chilly disapproval.

'Anyway, the hunt for the infected sausages was how it all started,' Trish said. 'Then he latched on to something bigger; more dramatic, anyway.'

She described the video and the news that Jamie Maxden had apparently committed suicide under the wheels of a pantechnicon parked outside the abattoir she had visited with Will.

'It was his death that first upped the stakes,' she said. 'Will couldn't accept that the man he'd known would ever have committed suicide. Then we recognized in the video one of the men we'd seen when we toured the abattoir itself. He'd seemed short fused then, and potentially violent. I have since discovered that he has done time for assault.'

Trish realized she hadn't been entirely honest and admitted a moment later that it had been she who had recognized Bob Flesker, not Will.

'Before you go on,' Petra said, making a note on her pale-blue lined pad, 'why did you go to this abattoir?'

Why do I feel as though I'm being interviewed in a police station? Trish wondered. What has Antony said to this woman to make her treat me like a suspect?

'There's a whole chain of reasons,' she said, before recapping them all.

'That's all very well,' Petra said, not making any notes, 'but why did *you* go, rather than just Applewood?'

Trish explained about Will's lack of confidence and her urge to help in any way she could. Hoping she didn't sound like a complete pushover, and wondering all over again how much he had not told her, she added a comment about her dislike of trotting around the country with one of her clients before the end of the case.

'That figures,' Petra said. 'Then what?'

Trish had never been briefed by Petra's firm, so she had no idea whether this hectoring attitude was typical. The one thing she could be sure of was that Petra was the best available. Antony only ever dealt with the best.

'Then he borrowed two hundred quid off me. I didn't know why he wanted it until he phoned me from France last night. He rang to tell me what he'd seen there, in case something happened to him.'

Trish looked at the solicitor, knowing she would think this casual loan to a man in Will's state quite irresponsible. It probably had been. But Trish couldn't grovel for absolution or comfort now. It wasn't dignified, and in any case there wasn't time for self-indulgence with Will under police guard in hospital. Instead, she described what he'd told her of his adventures at the French farm.

'Oh, yes, the only other thing was that right at the beginning he sent another sample of the doubtful sausages to some food-testing lab and the results came back negative. All they found were faint traces of a growth-promoting drug and bleach. I didn't understand the significance of the bleach at the time, but it excited Will.'

Petra nodded, pushed her rimless spectacles further up her small nose, and wrote a few notes. Laying down the pad and balancing her fountain pen on top, she said, 'And so is it your analysis that today's episode is part of his quixotic quest into the origins of the infected sausages, or some other, private, fight?'

Trish shrugged, not out of carelessness but because she had no answer.

'I wish I knew. At first I thought he was a vulnerable man, so open that he told me everything. That's clearly not true. I have no idea who this woman could be or what he was doing in her bedroom.' Trish shut her eyes and pressed her fingers into the lids. 'I wouldn't have thought him capable of killing anyone. But how do I know?'

'Indeed.'

Trish opened her eyes again. Petra's expression hadn't changed. 'I'm sorry I can't be more help.'

'Yes, it's a pity. As this stands, I don't think it's a story to share with the plods.'

'Probably not,' Trish said, fighting for her proper professional detachment. 'I can't see some hard-pressed DI wanting to delve into a closed suicide case and a possible international trade in contaminated meat at this juncture.'

Petra produced a small dry cough of laughter. 'I don't care about that. All I want to avoid is some over-dramatic DI deciding that you gave my client money and sent him charging down to Kent on a mission to wipe out the makers of the sausages you thought might kill your best friend. A story like that would screw up the case you're doing with Antony. It wouldn't help your reputation much either. And if that's tarnished, Antony's going to look a fool for putting so much faith in you.'

Trish was beyond comment.

'The police have got plenty to work on without that,' Petra went on. 'A sexy young woman wearing nothing but a negligee is found lying dead, while two strong young men tried to beat each other to death over her corpse. But it helps me to have the background. At least I'll know what I'm dealing with if Applewood starts to launch into any of this meat farrago.'

'Don't you think there's anything in his story?'

Petra stretched her face into a dolorous mask. 'Happily I don't have to decide. It could be true. I'd have thought it more likely to be a fantasy made up to impress you. That's the kind of thing a certain type of young man does.'

'Not often when he's dealing with counsel.' Trish thought her dry delivery would have made even Antony proud. She was glad to see that Petra did not really suspect her of sending Will off on his mission.

'Be that as it may,' Petra said, unimpressed, 'the only facts you have are that you visited an abattoir, in which there works a man who looks like one of the figures in a grainy film William Applewood sent you by email. He told you the film had been made by another man, who apparently committed suicide outside that same abattoir, but you have no proof of who shot the film. And Applewood provided the video only after news reports of the death were published in the local papers. It wouldn't be hard to make up the whole thing, would it? Particularly not when your own illness must have made you receptive to food-based scare stories.' She looked at Trish over slipping spectacles, then pushed them up her short nose again. 'As you'd have seen in an instant if this were your case and you were not emotionally involved with one of the participants.'

'May I get you some more whisky?' Trish asked coldly. She was not emotionally involved with Will. Nor could he have been trying to impress her. 'I did check the story about Jamie Maxden being found under the wheels of a meat lorry. It was true.'

'Of course it was. But Applewood had plenty of time to read it and work his fantasies around it before he offered them to you, hadn't he?'

'I'll be interested to hear whether you feel the same once you've met and talked to him,' Trish said. 'I'm sure he's more trustworthy than you think.'

To herself she added silently: at least, I hope he is.

'Let's hope you're right,' Petra said. 'Even if you are, this will definitely run better as a straightforward account of a summer afternoon's dalliance interrupted by a jealous rival.' Once more the glasses had slipped. The eyes that looked out over the top of them seemed colder than ever. 'The question is: which man was the rival?'

'I know,' said Trish, as she recovered from a sudden sinking sensation in her gut. 'Now, *would* you like more whisky?'

'Thank you, no. I have to drive into Kent.' Petra drained the glass Trish had given her when she arrived and stood up, fitting the fountain pen neatly into the inside pocket of her jacket. 'For what it's worth, I shan't pass this story on to Antony, and I'd advise you to keep it quiet too.'

Trish stood, waiting by the front door.

'He has a very high opinion of you,' said Petra, in a voice that suggested she did not share it.

A moment later she was out of the front door, leaving Trish to wrestle her way out of the outrage and fear that had dropped over her like a gladiator's net. When Petra was halfway down the iron staircase, Trish remembered Will's running down them himself. She called the older woman's name. Petra paused, then turned her head.

'You *will* let me know how it goes, won't you?' Trish said.

'Emotionally involved.' Petra beckoned. 'I knew it.'

Trish put the door on the latch and walked down ten steps to join her.

'You have to face it.' Petra's eyes were no longer quite so cold. There even seemed to be some pity in them. She put a hand on Trish's shoulder. 'Applewood could be a killer.'

Chapter 18

On Sunday morning Trish wasn't even tempted to lounge around having breakfast in bed. Feeling like death, she was up by eight and had to force herself to wait until ten before phoning Jamie Maxden's sister.

When the phone was answered, Trish introduced herself, then tried to make her questions seem legitimate by saying, 'I hadn't realized your brother was dead. I didn't see anything in the papers.'

'I don't know why not. I put an expensive notice in *The Times* with details of the service at the crematorium.' Mrs Blake's voice was jagged with grievance. 'Although I can't think why I bothered. There was only me there and the one editor left with any moral courage.'

That was a phrase Trish hadn't heard for a long time. She could sympathize with the bitterness in it.

'I'm sorry to rake over such painful ground, but . . .' she left a pause for the other woman to fill with polite reassurance. None came. 'But I wanted to ask whether you ever had any doubts about the inquest's verdict.'

'Why?'

There was music in the background, something disciplined and austere: Bach, probably, Trish thought.

'Because suicide seems so unlike Jamie,' she said, needing to be sure Will had been wrong about this.

'No. I meant why are *you* asking questions about it? What's your interest here?'

'Oh, I see.' For once Trish thought about lying, then decided only a version of the truth would get her what she needed. 'A friend of mine has been looking into a meat scandal he wanted Jamie to write up, and I need to be sure there isn't some kind of connection.'

'You can forget that.' Mrs Blake's voice hadn't softened.

'Why?'

'Because there's no doubt Jamie killed himself, and set the scene to ram home to all of us why he was doing it. That was typical. He always wanted everyone to know how much he suffered.'

'I don't understand.'

'Think about it. What happens in a slaughterhouse? Animals are driven to their death, just as Jamie felt he'd been driven to his.'

'But . . .'

'Listen! He goes to that abattoir in his own car and parks it in full view of everyone. Then he writes a suicide note. Then he fills his pockets with anti-cruelty literature and lies down under the wheels of a lorry easily big enough to kill anyone. You can't twist any of that to mean anything other than suicide.'

'Who did he write to?' Trish said, thinking she could easily produce a counter-argument, but then that was her training. 'You?'

'No. Jamie hadn't communicated with me for years.' There was a gulping sound, quickly stifled, and followed by a pause-filling cough. 'We . . . we weren't close. No, the letter was addressed to Nick Wellbeck, the news editor of the *Daily Mercury*, the one who came to the funeral.'

'Did Jamie type it?'

'Of course not. Who types a suicide note? It was handwritten in proper ink. That was typical too. Jamie made a fetish of loathing biros.'

'What did the note say?'

'I haven't got it. The police probably hung on to it. It went something like: "Didn't it occur to you that I've been phoning and emailing every day for weeks because I *needed* you, Nick? Couldn't you have spared me two minutes? Did I imagine it, or were we once friends? Well, I've had enough now. You'll regret refusing to take my calls."'

'I see what you mean about moral courage. I am so sorry, Mrs Blake.'

There was another gulp, then a sob, as though the sympathy had cut through her defensive bitterness.

'Why didn't he tell me it was that bad? He must have known I'd help, in spite of . . . Sorry. I haven't . . . There hasn't been anyone to . . .' Mrs Blake took a loud deep breath, then said more steadily, 'You're the first person who knew Jamie who's wanted to talk about what happened. Sorry.'

'Please don't be. It's always hard to deal with the things one did or didn't do when someone's dead,' Trish said, aching for her. It seemed awful to be taking advantage of her distress. But there were questions that had to be asked. 'And suicide must make that even worse. What happened between you to cause the split?'

'The usual story. We'd been very close as children, and it went on like that for longer than with most siblings. Then I fell in love with someone he loathed.' Mrs Blake was still fighting to get her voice in order. 'In the early days I used to try to build bridges between them, but when I had to choose I opted for my husband. Jamie didn't forgive me. I wish . . .'

Trish couldn't imagine doing something like that, but then she'd never had a brother anywhere near her own age.

'What was the problem between them?' she asked, forgetting the real quest.

'My husband is a civil servant, so he's constitutionally against any kind of freedom of information.'

And presumably, Trish thought with sympathy, against any discussion of powerful feelings like yours. What else could make you share all this with a stranger?

Mrs Blake sniffed. 'He thinks men like him should be allowed to get on with running the country in the best interests of the people, without having journalists causing panic and upset every time something goes wrong. He says they don't save any lives or put anything right. They just cause trouble.'

'It's a legitimate point of view, I suppose,' Trish said, 'but I can't see Jamie agreeing.'

'No. Where Miles sees a little disinformation as a small price to pay for public serenity, Jamie wanted every cover-up exposed and every perpetrator, however well-intentioned, vilified in the press.'

'You must have had a hell of a time between them.'

'By God I did.' Suddenly Mrs Blake sounded tougher. Maybe it wasn't only Jamie Maxden who couldn't forgive. 'I must go. Goodbye.'

She cut the connection at once, leaving Trish with a lot of unanswered questions: only some were about Jamie Maxden.

Sitting down at her desk, determined to do something to stop herself thinking about all the others, she started to search the Internet for his name. Soon she'd have to decide what, if anything, to do about the letter Ferdy had sent to Liz, and about the misery Liz had revealed when she'd come to the flat. But not yet.

To her surprise, there wasn't much to read about Maxden on the Net, although she was offered links to newspapers that had printed some of his old articles. Waiting for one to download, and watching the sunlight glinting on her stapler, she thought she couldn't bear to stay indoors. She printed off all the articles and took them out to read on the Jubilee Walk beside the river.

The tone of Jamie's work pleased her, with its passionate anger backed up by coldly reported fact. It wasn't only meat that obsessed him. He'd been able to produce diatribes on almost everything to do with the food trade, including farm pesticides and other chemicals. But his greatest fury had been expended on the BSE scandal. She found one article from the early 1990s, which ended:

> Sell-by dates were meant to stop us eating dangerous meat. No one told us the steak we bought might come from animals fed with exactly that. Farmers are being blamed, but it's not their fault. There is no legislation to control feed-manufacturers or force them to list the ingredients of their mixtures on the sacks that contain it. The farmers had no chance.
>
> Nor did we. Even now I see trays of 'braising steak' in supermarkets, so cheap it can only have come from milk cows past their useful life. Is there anything on the label to warn the consumer? Of course not. No one would buy it if they knew.
>
> If BSE has crossed the species barrier from the sheep whose remains were ground up to make cattle feed, it can also cross the barrier to us. Why did no one in government take steps to protect us as soon as the first cow died? How many people will die now because of that failure?
>
> And who will pay? No one except the farmers who lose their livelihood, and the parents who have to watch their children die from this terrible disease.

In spite of everything Trish knew about the steps taken to deal with BSE since Jamie Maxden had written his article, and the relatively small numbers of people who appeared to be at risk, she still found it frightening. George particularly liked braised steak, and he'd cooked it for her every winter since they'd met. Had they eaten the flesh of elderly cows riddled with an incurable, utterly devastating disease?

Trish read on, becoming increasingly uncomfortable.

On another occasion Jamie Maxden had produced a rant about the systematic closure of small local abattoirs, just like the one the Flesker family had owned.

> The result of all this will be not only poorer quality meat, more rural unemployment and more animal distress. There will also be a lot more under-the-counter slaughtering, with an inevitable rise in the supply of dangerous meat.
>
> This concern for food hygiene in small abattoirs is ludicrous in the light of the BSE disaster. That could have been controlled far more quickly if the officials and scientists had done the jobs we pay them to do. Instead, they fiddle about with slaughterhouse regulations that won't save a single life.

It was easy to see why his civil service brother-in-law had loathed him. But Trish still had doubts about the rest of what she'd heard from his sister.

Would anyone choose to kill himself outside an abattoir for the reasons Clare Blake had offered? Could anyone as angry as the writer of these articles ever have become so demoralized and unhappy that dying seemed a better option than fighting on? There was a school of thought that held suicide to be an expression of rage rather than fear or despair. Never having felt the urge to kill herself for more than a moment or two, even when the claws of depression had been at their tightest, Trish hadn't enough experience to help her judge. Maybe you could feel so hard done by that you believed only your death would get you the revenge you wanted, she thought.

For her, a victory like that would have been so Pyrrhic it wouldn't have been worth having. She'd have wanted to be alive to see her tormentors grovel in shame at what they'd done to her. Her reading of Jamie Maxden's work suggested that would have been his choice too.

Could the note to Nick Wellbeck have been a taunt rather than an expression of despair? A suggestion that Jamie had found an explosive – and provable – story he would be offering to some other paper because Wellbeck had refused to take his calls?

That would make sense of both the letter and the email he'd sent to Will. After all, he'd promised 'more later', which had never come. Would anyone write that if he were intending to kill himself in the way Clare Blake had described? Of course not.

One of Petra Knighton's warnings came crashing into Trish's mind. Had there been any proof that the film or the email had come from Jamie Maxden in the first place?

'Oh, stop it,' she said aloud. 'Why would Will bother to fake something like this? And how would he do it? I'm sure the film was real. And I'm sure it came from Jamie Maxden.'

A man walking his dog looked curiously at her. She realized she must seem mad, sitting in the sun with a heap of paper on her lap, muttering. She gave him a blinding smile. He looked even more worried and hustled his huge Dalmatian ahead of him.

Back in the flat, Trish searched for more information about the discovery of Jamie's body. The local paper that must have reported it and the inquest turned out to be the *Smarden Runner*, and that was not available on line. She let more questions well up in her mind. Who had planted the vegetarian leaflets on Jamie's body and why? They had proved highly successful decoys, completely misleading the police as well as his family. Jamie's articles had shown no interest in the animals that were slaughtered for food, only in the human beings who ate them, just as Will had suggested they would. Were there perhaps some militant animal rightists, who disapproved of Jamie so much they wanted to make an example of him?

No, Trish thought. That's absurd, too.

But she couldn't get it out of her mind. After half an hour, she reached for the phone and dialled the number of Jess and Caro's flat. The voice that answered was much slower and deeper than the one Trish expected.

'Is Jess there?'

'No. She's at the hospital. Who's speaking?'

'It's Trish Maguire.'

'Oh, hello, Trish. This is Cynthia Flag.'

'Hi.' She couldn't help the coldness of her voice. 'You might be able to help me if Jess isn't there.'

'If I can, of course I will.'

'What do you know about an industrial abattoir called Smarden Meats?'

'Nothing. Why?' Cynthia sounded quite untroubled.

'I just wondered whether there have ever been any vegetarian protests there, or any kind of rioting by animal rights activists. Sabotage. That sort of thing.'

'I wouldn't know. I'm not a campaigner.'

'Aren't you? I thought it was you who persuaded Jess to turn vegetarian?'

'What makes you think that?' The deep voice dripped with a mixture of sweetness and mockery.

'She turns to you whenever anyone asks a question about her dietary habits,' Trish said. 'You're practically living in the flat. She thinks you're wonderful. And you're a vegetarian. One doesn't have to be Einstein to make a connection like that.'

Cynthia laughed irritatingly. 'Come off it, Trish. I'm only here to give the poor woman some support while Caro's so ill. I suppose it could have been listening to me talk about what animals suffer that originally made Jess think she might prefer to stop eating them. What difference does it make?'

Trish wasn't sure, but she didn't trust Cynthia enough to explain why she was asking questions.

'None. I just thought if it had been you who'd done it, you might be able to explain why anyone who enjoyed food like steak tartare could change so quickly.'

'I think . . .' Cynthia paused, then began again, with a great deal less artifice in her voice. 'I know you're a good friend of Caro's, so it's fair to tell you. And safe. I think Jess felt in danger of being taken over by Caro's determination to make the whole world bend to her will. Becoming vegetarian gave Jess a chance to rebuild her faith in herself as a separate person.'

'That sounds a bit adolescent to me.' And it's not going to help unravel anything about Jamie's death.

'Only because you're as confident as Caro,' Cynthia said. 'You ought to try for a bit more sympathy for people who haven't got your advantages. Goodbye.'

And that puts me in my place, Trish thought, dropping the receiver back on its cradle. I wonder how much Caro knows about Cynthia's part in her life.

With the smear of Ferdy's odious letter to Liz Shelley still making her feel unclean, Trish knew she could never pass on any of her doubts. In any case, there was work to be done.

What she wanted was to go straight to Will's bedside in whichever Kentish hospital the police had deposited him and force him to tell her the truth about everything he had done since she had first told him about the contaminated sausages.

Suddenly she forgot her own needs. If he had asked the police to phone chambers when they took him to hospital, there couldn't have been anyone to tell his sister what was happening. She must be worried sick.

'In hospital?' Susannah said, when Trish had explained why she'd phoned. 'What's happened to him? He told me he was going away for twenty-four hours, and I just assumed he'd overstayed wherever it was.'

'He's OK. I mean, not too badly hurt. But it's a bit complicated,' Trish said, wondering how much to tell her. If Will had wanted his sister to know what had happened, he'd have asked the police to phone her, not chambers. But in her place Trish would have wanted to know everything. 'Could we meet? I know you have young children, so this may not be the best time, but . . .'

'Actually, my husband's with them. You're right, though: it would be difficult for me to get out. Could you come here? The children will need their supper soon, but we could talk while I cook it, if you don't mind the kitchen.'

'If you give me the address, I'll get to you as soon as I can. How's the parking at this time of day?'

'Free and safe, so long as you don't park in a residents' bay. Or a disabled space. Meters and yellow lines are all yours.'

Chapter 19

The kitchen was an elegant affair of pale oak and black granite with a curved glass cooker hood, which neatly dated its last makeover to three years ago. Nothing changed as quickly as fashions in kitchen fittings. Trish sat at a beautiful old gate-legged table in the middle of the room, admiring it as much as the amazing burgundy she was drinking.

Her first reassurance about Will's physical state had let loose an outpouring about how difficult it was to help him when he resisted everything you tried to do for him. She waited until Susannah had got it all off her chest, then said, 'What about his girlfriend? Can't she help?'

Susannah turned round from her pans on the Aga, a wooden spoon in her hand dripping tomato sauce on the white floor, like great drops of blood.

'What girlfriend?'

'Hasn't there been one? A woman who lives somewhere in Kent?'

'Ah,' Susannah said on a sigh of understanding. She dropped the spoon back in the pan and fetched a cloth to mop the floor. 'So that *is* why he wanted to borrow the car. I knew he was getting a bit of nooky, but I'd rather assumed it was you.'

Trish shook her head. 'I'm just the wig freak who may or may not help get him his damages from Furbishers.'

'I think there's a bit more to it than that.' Susannah smiled.

'He can't stop talking about you, and he grins like an idiot whenever he hears your name. It didn't occur to me you could have a rival.'

'What was it that made you think he could be . . . what was it you said? Getting some nooky?'

'Sorry. It was my father's expression. A whole lot of things. He looked sleeker.' Susannah turned back to her pots. 'And he was much less use about the house.'

'What?'

Susannah looked at Trish over her shoulder again. Mischievous amusement had driven out some of the anxiety from her expression.

'Haven't you noticed? When men are feeling a bit too beaten for sex, they turn all useful and caring. Then when things are going better, and the testosterone's rising, they start dropping their dirty clothes on the floor again and waiting for you to pick them up. It's a bloke thing.'

I suppose it is, Trish thought, glad that the eccentric regime she and George had devised for themselves avoided all such tactics.

Susannah tasted the contents of one pan, reached for the salt, added a bit, stirred and tasted again.

'Good. That's done. Rupert?' She raised her voice. 'Rupert! Could you get them to wash? Supper's ready.' She put the pan on a trivet beside the Aga. 'You're about to witness the hordes feeding. Do you mind if I lay the table round you?'

'Give me the cutlery and I'll do it.' Trish tried to fit Susannah's theory into what she knew of Will's activities. She hoped with a passion that surprised her that whoever had given Will his new sleekness, she wasn't the woman lying in some Kentish mortuary awaiting a forensic pathologist's saws and scalpel.

'Great.' Susannah produced a big bunch of knives and forks with bright-blue plastic handles. 'You still haven't said what's happened to Will to put him in hospital.'

Trish told her about the fight and the police, but not about the dead woman, and watched the tears edge out of the corners of Susannah's eyes.

'Oh, God. Not more trouble for him. It's so unfair. I can't bear it.'

'We're doing our best,' Trish said aloud, even as she thought, if he did kill that woman, nothing any of us can do will make a difference.

'I know. But . . .' Susannah grabbed Trish's arm and propelled her towards a large oil painting that hung on the far wall. 'That's what he lost when Furbishers ruined him.'

There was nothing grand about the painting, or about the building it portrayed. It was just an ordinary farmhouse, familiar from every county in England. Long and low, it was arranged as usual at one side of a big square yard, with barns and stables taking up most of the other three. The yard itself was filled with pale-brown Jersey cows waiting to be milked. They looked warm against the greyish stone.

More buildings could be seen in the distance with trees behind them, and in the foreground a flowery meadow sloped gently towards a narrow river. Below that, in the centre of the frame, a scrolled gilt cartouche announced the unpretentious name of the place: Manor Farm. Trish had never heard of the painter, and assumed he had been an amateur, probably working at the beginning of the twentieth century.

'Those are thought to be the original apple trees,' Susannah said, sniffing. 'Even though they have to be the reason we got our name, I didn't mind when Will sold them and the land. But it was different when the house went. I don't think I'll ever get over that. It was . . . well, home really. In a way that this never will be. Or anywhere else.'

'I'm sorry.'

Susannah produced a watery smile. 'It's much worse for him because he feels so guilty. All the time. I can see it in everything he does. That's why I was chuffed when I thought he was in love, even though it drove me mad when he ran the car dry of petrol and put bleach in the dishwasher instead of Rinseaid. I thought something was going right for him at last. Now this!'

'Mum, Mum. What are we having?'

Susannah stared at Trish for a moment, then scrubbed her eyes on the bottom of her apron, braced herself and turned to say brightly, 'Spaghetti, darling.'

'I'd better leave you to it,' Trish said, watching four small children clambering up on to the oak chairs. They looked so much the same age that she couldn't believe they all belonged to Susannah. Rosy with health and noisy with excitement, all four had the kind of confidence that comes only from a settled existence with contented parents, the kind of experience Kim Bowlby would never have.

'You will tell me as soon as you hear anything, won't you?' Susannah said, jerking Trish back into the present.

'Of course,' she said, trying to forget Kim.

'And could you explain it all to Rupert on the way out? I can't with all this lot earwigging.'

Susannah's husband walked Trish to the door and didn't comment until he'd heard everything she was prepared to say.

'Stupid bugger,' he said casually. 'I hope he *was* the victim this time. Susannah can't take much more. It seems to have been going on ever since the old man died and Will inherited the farm. One damn thing after another. But thanks for warning us about this one.'

'Before I go,' Trish said, 'could you tell me something?'

'If I can, of course. What d'you want to know?'

'How much of a friend to Will was Jamie Maxden?'

'Who?'

'A journalist. Will talks about him as a great friend. Didn't you know?'

'Never heard of him.' He twisted his head to call down to the passage to the kitchen, 'Sannah? You ever hear of a friend of Will's called Jamie Maxden?'

Trish heard her tell the children to eat tidily, then saw her emerging from the kitchen, wiping her hands on her apron.

'Of course. I haven't heard anything about Jamie for years,' she said, looking a little self-conscious. 'But he was OK, you know. A good bloke. At one time they were great mates.'

'How did they meet?' Trish asked.

Susannah frowned up at the ceiling, as though trying to bring back the memory. The children were shrieking with delight behind her. And there were splashing sounds, as though one of them was playing with his food or even throwing it.

'The Young Farmers' Ball, I think. It was donkeys' years ago. Has he popped up again?'

'No. He's dead.'

'Oh, Christ!' Susannah leaned against the wall. 'You're not going to tell me he was in this fight with Will, are you? I don't believe it. They were really close at one time.'

Trish was shaking her head before Susannah was halfway through her question. A crash followed by a scream made them all turn towards the kitchen. Susannah looked back at Trish. More screams made her say, 'Rupe, could you sort it? I'll tell Trish what she needs to know.'

'OK,' he said, but he looked puzzled.

Susannah scooped up a bunch of keys from a wooden bowl on the radiator shelf.

'Come on,' she said. 'I'll see you to your car.'

Outside, the air felt even warmer than it had indoors, and very dusty. Trish longed for rain to freshen it.

'How did he die?'

'There's a question over that,' Trish said, itching to know what was behind Susannah's odd intensity. 'But the inquest called it suicide. Why?'

She turned her neat face up to Trish, who saw that her eyes

were damp. 'Because they did have a fight once. But not nearly as bad as this one sounds.'

'Will and Jamie?'

'Yes. It was over me.'

'I don't understand.'

'Jamie and I had a bit of a fling, years and years ago. It kind of drifted into nothing, but we stayed friends. And when I was first married to Rupe, when things were really tough, I kind of . . . well, turned to Jamie. You see, Rupe had only just moved to the bank and later on I realized he'd been terrified of failing and being sacked. At the time, all I knew was that he spent about twenty hours a day there. I felt rejected.'

'That must have been hard.'

'It was agony. I can understand it now, but sometimes things bring it back – like the night you phoned and I bit your head off.'

Trish sympathized, but she had other things on her mind than Susannah's marital history.

'That doesn't matter,' Trish said. 'I didn't take it personally. What happened with Jamie?'

'I just wanted you to understand. I was very vulnerable because of the way things were with Rupe, and because Dad had just died. And Jamie was lovely.'

'You mean you had an affair?'

'Not really. But we did go to bed once or twice. And Will dropped in one evening, just as Jamie was dressing. Will had keys to the flat Rupe and I lived in then because sometimes he had to be in London overnight, seeing the lawyers about Dad's estate, and he used to stay. Anyway, he let himself in and saw us, not exactly fully clothed.'

'And Will let fly at Jamie? That doesn't sound like him.' They had reached Trish's car, but she didn't want to interrupt the flow so kept on walking beside Susannah further up Munster Road.

'He stared at him and said something like: "I'd thought I could trust you. How could you do it?" And Jamie just zipped up his trousers and said: "What're you talking about?" And Will hit him. Then Jamie hit him back. And for a minute I thought they were going to kill each other.'

'How did you stop it?'

'I screamed. I was terrified. It stopped them. Jamie stood there, staring at Will and said, "You should have trusted me." Then he took my chin in his hand and kissed me. He tasted of blood, so his lip must have been split, and he said, "Don't worry about this Suze. It's nothing." See you.'

'And did you? See him, I mean.'

'I never saw him again. And now he's dead.'

'I'm sorry.'

Susannah looked as though she'd just surfaced from a dive. She smiled politely. But her eyes were blank. 'I ought to get back. The children, you know. Will you be able to find your car?'

'Sure. Thank you.'

Susannah ran back down the road, then paused. Over her shoulder, she called, 'When you see Will, tell him to phone me if he needs anything. Anything. And get me a phone number so I can talk to him. It's important.'

'I'll do my best.'

When Trish got home at half past seven, the red light was flickering on her answering machine. She pressed Play and heard Petra Knighton's voice.

'I promised to let you know how things were going. It's not looking good for Applewood. As I told you, the other man is in a much worse way than he is, which makes the police highly suspicious of Applewood's story. Until they get the scientific tests back, they won't have a clue which of the two beat the woman to death. Even then the test results may not be conclusive. He sends his love, by the way.'

'Oh, shit!' Trish said aloud to relieve her feelings.

'The story he's told them, for what it's worth, is that he'd been in bed with the woman all day until she sent him out to buy bread before the shops shut. There'll presumably be witnesses who saw him in the baker's. When he came back, he claims she was already being beaten up. He launched himself at the man doing the beating and fought on until he managed to subdue him.

'Meantime, a neighbour had called the police. They're highly sceptical and think it's more likely that Applewood went berserk when he came back from the shops to find the other man on his patch and tried to kill them both.'

I don't believe it, Trish thought, pressing the button to save the message. Not Will. Not in a million years.

Now where did that come from? she asked herself, feeling as though the floor had turned to jelly.

She'd screwed up once before when she'd allowed herself to believe her father had murdered his lover. She couldn't bear to make the same mistake again.

It's still between us now, she thought. That's why Paddy hardly ever comes here. Maybe he's right to hate me for what I thought he'd done. What can it be like to know your own daughter believes you capable of killing another human being?

You had your reasons, she reminded herself.

There'd been plenty of those, including the violence she'd witnessed as a child. For years, she'd told herself that her father had simply abandoned her and her mother. But, since her mother had admitted that he had hit her, Trish had been allowing the memories to come back bit by bit.

Pacing around the empty flat as though it were a small cave in which she'd been trapped for weeks, she let the worst bubble up like hot lava through a crack in the earth's crust.

She must have been three or four, less than Kim's age, wearing striped pyjamas and a cherry-red dressing gown. Both her parents had been with her in the kitchen, and she had been furious about something. There wasn't anything odd about that: she'd always been an angry child. Whatever it was she'd wanted so urgently had driven her to tank on and on until she'd ignited a row between her parents.

Trish could still see her mother now, sitting on a low stool by the kitchen fireplace, with her head buried in her hands and her shoulders heaving. It was the only time Trish had ever known her cry. Paddy was standing over her, nursing his knuckles.

For years Trish had buried the memory and later told herself it was shock that had made her refuse to think about it. Only now could she admit that she had triggered the violence that night. More questions nagged at her, keeping her stuck in the past she'd tried so hard to escape.

Was it always me who drove my father to hit my mother? Was it my fault he left and she had all the responsibility and all the bills and all the angst of my growing up? Is that why I've taken on David, to compensate them both? Or to show that I can do it and so prove it wasn't such a monstrous burden for her?

Trish had walked right round the flat twice already and it wasn't helping. She took herself into the kitchen for the soothing ritual of making tea, but that couldn't stop the internal interrogation either.

Is it the old shock of what I saw Paddy do to Meg that makes me so frightened of male violence now? Is that the real reason why life with George works when it never worked with any of my other boyfriends? Was everything I said to Antony just a cover story? George eats his anger with all the food he insists on cooking, instead of shouting at me or leaving as they did. Did I provoke them so that I could prove no man could ever be truly domesticated, so that it couldn't be my fault Paddy left us? And did I head for family law for the same reason?

'Stop it,' Trish said aloud. 'You'll drive yourself mad.'

She thought of the landlord of the Black Eagle, providing a

kind of haven for men who couldn't adjust to life outside the army, a place where they could go and be, certain no one would try to make them talk about the mess in their heads. That was what she needed now. Work had always provided it for her in the past.

If you always had too much to do, then you couldn't think too hard about your wretched feelings. An empty evening like this one was a positive invitation to them to rise up and overwhelm you. Much better to get on and do something useful, like proving that Will Applewood was innocent, and get back a little confidence in your own judgement.

The best source of information had to be the news editor with enough moral courage to attend Jamie Maxden's funeral. Trish had no way of finding his home phone number, but it wouldn't be hard to find his email address.

Knowing how many emails he was likely to have when he got back to work on Monday morning, she headed hers: 'Jamie Maxden didn't kill himself'. In the body of the message, she added that she was looking for back-up information to add to her own and would like to talk. She gave her phone number in chambers, not wanting anyone who had anything to do with the *Daily Mercury* to know where she lived.

Will lay on the hospital bed with snuffling, grunting, snoring men all round him, trying to make sense of everything so that he'd be able to convince the hard-eyed old bag Antony Shelley had sent down. He wished it had been Trish who'd come to protect him from the police. She would have understood everything without having to be told. And she could have made the police believe her too. She could make anyone believe her. If only he hadn't muddled her phone numbers and given the police the one for her chambers!

Even the police were more sympathetic than the solicitor. After their first ferocious charge up the stairs in Mandy's house and all the questions they'd shouted at him then, he'd never have believed they could be kind. But once they'd seen the carnage, and the state he was in himself, they'd turned amazingly gentle. They'd got him here into the doctors' hands, for one thing, and the young one who'd been stationed in the corridor to keep him from running off popped in every so often to make sure he was OK. He also passed on what little news there was of the other bloke.

No one was worrying about *him* running off. He'd broken his neck when he caught his head on the open drawer of Mandy's dressing table. They said he was still alive, but it didn't sound as though he was in any position to talk, which was lucky.

Until Will knew exactly what had been going on at the abattoir, and how Mandy was involved, he didn't want the police trampling about asking the wrong questions and giving any of the gang the chance to destroy the evidence. Let them think no one knew what they were up to for a little longer, at least until he was on his feet again and could get to Trish.

Bob wasn't answering his phone. Tim had already left four messages at the flat and five on Bob's mobile, and he still hadn't phoned back. Ron wasn't responding either. They were probably still furious about the damage to the plane. But they had to get over it and come up with the cash they owed him. It belonged to him and he needed it.

The bank manager had already said he wouldn't provide any more credit. All Tim's accounts with suppliers had been frozen. He couldn't pay for fuel for the machines he needed to clean up the orchard or water the trees that were already shrivelling in the ghastly drought. Thank God, he'd still had enough to pay his casual pickers at the end of the harvest.

And thank God for his hens still laying their eggs for him, and for the veg in the garden, even if most of it had bolted or dried out. He wasn't going to starve, and Boney was being truly

Napoleonic now, catching most of his own food. There was a bit of the all-purpose dried dog food left in the rat-protected bin in one of the outbuildings, but it wouldn't last much longer.

Now that he'd deliberately crashed the plane, he wouldn't even be able to earn a few pennies taking photographs for the estate agents. He wondered if he were mad to think of pointing out to Bob how much damage he could do to the brothers if he didn't get his money soon.

Memories of the threats Bob had made in the pub outside Stubb's Cross told him he was indeed entirely mad.

Later that evening, Trish leaned out of the kitchen window in the soft dusk, to look over the rooftops and pigeons towards the cathedral.

She wished she hadn't wasted so much time excoriating herself for things she couldn't change now, even if they had been as bad as she sometimes feared. Except when she let herself think about them, she was a functional human being these days.

More than functional, she thought, looking back around the flat she had bought and furnished and hung with magnificently bleak paintings, paid for out of resources she had earned without help from anyone else. Whatever she had done to her parents, whatever her motives for the work she had chosen or the man she loved, there was no problem with any of it now. Past failings ought to be nailed down under the carpet and ignored.

Fears should be put there, too, so that you could get on with your life. The only problem was they sometimes escaped round the edges.

She played Petra Knighton's message again. As the solicitor's voice scraped out into the flat, Trish realized she'd cut it off too soon. The message didn't end with Petra's announcement that the man Will had fought was still alive. She listened to the rest.

'His name is Bob Flesker and he works at Smarden Meats. I

have, as you can imagine, enjoined my client to suppress all mention of his interest in that company when talking to the police. Whether this man's occupation is merely an unhappy coincidence or something worse, I will leave to your imagination. Goodbye.'

'Of course it's not a coincidence,' Trish shouted at the white-painted brick wall in front of her. 'And it means Flesker must have been the killer.'

Unless, she thought, sliding back into a chair as her legs gave way, Will was going after him and the girl got in the way. Or maybe she was part of whatever Bob Flesker has been doing. If she was the woman who'd been making Will look sleek and happy and behave weirdly at home, discovering that she was part of the conspiracy could have made him flip.

Trish dialled Petra's number and was surprised to be answered in person.

'Thank you for your message.'

'That's all right. I've no more news to give you yet, or I would have phoned you.'

'I know. I just wondered. You didn't put a name to the victim; the woman, I mean. Have the police told you who she was?'

'Yes.' There was the sound of scuffling paper. 'Her name was Amanda Turville, and she worked at a company called Ivyleaf Packaging.'

Trish had trouble getting out her thanks. A small voice in her head was muttering obscenities, over and over again.

Chapter 20

Antony was already in chambers when Trish arrived on Monday morning. He was looking uncharacteristically tentative.

'Hi,' she said, sweeping past him into her room. She'd been up since six, worrying away at various versions of what might have been in Will's mind when he'd spent the day in bed with a woman who worked for Ivyleaf and later found Bob Flesker in her bedroom. 'Have you been waiting for me?'

'Yes.' Antony's eyebrows had always been messy, with several extra-long, white hairs sprouting among the blond. Now he grabbed one and pulled it out with a vicious tug. Trish winced. 'I wanted to say how sorry I am that Liz came round to your flat. She says she accused you of . . . all sorts of things.'

Antony was not known for his apologies. He took the Disraelian line that they could only be signs of guilt. Trish wasn't sure how to respond to this one.

'She said you were kind and very sensible. So, thank you, Trish. And I'm sorry I landed you in . . .'

'It's OK, Antony,' she said, touched and touching his arm to prove her sincerity. 'You and I had fun, and luckily that's all we had, so I didn't have to lie to her.'

'Why are you so hung up on the idea of lies?' he asked. 'They ease so many things in life and do no one any harm.'

'That's just not true.'

'Why not?'

A frown bunched Trish's eyebrows. Was he trying to understand her or Liz?

'Because the lied-to feel manipulated and stupid when they find out the truth, as they nearly always do. And that makes them mistrust everyone and everything else. Not trusting people is a horrible way to live.'

He hunched a shoulder. He hadn't shaved carefully enough this morning and there were spots of blood on his collar. She hoped the oozing would have stopped before he changed in the robing room. You couldn't go into court as a silk with blood-spattered bands. Nor could you go in looking unhappy and humbled.

'I gather you were at Bar school with Ferdy Aldham,' she said lightly.

'So? Anyway, who told you?' Antony's dull eyes began to move, and the slackness in his face tightened a little.

'Someone with my best interests at heart,' she said. 'I also gather that the two of you have been conducting a sniping war ever since, and that this case is part of it.'

The familiar smirk tweaked the corners of his mouth. She'd never expected to enjoy seeing it as much as this.

'I thought you never cared who won or lost a case,' Trish went on. 'That's what you said to me last year, anyway.'

He laughed. 'It's true I don't usually. But I do hate being beaten by fucking Ferdy.' He stretched his spine, looking at least two inches taller when he'd settled back into his familiar stance.

'And what about the judge? Was Husking there with you both?'

'No.' Antony's eyebrows lifted into triangles, and he began to look entirely happy again. 'That would have been neat, but he's a good three years ahead of us. He's never been a rival either. When he saw he wasn't going to make it as a silk, the bench was pretty much his only option if he was to retire with any sensation of success. Why this interest, Trish?'

'I like to know what's going on. Tell me – truthfully this time – why you let Will Applewood run that day, when Ferdy was questioning him about his paranoia about the meat trade. I can't see how that fits into your war.'

His smirk deepened, but he said nothing.

'Come on, Antony. Was it because you wanted me to see how weird Will can be?'

He laughed. 'Darling Trish, how sweet! I know both he and I had the hots for you, but I'm not that unprofessional. No, poor old Husking had a bad scare a few years ago when he started falling over and forgetting things. He thought he'd caught variant CJD from eating beef. Ferdy must have forgotten, or possibly he never knew. I thought the experience might make Husking sympathize with Will's passions.'

'We'll see when we get the verdict, won't we?' Trish said, thinking there might not be all that much to choose between Ferdy and Antony as far as manipulation went. Maybe she'd drop the idea of reporting Ferdy to the Bar Council.

She heard someone walking along the corridor outside. Antony moved back and dusted down his suit.

'It won't be long now. We've only got Sally Trent's line manager, the Great Panjandrum himself, and then closing speeches.'

'D'you think we've got any chance?'

'I bloody hope so, all the trouble this case has given us both, but I'm not as sanguine as I was at the beginning. If it hadn't been for that sodding letter Will got from the Furbishers buyer, we could have had more confidence.'

'I know. But it was pretty ambiguous, wasn't it?'

'Depends how you read it. Let's hope Husking takes it our way. How is Will?' Antony moved towards the door. Trish reached for her gown, briefcase and wig box and followed him.

'I haven't seen him since the fight. Petra Knighton told me to keep out of the way, so I know nothing.'

'Good girl.'

'Patronizing git,' she said with all the affection it was now safe to show him, just as Colin appeared.

His eyes popped. Trish winked at him. Antony stalked past, well back into his usual all-conquering persona, paying no more attention to either of them.

As their little procession passed the door to the Clerks' Room, Steve Clay, the head clerk called Colin back. He looked at Trish, as if asking for permission to dawdle.

'It's OK. He won't keep you a second longer than you can spare, even if you have to run to catch us up. It'll be a brief of your own. Good luck, Colin.'

Like every other witness, Sally Trent's line manager, Martin Watson, confirmed that the statement in front of him was indeed his and reaffirmed its damning detail. Ferdy then handed him over to Antony for cross-examination.

'You gave all my clients' contracts to Ms Sally Trent for processing, did you not?'

'You can't expect me to keep the names of all your clients in my head,' he said, much more cocky than anyone should be in court.

A list of the clients was produced, shown to the judge, then handed to Watson.

'Looks fair enough,' he said. 'But if you needed me to swear, I'd have to check my files.'

'Why of all the six people in your department did you choose the youngest and most newly promoted for this work?'

He shrugged, which made his over-fitted pale-grey suit ride up around his shoulders. He seemed to be aware of it and unbuttoned the jacket so that it hung more loosely around his body.

'The contracts were straightforward and not particularly high value; a good bunch for her to start on.'

'Are you sure you didn't give them to her because she was the most malleable of your staff?'

'Say again?'

Antony repeated his question, adding a gloss in the unlikely case that Watson really didn't understand the word 'malleable'.

'No.'

'Then can you explain your instruction to her to draw out the negotiations.'

'I don't understand.'

'She has already testified in this case.' Antony turned to Trish, who had the relevant part of the transcript to offer him. He didn't smile or thank her; it was her job to anticipate his needs. He read out the admission Trish had winkled out of Sally Trent in court.

Watson coloured and shrugged again. He was sweating and slicked back his hair with both hands.

'She was a bit of a pushover, you see, my lord,' he said. 'And I was training her up. I thought she should get some proper experience of conflict before I let her loose on any big deals with important suppliers.'

And so it went on, with Watson showing himself to be just enough of a wide boy to explain his behaviour while still holding to the insistence that no one more senior at Furbishers had told him to do it. He was adamant that they had no policy of squeezing suppliers and would never have tried to sucker anyone into an unfavourable deal.

Antony's head was cocked at its most taunting angle as he stood up to cross-examine Sir Matthew Grant-Furbisher in the next session. Trish couldn't see Antony's face, but she knew the smile he must be showing the judge and the defendant: confident, intelligent, and offering an irresistible challenge.

'Now, Sir Matthew, as you know, the court has been told that Ms Sally Trent from your head-office contracts department was told by her line manager to spin out the negotiations on all small-supplier contracts she drew up. Why was this?'

'As *you* have heard, Mr Shelley,' Grant-Furbisher said, glaring, 'this was entirely contrary to company policy. Martin Watson, the line manager in question, has admitted he told her to do so out of some ill-judged personal attempt to train her in dealing with conflict.'

'Oh, yes? Are you expecting his lordship to believe that it was merely coincidence that this man's private enterprise allowed your company to make infinitely greater profits out of the claimants in this case – all thirty of them – than you would have done had they known the terms you were about to offer before they committed themselves to costly expansion?'

'Yes.' Grant-Furbisher had probably been trained on Disraelian principles too.

'I see.' Antony was far too experienced to look for a reaction from the judge, even though he was taking great care to make the cross-examination into a three-way affair to avoid excluding Husking. 'If Mr Watson's intervention was so ill-judged, what have you done to him now?'

'He has been disciplined.'

'How?'

'He has been demoted and moved to a less responsible position, where he can do no harm.'

'So you admit that he has done harm to my clients?'

'Certainly not.' Grant-Furbisher bristled, but his hands were still clasped loosely on the ledge of the witness box.

Nothing Antony asked could shake Grant-Furbisher, although there were several moments when he scratched the side of his nose in just the way George had described. Unfortunately it didn't help their case.

Throughout the session, Grant-Furbisher took the opportunity to make the point again and again that someone of his eminence had no day-to-day knowledge of employment issues, or indeed contractual ones. The message that came over loud and strong was: I am much too important to be questioned in this fashion.

Trish thought she could see subtle signs that Husking didn't like him any more than she did. That was encouraging in a case that was going to depend entirely on the judge's assessment of the balance of probabilities. He *has* to come up with the right verdict, she told herself. Manipulative, lying businessmen can't be allowed to get away with making huge profits by ruining people like Will.

But why hadn't Will warned them about the oral protest he'd made to Arthur Chancer, the buyer? If they'd known about it in time, they could have countered Ferdy's argument before they even heard it, which would have been far more effective than trailing along behind, trying to clean up the mess.

Oh, damn you, Will! she thought. Why couldn't you have been straight with us? How many other lies have you told?

Grant-Furbisher was the defence's last witness, and the judge decided to rise for the day before hearing the closing speeches. Once he had left the bench, Colin appeared at Trish's side. He hadn't come back to court for the afternoon session. Now he was looking almost as agitated as Will had on the day he'd discovered Jamie Maxden was dead.

'What's up?' Trish said, noticing that Colin didn't go straight to the heaps of folders on her bench to load them on to the trolley as he usually did. 'Is it the brief Steve gave you?'

'Yes. It's an immigration case,' he said, scratching his cheek nearly as savagely as Grant-Furbisher. 'When he first told me, I was over the moon. Now I've read the papers, I can't think why he gave it to me. I'm not nearly experienced enough for something so important. Why is he doing it, Trish?'

'Because he has to find out whether you're likely to crumple under pressure,' she said, deeply sorry for him but trying to inject some realism into his misery. Sharp memories of the fear she'd felt in her own first few cases made it hard not to show her sympathy. 'Chambers doesn't normally take immigration cases, so if you do screw this one up, you won't do any serious damage to our reputation.'

'What if I don't manage to make them give him asylum?' Colin clearly hadn't heard a word she'd said. He looked like a man trapped in the path of an advancing tank. 'He'd have to go back, and he was tortured, Trish. He's a doctor, you see, and they arrested him when he spoke out against the brutality of his country's regime.'

'Colin, don't look like that. However awful your client's possible suffering, you have to put it right out of your mind; otherwise you'll get bogged down in your own emotions, and won't be able to do your job properly. It's important for him that you keep your distance. OK?'

He wiped his lower lip with his teeth, as though he'd had to learn not to be dribbly as a child, looking almost as vulnerable and frightened as Kim. 'I'll try. Will you help me?'

'Of course. That's what I'm here for. Do what you can with the papers, work out how you're going to manage the case, then come and run through it with me.' What was it she'd wanted her pupil-master to say in those far-off days of quite nauseating terror? 'You'll be fine, Colin. You're a bright chap, and you've watched enough trials to see how they're done. Now, could you help me with the files? We need to haul them back.'

As they walked to Plough Court behind Antony, not talking of anything much, Trish thought of how Colin must be feeling. The brain-emptying terror had been all but unmanageable for her, too, and her client hadn't been in anything like such danger as his. But she'd found a way to get over her fear. Colin would too. Or he'd leave the profession. There was no other option. She was surprised to find herself so ruthless, in spite of her sympathy. Presumably all the tough senior juniors and silks who appeared so impervious had once felt like this too.

The ruthlessness helped, though, when they reached chambers and Steve put his head out of the Clerks' Room as she passed.

'Trish? There's a message for you, from a man who said he was too busy to wait to be put through to your voicemail.'

'Pretty arrogant! Who is he?'

'Said his name was Nick Wellbeck and you're to call him straight back. I put the number on your desk. You will ring him, won't you? Don't forget, even when you hate someone, it costs nothing—'

'To be polite, I know.' She smiled at his rehashing of a favourite Churchillian saying. She'd never yet thrown back the one about how useful it is for uneducated men to read books of quotation, but there had been occasions when he'd been so difficult that she'd been tempted. She watched Colin sit down at his table at the far end of her room and stare blindly at his papers.

He will get over it, she thought, particularly if he plays enough squash and wins enough matches. She picked up the phone on her desk.

'Nick Wellbeck?' she said when she'd been through the switchboard and a secretary. 'This is Trish Maguire.'

'Ah. Good. Then you can explain your email. Is this some kind of sick joke?'

'Far from it. I thought you might be glad to know that there's reason to doubt the inquest's verdict of suicide. I am almost sure Jamie Maxden didn't kill himself.'

'Who put you up to this?' His voice cut.

'No one. I just thought we might be able to help each other because I'm sure you don't believe Jamie killed himself any more than I do. But I can't find anyone else of that persuasion.'

'So you want to meet?'

Was she mad to be contemplating getting into bed with the

Daily Mercury? She'd loathed the paper for years, for its sanctimonious views about the proper place of women in society, its lack of tolerance of any kind of individuality, and its vindictiveness towards anyone who flouted its shibboleths. But if she had no way of finding out what she needed to know except by talking to its news editor, she'd have to do it.

'That would be great.'

'Do you people still drink in El Vino?'

'We do. Meet you there in, what? An hour?'

'I'll be there. How will I know you?'

'Tall, thin, dark hair, white face, black suit. What about you?'

'Much the same, except I'm going grey and won't be in a suit.' His tone had softened. 'I'll be carrying a copy of the paper. I don't suppose there'll be many others there.'

Trish was smiling as she put down the phone. Colin didn't look up. She could see he was scraping at his left thumb with all the fingernails of his other hand as he tried to read his papers.

Chapter 21

Trish had never known El Vino so empty. A few nervous-looking strangers sat uncomfortably in the long-seated leather chairs. There was no one bearing a copy of the *Daily Mercury*, so she chose a free table and read through the familiar wine list, before ordering the claret she always had and some biscuits. The usual fruity chatter was absent, and the few drinkers were talking in voices so low and shy they couldn't have belonged to any barrister.

'Trish Maguire?'

She looked up to see a tall man with grey hair and a face that looked far kinder than she'd have expected of anyone with any kind of responsibility at the *Mercury*.

'Yes. You must be Nick Wellbeck.'

'I am.'

She poured him a glass of wine and thanked him for coming, adding, 'Clare Blake told me that you were the only editor with the guts to go to her brother's funeral. That's why I thought you'd be the best person to talk to now.'

He sniffed the wine, then drank a little, watching her all the time, as though probing her expression for signs of sincerity.

'So what do you think Jamie was doing under that meat lorry if he wasn't trying to kill himself?' he asked at last.

Trish put forward a few theories, adding, 'I know there are security cameras outside the abattoir because I saw them there, but I don't have any way of finding out whether they were working that night. I thought you might—'

'They were working,' he said. 'They always are, twenty-four seven. Anyone known to be involved in killing animals needs good security, but Smarden couldn't afford to have people watching the monitors all the time, which is why no one noticed that the parked lorries completely blocked the camera's view of the relevant part of the forecourt.'

'Shit,' Trish said, thinking: so you've been making enquiries, have you?

'As you say. They tracked Jamie's car arriving and clearly recorded the number plate, but very little more. He wasn't particularly visible behind the wheel, but it was clear there was no passenger, and there was no sign of anyone else around on foot that night.'

'That's something,' Trish said. 'But if the lorries blocked the camera's sight lines, anything could have happened behind them.'

'True. But with no films, no evidence, and not even a body any more, there's no way anyone will ever know what it was or be able to prove it. I assumed you had something from another angle. I didn't realize you were just fishing when we spoke.'

She was surprised he didn't sound angrier. In his place she'd have been furious. He reached for the bottle and refilled their glasses before looking round the room.

'This takes me back. I haven't been in here for years, but it was our local in the old days.'

'I know. Did Jamie ever drink in here with you?'

'Sometimes.'

'So you were friends, just as Clare told me?'

He looked across the table, and Trish realized why he wasn't angry. He hadn't come for information about what Jamie could have been doing outside the abattoir. All he wanted was release from the fear that he might have pushed a friend into suicide.

She could understand that. One of her neighbours in halls had hanged herself while they were both in their second year at university. They hadn't been close friends, and Trish had had no warning of what the woman planned to do, but she'd still felt guilty for not having intervened to save her. Even now, nearly twenty years later, the memory could make her heart race and her palms sweat.

'Yes, we were friends,' Wellbeck said. He drank again. 'But we fell out over a story he faked. He couldn't forgive me for pulling it, and I couldn't forgive him for making me do it.'

'You cut him right out of your life, just for that?'

'"Just"?' Now Wellbeck was angry. 'There's no bloody "just" about it. Invention is the one unforgivable sin in any investigative reporter.' His face had set like cement. There was nothing kind or sad about it now. He drained his glass, then refilled it for the second time.

'How d'you know he faked it?'

'Because he had nothing to give us to support what he'd written when the lawyers asked for it. No documentary evidence. No identity for the source he'd claimed he was quoting.'

'Couldn't he have been protecting the source?'

'No.' Wellbeck had put down his empty glass and was examining a hangnail, so Trish couldn't see his eyes. 'At the paper we're used to dealing with anonymous informants. It happens all the time. We know how to protect them, and the journalists who quote them. Jamie had no reason to refuse to give *us* the name. The fact he never did, even when he must've understood what he'd done to his career, has to mean there'd never been a name to give.'

'What was the story about?'

'Meat, of course. Infected meat. Jamie hardly ever wrote about anything else.' Wellbeck left his nail alone and reached for the bottle again. 'He'd been after one particular farmer for years. The story was about how the bloke was regularly selling dangerously diseased animals to—'

'The abattoir where he was found dead?' Trish said quickly. 'Smarden Meats?'

'What on earth makes you say that?'

'Because I've seen so many coincidences these last few years that I've come to expect them everywhere. And dread them.'

'You don't have to worry this time. The slaughterhouse he wrote about was up north somewhere, and tied in with the head of a local authority central purchasing department. He was responsible for ordering all the foodstuffs for schools, old-people's homes, and so on.'

Trish thought she knew what was coming now. The *Mercury* had always had it in for corrupt councils, particularly if they were dominated by the Left.

'Jamie's article alleged that this farmer from the Hampshire borders was sending meat from diseased animals up north to sell cheaply to the central purchasing department. It was a scam that saved his vets' bills, brought him in a little profit, *and* balanced the council's books.'

'And who cared if the school children and old people got ill?'

'Exactly.' Wellbeck shot Trish a tight smile. 'It would have been a great story, just up our street – if only it'd been true.'

A new party arrived, four men and one woman, and looked nervously around. One of the men pointed to an empty group of chairs, but the atmosphere was too daunting for the rest. One said something about a pub and they turned tail.

'How did he suggest they'd got away with it?' Trish asked when the door had shut behind them again. 'I know record keeping has been tightened up a lot, but didn't livestock have to be registered even then?'

'Can't remember the details. I have a feeling Jamie claimed the paperwork had been doctored. And in those days farmers were allowed to bury dead livestock on their own farms. Maybe that's what he said he'd done.'

'But Jamie didn't produce any evidence of that? Or the doctored paperwork?'

Wellbeck grimaced. 'What do you think?'

'No, then.'

'Exactly. Even one supporting document would have made all the difference. But on this story – unlike all the others he'd ever written – Jamie was like a lizard: every time we thought we'd got a grip on him, he'd shed his tail and whisk away into hiding. We were left with the equivalent of a bit of worthless shrivelled skin.' He drank again. 'Even that was better than what might have happened.'

Trish finished the wine in her glass too. 'Which was?'

Wellbeck looked at her, then at the bottle, then back at her. He shrugged. 'What does it matter now, six years on? The farmer had a stroke the day we'd been planning to run the story. Can't you just see our rivals' headlines if we'd gone ahead?'

'*Daily Mercury* hounds honest farmer to death, you mean?' she said, trying not to see the coincidence that was hitting her in the face. She'd always known there would be one somewhere. This one could explain a lot. Nick Wellbeck might be certain the story had been faked; she wasn't so sure. Her mind began to spin faster, throwing up ideas she couldn't bear to acknowledge.

Wellbeck laughed, so she must have hidden her feelings well enough. 'I think they'd have found a wittier twist than that. It's a rare talent, writing front-page tabloid headlines. Shall I get another of these?' He tapped the bottle.

Trish shook her head. 'I've had more than enough, and there's still at least a glassful left.' She poured it for him and made her excuses.

Within minutes, she was out of the door and hurrying across the bridge, hungrier than she'd ever been in her life. She didn't want to think about Jamie Maxden or the Hampshire farmer who'd supposedly peddled diseased meat and died of a stroke six years ago. Or the real reason why Will had hit Jamie Maxden in Susannah's bedroom. All she wanted now was food. The El Vino biscuits had been the first things she'd eaten since breakfast and they hadn't been nearly enough.

Tomorrow, when she'd got used to the idea, she could phone Susannah for confirmation, but until then she wasn't going to let herself think about anything. There were sums here she didn't want to do. One way of avoiding them for a while would be to visit Caro. Maybe food could wait.

When Trish reached the hospital, she found that Caro had been moved again. She was sitting up and sipping water from a beaker. There were no longer any drip tubes attached to her arms. A towering bunch of roses and delphiniums soared up from her bedside locker.

'You look great,' Trish said. 'And those are fantastic flowers.'

'Aren't they? Andrew Stane brought them today.'

'What's the news of Kim?'

'Not a lot. She's settling with her foster mother, apparently, but still having nightmares most nights. She wakes the whole house with her screaming. And she's clammed up again. Neither the psychiatrist nor the social workers have managed to persuade her to say anything else. You were unique in getting through to her, Trish.'

'How does Mrs Critch cope with the screaming?'

Caro wagged her head from side to side in a gesture Trish knew well. It wasn't encouraging.

'So far she's bearing up, and spooning in the Calpol, but Andrew says he's afraid that if Kim doesn't let her sleep a night through soon, her benevolence is going to crack.'

'Like Crossman's,' Trish said grimly. 'I'm sure now that it was the screaming that got to him. I keep wondering what it was he threatened to do to the baby when Kim woke him in the night.'

'Why are you so sure he did? Isn't making her stand naked on the box at the end of his bed enough?'

'I don't think so. Horrible though that is, I don't think it's enough to explain the intensity of her terror.'

'You may be right. But whatever else there was, it's over now. Kim's safe, Trish. Thanks to you. You can stop worrying about her. And the unit is keeping a very close eye on the baby.'

Trish couldn't stop herself sharing some of Pete Hartland's outrage that no one was going to able to punish Crossman for what he'd done. She hated the thought that Kim was going to have to live with her terror. There were people who thought that counselling for post-traumatic stress only made the condition worse, but she still believed that children needed to talk about what had been done to them.

'How's Pete Hartland?' she asked and wished she hadn't as the anxiety pulled at Caro's face and made her look suddenly twice her age.

'He terrifies me, Trish. I've made everyone in the unit promise to keep an eye on him too, and so far he hasn't done anything. But he talks more wildly every time I see him.'

'I did my best.'

'I know. I didn't mean to criticize you. I'm really grateful that you tried to help. I wish I could get him sent on leave, but I've tried that and they won't wear it. With me out of action, there aren't enough bodies in the unit as it is.' She gritted her teeth. 'As soon as I'm out of here, I'm going to have to find a way to get him transferred. Child protection is all wrong for him.'

'Why?'

Caro shook her head. More professional secrets, Trish thought. Then Caro said despairingly, 'The trouble is, they've seen how good he is at it and haven't understood that's because he minds too much. They can't see the danger.'

*

Trish wrenched open the door of the freezer, hoping there might be something she could thaw in the microwave. The frost-free shelves were much fuller than she remembered. Rootling through the neat packages, she found something labelled 'seafood pancakes' in George's handwriting, along with instructions to microwave them for five minutes, then rest them, then give them another two-minute blast.

They hadn't been there the last time she'd looked, which must have been the day she'd stowed away a boxful of Snickers ice-cream bars for David at the beginning of the school holidays. There were other unfamiliar wrapped packages, too. She took out several and saw a neat label on each one, naming the food inside and giving instructions for heating or cooking it. George must have been so sure she'd starve without him that he'd had a marathon cooking session and secretly filled her freezer before he left the country.

Once that would have exasperated her; she would have taken it as a signal of control or reproof or something. Now she was just grateful. And hungrier than ever.

She was halfway through the second dill-flavoured fish pancake when the door bell rang. Since it wasn't likely to be Liz again, and nearly all her friends were on holiday, it was probably someone selling low-grade dusters for ludicrous prices or perhaps a charity collector. Either way, she wasn't going to interrupt herself to answer. She sat tight and forked up another huge mouthful.

'Trish!' She recognized Will's voice at once. 'Are you there?'

She swallowed in a hurry, but half the food stuck in her throat.

'Trish? Trish, I *need* you.'

Not again, she thought, knowing she'd never be able to resist that particular plea. She told herself that whatever the significance of Nick Wellbeck's information, whatever the justification for Petra's warning, Will was still the man she'd instantly liked and wanted to protect. But she couldn't move.

'*Trish*.' He'd pushed open the letterbox now. Even though he wouldn't be able to see her, he'd see the lights and smell the food and know she was there.

He'd broken a man's neck. He might have killed a woman. And he'd lied to her. Could she persuade him that she still believed in him? If not, it would be better to pretend she was out, however unconvincingly, than let him in and risk provoking him.

But what if he *were* innocent? With his sensitivity to criticism, he'd know why she hadn't opened her door. What would that do to a man so raw, so attuned to the slightest hint of dislike or contempt?

'Trish, please.'

'Coming,' she called as soon as she'd got the mouthful down. 'Sorry, I was choking.'

The latch seemed stickier than usual, but she managed to turn it eventually and opened the front door far wider than she wanted.

Will had one arm in plaster and several bits of transparent wound tape across abrasions on his face. His bottom lip was swollen as though one of his teeth had been driven into it, and he had a black eye. He was also leaning against the wall, a stick dangling from his good arm. Looking down, she saw that his left ankle was plastered too. She stood aside to let him in.

'It's wonderful that they've let you go,' she said, struggling for the right amount of enthusiasm, and not specifying whether it was the hospital or the police she meant. 'Fantastic. Come on in and I'll heat you up some food.'

'Can I really come in?' He sounded as uneasy and unthreatening as ever.

'Yes.'

'Thank God.' He stumbled as he crossed the threshold and landed in her arms, as the stick clattered to the ground. 'Sorry. I wasn't sure if you'd—'

She had to hold him for a moment to stop him crashing to the floor. Swaying under his weight, feeling the thud of his overstimulated heart all through her body, she used both hands to get him upright and balanced, before bending to pick up his stick. Touching him made her teeth clamp tight against each other.

'Here,' she said, making herself relax. 'Come and sit at the table, if you can. Pour yourself a glass of wine, and I'll go and get you some food. OK?'

He was wiping his eyes with the back of his hand, as though something had hurt so much in the fall that it had made them water.

'Great. Thanks.'

It was a relief to be out of sight in the kitchen. She could hear him lumbering around the table and manoeuvring his body and the stick so that he could lower himself into a chair. She still didn't know what to think, or whether to ask him questions now. All she knew for certain was that he couldn't do her any physical harm in this condition.

Later, when he had eaten and they were sitting over the wine and a bowl of rich, dark, imported cherries, in an atmosphere heavy with suspicion and fear, she asked him how he felt. It was a silly question, but someone had to say something.

'Like shit,' Will said. He let his eyelids lift and looked directly at her.

Trish had never seen his face so hard. Even when he'd been worried or frightened, he'd been able to produce a smile of sorts. Now, it seemed all masks were off.

'The police have said they'll want to talk to me again,' he went on, 'but at the moment they seem prepared to believe I didn't kill Mandy.'

Trish fought down the question that surged up her throat, asking instead, 'Who was she, Will?'

'A girlfriend? A source? A threat? I don't know,' he said,

looking away, towards the window that framed the tower of the cathedral. Soon the light would go, but for now it was washing the stonework in a warm, golden glow. 'That's the trouble. I just don't know.'

'How did you meet her?'

'When I went to Ivyleaf in search of information about the sausages. She's . . . She was the receptionist there.'

'And you became friends?' Trish suggested when he left it at that.

'More than that.' He looked back at her. A faint flush seeped along his cheekbones. 'I couldn't believe it at first, but she . . . she took me to bed. I'm sorry, Trish . . . But that's what happened. She seemed so sweet, so cuddly, that I felt awful for trying to get information out of her. Now it looks as if she was at it, too. All the time.'

Trish poured more wine into his glass and attempted a teasing tone of voice to hide all the inferences she was trying not to make about the way a man as vulnerable and emotional as Will might react to this kind of betrayal. 'There's nothing to apologize for. And I can't believe you were reluctant.'

'I wasn't.' Will blinked several times, then gulped some wine. 'And I shouldn't have been so surprised to find she knew Bob Flesker. Or so angry. I mean, they worked for companies that did business together, but I . . .'

'Don't make yourself go through it again, Will,' Trish said, knowing she couldn't hear a confession from him and not do anything about it. 'You look exhausted, and you must have had to tell the story too often by now.'

'Yes. But you need to know. I have to tell you.' His voice was rising in excitement and his hands were clenched. Even the one at the end of his broken arm tightened into a fist. Those were the hands that had broken Flesker's neck. She forced herself to look away from them and smile into his face. 'It won't take long. Please listen, Trish.'

'OK.'

So he told her the story she'd already heard from Petra. Everything was the same, even the words he used. Trish recognized them all, sensible, disciplined, convincing in themselves, and now so obviously rehearsed they made her shiver.

'I could never have hurt Mandy,' he ended, 'even to save my own life.'

'Good.'

'You do believe me, don't you?'

Why did that sound so much more like a threat than a plea? Trish wondered even as she tried to put her mind into the right condition to answer.

'By God, you don't. What have I ever done to you to make you think I could . . .?' His voice failed, but his eyes looked flinty.

She looked straight at them and forced herself to lie with yet another smile, hating what she was doing. 'Of course I believe you. Don't be silly, Will.'

'That's OK then. Good,' he said, letting his hands flatten. She felt her lungs inflate again. 'So, what are we going to do about Ivyleaf?'

'I'm too tired to think about that now, and there are other priorities. Once the case is over, I'll help you sort out a dossier, with all the facts and supporting evidence clearly laid out, to submit to the Meat Hygiene Service or the Food Standards Agency. They're the people to get the whole Ivyleaf operation shut down for good.'

'It can't wait that long. It's cost too much to get this far. Mandy's dead. Trish, we have to—'

'It *has* to wait,' she said grimly. Then she made her face and neck soften again. 'And you have to get home now. Does your sister know the police have let you go?'

'She doesn't know they ever had me.' He was leaning across the table now, peering into her face. 'Unless you told her.

Christ! You did, didn't you? Trish, why have you turned against me? I thought you were on my side.'

'Come on, Will, don't look at me like that. I am on your side. Of course I am. I didn't say anything to Susannah about Mandy; only that you'd been in a fight and were in hospital. Someone had to tell her that much, to explain why you weren't coming home.'

'Bollocks. This is nothing to do with her. She's not my fucking keeper. What gave you the right to interfere?'

The only way of keeping this within safe limits was to behave as though Will were ordinarily angry and she still sure he was real and honest and safe.

'You're living in her house,' she said quietly, 'and she's concerned about you. You'd better ring her now, then I'll call you a cab.'

His nostrils flared, but he didn't say anything. Every self-protective instinct screamed at Trish to get him out of her flat fast, before this got out of hand. She almost pulled the kitchen phone off the wall.

'Sorry, love,' said her local minicab company. 'Hour and a half wait. It's a busy night. Shall I book you in for then?'

'No, thanks. Don't worry. I'll try someone else.'

All the numbers on the cards stuck round the phone produced similar results. Everything she'd eaten and drunk was rocking around in her gut, making her feel seasick.

'Don't worry, Trish,' Will said from right behind her, making her jump. How had he moved so quietly with his plastered leg and his stick? 'I can crash on one of your sofas. They're big enough. And I won't disturb you.'

'With all your injuries, you need to be safe at home in your own bed,' she said, grabbing at the excuse. 'I haven't had that much to drink, I'll drive you back to Fulham.'

Tonight was obviously the time for breaking all her rules. But she knew she wouldn't sleep if she had Will in the flat, even in his wounded state. She nipped into the kitchen to grab a handful of coffee beans to chew to keep her mind focused and urged him out of the flat.

Chapter 22

The edges of the road wouldn't keep to their place as Trish drove back home from Fulham. Light from oncoming cars ballooned in her eyes. Her hands were clutching the steering wheel more tightly than at any time since she'd first learned to drive. She tried to reckon up how many glasses of wine she'd drunk tonight as a way of focusing her mind.

There'd been the bottle in El Vino, but Nick Wellbeck had drunk most of that, although she hadn't been able to stop him refilling her glass when she'd finished it the first time. She'd left it there on the table though, and scooped up handfuls of biscuits. Or was handsful? Her hands were definitely full of steering wheel and guilt for this irresponsibility.

What had happened to the Trish Maguire who believed in the law and control and accepting the consequences of whatever you did?

She kept swerving away from all the ideas she couldn't bear to confront, just as the car veered from the line it was supposed to take. It jolted suddenly, as though she'd run over a brick or a branch or something in the gutter. She wrenched the steering-wheel back to the straight. But she'd been too violent and the car charged towards the next corner at quite the wrong angle.

Correct it gently, she told herself, coming back to life and sanity just in time to avoid bouncing off a row of very expensive parked cars.

This couldn't go on. She checked in her mirror, making a great labour of it. There was nothing behind her, so she stopped in an empty space by the pavement, and applied the handbrake as tightly as if she'd parked on a one-in-three hill. Then she took her feet off the pedals. The car jolted forwards as if it had been hit by a truck. Still no one in the mirror. She'd left the car in gear.

Pressing down on the clutch again, she waggled the gear lever to make sure it was free, then she turned off the engine, pulling the key from its lock. A minute later, she was out in the fresh air, weaving slightly. It was a pity it wasn't colder, to shock her into sobriety, but the day's heat still hung about her head and wafted up from the tarmac.

She was sure she shouldn't be as drunk as this. A glass and a half in El Vino and two at home. That might be too much for any driver, and more units than a woman should take in one day if the health experts were to be believed, but it wasn't nearly enough to make her behave like this.

The edge of the Embankment was comfortingly close. She lurched towards it, and leaned with her arms crossed in front of her, to gaze at the Hungerford Foot Bridge. She wasn't used to seeing it from this side.

Her wobbly mind played around the blue light on top of each bunch of steel wires keeping the bridge suspended in the air. The bunches looked like transparent tents. What genius had been able to envisage this fantastical arrangement of wire, darkness and blue and white light? Each component was ordered and severe on its own, and yet together they were magic. And what a blue! Not navy or royal or turquoise or French or powder or any other kind of paint-card shade; just blue. Perfect.

Trish's ears were still buzzing, but her sight was steadying, and the hardness of the stone she was leaning on helped bring her back to her senses.

It wasn't only the drink that had thrown her so wildly off

course. There was also the suspicion that had been growing like a fungus in her brain since the meeting with Nick Wellbeck. She still didn't want to think about it. Her subconscious would probably find ways to make it less awful if she could leave it alone for a few more hours.

'Why didn't he tell me?' she asked the moon, which couldn't have cared less. 'He told me about his wife; about how much he hated farming and all the quarrels he'd had with his father. He even told me about his father's stroke and what he felt after that. Some of it, anyway. So why the hell didn't he tell me the truth about Jamie Maxden and his article about the illegal meat that must have come from Manor Farm?'

She'd known almost from the start that Will was cleverer than he usually let himself appear. Now she had to face the fact that for all his extravagant outpourings of words and emotion, there'd been more than one secret tightly withheld in his brain. What else might there be?

What if he hadn't sold the farm because he'd hated getting up in the raw dawn for milking every day, as he'd claimed? What if he'd done it to make sure that no hint of a scandal about the meat from those same cows could damage him? What if he'd blamed Jamie Maxden's investigation for his father's death? What if he'd been biding his time ever since, taking pleasure in the ruin of the journalist's career, until he could exact the maximum revenge? How much of the stories he'd told Trish had he invented?

Her mind kept lurching away from the rational. She was usually much better at analysis than this. The idea sobered her a little and she decided that Will couldn't have been after revenge or he'd never have involved her in his drama.

Unless he was a lot more subtle than she'd guessed.

'You all right, love?'

Trish pushed herself away from the supportive granite and looked round into the concerned face of one of a pair of

Community Support Officers. They were dressed in dark-blue uniforms with fluorescent yellow jackets on top. She couldn't remember whether they had powers of arrest or any responsibility for traffic control. But maybe it didn't matter. They couldn't have any idea that the lanky dark-haired woman talking to herself as she mooned over the river could have had anything to do with the smart Audi parked on the opposite side of the road. Or that she might have been driving a murderer home to his caring sister in Fulham.

'I'm fine, thank you,' she said, watching her best warm, high court voice relax them. 'I was just walking off dinner and admiring the bridge. Isn't it wonderful?'

She assumed that would send them on their way, reassured that she was a harmless local eccentric.

'Fantastic,' said the second officer, in a rich Birmingham accent. He poked his chin towards the bridge. 'Doesn't look so good in the day, but at night it's the best new landmark in London. Knocks spots off the one by the new Tate if you ask me. And as for that Gherkin! Words fail me.'

Trish nodded, words having failed her in a much more literal sense.

'Take care now,' said his partner, and the two of them set off with the steady swinging trudge that would carry them over the rest of their beat without too much damage to their calf muscles or the soles of their feet.

No wonder the London police were called plods, Trish thought, watching them. That's exactly how they must have walked in the days when they still patrolled the beat.

She waited until these two had turned off the Embankment and disappeared. Then, almost sober, she turned back to face the river, wishing she had someone to consult about Will. But Antony was impossible; Caro, too ill and in any case too tied in with her police colleagues; and none of her other friends would be able to help with something like this, even if they were still in London. It would be far too complicated – and expensive – to try to explain it all to George over the phone.

This was the flip side of the freedom that had given her back her wings. She'd forgotten what it was like to feel so lonely.

Loneliness has nothing to do with the physical absence of your lover, she decided. It's being in a place where there are no landmarks because someone you trusted has destroyed them all. It's a place where time doesn't move and there's no warmth and no safety. And the only way to avoid being there is never to trust a living soul.

One person might have been able to help, if only she hadn't cut herself off from him. But how could she go to her father now? It would be impossible to say, 'I've let another violent hurt man get through my defences. I've come to care about him. Now, I think he could be a killer. If he isn't and knows what I think, I'll hurt him nearly as badly as I hurt you. What can you tell me that might help?'

At last, she got back in her car and drove with the utmost caution back to Southwark.

Next morning in court, she sat behind Antony, waiting for Ferdy Aldham to make his closing speech in defence of Furbishers Foods. She didn't have the headache she deserved for last night's excesses, but she couldn't get the thought of Will out of her mind.

Right from the beginning she had prided herself on picking the real facts out of his torrents of impassioned words. Had she in fact heard only what she'd wanted to believe?

What if his pleasure in her various summaries had been triumph at having so comprehensively deluded her? There had always been a distance between the friendly country-bumpkin persona he often affected and the sharp mind she knew it hid. She should have had the sense to probe more deeply before she had embroiled herself in his games.

Have I backed the wrong horse all along? she thought. If I have, then what does that say about the case? We *have* to win it, but if Will has lied, then what satisfaction could there be?

'And so, my lord . . .' Trish woke up to the fact that Ferdy must have been speaking for at least ten minutes. Thank heavens Colin was obediently writing notes of everything. She'd have a chance to read what she'd missed.

'And so, my lord, we have here a group of small food producers, unfamiliar with the normal trading practices of major supermarkets and consequently unable to distinguish between their own enthusiasm and the realities of large-scale business,' Ferdy said, flicking his papers disdainfully away from him, before launching into a panegyric of Furbishers' importance and benevolence.

Trish settled down to concentrate and mentally redraft aspects of Antony's speech to counter the few points Ferdy made that they had not expected.

At the end of the day, it was a relief to go back to chambers for the post-mortem. The last thing Trish wanted now was to be in the flat and accessible to Will. She'd had her mobile switched off all day and planned to keep it that way. It was a pity Liz Shelley was back; otherwise, Antony might have suggested going out for dinner again. Still, Trish could always drop in and see Caro and find out if there were any more news of Kim.

The meeting in chambers didn't take long because there was so little Ferdy had adduced in his speech that they had not foreseen. Trish was walking up the hospital stairs at half past six.

She'd given up waiting for the lifts long ago. They always seemed to be monopolized by people going up and down a single floor. She pushed open the swing doors that led from the main passage into the ward and saw Caro, walking slowly towards her, held up by Cynthia Flag.

'Hi, Trish! Don't you think I'm doing well?' Caro called.

'Brilliantly. How are you feeling?'

'Much better. I can't tell you how different it is now. I even think they're going to let me go home soon.'

'You mustn't rush it, Caro. It would be madness, having been through all this, to risk a relapse.' Cynthia said. 'Hello, Trish, how are you?'

'I'm fine. We're almost at the end of the case. Just our speech, then the verdict.'

'Will you go out to Australia then?' Caro asked.

'Not worth it. George and David are due back at the end of the week in any case.' Trish found herself smiling at the prospect.

'Caro, would you be all right if I left you in Trish's hands now? I ought to get home and she can take you back to your bay.'

'Of course, darling. Thank you.' Caro kissed her.

'Nice woman,' Trish murmured when Cynthia had gone. 'How did you meet?'

Caro laughed, seeming almost back to her usual self. 'She's a probation officer. I found her when I first came to London. In fact, she and I were together for a while. She was my first, taught me what it was all about.'

'Ah. I see. I must say, she's gorgeous.'

'Isn't she? But that's a recent development. She wasn't confident enough to let herself look like that in those days.'

'How's Jess?'

'Hanging on. It's a pity she hasn't got any work at the moment; that always cheers her up. Being around the flat all day, waiting for her agent to call, means she hasn't got any distraction from her frets. That's why Cyn moved in. She promised me she'd look after Jess until I could get home.' Caro looked at her feet, then said, 'I owe Cyn a lot more than I realized till now; taking care of Jess is only part of it.'

'It looked to me as though she was doing a good job,' Trish said, aware that yet again she'd been making wildly inaccurate judgements on inadequate evidence. She'd never do that on a case. When was she going to learn to apply the disciplines of her work to her personal relationships? Life would feel a lot safer if she started to do that. 'I'd wondered how she came to be there.'

They were back at Caro's bed now, which was lucky because she was beginning to tire. The colour had gone from her face and she was trembling. As she lay down, she said, 'Did your meat man ever find out anything useful about the sausages?'

If Caro had been well, and if Will had not been facing arrest for murder, Trish wouldn't have been able to resist confiding in her. In normal times, there were few people whose judgement she would rather trust. Now it was crucial to keep within the limits set by their different roles. Caro had always put her work ahead of every personal consideration. She wouldn't be able to listen to anything that might help her colleagues in such a serious investigation without passing it on to them. Trish's professional rules were equally stringent, but different. For the moment, she had to keep her anxieties about Will to herself.

'He hasn't found out anything yet,' she said lightly, 'although he's still got all sorts of suspicions. But it's looking more and more likely that it was some kind of local contamination, confined to that particular packet of sausages. That's why the bugs attacked only you and me.'

'I still don't know why they went for me so much more ferociously than they did you.'

'One of the nurses here suggested stress,' Trish said lightly and watched Caro's face close in. For her, stress was tantamount to weakness and she'd never admit to that.

This was clearly not the moment to ask for news of Kim or Pete Hartland.

When Trish eventually got back to the flat, she switched on her mobile in case there were any urgent messages. Will's voice was the first she heard.

'Trish, I'm sorry I lost it yesterday and shouted at you. It wasn't fair. I'd had a hell of a time, but I know it's not your fault. It was wonderful to see you last night. I'll never forget . . . Sorry. Bye.'

The next was Petra Knighton, sounding as dry and aggressive as ever. 'As I expect you know by now, your protégé and co-investigator has not been charged with anything as yet. The police are waiting until they get an analysis of the blood spatters. And there were plenty of those. The signs are that the other man will live, but he is still not in a state to be interviewed.'

'I can't just leave it like that,' Trish muttered, staring at the tiny phone that nestled in her hand like a scarab.

There wasn't much she could do until after Antony had given the closing speech. Then they were bound to have at least a day – probably more – while the judge considered his verdict, so she could start to make proper enquiries then. In the meantime, she could at least phone Susannah for confirmation of the date of her father's death.

'It was almost exactly six years ago. The twentieth of next month. Why d'you need to know?'

'Just confirmation,' she said, without offering any explanation. 'And I didn't want to bother Will with questions while he's so vulnerable. How does he seem to you?'

'Morose. He won't tell me anything about what happened or whether he's facing more trouble from the police. Do you know?'

'No.' It wasn't quite a lie, but Trish still hated saying it. Remembering Will's reaction to her indiscretion last night, she knew she couldn't tell Susannah any more now. 'Still, we shouldn't have too long to wait for the Furbishers verdict. The judge must be pining to get shot of the case. Everything will look different once we've got the verdict.'

'Only if it's in Will's favour. And he doesn't think it will be. If it isn't . . . if he doesn't get any damages—' Susannah gasped. 'Oh, God! I don't know what we'll do then. I must go.'

Trish switched on her laptop and ran Jamie's film again, wishing there were more landmarks to be seen around the airstrip. If she could find that, she could almost certainly find the pilot, who, Will believed, was the man who'd protected him from discovery in France. So far, Trish had no proof that anything in Will's story had been true. If she could check that out, she might feel better.

Had she backed the wrong horse? Susannah's anxiety was as nothing to Trish's dread.

Chapter 23

'And so, my lord, I submit that Furbishers Foods has consistently operated a policy of deliberate breach of contract,' Antony said, without any emotion at all. He almost sounded as though he didn't care. 'They have put my clients in a position of maximum financial vulnerability in order to squeeze out the last drop of profit for themselves. Taking immense pains to ensure that there was nothing whatsoever in writing about what they now claim to have been only the first of two contracts in each case, Furbishers proceeded to allow my clients to believe that they had a contract that would last for several years. At the same time, as you have heard, Furbishers' head-office staff were deliberately spinning out the negotiation of the paper contracts my clients had been told, orally, were a mere formality to confirm what had already been agreed.'

Trish watched Mr Justice Husking as carefully as any hen overseeing its chicks, but she still couldn't discern any change in his expression. Antony paused for him to catch up with his notes. The judge eventually looked up and nodded for him to begin again.

Antony ran through the actions Will and the others had taken to deal with Furbishers' initial interest and then to fulfil the orders. Trish didn't see how anyone who heard Antony could find for Furbishers, but then she was wildly prejudiced in his favour. She glanced at Ferdy and his junior, who were carefully looking unworried. No one from Furbishers was in court today.

At last it was done. Mr Justice Husking thanked counsel and announced that his verdicts would be delivered in two days' time, which was about as quick as any judge could possibly be.

'Celebration lunch, Trish? Colin?' Antony said as soon as the judge had left.

'Yes, please,' Trish said.

She was itching to find out more about the pilot and the airstrip, but she couldn't turn Antony down, and she knew Colin would never lunch with him unless she were there too. Colin looked as though he'd barely slept, which must mean he was worrying over the papers for his immigration case. Somehow, Trish had to show him that even though stringent preparation was essential, so was clinging on to real life. And squash.

Antony took them to the Garrick, which might not have been quite as empty as El Vino had been but was much more sparsely populated than usual.

As soon as they'd ordered, Antony asked Colin whether he'd come to any conclusions about the area of law he wanted to go for. He blushed.

'Actually,' he said, 'commercial. I'd always thought it would be a dry business, all about money.'

'Isn't it?'

'Not the way you and Trish practise it.'

Antony laughed, and toasted her in the club's claret. 'That's Trish. I don't go in for her kind of sympathy. There aren't many of us who do. How *is* Will Applewood, Trish, now that he's at risk of a murder charge?'

Colin looked from one to the other, as if still trying to decode their subterranean messages. It occurred to Trish that he knew nothing about Will's disaster.

'Verbally aggressive,' Trish said.

'So long as it's only verbal, I don't mind,' Antony said. 'If it looks like getting physical, I want you right away from him. At once. Understood?'

'All right. But there's not much he can do to anyone now, with one arm and one ankle in plaster.'

'I wondered why he wasn't in court.' Antony turned to the gaping Colin, smiled and added: 'You'd better fill him in, Trish. It's not fair to keep him hanging like this.'

A waiter brought their food as Trish gave Colin a version of what had been happening. He was too tactful to ask questions or make any connection with the research he'd done for her. At the end of her explanation, he moved the conversation on to his own immigration case.

'Your client sounds quite desirable,' Antony said, refilling Colin's glass. 'So I hope you manage to win for him. But some of the people trying to sneak in are an infection of the body politic. Rather like your food-poisoning bug, Trish, but considerably more dangerous.'

Could that sort of infection be relevant to her own enquiries? she wondered, suddenly aware of a whole range of new possibilities. Could the smuggling out of mucky meat be only a sideline to the real business of bringing in live bodies of people rich enough to pay for their journey and with an unusually strong need to evade every possible kind of immigration control? That would make infinitely more sense – and infinitely greater profits.

Was 'the rest' that Jamie Maxden had promised to email a film showing illegal immigrants descending from the plane? It sounded more than possible, and it made Trish want to find the pilot fast.

That afternoon, while the judge started to ponder his verdict, Trish trawled through all the notes she'd made of Will's telephoned story, coming upon the reference to a farmer near Smarden, who was thought to own his own plane. She phoned the Civil Aviation Authority to ask for the names of all farms with airstrips within a radius of thirty miles of the town.

'We don't have that information available,' came the polite reply.

'What? You must.'

'No. Private planes can be flown off any piece of grass: your own front lawn, if it's big enough. We don't regulate them.'

'What about the planes? They must be registered.'

'Yes. They all have to carry a five-character identification. The first is the prefix that identifies the country. Ours is G. Then there's a hyphen and four other letters.'

That must have been the illegible marking she'd seen on the plane's fuselage in Jamie's video.

'I haven't got the identification, I'm afraid,' Trish said. 'So if you could just look through your lists for any planes registered to addresses . . .'

'That's private information. All I can tell you is whether any particular named individual has a private pilot's licence. Nothing else. If you haven't got a name, I'm afraid I can't help you.'

All Trish had was a first name – Tim. She contemplated the smears on the glass in front of her. It was more than time the window cleaner had another go at them.

'Then, do you have any specific rules about amateurs flying? That might help me.'

'No. There are no rules for private aircraft flying in uncontrolled airspace, that is below five hundred feet in congested areas and one thousand five hundred in uncongested ones, except that the pilot must have the relevant qualification.'

'So what happens if someone's flying into the country at night? I mean, don't air traffic controllers monitor who they are and where they're going?'

'Not if they're flying in uncontrolled airspace. Private aircraft there, in daylight or after dark, operate on a "see and be seen" basis. That is, it's up to them to keep out of other aircraft's way.'

'Thank you,' Trish said, although she wanted to curse. She couldn't believe it was so easy to hop in and out of any country in the world. No wonder the asylum problem was so bad.

She put down the phone to re-read the notes. There was nothing in them to show what legitimate use the pilot had for his plane and so there was no obvious way of tracking him down. It was beginning to look as though she would have to drive down to Smarden and cast about for local information.

Through the smears on the window she could see the sun still shining as brightly as it had for the last six weeks. It seemed eccentric to long for rain, but the relentlessness of the dazzle was getting to her, and the dust in the streets choked everyone. She looked out her sunglasses and a bottle of water, collected her laptop, and set off.

It wasn't hard to find and identify the pub nearest Smarden Meats, which Will had mentioned in his notes. That was where he'd heard a group of one-time farmers talking about their bed-and-breakfast businesses and the friend who owned a small plane. A notice told her that the pub closed after lunch and wouldn't be open again until the evening. Trish cast around the village and its outskirts until she found a sign for one of the bed-and-breakfast operations.

She didn't much like driving her Audi down the potholed drive, but there were no sinister sounds of the axle cracking on any obstruction and no obvious damage. At the bottom of the lane was a perfect Kentish farm, with an oast house, lots of white paint, and a small apple orchard to one side. Chickens were clucking somewhere and bees buzzing. It looked like an illustration from a children's book.

The woman who opened the front door had dressed herself to match with a voluminous blue and white gingham apron over her sprigged cotton dress. She looked hot, but welcoming.

'Hello,' Trish said, 'I was passing and I saw your sign. I'm thinking of bringing the family to Kent for a week at the end of August. I wondered whether you take bookings and how much you'd charge.'

'Come in and have a cup of tea and a look round. I'm making apple jelly with the windfalls at the moment and I don't want it to burn. D'you mind?'

'Not at all. How kind.'

The kitchen was all the exterior had promised and Trish was soon sitting at the big scrubbed table with a mug of strong tea and a slice of thick dark fruit cake while the farmer's wife tested the temperature of her jelly. The scents of apple and sugar mingled with preserved meats and cheese to bring a Fortnum & Mason style smell of incredible luxury into this childhood paradise. Trish wondered whether the kitchen had looked like this in the days when it had been the centre of a working farm.

'How many of you would there be?' asked the farmer's wife.

'Three, if we come. My only worry is about my half-brother. He's ten and he's never lived in the country. I'm worried he might be bored. Are there any stables round here, where he could have riding lessons?'

'Plenty. And there's canoeing on the river. Most boys like that, I've found. We've got bikes, too, and he'd be welcome to borrow one.'

'That would be great.' Looking around the kitchen, Trish was beginning to think she really might bring David here for a while. It would do him good to experience a way of life that was so different from anything he'd ever known. She reminded herself to get on to the real questions before she lost herself in the other woman's fantasy world.

'What about more exotic things: hot-air ballooning or flying or something? He's always talking about a friend of his whose father has a plane. I wouldn't know where to begin to find that.'

The other woman was pegging a curious cone-shaped flannel bag to the legs of an upturned stool. Then she put a large earthenware bowl below it and proceeded to pour her boiling, apricot-coloured liquid through the bag. How odd that apples should turn that colour!

'There, that'll clear nicely and I can concentrate.' She put the jelly pan in the sink and ran cold water into it, before pouring herself a mug of tea from the big brown pot she'd put out for Trish. 'Ballooning? I've never heard of anyone round here with a balloon. But they give flying lessons at Lydd Airport, down towards Dungeness, and run charter flights. That'd be the place to go.'

Shit, thought Trish, keeping the smile on her face. A legitimate airport was the last place she wanted.

'That would be great,' she said, smiling as she lied. 'I'll look them up. Is there much recreational flying here?'

'I don't know.'

'You see I've been reading about how there are lots of little airstrips in Kent. I wondered who could be using them. It can't be crop spraying. There aren't those sorts of fields here.' This could take for ever, Trish thought, and the woman was beginning to look suspicious.

Trish moved the conversation on to the date of the house and how full it was at the moment. Soon, she was being shown around some beautifully kept bedrooms, with high, plump beds positively smothered in huge soft pillows cased in pristine linen. She almost promised to take two of the rooms for the last week in August, but got away without making any definite commitment.

None of the next three farms she tried were half as alluring, and none produced any information about local aeroplanes or night flights. Her cheeks were aching with the smile she'd had to keep on her face, and little hammers were banging behind her eyes. The petrol gauge in the Audi was showing empty and the warning light glared at her from the dashboard.

Stuck in the middle of a tangle of tiny country roads, she had no idea which direction would take her to the nearest garage. She didn't want to drive even deeper into nothingness and run out altogether. Feeling a fool, she stumped back up the garden path to knock on the door of the last farm.

'I'm sorry to bother you again. I just wanted to know where's the nearest place I could get some petrol.' She waved at the car, which looked horribly urban and out of place, even with the Kentish dust fanning along the sides.

The owner of the bed and breakfast directed her to a town five miles to the west, where she'd find a twenty-four hour petrol station.

'Thank you.'

'That's all right. I was thinking after you'd gone that if you wanted more information about how to get your brother up in an aeroplane, you could ask Mr Hayleigh.'

'Who's he?'

'He has a cherry farm on the edge of the Marsh, only about two miles from here.'

It was in the opposite direction from the garage, but Trish's blood was up now and she wasn't going to abandon the hunt.

'He takes aerial photos too. He might be able to help. I don't know if he takes passengers up ever, but you could always ask.'

Thirty minutes later, with her car's tank filled to the brim with petrol, Trish was leaning against a sagging post and rail fence, with her laptop balanced on the post. She was running Jamie Maxden's film and trying to decide whether the buildings that formed big black lumps in the distance on the far side of the field could be the same as the orangey-red ones she saw in front of her, looking warm and comfortable in the late sun.

She was never going to be able to swear to it, but they looked pretty much alike to her.

There was no sign of any aeroplane and, from where she

stood, she couldn't see anything that looked especially like an airstrip, but this was the place to which she'd been directed, and it had plenty of empty fields. It wasn't a farm; more an enormous orchard. There was no sign of any animals, although she could hear the ubiquitous chickens clucking somewhere.

Some of the outbuildings had open sides and protected various tractor-like machines. Others were closed and might easily contain a small aeroplane.

Trish clicked the computer shut and locked it away in the boot, before making her way round to the front of the farmhouse. There was no answer to her knock at the door, so she took that as an invitation to explore.

A frenzy of barking stopped her before she'd done more than put her hand to the double doors of a building that looked like a stable. She turned hurriedly to see a wild bunch of red-gold fur careering towards her, its ears flying. The noise of its warning was indescribable, and its bottom waggled in a frenzy of excitement. All Trish knew about dogs was that a wagging tail meant the animal was friendly, but this one seemed positively aggressive in spite of its tail. That the barks were warnings, threats even, was obvious.

She put her back to the stable doors and called encouraging, breathlessly friendly comments to the animal. It didn't touch her, but it stopped only a foot away, still barking. Its ears were back now, and its yellow teeth were bared.

'Boney!' came a stentorian shout from the far side of the buildings.

Trish leaned more comfortably against the wooden doors.

'Boney!'

The dog didn't move, but it stopped barking more than two or three times a minute. A man came towards her, wearing a blue checked shirt tucked into torn cream corduroys, which were themselves stuffed into knee-high dusty gumboots. His sleeves were rolled up above his elbows. His forearms looked tanned and powerful.

'Can I help you?'

'I hope so. I'm looking for Timothy Hayleigh.'

'I'm Hayleigh.' He smiled. 'Have we met?'

'No. But I need to talk to you.' She looked at the dog, and told herself there was no reason to be frightened of either of them. She smiled yet again.

He was looking puzzled but not at all worried. 'What about?'

'Jamie Maxden.'

'Oh, God!' The exclamation was out before he could control it. He bent down to pull the dog nearer his leg and stroked its head. 'I knew someone would come one day.'

Trish didn't think she would have much trouble getting him to talk.

Chapter 24

'You'd better come in. What did you say your name was?'

Trish didn't answer as she followed him into a drawing room that couldn't have been altered in fifty years, and he didn't ask again. Bulging sofas covered in thick cretonne stood either side of a logless fireplace. A vast Edwardian carpet in shades of blue, beige and pink covered most of the parquet floor, and there were china lamps with pleated silk shades on dusty mahogany tables all around the room. Dim watercolours, hung much too high, decorated the plain cream-painted walls. A glass-fronted cabinet on little bow legs stood against one wall, displaying flowered china behind its foggy panes.

'Why don't you sit down and I'll make some tea,' he said.

'Thank you, but there's no need.'

'It's no trouble. I won't be long,' he said, clumping out in his boots. The dog made to follow him. 'Stay, Boney.'

Trish sat in a stiffly uncomfortable wing chair beside the cold ash-heap that almost filled the fireplace and spilled forwards on to the cracked hearthstone. She heard chinking sounds in the distance, then an oath. Trish smiled at the dog, who glared at her. The tea-making seemed to be taking an extraordinarily long time.

At last, the drawing-room door opened, pushed aside by the corner of an old-fashioned wooden tray. Tim Hayleigh had changed out of his boots, which might have explained some of the delay. He fussed about pouring tea, then sat in the chair opposite hers. She waited for him to speak, but he simply sat, looking as though he expected her to hit him.

'A copy of a film Jamie Maxden shot of your farm one night has come into my possession,' she began.

'Only a copy?' he said quickly, leaning over his corduroy-covered knees and grabbing hold of the poker.

Trish saw it had an enormous brass knob at the handle end. She stared at it, then up at his face. His black eyebrows formed one continuous line across his frowning forehead.

'What?' he said, more puzzled than aggressive.

'I just thought you might put the poker down,' she said, measuring the distance to the door. She did not think he was about to start belabouring her with the poker, but she had to be sure before she said anything that might trigger an outburst of temper.

'Oh, sorry. Yes.' He laid it back in its brass rest, beside a matching hearth brush and a set of bellows. 'Boney!'

The dog ambled to his side, looking like a friendly rug. Trish wondered how she could ever have been afraid of it. It sank down by his chair, front legs stretched ahead of its pointed face. But its beady black eyes stared at her, as if warning her not to take too many liberties. Hayleigh's hand rested on its head.

'Who else has copies?' he asked.

'Quite a few interested parties, all of whom know where I am.'

'How did you find me?'

'It wasn't difficult,' she said, editing out all the memories of the miles she'd driven down unidentified roads to farm after farm, finding nothing. 'Just as it wasn't hard to find out about the carcasses from Smarden Meats that you fly out to Normandy.'

'Oh, Christ!' His voice throbbed. 'You've got to get out of here.'

'I can't go yet. We've a lot to discuss.'

'You don't understand.'

Trish saw that he was no longer looking at her, rather over her head towards one of the long windows. She could hear an engine, too, and tyres crunching over gravel.

'Who is it?' she asked quickly.

'You don't want to know, and he mustn't find you here. Oh, Christ! It's too late for you to get away and he'll see your car.' Hayleigh flung himself over to a door in the wall behind the log basket.

He opened it, revealing a small study, with a battered desk and piles of paper all over the floor. There was another door in the far corner, and a long window overlooking what must once have been a formal garden but was now a mass of weeds and wildflowers.

'Get in here and keep quiet. I'll think of a story to explain the car.'

They heard a door slam.

'Come on.'

The terror in his face made her move. Pressed against the wall, keeping out of sight of the window, Trish breathed in mouthfuls of dust.

You stupid cow, she thought. Just because *he's* not dangerous himself, that doesn't mean the rest aren't. He must have phoned one of them while he was making the tea neither of us wanted. Oh, sod it!

The dust was making her throat tickle. She knew she could neither cough nor sneeze. Her mouth was drying out and her eyes leaking all the moisture her throat needed. Now, if ever, was the time to exercise the self-discipline she'd forced herself to learn over so many years.

'Ron,' she heard Hayleigh say through the door. 'Thanks for coming.'

'What's that car doing in the drive? Whose is it?' The new

voice had a thick country accent. It did nothing to disguise the sharp note of aggression.

'A woman. God knows who she is. Knocked on the door all polite to ask if she could leave it there while she took her dog for a walk. Didn't want to risk leaving it on a road as narrow as this.'

Good, Trish thought. That's a good story. Well done, Tim, but what is it he's setting me up for?

'How long ago?'

'Twenty minutes, I suppose. She said she wouldn't be more than an hour.'

'OK, so we've got a safe margin of twenty minutes. What do you want that's so urgent you've left me all these messages? People are beginning to talk.'

'It's the money.' Tim sounded hopeless. 'I've told you over and over again that I need it. I had to come to you because Bob won't talk to me.'

'Haven't you heard?'

'Heard what?'

'The police have got him.'

'Oh, God. No. How? Why?'

'Because the stupid, violent arsehole killed Mandy. I can't believe you don't know anything about it.'

Trish sagged against the wall behind her. Fear was replaced by a vast upswell of relief that made her head sing. Will hadn't done it. Will wasn't a killer. Her drunken drive through London had been as unnecessary as it had been stupid. Suddenly the wall felt as soft as her expensive goose-down pillows. She didn't really care about anything now.

'Who'd tell *me*?' came Hayleigh's voice through the door. 'Neither of you have answered any of my calls, and there's no one else. I don't get the papers any more.'

'Stop asking so many sodding questions. There isn't time. Bob found out she'd been seeing someone else.'

'But she was your girlfriend, not his. Why would he worry?'

'Shut the fuck up and listen. He thought I hadn't been keeping a close enough eye on her, so he phones one day from the meat works to offer her a lift home. They tell him she's already there, with a migraine. So he goes round to see if she was telling the truth, and . . .'

'Why wouldn't she tell the truth?'

'He thought she'd changed sides. He didn't believe she was only bonking this other bloke because I'd asked her to, so that we could find out how much he knew.'

'What? What other bloke?'

'He came to the pub one day and was asking the customers all about the meat works and Ivyleaf. It was too much of a coincidence. I knew he knew something, so I had to find out how much. After I'd given him directions to Ivyleaf, I phoned ahead so that Mandy was ready for him.'

'Your own girlfriend?' Tim's voice wasn't nearly as disgusted as Trish's would have been.

'Oh, Mandy was up for anything that would help us. Or I thought she was. But Bob thinks she'd fallen in love and started telling all. He claims that when he questioned her, she confessed that she'd given this bloke the address of the French farm. I still don't believe it. But that's Bob's excuse for hitting her. You know what he's like when he starts in on someone – it gets out of hand. The fucking bastard killed her.'

Trish wondered if it could have been Tim who'd spotted Will at the French farm and hidden the fact from everyone else. He didn't interrupt Ron.

'Then the other bloke comes roaring into the cottage and gets into a fight with Bob. They both end up in hospital, with the police watching the pair of them.'

'But don't you . . .?'

'Listen. They've let the other bloke go, so they must know more than they're saying. Bob's bound to go down for Mandy's murder, and he'll try and take us with him. So we've got to shut down everything. Now. That's why I came. You've got to make sure that plane of yours doesn't show you've been flying across to France. And when they come asking questions, deny everything. Can you do that, Tim? It won't be long before they tie the journalist's death to Bob, so you could do a lot of time too, if you don't keep your mouth shut. Can you? Come on. Think about it. Can you do it?'

'Christ! I don't know. I'll try. But I need my money.'

'You won't get that for a long time.'

'But I *need* it, Ron. That's why I—'

'Get this into your thick head. If they believe Bob's story, they'll come looking for the cash. So if you haven't got any, that'll be one more reason for them to believe your denials. Got that?'

'But I need it, Ron, to keep the place going.'

'Tough. Now, keep quiet; look stupid when they ask questions; and don't try to find me. You'll get your money in the end. When it's safe. And don't go letting any more strange women park on your land. That's just stupid.'

Boney started barking again, furiously, as though picking up a threat.

'Ron, she's . . .'

Trish pressed herself against the papers. The words 'you fool, you fool' beat in her head like a metronome as she waited for Tim Hayleigh to pluck up the courage to betray her.

'Keep that animal quiet; don't let it follow me. And don't look so frightened. If they see you looking like that, they'll know it was you.'

'Ron!'

No, shrieked something in Trish's head. Don't call him back. Let him go.

There was no answer. Holding her breath, Trish heard footsteps on gravel. At least she thought she had, but then there was silence. She couldn't hear anything from the room next door. Had Tim Hayleigh gone and left her here? Had he run out after the man he'd called Ron to get him back?

An engine sounded, then gravel spurted from under rubber tyres. Trish waited. Footsteps sounded on the other side of the door. A wave of dizziness warned her she hadn't breathed for far too long. She let herself fill her lungs again, then felt her throat clutch into a spasm as the dust choked her.

She wrenched open the door, but she couldn't see anything through her streaming eyes. When her vision cleared, and the coughing had stopped wrenching her throat and chest, she looked at Tim Hayleigh.

He was sitting in the wing chair, with the dog in his lap, both arms wrapped round it, rocking to and fro.

'What'll become of me?' he asked.

'First tell me where I can get some water,' she said, one hand still stroking her throat. 'Then we can sit down again while you tell me exactly what has been going on. I'll give you whatever help I can.'

'You must have heard what he said.'

'I did. Is that why you phoned him? So *you* wouldn't have to make any kind of confession to me?'

'I don't know what you mean.' He had his head buried between the dog's ears now. Trish thought he looked pathetic, but she needed his information too much to let that get in her way. She was no longer in the remotest bit frightened of him. 'Tell me where the kitchen is.'

He told her and she left him to his canine comforter. The kitchen was the most disgusting place she had seen in years. The floor was covered with linoleum so old it had been worn into holes, in which she could see fat and crumbs and mouse droppings. The sink was full of dirty crockery, and plates of half-eaten food were dotted about all round the room. Ancient cobwebs hung from the yellowed ceiling and brown stains and drips disfigured every vertical surface. If anyone were to get food poisoning, it should have been the owner of this place.

A row of oily glass preserving jars stood on a shelf beside a streaked can and a glass bowl of what looked at first sight like maggots, but which proved to be white string wicks. Clothes were draped over the back of every chair and thick socks hung on the rail in front of the range. The smell was gross. Trish decided her throat could heal itself without any water that had come anywhere near this room.

She looked round and saw that Tim had followed her.

'You need a doctor,' she said.

'I need a cleaner. But I can't afford one.'

That was probably true, but she thought no adult who was not suffering from clinical depression could have allowed any part of his home to get this bad, however poor or busy he might be. Some of her other feelings slipped away in a wave of sympathy.

'Let's go back to the drawing room. Have you got a pen and some paper?'

Looking dazed, he nodded.

'They're for you,' she said, when he offered her a dusty pad and a biro with a chewed end, 'to write down exactly what has been happening, starting with Bob and Ron.'

'They're brothers. Bob's the elder and the leader.'

'Are you sure?'

'Of course. Ron's hopeless. Lazy. He just does what Bob tells him, when he's not working the pub, that is. Bob's a skilled slaughterman. Ron just pulls pints, and helps us out when Bob needs an extra pair of hands to load the plane.'

This wasn't the moment to talk about the commanding tone of Ron's voice or his assumption of absolute authority over Tim.

'OK,' Trish said, smiling her best client-soothing smile, 'then when you've put that down, write what you know about the carcasses Bob took from the abattoir.'

'It wasn't stealing.' He gazed at her, looking like David when he was afraid she was going to reprimand him for a bad school report. 'They were only going to be made into pet food.'

'Why?'

'Because one of those bloody vets condemned them.'

'You mean they were infected?'

'Only marginally. Probably not even that. There was plenty of meat on them that was edible. We – Bob – rescued them from burning. There are a lot of hungry people in the world, you know.'

'Not many in Kent or Normandy,' Trish said before she remembered the men on the street barbecuing their pigeon. 'How did Bob hide the fact that he'd nicked them? Aren't the vets supposed to oversee the disposal?'

Tim shrugged. 'All I know is that he once said he had to pay pet food people to turn a blind eye. Maybe that's what happened. I don't know.'

'How could there be so many carcasses? Such a reliable supply?'

'I don't know that either. Maybe Bob got some from other slaughterhouses. Maybe he sometimes nicked ones that hadn't been condemned. There's no point interrogating me.' His voice was rising with every word. 'I don't *know* any more.'

'OK. Then what happened to the meat after you'd flown it to France?'

'I don't know that either.'

'Come on! You can't expect me to believe that.'

He looked the picture of puzzled innocence. 'It's true. I was like a kind of taxi. They came to me about eighteen months ago – the Flesker brothers – they told me they had this regular source of meat they had to get out of the country without anyone noticing. They'd heard I had a plane and they wanted to hire it and me once a week. I thought about it for a bit, then said yes. OK, so it was illegal. But I needed the money, and it didn't seem too serious – a bit of nicked meat. I flew the packages across to Normandy, and the people over there took it off me. That was the end of my role.'

Trish looked at him as if he were a witness under cross-examination. 'Apart from the people you brought back with you.'

His mouth opened. 'People? I didn't bring back any people.'

'Oh, come on, Tim. You can't expect me to believe it was worth anyone's while to go to all that trouble for a one-way cargo of iffy meat. That's the kind of thing being sold from the backs of vans and in little markets all over the country.'

'I didn't bring back any *people*,' he said with the kind of emphasis that told her a lot.

'So what was it you brought back? Come on, Tim. I know there was something.'

He chewed his bottom lip. His eyes begged her to let him off, and Boney yelped as Tim's hands tightened in the golden fur.

'It was boxes. Heavy boxes. At first I didn't know what was in them. Then one night we dropped one when we were unloading, and I saw . . . well, they were guns. Not proper guns: shotguns or rifles. They were street guns.'

So, this was 'the rest' that Jamie Maxden had intended to film.

'And what happened when you got them back?'

'Ron took them away in his van.'

'Ron, not Bob?'

'That's right.'

'OK, Tim. Write it all down,' Trish said, certain now that Ron had been the boss, 'and take it to the police.'

'But I'll . . . they'll . . . I was there when . . .'

'When Bob killed Jamie Maxden?' she suggested.

Tim hung his head over Boney's.

'Yes. And it was he who thought of the veggie leaflets and the placard. They'd been left behind after the last protest at the meat works. I don't know why he kept them.'

'The sooner you confess what you have been doing, the less trouble you're likely to be in.' Trish salved her conscience with difficulty. But he was not her client and Will, still technically under suspicion for Mandy's murder, was. He was the only one whose interests she had any kind of duty to protect. 'If you make the police come to you, you'll have a much tougher time. Go to them freely, give them the evidence they need of what Bob and Ron have been doing – and making you do – and you'll stand a reasonable chance. They'll provide you with a lawyer.'

'Oh, Christ! Will you help me?'

'I'll help you draft your statement,' she said, fighting every instinct that urged her to do much more for him. 'And if you've got a fax machine, or a photocopier, I can take a copy for safety.'

It took an hour to elicit the facts he had and help him organize them all into a coherent narrative. Trish read it, then looked up.

'You've missed a bit out.'

'What d'you mean?'

'The bit about Jamie Maxden's laptop, which was your main contribution, wasn't it? I can't believe Bob typed those emails to the suicide websites, and Ron wasn't there. So it had to be you.'

The blood ebbed away from his face, leaving it grey.

'They say prison isn't much worse than a minor public school,' he said at last. 'And at least I won't have to worry about paying the bills there.'

Trish had no comfort to offer him. He looked round the room and sighed. 'Will you come with me to the police? Help me talk to them? Please.'

'I can't. I can't be involved in any of this.'

'But you are involved, aren't you? Somehow.' His face narrowed, as though two huge hands had pressed against his cheeks and squeezed. 'Who *are* you?'

Trish was already on her feet and half way to the door. She looked back. 'I'm just a friend of a friend of Jamie Maxden, who Bob kicked to death while you watched and did nothing to save him.'

'Oh, Christ! You've got to help me.'

'I can't. Go to the police, Tim; they're the only people who can do anything for you now.' She thought of Nick Wellbeck, who would love to hear this story and would probably pay well for it. Looking around, she could see how much money Hayleigh needed.

'I can't go to them.'

'You have to.'

'No, I mean, I can't *go* to the police; I haven't any petrol in the car.'

'You could always phone them. If you say you've got information to give them about Mandy's murder, they'll probably send someone to talk to you.'

She waited while he made the call, and heard him explain that he'd seen Bob Flesker kick Jamie Maxden to death. It was clear from his answers that the officer at the other end was highly sceptical. But eventually Tim said, 'No, I can't come in. My car's not working. All right, yes, I'll be here if you send someone.' He put down the phone.

'There is one other thing you could do,' Trish said, 'to help yourself. It might earn you some money too.'

He looked puzzled, as though the idea of anyone paying him anything was impossible.

'There's a newspaper editor, who would love to know what happened to Jamie Maxden. I expect he'd pay quite well for any information you can give him.'

Tim hid his face in Boney's fur again. When he looked up, his eyes were calmer.

'Thank you. I can't tell you how—'

'Don't worry about it. Just forget that I was ever here.

He's called Nick Wellbeck and this is his number. Now, I must go.'

She used the hands-free to call Will from the car, as she was negotiating her way back through the twisting, featureless, lightless lanes. He wasn't in, but Susannah answered and told her that Will was round at the doctor's.

'Is he OK? I mean is there anything else wrong?'

'Splitting headaches. He's never had them before and they've only come on since he was let out of hospital. I bullied him to go to the doctor.'

Her voice went up at the end of the sentence, as though she was asking for something.

'Quite right, too,' Trish said, hoping that was what she'd wanted. 'Will you tell him when he comes in that I've found the airfield and I've got the whole story behind Jamie's video. I can meet him somewhere, or tell him over the phone or whatever he wants.'

'I'll tell him. I don't understand, but I'll tell him: you've got the airfield and the story. Is that right?'

'Pretty much. Thank you.'

'D'you know when you'll get the verdict in Will's case?'

'Should be Friday.'

'Oh, God! I don't know how he's going to be able to sleep till then. Or me, either.'

There was nothing Trish could do about that, so she said goodbye, and switched off the phone to concentrate on driving.

The lit-up motorway beyond acres of dark fields was a welcome sign that she was at least going in the right direction, but it took her another half hour to get on to it. After that, it was simply a question of keeping herself awake and concentrating until the motorway ended in the muddle of the south London suburbs.

Not much to her surprise, Will was waiting for her again, this time sitting down on the iron steps with his plastered leg stuck right out in front of him.

'You didn't tell Susannah where you were when you phoned,' he said, levering himself up with his back against the wall, like a mountaineer in a chimney. 'I was beginning to wonder if it was Scotland.'

Trish bleeped the car's locks and ran up the stairs to help Will upright and plant a kiss on his cheek. He put his good arm around her shoulders and looked down into her face.

'How very nice, Trish!'

She couldn't tell him it was an apology for all her terrors, so she just smiled. He bent his head and kissed her full on the lips. She waited a second, then patted his cheek and pulled away.

'Come on in,' she said cheerfully. 'I've got so much to tell you.'

There were eggs in the fridge and butter and some old Parmesan, so Trish made an omelette, while Will balanced against the kitchen worktop to open a bottle of soft, woody Rioja. As she cooked, she told him what had happened that day and what she'd found out.

He listened without asking any questions, holding out each plate in turn when the omelette was ready. When he'd eaten his share, he wiped a piece of bread around the plate and looked up as he swallowed it.

'So at least I don't have to blame myself for *Jamie*'s death.'

'Of course you don't, Will. What on earth do you mean?'

He looked at the last scant smears of egg and molten cheese on his plate. 'I thought I would. Like I have to with Mandy. If I'd never gone anywhere near her, she would never have been killed. It's my fault, Trish. I've done it again. It keeps happening. I get angry and people die.' He grabbed his glass between both hands. 'If the case doesn't go our way . . .'

'I still think it might.'

'Don't try to comfort me. This is important, Trish. If we don't get the right verdict, keep away from me. I'm not safe to have around when I'm angry.' There was the sound of a car hooting in the street. 'That'll be my cab. I ordered it so there'd be no risk of you having to drive me home. Rupert said I could put it on his account.'

Trish had plenty more to ask him, but it was all so difficult that she wasn't sorry when he'd gone. She took her time washing up the plates and pans and swabbing down the kitchen surfaces, trying not to take any of her fears too seriously.

Next morning, she phoned Petra Knighton and described what she'd done.

'I thought you'd agreed to stay out of this, Trish.' The solicitor's voice was arctic.

'Yes. But once I realized the police might never get enough evidence to clear Will, I knew I had to try. I know how many murders they fail to solve. Shall I fax you the statement made by the pilot?'

'I suppose you'd better. But, you know, you've been underestimating the police.'

'How?'

'Their bloodstain analysis has proved it could not have been Applewood who killed the girl, so it is likely they've already accepted his story.'

'Thank God for that.'

'Yes. But I would advise you to acquire a little more faith in temporal authority next time. Goodbye.'

Snubbed and feeling like a fool, but still glad she'd intervened, Trish phoned Nick Wellbeck.

'What have you got for me?' he asked as soon as she'd given her name. That didn't sound as though Tim Hayleigh had been in touch with him, so she thought she'd better tread warily.

'It'll be sub judice any minute now,' she said, 'but it seems that Jamie Maxden was on the trail of a small private gang of meat and gun smugglers based in Kent. It *was* a real story. One of the perpetrators – who may have killed Jamie – is in police custody at the moment.'

'And?'

'And nothing.'

'Is that all you're going to tell me?' he said in a voice so tough she was glad she was not one of his employees.

'It's all I *can* tell you.'

'And what is it you want for your information? How much?'

'Nothing but confirmation that the farmer in the story Jamie sold you six years ago was called Applewood, Peter Applewood.'

'If you know, why are you asking?'

She put down the phone. The source Jamie had protected at so much cost to himself had to be Will. It explained so much about Will, and his motives and his misery. And it made far more sense of the fight in Susannah's bedroom than her version. Would it help Will to have it brought out into the open now? Or would it make him even more ashamed of himself? More desperate?

This was Kim all over again. Did it really help people to push emotional stuff under an imaginary carpet and pretend it didn't exist? Or was it better to bring it out into the open so they could see it wasn't as terrible as they'd once thought? That would only work if the thing that frightened them wasn't as bad in reality. What would happen if it were worse?

An impulse came into her head to phone her father. At first she couldn't understand it and put it off by making a pot of coffee. That displacement activity didn't last long and she was soon dialling his mobile number.

'Paddy Maguire.'

'Paddy? It's Trish.'

There was a pause. Then he said, 'And how are you, then?'

'Fine,' she said, then corrected herself. 'No, actually I'm not. I'm eaten up with guilt about what happened after David's mother was killed.'

'So you should be. But it's two years now. I've nearly got over it, and if I can, so can you.'

'I'm glad you have.'

'Was that all? Because I've a lot to do today.'

'No. First I wanted to know if you'd come to dinner with me on Saturday. It's my last night of freedom before George and David get back from Australia.'

'Saturday is it? All right. Bella will be away, so it'd be just you and me.'

'Great.' That would definitely make it easier to have proper peace talks with him.

'What's the second?'

'This is going to sound aggressive and it isn't meant to.' She waited for permission to continue, but he wasn't going to give it. 'I wanted to ask about an episode in the kitchen in Beaconsfield when I was a child.'

'I don't know what you're talking about.'

She tried again. 'I'd made you furious with Meg and I think you hit her. I can see the aftermath and the prelude, but I can't see the actual blow. Did you, Paddy?'

'Why haven't you asked her?'

'Because that seemed cowardly. Tell me. Did you?'

'I did.'

'I'm sorry.'

'*You*? Trish what is all this breast-beating? It's not like you.'

And it's not like you to talk in perfect English without the synthetic Irish brogue you usually put on whenever I try to discuss anything that embarrasses you, she thought.

'I've just been feeling guilty about that, too. Because it *was* my fault. I made you angry with each other. That's why you left, wasn't it?'

'This is stupid. We've been here before and I've told you why I left. You were not responsible, Trish. Hasn't all your work told you that it's never the child's fault? At three or four or whatever you were when I hit your mother in front of you, you were not of an age to be responsible for your parents. You know that. Stop wallowing. I'll see you on Saturday.'

It's never the child's fault, she repeated to herself in Paddy's voice. She hoped that Andrew Stane or someone from his team was going to be able to get that through to Kim soon, and to Daniel Crossman before he started putting his son in the space Kim had occupied in his mind.

Chapter 25

On Friday morning Will fought for the sleep he'd always been able to pull over himself in the past like an extra pillow. But now that there was time, there was no sleep to be had. Susannah had knocked on his door an hour ago, wanting to cook him breakfast and make him talk and give him the benefit of her wise counsel before he went into court to hear the judge pronounce on whether or not he had a future. But she didn't know what the judge was going to say any more than he did, and anything she could say was going to make it worse.

'Andrew? It's Trish here. Have you got any more out of Kim yet?'

'Not a thing. Why?'

'Because I've been thinking a lot about her and I want to talk to her again. Caro said no one else has been able to get anything out of her. I think I know now what must have been going on, and I'm sure I can help her tell us. Could you get her back to that interview room?'

There was a pause. 'I could try. What have you found out? Have you been investigating Dan Crossman, Trish?'

'No.' She wiped her lips and picked up her coffee again. 'But I think I know what's been driving Kim.'

'What?'

'Don't make me say it. If I'm wrong, it'll muddy the waters

for ever. If I'm right, it's better that you should hear it direct from her first, rather than worry about my having put words into her mouth. OK?'

After another pause he eventually said, 'I'll see if I can get her here today. What time? Four thirty again?'

'That would be great. We're due in court for the judgment this morning, but it won't take that long.'

'I'll have to phone her foster mother.'

'I know. You've got my mobile number. Just ring it and leave a message if there's a problem.'

Caro lay against cool, white linen pillows, sipping the lemon-and-ginger tea Jess had made for her. This was no mass-produced teabag drink. Jess had pared the zest off a lemon and infused it in boiling water with a spoonful of grated fresh ginger. She was sitting on one of the window seats, looking out at the street, reporting anything interesting to Caro.

'Is Cynthia coming round today?' Caro asked. Jess turned her head and smiled.

'I don't think so. D'you want her? I could easily phone.'

'No. It's just that she hasn't been round much since I got back. Is she angry about something?'

Jess's smile widened. 'I think she doesn't want to get in the way. She knows how much we both depended on her in the crisis. She doesn't want to make us feel we have to pay her back by including her in everything now.'

'That doesn't sound like Cyn.' Caro frowned. 'She doesn't believe in tit for tat. Not in anything.'

The phone rang. Caro, still worrying, picked it up to hear Andrew Stane asking how she felt. She mouthed his name to Jess, who nodded and turned back to the street.

'I'm much better. Thank you.'

'Caro, Trish Maguire thinks she has an answer. I've fixed for Kim to come back for one more interview in the psychiatric unit this afternoon. D'you want to be there? Are you up to it?'

'When?'

'This afternoon at four thirty.'

'Sure. I'd love to come. Did Trish say . . .?'

'She wouldn't say anything. Told me I ought to hear whatever it is straight from Kim.'

All Caro's facial muscles softened. 'So there's no question of undue influence. That's like her. Andrew, would there be room for Pete Hartland? He's been so much involved, I think he ought to hear it, too.'

'OK. D'you want me to summon him?'

'Would you? Thanks.' Caro put down the phone and set about explaining why she was going to leave the perfect lacy whiteness of the flat and the convalescence Jess had designed for her.

'Well, Trish, this is it,' Antony said, as they stood outside the court, in their gowns and wigs. 'How d'you feel?'

'Numb,' she said, lying for once because to talk about how she felt would threaten her self-control. He looked so sceptical that she added, 'Too much has happened in the last few weeks to be able to feel anything much.'

'That's my line,' he said. 'Cheer up. We've got a good chance. And you must look more confident for the clients, even if not for yourself.'

All thirty claimants were here today, most with their husbands or wives. Will had come alone. He'd already told Trish that Susannah had wanted to be with him, but he'd needed to do this on his own.

Trish knew he didn't have much confidence in the outcome, and she wished he had someone to stop him taking failure too seriously. Without his sister, or any friends, she'd have to talk him down herself, however seriously he'd meant his warning to avoid him when he was angry.

Something spiked in her mind. How could she have let this case come to matter so much? It had started so lightheartedly. Looking back, she could hardly believe the casual teasing she and Antony had indulged in at the beginning.

'It's not that bad,' he whispered. 'Liz has decided she's over-reacted and has taken the kids back to Tuscany. I'm to join them next week. You and I can have a celebratory or consoling dinner tonight. It's only a case, Trish.'

No, it isn't, she thought. It's Will's life and my self-respect. She thought of her own advice to Colin and knew she'd fallen into a trap she should have been experienced enough to avoid.

The usher appeared and beckoned them in. The claimants formed an orderly procession and marched in behind their solicitor. Some looked as if they were facing a firing squad; others as though they were already in a victory parade. Trish and Antony followed them, side by side with Ferdy Aldham and his team.

Only Colin was absent, hard at work on the papers for his immigration case. It wouldn't come to court until the beginning of next term, but he was determined to do everything he could to get the right verdict. Trish hoped he'd win, for his own sake as well as for the tortured doctor's. After all, he had been completely law-abiding in his attempts to get into England, and he had suffered terribly.

The idea of them made her think of the guns Ron Flesker had been bringing into the country. She hoped Tim's approach to the police meant they would go after Ron. They already had Bob Flesker, who would almost certainly be convicted for the two murders he'd committed, and he and Tim would probably have to answer charges for the meat smuggling, but that would be it. Responsibility for the most lucrative – and dangerous – kind of smuggling would dissolve.

Trish tried not to feel a failure for not having done anything to stop Ron getting away with it. That was the worst of crime:

the biggest criminals escaped with their profits and left the little scruffy ones to do the time.

Everyone in court stood as Mr Justice Husking swept in through the private door behind the throne-like bench. The lawyers bowed their bewigged heads to the notion of justice rather than to the man himself. After all, he'd been the failure, the one who was never going to make the millions Antony and Ferdy pulled in every year. They'd never liked him, but he wasn't worth the kind of war they fought between themselves, so they found it easy to be polite to him.

Feeling bolshier than she had for years, Trish straightened the fronts of her gown and settled down to concentrate on the judgment.

'. . . and Furbishers Foods contended that the claimants had ignored the inescapable fact that the oral contracts were on terms that had nothing to do with the longer-term relationship they were intending to set up,' Husking was saying, as he began to unravel the evidence he had heard.

Trish heard someone in the claimants' bench gasp. She hoped it wasn't Will. She'd tried to warn him of what this would be like. 'It'll be as bad for you,' he'd said, but she knew he was wrong. Unlike her, he didn't know the jargon or the reasons for the long-winded synopsis of everything that had happened in the past weeks.

'While the claimants held that Furbishers had never mentioned the fact that there were two distinct and different contracts being discussed.'

She turned her head to see Grant-Furbisher glaring at the bench. His red face had a faint sheen of sweat, but that had to come from the heat rather than from fear. What would it matter to him, how the verdict went? If he lost, his business would have to pay damages to the suppliers who'd been ripped off and Furbishers' share price would fall a point or two tomorrow. But he'd lose nothing personally. His fortune, and his family's, was so big that the dip in the value of their shares wouldn't matter. He had so much that he gave millions to charity every year. Even if he'd had to pay the damages himself, he wouldn't exactly go hungry. But he would lose face. Maybe, if you were as rich as he, and as ridiculous looking, that mattered.

'This contention of the claimants would have carried more weight, had it not been for the alleged protest by Mr William Applewood after the first, oral, contract had been offered to him.'

Oh, shit, Trish thought. Here it comes. Husking is going with Furbishers.

She could only see the side of Ferdy Aldham's face from where she sat, but she knew it would show neither fear nor excitement. Like Antony, he would be impassive. Husking began to speak again. Neither of the silks moved to recross their legs or arrange their gowns or wigs during the whole two hours of the painstaking assessment of the case for both sides.

Trish tried to keep her mind in the same kind of order, but she felt it swinging one way, then the other, with the judge's summing up. She wasn't used to feeling like this. She tried to hold on to her faith in the moments when Husking showed warmth towards the claimants, but there were all too many when his sympathies were clearly with the defendant.

At last he reached the end and allowed a small, grave smile to disturb the stiffness of his expression.

'And so, I find in favour of the claimants.'

Trish couldn't resist a quick look over her shoulder at Will. She wasn't going to display unseemly triumph, but she wanted to share the moment with him. He beamed at her like a child on his birthday. Then he mouthed the words 'thank you'.

She looked back towards the judge, quite satisfied.

Antony was on his feet as soon as Husking had awarded their clients every penny of the damages they'd claimed, with interest to be calculated from the date each had received his written contract. Husking nodded to Antony, who then formally asked for costs to be awarded against Furbishers.

As Ferdy got to his feet to protest, Trish hoped Will would understand that if the judge didn't award costs against Furbishers, some of the damages would have to go in settling the claimants' legal bills. Quite a lot, in fact. It could come as a whole new blow if Will were faced with vast fees to pay just as he believed himself free of all his debts.

She waited, directing all her attention at him to wake him out of his stupor of delight. Eventually he saw her and she watched as awareness dawned. Satisfied, she turned back just in time to watch the judge as he gave costs against Furbishers, as easily as though he'd always intended to do it. And not just standard costs either, but the so-called indemnity costs, which were awarded only when the court considered there had been improper conduct on the part of the paying party. That must be punishment for the long, fruitless, and quite unjustified procedural argument they'd launched, which had made the case overrun in the first place.

The hardness of the bench helped Trish to hold on to her assumption of calm. Not for her and Antony the exuberance of some of the clients, who were hugging each other. It was a point of honour to remain unmoved, whatever happened to the case. But when the judge had retired, Antony did turn, elbow propped on the back of the bench, to nod briefly at her.

'You did well, Trish. Thank you.'

She smiled. 'It was fun. Not the last bit, but the rest.'

'So, we have dinner tonight?'

'I'm not sure. I ought to see Will.'

'Be careful, Trish.'

'What d'you mean?'

'He thought you were the only woman for him at the start of the case. Now we've won him the best part of three million pounds plus costs, you're going to seem like the answer to all his prayers. You'd better tell him you're dining with me.'

'I'll let you know. I have to see someone else between now and then. I'll phone you.'

He nodded and turned to face Ferdy. Neither of them spoke, but there was a tightness about Ferdy's full lips that said everything.

Trish and Will were sitting on a bench in the Temple garden. She still had her red brocade bag with her, stuffed with her gown and wig, and her black linen suit felt much too formal for this part of the day, and much too hot. Will had dumped his jacket in a bundle on the bench and he'd pulled down his tie and undone the top two buttons of his shirt. His plastered leg was stretched out in front of him.

'And so now I can tell you, Trish. I love you. I need you in my life.'

'Will, I . . .'

'No, listen. I know I didn't help myself by sleeping with poor Mandy, but it was a kind of aberration. All part of the horror of what was going on. I didn't believe I'd got a chance of winning the case, so I didn't think I could ask you out.'

'But . . .'

'Wait, Trish. And listen. For once it's me that's got to talk. Like I said, I need you, and you don't hate me, do you?'

'Of course I don't, Will.' It was the truth. 'But . . .'

'In fact I think it's more than that. You see, you've always been sweet to me, even that night when you were frightened because you thought I'd killed Mandy. That made me see you might need me as much as I need you. So I thought we ought to make plans to see each other.'

Trish put a hand on his good arm, as though only by touching him could she make him hear her.

'Will, you must listen. I like you a lot. I think you've had a hell of a time and borne up incredibly well. I think you're kind and clever and brave. But I can't go out with you.'

He turned his head away, swinging his functioning leg in a vicious kick at the side of the bench. 'Is it because of what I did to my father?'

'You mean telling Jamie Maxden about how your father disposed of diseased meat to the local authority up north? No, Will, that's not why.'

He lifted his head as if he'd just heard a shot in the distance. 'So you did know. I thought you did. When did you find out?'

'When I was trying to discover whether Jamie could have killed himself. I stumbled on it by accident, but it made such sense that I believed it straight away, as it made sense of the fight you had with Jamie after you found him with Susannah.'

He stared up at the sky. She thought he was trying to keep tears inside his eyelids.

'It was the worst thing I've ever done, including getting Mandy killed. I was so angry with him that I just handed Jamie all the information he'd wanted for so long. The deal was that he would never – ever – tell anyone it came from me. That night I thought he'd broken his promise. But he hadn't. He stuck to it right to the end. Not many men would have. And you know what happened: it ruined his career. Indirectly it led to his death too.'

'Did anyone ever know that you'd given Jamie the information?'

Will looked at her for a second. She'd never seen such misery in his eyes.

'Only my father. God knows how he found out. Maybe it was just a guess. But he came rampaging into the farm office, where I was filling out some of those interminable ministry forms, and started yelling at me. That's when he had the stroke. If I hadn't done it, he'd probably still be alive.'

He shook his head from side to side, as though he couldn't

bear the weight of his memories. At last he looked back at her, with the tears sliding out of his eyes. 'Maybe you're right to have nothing to do with me. Three people have died because of me.'

'It's not that, Will.' She touched his arm again, and felt the tendons as hard as they'd been on the day he had to give his evidence. 'I have someone already.'

'*What?*'

She couldn't work out whether rage or surprise was making his voice so rough. She had to work hard not to edge away along the bench.

'It's true,' she said gently. 'He's called George Henton, and we've been together for nearly six years now.'

'But you don't wear a ring. And there's never been any sign of him in your flat. Or in the way you live. Everything about you announces your single status.' He rounded to face her again. 'It's not *fair*, Trish. You let me fall in love with you.'

'I'm sorry.' It was all she could say as he fought for the right words to tell her what she'd done to him. They didn't come so, as usual, she had to try to help.

'Will, don't look like that. You've won your case. You've been vindicated. Everything you did and said and felt about Furbishers has been publicly applauded. You and all the other claimants you brought together will be put back into the financial position you were in before Furbishers screwed you. That's a huge thing to have achieved. You can start again, and this time you'll know how to protect yourself better.'

'But I won't have you.' He pushed and pulled himself up off the bench. She just caught the last words. 'None of it'll mean anything without that.'

She watched him hobble away, wishing she'd been able to help. But he wouldn't have been able to hear anything she said at the moment, and she had to get her mind clear so that she could talk to Kim.

*

Trish had avoided lunch. She didn't want her mind fogged with food or drink when she came to talk to Kim, but emptiness was making her stomach rumble. She hoped it wouldn't worry the child.

At exactly half past four the door to the interview room opened and Kim appeared with Mrs Critch. They were still not holding hands. Trish smiled at the woman, who sat down near the door, leaving Kim standing in her neat red dungarees and red-and-white striped shirt.

'Hello, Kim. D'you remember me? I'm Trish Maguire.'

The blonde head bowed in silent acknowledgement. She didn't look any different from the last time they'd met. There were still dark-violet crescents under her eyes.

'Come and sit down.'

'D'you want me to do a painting?' Kim asked in a whisper.

'Not this time,' Trish said quietly.

When they were sitting opposite each other at the small, scarred table, Trish put her hands on the surface, balancing her wrists on the edge. Kim kept hers in her lap.

'Kim, I need some help.'

The child didn't look at her.

'I am trying to save your mum.'

Kim's eyelids flew up. Her lips remained tightly closed.

'What happened to her when you made a noise in the night?'

Kim's face crumpled, but she held on, breathing hard through her nose.

'I know you're frightened that something even worse will happen if you talk to us, but we can't help her unless we know everything. Do you understand that, Kim?'

Kim shook her head. Tears flew out of her eyes. Still she didn't speak.

'You said that Daniel made you stand on the box after you'd been screaming in the night. Is that right?'

She nodded.

'Was there more than that, Kim? Did something else happen?'

The tight, chewed lips didn't open.

'What did he say when he first told you to stand on the box?'

'That if I couldn't go to sleep without screaming when I had a bad dream, then I'd better not sleep at all.'

'So he made you take off your nightie and stand on the box to make you stay awake?' This wasn't a leading question, only confirmation of what Kim had already told her.

'Yes. With the window open behind me.'

'So you got cold?'

'Yes.'

'Did you sometimes go to sleep anyway?'

'Yes.'

'What happened then, Kim?'

She looked across the tiny table, her eyes imploring Trish to stop.

'Kim, we have to know what happened so that we can help. And we can help. I promise you.'

'He said he'd kill her if I told.'

Trish held in her reactions and her fury with all her strength. It felt like the most enormous physical effort she had ever made. If Daniel Crossman had been standing in front of her, she might not have been able to keep her hands off him.

'Who, Kim? Who did he say he was going to kill?'

'My mum.'

'Did he say how?'

'With the knife.' Tears were sliding out of her eyes now. She wiped the backs of both hands against her face.

'Which knife, Kim?'

'The vinyl one,' she whispered, 'with the red handle. He keeps it in the drawer by his bed.'

The stillness in the room was absolute. Trish had never known anything that took so much self-control.

'Have you seen it?'

Kim's eyelids lifted again. Through her tears, she looked at Trish as if she were a fool.

'Of course. It's what he uses when I fall off the box.'

'When you go to sleep?'

'Yes.'

'How does he use it?'

The silence lasted for nearly five minutes. It felt like eternity. Trish knew she mustn't ask anything else or offer any more reassurance; Kim had to do this on her own.

'When I go to sleep and fall off the box,' she said at last in a tiny voice, 'he makes me watch while he cuts my mum.'

Trish fought to get herself and her voice back in order. No wonder Kim had twice run away from home. That must have seemed like the only way to save her mother since she couldn't stop herself falling asleep, even naked in the cold blast from an opened window. No wonder she hadn't told anyone about what happened.

When she could speak again, Trish said carefully, 'You have had a very frightening time, Kim. And you have done everything you could. I would never have been able to be as strong as you. Your mum probably sometimes seemed cross with you, but you have been a very good daughter. It's not your fault that Daniel hurt her. It's Daniel's fault.'

Kim leaned forwards until her whole torso lay on the table. Her back heaved with the hugeness of her sobs.

Andrew flung his arms around Trish, just as she'd wanted to hug Kim.

'Only you could have done it. What is it about you that makes these children trust you when no one else can reach them?'

'I don't know, except that I never lie to them. And I care.'

'It's more than that: a kind of witchcraft.'

She shook her head, thinking of some terrible stories she'd

heard of children from alien cultures, whose relatives had beaten and killed them to exorcize evil spirits and black magic. 'You shouldn't even think like that in your line of work, Andrew, let alone talk about it. It's wrong, too. There's nothing in what I do except experience, mixed with sympathy and some good guesses.'

He put up both hands in surrender. 'OK. Whatever you say. I don't care what it is, so long as you keep doing the work. You mustn't give up, Trish, however much you can earn elsewhere.'

'That's not why I don't do family law any more,' she said through her teeth, which made him apologize and back off.

'How *did* you know, Trish?' Caro asked later, when Andrew had gone and Pete Hartland was on his way back to the police station to organize Daniel Crossman's arrest. Trish was sipping a mug of strong tea. All she could think about was Kim and how she was ever going to move on from this.

'I kept finding myself thinking about guilt and people's responsibility to – and for – their parents, and suddenly it seemed obvious. I'm only sorry it took so long.'

'That's not your fault. We should have known. We should have seen. The Stanley knife was there when we searched the flat, but it was in a tool box and it didn't look out of place. He said he'd been using it to cut new vinyl tiles for the bathroom. We should have examined Mo, instead of just the children. There must be scars all over her.'

'You're child protection officers; your minds were on them. Don't beat yourself up about this, Caro.'

'Easier to say than to do. I can't tell you how much I owe you, Trish.'

'No, you don't.'

'It's not just Kim,' Caro said, looking as though she found words as hard as the child had done. 'It's the E. coli, too. I infected you, and it's only good luck and your immune system that saved you.'

'That wasn't your fault, Caro. You only cooked the things.'

Caro took a deep breath. 'This seems to be confession time all round, Trish.'

Oh, don't, she thought. Don't tell me you contaminated them yourself. How? Why? Aloud she said, 'I don't understand.'

'I didn't either until today, but I've just had Cynthia weeping all over me in an orgy of self-recrimination.'

'Oh, yes?' Trish was beginning to feel dangerous.

'You have to try to understand. She feels a kind of proprietary interest in my welfare. She said she knew Jess and I were going through a bad patch, and so she . . . Oh, shit! Even now I can't believe it.'

The danger inside Trish was welling up to crisis point. 'Are you telling me she deliberately made you ill? With E. coli 0157?'

'Yes.'

'But why, Caro?'

'She had no idea it could be so dangerous. She just wanted me to be ill for a while because she thought Jess and I would do better, in her words, "If Jess understood her own strength", and if I was forced to admit my weakness. Apparently when Cynthia and I were together I hurt her by putting her down all the time. I didn't know I had. But that's how she felt, and she says now that it's why she left me. She said she could see me doing the same thing to Jess, and she couldn't bear me to lose another relationship that mattered.'

'So she poisoned you out of love, did she? Charming! And how did she do it exactly?'

'E. coli is usually caused by faecal contamination of food,' said Caro with absolutely no emotion in her voice. 'You don't want to know any more. Believe me.'

Trish shuddered. 'I may be able to believe that, but not that any friend of yours could take such a risk with your health. Sod it, with your life. How *could* she, Caro?'

'I told you. She didn't realize how dangerous it could be.'

'Oh yeah?'

'I believe her. I think.'

Trish suppressed some instinctive questions about revenge and obsession and irresponsibility and asked instead: 'What are you going to do about her?'

'I don't know. That's for another day. But I knew I owed you the truth.'

So it was nothing to do with Smarden Meats, Trish thought, or Ivyleaf Packaging. Will need never have gone anywhere near them, and Mandy could still be alive.

But the Flesker brothers would still have been smuggling meat out of Kent and bringing guns in, and Jamie Maxden would still be dead. Kim might not have found a way to tell her story. There were never any easy answers.

Trish's phone rang. Without thinking, she picked it up to hear Antony saying that he'd booked a table at the quiet old-fashioned restaurant where she'd had asparagus and he coquilles Saint Jacques. He would meet her there at eight, he said, and didn't wait for an answer.

Epilogue

The long flight was on time on Sunday morning. George and David stretched themselves as they walked from the plane into the terminal.

'Can you get a trolley, David?' George said as soon as they were through passport control and into the baggage reclaim hall. He was scanning the screens for signs of their flight number, while he rolled the stiffness out of his shoulders. 'I'll get the bags off the carousel.'

'Sure,' David said with his new cocky grin.

His teeth looked fantastically white against the golden tan. It might have been winter in Sydney, but the weather had been glorious. George hadn't felt so well in years. He'd never seen the boy so perky.

'Will Trish be here?' David was having difficulty manoeuvring the heavy trolley, which had uncooperative wheels, but he didn't appear to mind.

'I hope so. The case is over and she promised she would be, so if she isn't we can make the most enormous fuss. Look, isn't that your bag?'

They both leaned forwards to grab the red nylon rucksack that held David's books and games. George gave way. David hauled it on to the trolley.

'D'you think she's going to like the gum-tree pot pourri?' he asked anxiously.

'I'm sure she will. It'll give her a faint flavour of what she's been missing.'

Four minutes later their suitcases had appeared too. George loaded them on the trolley and pushed it towards the 'nothing to declare' channel. They got through without being challenged, then searched the thick crowd of people waiting outside. Cab drivers stood with name cards held up in front of them, hiding the faces of the people behind them.

George felt David tugging at his arm. 'Look! Look! She *is* there. Trish!'

George followed his pointing finger and saw her. Trish's dark eyes were blazing in a face that had far more colour than usual. Her lips curled in the best welcome he could have hoped for. She was wearing soft scarlet trousers he'd never seen, and a loose cream-coloured shirt. He abandoned David and the trolley.

She felt wonderful, too. Hugging her, he could feel that she was laughing. And that she wasn't wearing a bra. She said his name, as breathless as he felt. It was he who pulled back eventually to remind her that David was there.

'Hi, Trish,' he said in his best new voice. 'You look awesome.'

'My Australian brother! I hadn't realized you could catch the accent so easily.'

'He puts it on, don't you, Dave?'

'Only sometimes. Did you bring the car, Trish? Or are we going back by bus?'

'No, we've got the car. It's in the multi-storey. Let's go. Did you have fun?'

'Yeah.' David made sure there was room for him and squeezed up on her other side. 'It was fantastic. The cousins were great. And they had these friends over all the time. They've got a pool, you know, in the garden. We used to spend all day in it. And we had barbies nearly every day.'

*

Trish let him prattle on, asking questions and commenting on what he told her, while her heart raced. Every so often she would glance up at George to show how much she wanted to say to him. He had one hand around her shoulders, while he guided the laden trolley with the other, but sometimes he couldn't stop himself stroking her hair.

Suddenly she understood what the appalling Cynthia Flag had meant when she'd talked about Jess and Caro holding each other up. For two years Trish had felt it was her responsibility to keep both George and David happy, submerging herself and her own needs to do it. None of them had been happy. Now she understood how destructive that vast effort had been. All the three of them had needed was the freedom to be who they were, without distorting themselves to fit into someone else's design.

How odd that Cynthia, having been aware enough to understand that, could have been capable of anything so dangerous!

There was a pause in the story of David's adventures, while he bent down to retie the dragging laces of his trainers. George took quick advantage of it.

'You look quite different, Trish. Absolutely fantastic. You've been voyaging through strange new worlds, too, haven't you?'

She thought of everything that happened, Antony's proposition and Will's declaration, Caro's near death and her own extreme fear. There'd been Kim, and the case. And there'd been the extraordinary evening yesterday with Paddy, when a lot of old hurts had been eased. One day, she'd tell George most of it. But not quite all.

'In a way. You wouldn't believe the half of it.'

In spite of the crowds all round them and David's fascinated expression, George ignored the luggage trolley, took her face between his hands, and kissed her. At last he let her go.

'Try me,' he said.